For the
LOVE of

MARY

A NOVEL

Christopher
Meades

Published by ECW Press
665 Gerrard Street East, Toronto, ON M4M 1Y2
416-694-3348 / info@ecwpress.com

Library and Archives Canada Cataloguing in Publication

Meades, Christopher, author
For the love of Mary / Christopher Meades.

Issued in print and electronic formats.
ISBN 978-1-55022-974-5
ISBN 978-1-77090-827-7 (pdf); ISBN 978-1-77090-828-4 (epub)

I. Title.

PS8626.E234F67 2016   C813'.6   C2015-907264-6
C2015-907265-4

Editor for the press: Jen Hale
Cover design: David A. Gee
Cover images: hand of god © estelle 75/iStock; stars © juliannafunk/iStock
Type: Rachel Ironstone

The publication of *For the Love of Mary* has been generously supported by the Canada Council for the Arts which last year invested $153 million to bring the arts to Canadians throughout the country, and by the Government of Canada through the Canada Book Fund. *Nous remercions le Conseil des arts du Canada de son soutien. L'an dernier, le Conseil a investi 153 millions de dollars pour mettre de l'art dans la vie des Canadiennes et des Canadiens de tout le pays. Ce livre est financé en partie par le gouvernement du Canada.* We also acknowledge the Ontario Arts Council (OAC), an agency of the Government of Ontario, which last year funded 1,709 individual artists and 1,078 organizations in 204 communities across Ontario, for a total of $52.1 million, and the contribution of the Government of Ontario through the Ontario Book Publishing Tax Credit and the Ontario Media Development Corporation.

Canada Council   Conseil des Arts
for the Arts   du Canada

Canadä

Ontario
Ontario Media Development
Corporation

ONTARIO ARTS COUNCIL
CONSEIL DES ARTS DE L'ONTARIO
an Ontario government agency
un organisme du gouvernement de l'Ontario

Printed and bound in Canada by Friesens
1   2   3   4   5

MIX
Paper from
responsible sources
FSC
www.fsc.org   FSC® C016245

To Claire

Author's Note

The end of chapter 26 is based on a very old joke about a nun and a priest. Many variations of this joke exist, with most having something to do with a car and a made-up Bible verse. I would quote the source, but the drunken lout who first came up with the joke in a pub some one hundred years ago has (most likely) long since walked through the Pearly Gates.

I've taken some liberties with the release dates of video games, but never fear, I've only shifted the dates by months, not years.

Also, apologies to my father, a man of infinite patience, for repeating here the true story of the first time I ever caught him swearing.

1
Christmas in July

Before the signs caused all the hoopla, and well before our little rivalry made national news, I'd heard great things about the new church across the street. They had air conditioning, a banquet hall and an air-hockey table in the basement.

My family went to the Passion Lord Church of God, a place my mother called "exclusive," which was another way of saying it was sparsely attended. We were the small church in town, our little ramshackle country house of a chapel sitting kitty-corner to the newer, modern Church of the Lord's Creation. While our choir was composed mainly of retirees with varying degrees of memory loss and halitosis, the Church of the Lord's Creation had a rock band with a drop-dead gorgeous female lead singer and a guitarist who could play note-for-note any solo from Metallica's landmark 1991 *Black* album.

That was the first point of contention between our two churches: the sheer noise their band made. At our church's Saturday picnic, my mother was talking about it as she took sandwiches out of the cooler and set them on the picnic table.

"I'm going to call the sheriff again," she said. "This time I'll make him show me the noise ordinances on the books."

Everyone within five feet of my mother looked away. If

they made eye contact, she'd go on about the noise for an hour.

My father bit into his peanut butter and jam sandwich and immediately spat it out onto his plate. "Tarnation, Margaret!"

Right away I knew what he was yelling about. Mom had put raspberry jam in his sandwich again. My father — name Donald: bald, stout and capable of picking a cooked Safeway chicken clean with his own two hands — hated raspberry jam. He preferred strawberry and had, for years now, insisted my mother put strawberry jam in his sandwiches. Only, Mom refused. This was her line in the sand. She gave Dad a dirty look and continued setting out bags of chips next to the sandwiches.

"We're a raspberry jam family," she said. "If you don't like it, you can go live with the heathens."

Dad's face turned red. "I bought a jar of strawberry jam last week and put it in the cupboard next to the Oreos."

"I know," Mom said. "I threw it away."

"Why?"

"Because our house is too small to fit dozens of jams and marmalades."

And there was my mother's thesis statement, an unsubtle one at that. She was straight-up telling my dad we needed a bigger house. For as long as I could remember, this was the central issue in their marriage. My mother wanted a house with a state-of-the-art kitchen, one with an island for chopping vegetables, a stove with more than two settings (lukewarm or scorch-the-roast-beef hot), flooring that wasn't the color of ten-year-old mustard scrapings and a multitude of cupboards in all shapes and sizes. And my father wouldn't, or perhaps couldn't, pay for one. To punish him, my mother limited the kinds of food she'd allow in the house. We could have bacon in the refrigerator, but we couldn't have maple-cured bacon. We could have Lean Cuisine frozen pizzas but none of my dad's favorite late-night Pizza Pops. And definitely no strawberry jam. My father was in the unenviable position of being starved out of his own house.

Dad lowered his voice. "Tarnation, Margaret. We've already discussed this."

My mother turned away and yanked a banana out of my sister's hand. Caroline looked shocked at first and then she made a sad face, like a snowman whose coal smile had melted into a frown.

It troubles me to say this, but Caroline was completely incapable of eating a banana in a non-erotic way. She couldn't help herself. She once confessed that this was an involuntary impulse, which sounded strange to me. After all, no one was forcing her to eat long, phallic-shaped fruit in the first place. Still, she was adamant. There was no manner in which she could consume a banana without, at least for the first few bites, treating it like an appendage dangling from George Clooney's nether region. My sister, Caroline, was like a drug addict with no desire or capacity to disengage from her self-defeating behavior. Her phallic banana-eating made our family's attendance at church picnics uncomfortable. At least for me and my mom. I'm not sure anyone else noticed.

It was July 20, 1996. I was fifteen and skinny with a peach-fuzz moustache that had become both a matter of pride for me and a great conundrum for my mother. At least twice a week, she and my father would openly debate whether or not they should force me to shave it off.

"The boy is fifteen and he looks like a '70s porn star," Mom would say.

3

My dad would shake his head. "As soon as you start shaving, it grows back in thick like a patch of weeds. Is that what you want?"

And here is the ultimate issue with debating — each side only gets more firmly entrenched in his or her own point of view. Especially after pounding back a full box of Hochtaler wine. (*It's always a good year.*)

Caroline was eighteen and had no such follicle issues. She'd been shaving, plucking, trimming and/or waxing every hair her body dared to grow for the past four years and, as a result, when she walked along the beach in her yellow polka-dot bikini, she looked like a little girl. With breasts. And a banana-sucking problem. Which, according to my mother, always drew attention from "the wrong kind of people."

At this point, wrong kind of people or not, we would have been glad to have anyone attend our picnics. There were fewer than forty people gathered in the park across the street from the church. A few years ago, three hundred would have shown up. It was an irrefutable fact: the Passion Lord Church of God was losing members left, right and center to the Church of the Lord's Creation.

For most of my life, our little church at the corner of Ascott Street and Jedidiah Avenue was the only religious game in town. Years ago, when I was still in grade school, some optimistic soul had built a mosque on the other side of the railroad tracks. What that one devout Muslim failed to realize was that Parksville was 99.99 percent Anglo-Saxon white. The mosque was now a credit union and the town was still white, more or less, today.

There were a few black families in our neighborhood, and an East Indian named Pushkar had moved into one of the big houses on Tantamount Avenue. Pushkar operated the local AMPM convenience store, which frustrated my father to no end. Despite the occasional redneck catchphrase flying out of his mouth, my dad was as progressive as any red-blooded male in a red state had ever been, and he often wondered out loud why the one East Indian family in town had to run a convenience store.

"It's a stereotype, Margaret," Dad would say. "If he were a doctor or a lawyer, he could help change people's opinions."

"I'm sure there are thousands of doctors and lawyers in India," Mom would say.

"But that's my point. Why can't *they* immigrate our way?"

"They do, dear," Mom would say. "But our government doesn't recognize their licenses, so they end up driving taxi-cabs in New York City."

My parents would talk like this for hours, circling the same subject like a gumball orbiting a funnel. Only, unlike a gumball — which ultimately succumbs to gravity — they never arrived at a destination. There was really no point in interjecting. If they weren't listening to each other, I highly doubted they would listen to me.

The one person my mother listened to was Reverend Richard. With his grayish-white beard and year-round sun-burnt complexion, Reverend Richard looked like a reverend, in the way that it would have been weird to see him in any other occupation, such as the guy bagging your groceries or ticketing your double-parked car. There was something rev-erential about him that came through in his eyes, something about the way he wore his black suit and white collar that made it feel like he was born into his profession.

At our pious picnics, however, my image of him came undone. Reverend Richard would wear pleated khakis and a golf shirt with a tiny insignia of an alligator or a sailboat. It made him look ordinary . . . human even. If I were Reverend Richard's stylist (if such things existed for small-town clergymen), I would have advised him to stay away from anything other than his priestly frock. Even at bedtime, he should only have been allowed to wear pajamas that were black with white trim.

However he dressed, Reverend Richard had a deep, almost sacred tone of voice that came through whenever he spoke of his little church's dwindling congregation.

When construction of the Church of the Lord's Creation had started four years earlier, none of us could believe its sheer size. It looked like the building blocks of an ancient Roman amphitheater as they poured those first concrete pillars. As the workers hammered and poured and fused and erected the goliath building, its shape started to form and we could all see what we were dealing with. It was a giant steeple with an enormous multi-room, multipurpose building underneath.

For Reverend Richard, the swift erection of that steeple must have made him feel like he'd been fishing in a rowboat, happy as a clam, until some stranger pulled up in his yacht and threw three dozen lines into the water. I was only eleven when construction started, but I remember wishing I'd been a giant, so I could yank off random sections of the building and chomp down on them, the way the Fraggles did to the Doozers' scaffolding, only ferociously, like an ogre gone wild. The giant me would bite off chunks of their baseboards and pillars and delight in watching the workers run and scream.

That was how I felt during construction. Once the building was in place, dwarfing our small church, stealing the very sunlight from the air every summer's day during the three o'clock hour, I didn't give it much thought. It was just a large building next to a small building I visited once a week, a place where I mostly sat in silence and replayed that week's TV shows over again in my head. I didn't actually listen to the sermon. I was just a warm body filling up a seat in the pews — a warm body in that I was there but not really there, like one of those stars the newspaper said that telescopes could see but had actually burnt out millennia ago.

Originally, the Church of the Lord's Creation wasn't even supposed to be built in Parksville. Years ago, word had spread of an alternate location in the nearby city of Springfield that was the new church's first choice. Rumor had it that just before construction was scheduled to start, the reclusive oil baron who'd been financing the project did a sudden about-face and picked Parksville instead, choosing to retire in peace to a quaint small town. Rumor also had it that the oil baron suffered a massive heart attack hours after he wrote the check to finance the church of his dreams, leading to lots of money and no captain to steer the ship.

My mom called shenanigans, refusing to believe the mysterious-benefactor story and suggesting instead that a syndicate of big-city charlatans and back-alley swindlers had taken out a series of high-interest loans from multiple financial institutions, some as far away as Kuwait, all for the purpose of laundering mafia money through her precious little community. My dad said that both stories were "complete and utter malarkey," and told Mom that if she was so interested in exposing the truth, she should call Crime Stoppers.

In the end, it didn't matter. All the conjecture in the world couldn't stop the Church of the Lord's Creation from coming to Parksville. It would still be okay, Mom insisted, as they were planning on erecting the new building all the way across town.

As luck would have it, the Church of the Lord's Creation switched building sites a second time because of a single gravestone found while excavating the weeds in the vacant lot they'd selected. I'd never seen the gravestone, but apparently there was a woman's name (Agnes Petrich), an occupation (seamstress) and a date (New Year's Eve, 1897), and that was enough to spook the Church of the Lord's Creation to move all the way across town. Often, late at night, when the Hochtaler sweats kicked in, my mom would curse Agnes Petrich and her pre-indoor-plumbing life and death (which Mom assured us was likely from a mixture of syphilis and gout). If it hadn't been for that one long-forgotten skeleton, the big church never would have been erected across the street. The sunlight wouldn't have been stolen. Everything would have been just the way it always was.

The first to jump ship were the Wittys. It was the second Sunday after the church opened, and I can still remember my family getting out of our car and spotting the Wittys exiting their vehicle in the parking lot across the street. They weren't even ashamed. Where was their contrition? Their remorse? Where was their humanity? Joan and David Witty simply stepped out of their Subaru, removed their young children from their car seats and brazenly walked into the other building for Sunday service, without a single thought as to how this might affect their eternal souls.

My mother could hardly contain herself. I remember her wishing out loud that the Witty children be plagued with the same pox that afflicted Agnes Petrich. In retrospect, hoping that small children catch syphilis — or, at the very least, burst out in all sorts of inflamed pustules — probably wasn't the nicest thing my mother ever said, but we were all so stunned. The Wittys had abandoned Reverend Richard.

Judases! Each and every one of them.

The next to go were the Craigs. Then the Knox family. The parishioners toppled like dominoes. In less than three months, our little Passion Lord Church of God's throng was cut by two-thirds. It was like watching patrons flee a corner store only to bustle through the doors of the newly constructed Walmart. And while none of us should have been surprised, most of us were. Even Caroline and I, who went to church only because our mother insisted, were offended.

My best buddy since grade school, Moss Murphy, attended the new church with his parents. He described the place as "wicked freaking awesome like you wouldn't believe." Besides the air conditioning to keep you from sweating through your shirt, the air-hockey table in the basement turned out to be only the tip of the iceberg. To hear Moss Murphy describe it, the new church basement was like a Chuck E. Cheese's where all the games actually worked, only you didn't need to use a token each time you wanted to try the mini-bowling.

One evening when Reverend Richard was at our house for dinner, he asked Moss Murphy what the sermons were like.

"They're good, I suppose," Moss Murphy said.

"But what specifically are they teaching? How is Minister Matthew? Do the parishioners look happy? Do they look fulfilled?"

Moss Murphy stared at Reverend Richard like a deer caught in the headlights, his eyes widening with each passing second. Before his pupils could take over his entire face, Reverend Richard placed a consoling hand on Moss Murphy's shoulder.

"Don't worry, Moss. Just follow where your heart takes you."

Moss Murphy nodded his chubby cheeks and walked into the other room, his heart taking him to a half-finished bag of cheese puffs.

Reverend Richard's faith in his remaining flock, were it to have faltered — momentarily or for keeps — never wavered in public. At least, I never noticed it wavering in public. This was the summer I became awake, the dividing line between my youth and adulthood, the summer I was saved. And not saved in the way one might think. Suffice it to say, during those warm July days in 1996, Reverend Richard could have come into the church weeping or cursing or wearing an enormous fruit hat, and I might not have noticed.

That Saturday afternoon, however, I did notice him place a white-trimmed Santa Claus cap atop his head.

Our pious picnics usually had a theme and this one was no exception. It was Christmas in July. Sort of. No one had gone to the trouble of baking a turkey or whipping up some mashed potatoes, or even wrapping any presents. A pint-sized Christmas tree sat on one of the picnic tables, and Mom had discovered some miniature candy canes in the back of our front hall closet and placed them in a festive snowflake-covered bowl. Another lady set up a makeshift manger scene using the porcelain figurines she kept in the back window of her car, and my Uncle Ted had brought his own mistletoe. Other than that, the only way you could tell we were celebrating Christmas in July was by looking at Reverend Richard.

"Thank you all for coming on this beautiful day," he said to the group. Reverend Richard adjusted his Santa Claus cap and glanced up at the bright, sunny sky. "Merry Christmas in July," he said, and everyone laughed. "In these rapidly chang-ing times, it's important for us to meet outside the church walls, to break bread — or sandwiches and fried chicken, as it were — with one another and to understand that God isn't just some mythical figure we pray to once a week, but a part of our lives we honor every day, with our acts of kindness, with how we interact with our neighbors and brothers, with how we speak and think and love one another.

"Now, Nancy, does everyone have a glass?"

He cast a glance at Nancy Sylvester, the heavyset assistant church secretary currently scampering around handing out juice boxes and cans of Diet Sprite. Rumor had it that in her early twenties, Nancy Sylvester was caught stealing a pack of Duracell Triple-A batteries from RadioShack and resisted arrest to the point where she — and the details are fuzzy here — was either pepper-sprayed by a mall security guard, bitten on the leg by a police dog or both. Mom said that after the RadioShack incident, Nancy Sylvester threw herself on the mercy of the Lord. That's why she volunteered to assist the church secretary, to serve out the remainder of her days in eternal toil and penance.

Nancy Sylvester surveyed the group. "I think we're good," she said.

Reverend Richard lifted his glass. "I promise, this isn't filled with Kool-Aid," he said, eliciting a few scattered chuckles from the adults. Just as he was about to launch into a toast, a loud noise rang out from the other side of the street. Our heads turned in unison. It was a single screeching guitar chord, followed by a clash of cymbals and then the beating of a bass drum, all coming from the Church of the Lord's Creation. The band was practicing. And they were even louder than on Sundays. Without the audience to complain, the band members turned their amplifiers up as loud as they could. It was as if they were playing right under our noses.

And not spiritual music. I recognized the song immediately. It was "Kickstart My Heart," the fifth track on Mötley Crüe's seminal *Dr. Feelgood* album. The band was on fire. Much to Reverend Richard's chagrin, it sounded just like being at a heavy metal concert.

He raised his glass and said simply, "To our continued good health under the Lord."

End of speech.

The picnic went well. They usually did. There was a three-legged race and a wife-carrying event. My dad persuaded Mom to do the three-legged race with him, while my sister flat-out refused to hop on our Uncle Ted's back as semi-incestuous participants in the wife-carrying event. Later, my mom led the group through some Christmas carols. I only mouthed the words while Caroline spent her time imitating Nancy Sylvester's surprisingly high soprano on "O Holy Night." We only made it through three songs before Reverend Richard decided it was too hard to hear ourselves over the band across the street.

"Another three-legged race, anyone?" he said.

After blistering through an hour-long set consisting of a few Smashing Pumpkins songs, Journey's "Don't Stop Believin'" and some more Mötley Crüe, the band stopped playing and it began to feel exactly like any other summer's day in the park. Children swung from the monkey bars. Caroline flirted her way into acquiring a can of Coors Light from one of the dads and I'd managed to drink, in order: a Tangerine Wavelength Fruitopia, two juice boxes and a long-expired Crystal Pepsi. It was official. I was completely hopped up on sugar. And I really needed to pee.

"Caroline, come with me," I said.

"No way." She flipped her hair in the air and polished off the last of the Coors Light.

"Come on, I bet you have to pee. If you really think about it, you need to pee. Bad."

A short thin line formed between Caroline's eyes. "Argh. I do need to pee," she said.

The two of us were walking across the street to use the washroom in the church basement when everything changed. We saw it — the giant sign in front of the Church of the Lord's Creation, the one that for over a year now had sat dormant, like a ginormous scoreboard at a baseball game that someone had forgotten to plug in. It had finally been turned on and it was like looking into the biggest television set I'd ever seen. Only, there weren't any moving pictures. There was just a single sentence in big bold letters.

Caroline and I looked at each other and then back up at the sign again.

"I'll get Reverend Richard," she said, and took off running.

It didn't take her long. The picnic was only fifty feet away. The entire congregation hurried over. First Caroline, then Reverend Richard, then all the rest. Aside from my mother cursing under her breath, we all stood in stunned silence.

To understand why we were all so dumbfounded, one had to look at the tiny, dilapidated sign on the Passion Lord Church of God's front lawn; the words Reverend Richard had selected, the ones Nancy Sylvester had diligently put up by hand a week ago. Inspired by the theme of this week's picnic, our little sign read:

CHRISTMAS IS ONLY 5 MONTHS AWAY.
REMEMBER . . . SANTA'S WATCHING!

It was a kind remembrance. An offhand refrain. A wholesome little ode and, most importantly, a reminder for the children of Parksville to be good all year round.

As a group, we turned our heads, read our little sign and then looked back at the mammoth colored lights across the street.

The sign read:

THERE'S ONLY ONE TRUE MESSIAH
AND IT SURE ISN'T SANTA.
READ THE BIBLE, PEOPLE

My dad put his hand on my shoulder. Mom wrapped her arms around Caroline, while Reverend Richard looked as white as a ghost. He took off his Santa Claus cap and stared along with the rest of us.

We all knew instantly. This meant war.

2
Long Driveway, Small Kitchen

If you ask me, our house wasn't all that small. Compared to a single-family dwelling in war-torn Croatia, it was a palatial estate. But compared to the other houses on the street, it wasn't especially big. My sister and I each had our own room. My mom even had an office from which she'd long been halfheartedly running a ceramics business. There was a fair-sized living room in which the family would watch television, and in front of our house, a long winding driveway led up to our front door. The one problem, as well as the focal point of almost every discussion between my mother and father, was the tiny kitchen space.

Whoever designed our house must not have been interested in fine cuisine because, with the inclusion of a small table and four chairs, there was barely room for three of us to stand in our kitchen, let alone for two people to cook together. My mother had long dreamt of cooking in a kitchen like the ones she saw in *Martha Stewart Living*. Visions of arched ceilings and wood-paneled twin subzero freezers danced through her head. Mom wanted a Crock-Pot, a wok, a waffle iron and a state-of-the-art food processor to all fit on her kitchen counter at the same time and still have room left over to comfortably chop vegetables while chatting on the cordless phone. That was her dream.

It was also my father's nightmare. He had long refused to build my mother a new kitchen, citing zoning permits and the structural integrity of the existing walls. No matter how adamant my father was in his justifications, we all knew the real reason for his reluctance: money.

My father managed a school bus rental company, employing a fleet of eleven buses and a rotating cast of eight or nine drivers that covered schools in three townships. He was the first one a neighbor would call if they wanted someone to look over their proposal for a bank loan. He was also the last person anyone would call if they needed something fixed around the house. My father had long decided that (a) a brand-new kitchen "wasn't in this quarter's budget" and (b) if my mom wouldn't let him do the work himself, there would be no way to control costs.

Against all reason and with no empirical evidence to back up his claims, Dad considered himself a handyman. He'd even started doing little projects around the house to prove his worth. Dad started with the bathroom downstairs. He cut the tops off empty milk containers and duct-taped them to the bathroom wall: one for hair supplies, the other for my sister's feminine hygiene products. In a moment of inspiration, he'd taken down the toilet paper dispenser and replaced it with four separate spokes on which four rolls of toilet paper now sat, just in case "Montezuma gets his revenge at home." Somehow, and perhaps mistakenly, he'd fused the overhead light and the ceiling fan together, causing the light to spin in dizzying circles, such that, whenever Caroline sat down to use the facilities, she would complain of mild migraine headaches.

I could never quite figure out whether my dad was some kind of evil genius, doing an abysmal job on purpose, or whether he was genuinely incompetent. But one look inside that bathroom was all my mother needed to realize her husband would only make her kitchen situation worse.

The stalemate continued.

Inside the tiny kitchen that Saturday night, the talk as we sat down to dinner was about the electronic billboard.

"It's an abomination," my mother said.

"You can't let those people get your goat," Dad said. "That's what they want."

"Well, if they want my goat, they've got it."

Caroline looked up from her spaghetti and meatballs. She'd barely touched her meal. Caroline usually waited until after dinner on a Saturday night to get ready to go out, but tonight she was already dressed up to the nines in a pair of short jean shorts and a 1988-era Madonna black bustier. Her makeup was caked on. Her fingernails had little hearts on them, something she probably thought boys noticed, but I knew they didn't because they'd be too busy staring at her ultra-tight, strapless top.

"They probably eat goat," she said. "They probably sacrifice goats at a big altar inside their great hall."

Now Caroline was trying to get my mom's goat. What she didn't realize was that someone already had Mom's goat and when someone had my mother's undivided attention, it was very difficult to tease her.

"It wouldn't surprise me if they did," Mom said.

Dad poked Caroline in the arm with his fork.

"Ouch!"

"There's no need to throw fuel on the fire, young lady," he said.

Dad's utensil attack notwithstanding, the fire was already lit underneath my mom. She was beyond reasonable discourse.

"If they had a volcano, they'd probably sacrifice virgins there too," Mom said.

"Well, Caroline's safe then," I said.

Caroline poked me in the arm with her fork, forcing my dad to poke her a second time. My mother didn't seem to notice.

This is what that big church wants, I thought. *All of us poking each other with forks.*

"There has to be a bylaw of some kind," Mom said. She set her meatballs down and looked directly at my dad. "You're the expert on zoning laws in this county. Care to tell me exactly how they were able to put up a flashing electronic sign?"

My dad hummed and hawed.

Caroline snickered.

"I never claimed to be an expert, dear," Dad said. "I only looked up *residential* zoning laws and applications."

"Isn't the church in a residential neighborhood?"

"Well . . ."

"Well," Mom said. "It sure as shooting isn't an industrial neighborhood."

My father was backed against a wall (metaphorically — in reality, it was my sister's chair that was pressed up against the floral wallpaper). He looked to me for help, only I was useless to him because (a) I thought it was kind of funny, (b) I wanted to see what happened next and (c) I was too busy thinking up another snide comment about my sister's long-lost hymen. My dad had to think fast.

He pointed out the window. "Look! The Deck Girls are doing their laundry."

Mom and I looked out my mother's narrow kitchen window. Caroline turned around to see.

Outside our window, less than forty feet away, Lydia and Leah Fontaine were doing their laundry on the back deck of their father's house. This had been going on for months now. The girls' father, a stubborn man with a stubborn nose and a stubborn chin and sunbaked freckles around his eyes, had kicked them out of the house. They were eighteen and twenty years old and neither of them had yet to amount to anything.

Lydia, the younger sister, had been convicted three times of various misdemeanors relating to drug and alcohol abuse. If the statistics they taught us at school were to be believed — that the average person drives drunk at least eighty-seven times before they're caught — that means Lydia had driven under the influence approximately two hundred and fifty times, give or take, before her third strike landed her in hot water. That's a lot of inebriated driving, by anyone's standards. The third time she got caught, she also ran a red light and, while attempting to flee a field sobriety test, accidently sprinted into a busy street, forcing a startled driver to crash into a lamppost. The startled driver escaped the car wreck uninjured, only to (as my father put it) "freak out of her gourd" and clock a severely inebriated Lydia over the head with her newly detached side-view mirror. The police had no choice but to haul both women off to jail for the night.

Litigation was still pending.

Leah, the older sister, wasn't quite as rotten an apple. However, she did get caught writing a bad check once at

Target. While charges were never filed, local gossip spread like wildfire. Later that same year, her father lost all faith in her when she failed out of community college (which my mother insisted is almost impossible to do). Leah was unceremoniously kicked out of the house the same day her sister got the boot.

They didn't go far. The Deck Girls' mother was sympathetic to their plight and allowed them to live rent-free on the back deck of the family home, provided they only enter the house for bathroom emergencies and that the girls "get their act together before the Rapture," which, according to their hippy-dippy mother, was supposed to arrive in December 2012. The Deck Girls had essentially been given a sixteen-year reprieve, something they used to erect tents on their father's deck and set up a rummage-sale hot plate that served as equal parts fire hazard and weapon of choice were they to argue, which happened a lot.

Despite being two years apart, the Deck Girls looked alike, the only differences being that Leah had enormous breasts and a lisp, while Lydia plucked her eyebrows so thin it looked like a single pencil line had been drawn over each eye. Other than that, you could barely tell them apart.

My father must have been thrilled when the Deck Girls moved outside, because he often brought them up to distract my mother. Mom hated that the Deck Girls had become such a public spectacle and could usually be distracted into ranting and raving about how the police should come and shut down whatever lesson their father was trying to teach them.

Today, however, she was in no mood.

"Yes, the Deck Girls are washing their brassieres. How very tantalizing," she said. Mom looked at Caroline. "This is exactly why you need to stay in school."

"I never left school," Caroline said. "It's summer break. I start beauty school in September."

"Ha!" Dad said.

"Excuse me?"

"Why anyone needs to go to school to learn to put on makeup is beyond me."

Caroline put her arms on the table, exposing them to possible fork attacks. "Did you know that good makeup artists can earn up to a thousand dollars a day?"

"That's impossible," Dad said.

"It's true," Caroline said. "Look it up on the internet."

"There will be no internet in my house, as long as I'm alive," Dad said.

Caroline stood up. "I'm leaving."

"No one leaves until we finish dinner," Mom said.

"I have a date," Caroline said.

"With whom?"

"Phil."

"And what are you planning to do?"

"Make babies in the back seat of Phil's car," I said.

Caroline almost picked up her fork to stab me. Instead, she leaned into my ear and whispered, "At least I didn't spend twenty minutes humping a pink loofah in the shower this morning."

I gave Caroline a dirty look. *How did she know?*

"No whispering," my dad said.

"Yeah. No whispering, Caroline," I said.

My father turned to me. His eyes drew together, like pendulums stuck in the center of a swing. "As for you, Jacob, you've said two things this entire conversation and both of them were mean shots at your sister. Maybe you should try saying something nice for a change."

I expected my entire family to continue arguing, for my sister to sneak in a second comment about my extra-long showers, for my mother to rail against the Deck Girls or their father or some golden sign speaking blasphemous words in the parking lot across the street from her beloved church. Instead, they just stared at me. The stare only lasted a few seconds, but I could tell they were disappointed. My father might have been backtracking and my mother might have been raging a little and, without question, Caroline was exaggerating about how much money she was going to make right out of school, but I hadn't ventured a single worthwhile opinion during the entire conversation, and when I stopped to think about it, maybe it's because, at that moment in time, I didn't have one.

"I'm sorry," I said.

"Look at your sister and say that."

"I'm sorry, Caroline."

"I'm still leaving," Caroline said, and walked away.

My dad was about to protest when my mom put her hand on his shoulder. They shared a look and then watched Caroline walk down the hall. We heard her zip up her tall boots and the front door slam shut. My dad stabbed a meatball with his fork and twirled his spaghetti around it. He shoved the biggest bite he could fit into his mouth. Meanwhile, my mother had lost her appetite. I could see it in her eyes — that fluorescent sign was driving her crazy.

"What Nancy Sylvester put on the church's front lawn was lighthearted and fun, a way of reminding children to be good all year long," she said. "And then that holier-than-thou Church of the Lord's Creation has to go and put down Santa Claus. Who doesn't like Santa Claus?" Mom looked me straight in the eye.

"Um, bad people?" I said.

She turned to face my dad.

His eyebrow twitched. For a second, it looked like Dad might not come up with anything. Then he said, "Heathens?"

Mom nodded. "Exactly."

We ate in silence for almost a minute before Mom got up from the table. She glanced out the window, past the Deck Girls and into the marbled sky, then over at my dad, who was trying not to make eye contact. Mom took a sip from her glass of wine. Every muscle in her body tensed up.

"If they're looking for a fight, they've got one," she said.

"This will all blow over," Dad said. "I'm sure cooler heads will prevail."

Mom shook her head. She downed the rest of her wine. "No, Donald. The righteous will prevail."

3
Casting the Second Stone

At church the next morning, everyone was in a tizzy. A revolution was at hand and the devout disciples were up in arms. Alliances would be formed! Illicit events would be reported! Vengeance would be had!

Only, Reverend Richard didn't seem to care.

At least, outwardly he seemed not to care. I could never tell what was going on inside that man's head. He came out to a congregation buzzing about who was responsible and what should be done. If he'd been even one-tenth as outwardly outraged as my mom, the entire lot of us would have stormed the giant church doors that very afternoon. Only, he wasn't about to let the inmates take over the asylum. Reverend Richard instructed the seven-person choir to sing a rather solemn hymn, and when they were done and the chatter still hadn't subsided, he instructed them to sing it again, this time "with feeling." The two hymns in a row extinguished the chatter bugs' flame a little.

Reverend Richard stood on his velvet-covered platform, stared at the congregation and, in his sternest voice, said, "Simmer down!"

The chatter ceased immediately and Reverend Richard cleared his throat.

"Tolerance," he said. "I've never liked that word. What does it mean? To tolerate. Someone with great tolerance is said to have the capacity to endure the actions of others. But who are we to say their actions are wrong? Is it not up to the Lord to decide?" He pointed at Candice Collington in the front row. For weeks now, Candice Collington had been distraught over the passing of her beloved basset hound Rex. "Mrs. Collington, do you remember our Bible study from last week, the book of John, passage 8:7?"

Candice Collington looked from side to side and then straight up at Reverend Richard, a terrified expression on her face.

Reverend Richard smiled. He stepped closer. "Don't be nervous. You remember in the book of John, at the Feast of Booths, the authorities apprehend Jesus and he says, 'Let anyone among you . . .'"

"'Let anyone among you who is without sin be the first to throw a stone,'" Mrs. Collington said, clapping her hands together and smiling wide.

"Yes," Reverend Richard said. He looked out at the congregation. "We all know that verse. It's one of the most famous verses in the entire Bible and definitely one of the most quoted. I've seen those words on church walls in England. I've seen them engraved on ceramic plates. I've seen them sewn into sashes and even tattooed on a convict's arm. But what people fail to recall is that Jesus wasn't speaking in generalities there. He was talking about a woman, an adulterous woman. The authorities were trying to entrap Jesus. They were trying to get him to impose his own moral authority over her and then declare our Lord and Savior a hypocrite.

"Jesus was too smart for that. He didn't just say, 'Let anyone among you who is without sin be the first to throw a stone.' Rather, he said, '. . . be the first to throw a stone *at her*.' This is an important distinction." Reverend Richard pointed out the window, where the warped image of the Church of the Lord's Creation could be seen through the stained glass. "Don't think of our neighbors as our enemies. Don't think of them as conquerors. Think of them as people. Life is too short to worry about signs.

"And as to whether Santa Claus was the Messiah? I'm sure we all know the answer to that question. Christmas is important. But it's not important enough to get into a war of words with our neighbors, especially when it's five months away." He cleared his throat. "Now, I had a sermon planned today on the purpose of forgiveness and I don't think a little controversy should divert us from that very important lesson."

With that, Reverend Richard launched into a long, well-rehearsed sermon, of which I didn't listen to a single word. I was too busy watching the faces in the crowd. Mrs. Collington was still all smiles, her contribution to that morning's sermon having temporarily derailed her grief over the loss of her best friend. However, Nancy Sylvester, sitting three seats to my left, was staring straight ahead, her lips trembling. The woman to her right had her fist balled so tight you could have put a piece of coal inside and produced a diamond in under an hour. A few of the men in the congregation looked rather solemn, but it was the women who looked upset.

My mother's jaw was clenched. I'd seen this look before, that night when my father came home from a bachelor party smelling of perfume, whiskey and shame, unable to explain the patch of stripper glitter on his shoulder. My mother's jaw had remained clenched for the better part of three weeks, until ultimately Donald won Margaret over with contrition, sweet talk and (what I chose to believe was) a loud, late-night session of furniture rearrangement in the master bedroom.

Reverend Richard's wise words aside, Mom wasn't going to let this sign controversy slide. And neither were her friends.

4
Orange Fingerprints Everywhere

Moss Murphy was my best friend.

I had other friends, of course. There was Calvin Cockfort, who was forced to endure the daily indignity of not only having the word *cock* in his last name, but also the word *fort*. The mere sound of his name provoked the image of multiple penises being used to erect an outdoor structure of some kind. I always imagined them forming a teepee, but if someone suggested a phallic log cabin, I wouldn't have argued. Calvin Cockfort's parents owned the shoe-repair kiosk in the mall, and while we'd been friends for a few years, we mostly hung out at school. Never at home. Calvin made a strange snorting sound, like a goat seeking attention from an inattentive farmer, and while I was never sure if this was a habit or some physical compulsion he couldn't control, it was constant and distracting and ultimately reason enough not to invite him over to the house.

Then there was Brent Spader, who wore a back brace and aspired to be a world-renowned rap superstar. Most of Brent's raps were about his debilitating scoliosis, and while Brent had all the talent in the world, he could never find a place to practice dropping his funky beats. His mother wouldn't let him do it in the house and the principal frowned on students "shucking on them hoes" in the hallways. Brent was mostly my friend because his locker was next to mine, and while we often chatted about who was the greatest rapper of all time — the general consensus being that it was Biggie Smalls (Snoop Dogg and Tupac notwithstanding) — Brent and I never had much to chat about besides rap music. There was only so much a small-town white kid like me could contribute to the debate over who ruled the streets, the Bloods or the Crips.

I could probably come up with a list of other friends I had when I was fifteen, kids who sometimes came around the house or guys I hung out with at school. But Moss Murphy and I had become pretty much inseparable. We were friends mostly because we lived so close to each other. When you're fifteen, it's almost impossible to ignore the kid who lives across the street. The convenience is such a selling point that a friendship is almost non-negotiable. Moss Murphy and I had been walking to school together since fourth grade.

Prior to that we were sworn enemies.

The nine-year-old Moss Murphy used to sit on my head and fart. And I used to scream. That was pretty much the extent of our relationship when we were younger. It was a rather one-sided relationship and definitely not built on anything like trust or mutual respect or the enjoyment of each other's company. Moss Murphy was a chubby kid and he used to delight in grabbing me in a bear hug, wrestling me to the ground and passing gas on my face while calling out what he'd eaten for lunch.

"Chimichangas!"

"Enchiladas!"

"Tostadas!"

"Wonton soup!" (Not all dishes were of Mexican origin.)

Yes, the young Moss Murphy was a bully. For years, he picked on me every chance he got, until one morning when everything changed. Moss Murphy was standing on his front lawn, watching his dad wash his rusted 1982 Trans-Am, when my father and I walked out our front door. Typically at this point in the day, Moss Murphy would call out the various odors he planned to unleash on me later in the afternoon.

On this particular morning, he just stared at me in stunned silence. I was wearing my karate uniform, complete with my yellow belt and two gold stripes I'd earned the previous week. Moss Murphy took one look at me and clammed right up. I climbed into the car with my dad and we drove off.

Later that afternoon, our doorbell rang and I was surprised to see Moss Murphy standing at my front step with a basketball in his hands.

"Do you want to play twenty-one?" he said.

At first I thought it was some kind of trick. Only, Moss Murphy's expression was sincere. His mean, gap-toothed scowl had been replaced by a semi-nervous kind of smile.

"Sure," I said.

We went outside and shot some hoops and that was that. We'd been best friends ever since. The karate-outfit-necessitates-friendship incident taught me that you don't really need to fight to gain respect in this world. Only the threat of physical violence is required. I finally understood what all those rogue nations in the Middle East had been thinking during the early 1990s. They didn't want nuclear weapons so they could blow up the continental United States (well, some of them did, but that's another story). They wanted nuclear weapons so that the big countries on the block would stop sitting on their heads and farting.

Moss Murphy and I were both addicted to video games. From ages ten through fourteen, we would play up to nine hours of Nintendo a day. Our personal favorites were *Dr. Mario*, *Pin Bot*, *Punch-Out!!* and (believe it or not) the 1986 version of *Donkey Kong Jr. Math*, in which each player attempted to solve some rather modest mathematical equations as a monkey swinging from a series of vines.

For a long time, I thought *Tetris* was my one and only video game love. Designed by a Russian, it was so addictive the term *Tetris Syndrome* was coined to describe the game's hypnotic effects. I used to dream in *Tetris* blocks. On more than one occasion, I woke up with night terrors about left-facing L-blocks that refused to fit into the right side of a puzzle.

Tetris even entered my teenage sex fantasies. In eighth grade, my social studies teacher, Ms. Tarvis, would often wear revealing tops. They wouldn't show off her breasts or anything. Ms. Tarvis wore modesty panels, which were essentially cleavage-blocking patches ladies used to cover up their boobs. Ms. Tarvis wore leopard-print panels on Mondays and tiger prints on Wednesdays. Friday was all about the lace.

Ms. Tarvis's shirts were revealing in the midriff area. She was a youngish-looking thirty and super fit. She looked like she did cardio and Pilates, or at least a ton of sit-ups, and each time she put her hand in the air, her shirt would ride up and I'd see a little bit of her bellybutton. It was awesome. I could have stared at Ms. Tarvis's exposed midriff all day. Only, *Tetris* got in the way. I used to imagine blocks sliding into her bellybutton. Square ones, L-shaped ones, even the big long four-piece sticks. Each time, I would shake my head and rub my eyes. This wasn't right. I should have been imagining taking Ms. Tarvis in my arms and laying her down by the fire, ravishing her like a beast and calling her "Lois" (which, incidentally, was not her real first name).

That's what Brent Spader did, sitting beside me. That's what all the other boys in class were thinking. But me, I was sitting there fantasizing about how many *Tetris* blocks I could symmetrically insert into the woman's bellybutton.

I tried going cold turkey with *Tetris*, only to come back to it time and time again. I might have stayed addicted if not for the release of the Nintendo 64 and its flagship game, *Mario Kart*. Once I unwrapped the cellophane from the N64 *Mario Kart* case and placed it in the console, any hope of getting the video game monkey off my back was completely lost. Moss Murphy and I played *Mario Kart* every single day in his basement. Sometimes I would even sneak across the street after my parents had gone to sleep and play *Mario Kart* until the wee hours of the morning.

Once or twice during my late-night prowls, I bumped into Caroline sneaking out herself. The two of us would see each other in the hallway, me holding my favorite red N64 controller, Caroline wearing bright blue eye makeup, a spandex shirt and her thigh-high hooker boots. We'd share a look. Then, without a word, we would slip out the front door. Caroline never asked me where I was going and I never asked her (although I always assumed it involved the flatbed of a pickup truck and a guy in a Whitesnake jacket).

The reason Moss Murphy and I played video games exclusively in his house was because for years, my mom wouldn't let him past her front door. Moss Murphy was a messy kid, apt to spill at any moment. Dust followed him everywhere, like Pig-Pen in *Peanuts*, only with a burgeoning sour-milk body odor that manifested sometime around his twelfth birthday. My mom's chief complaint about Moss Murphy was that his fingers were always covered in a sticky orange paste from eating too many Cheetos. She actually had a point. There were orange fingerprints everywhere in Moss Murphy's house. Besides Mexican food and the occasional bowl of Chinese soup, I'd never seen Moss Murphy eat anything other than chocolate chip cookies and Cheetos.

The Murphy family rarely came over. My mom found Mrs. Murphy pleasant enough, but she objected to the family owning a ferret (which Mom openly called a "cat-snake"), and moreover, it gave her the willies that a critter named Roscoe was allowed to run free in Mrs. Murphy's spacious kitchen. Still, they were neighbors, and Mom, being a good Christian, would occasionally invite them to dinner. Each time, about an hour before they arrived, she would go into a panic and start cleaning the house from top to bottom, as though a preemptive surface clean with Lemon Pledge would somehow thwart the mess Moss Murphy was destined to make. She even had a special blanket she draped over a chair, the rather unimaginatively named Moss Blanket, one made completely of polyester, easy to clean and almost entirely flame-retardant. Mom used to steer Moss Murphy toward the Moss Blanket by placing a bowl of sour candies on the table next to it. It worked every time.

For years, I didn't share my mom's concerns. If Moss Murphy wanted to be sticky and smelly and covered in processed cheese, so be it. Who was I to judge? Then we hit high school and very quickly, almost within the first week of class, I noticed something. None of the girls would anywhere near him. Moss Murphy's chubby cheeks, his mild-to-moderate body odor and orange-stained fingers were acting as a teenage-girl repellent. This didn't just affect Moss

Murphy. It affected me as well. How could I hang out with the only kid in school who made girls run the other way?

Teenage girls smelled like strawberries and candy apples and they had pretty eyes and the softest skin, and all I can remember is wanting to touch them and smell their hair and go to the mall to buy them pretty things. Moss Murphy's hygiene would interfere with all of this.

One afternoon I tried to do something about it. I thought I'd start at the root of Moss Murphy's problems: his weight. He wasn't quite obese, but he was well on his way to becoming one of those enormous old guys who rides a scooter around Home Depot while resting a coffee and a danish on his giant stomach.

I couldn't just say anything outright. Even as a teenager, I knew that confronting someone with a direct accusation like "You're fat" only makes them defensive, and for some reason they feel compelled to start pointing out all the things wrong with their accuser rather than looking within and wondering how their weight had reached such titanic proportions. I would have to use my people skills, indirection and perhaps even a little marketing savvy.

Moss Murphy and I were playing *Mario Kart* in his basement. He was drinking a Dr Pepper and eating Cheetos out of the bag. I waited until we reached the Moo Moo Farm level.

"Do you know Mr. Francis, the history teacher?"

"The one with the goiter on his neck?"

"Yeah, him," I said. "Today he told us that if the average American gave up drinking soda pop, they'd lose twenty-five pounds within a year."

Moss Murphy sent a turtle shell hurtling toward my character's head. "I'd rather die."

34

"What?" I said.

"You heard me — I'd rather die than give up my Dr Pepper."

"That's what I'm saying. You're going to die if you keep drinking all this soda pop. It's a statistical probability."

Moss Murphy beaned me with another turtle shell. "Don't worry. I'll beat the odds."

Things were not going as planned. The conversation had just begun when I thought of something that had never occurred to me before. To fix a problem, a person needed to admit they had a problem. And the people with the worst problems were the least likely to admit they had any.

"How are you going to beat the odds?" I said.

Moss paused the game and flashed a chubby-cheeked grin. He ran his fingers across his jaw, leaving a thin layer of cheesy flakes behind. "With my natural charisma."

I shook my head and wondered why I was so concerned about the health and welfare of someone who used to fart on my head.

Strangely, in the days that followed, Moss Murphy figured things out for himself. Sort of. He just needed a little prompting.

5
The Cure for Burgeoning B.O.

It was the Wednesday after that Sunday sermon, four days after the electronic sign lit up and six weeks into our summer holidays, when Moss Murphy and I headed over to the mall, partly to look at the new N64 games we couldn't afford, but mostly to talk to Shotgun, the local burnout who worked at Sore Thumbs, the local games store. Shotgun was unlike anyone I'd ever met. He smoked pot, and not just a little pot. He was what Dr. Dre would have called *chronic*. Shotgun said "dude" at the end of every sentence and he knew every single cheat code, bug and hidden level in every video game released since 1984. His nickname was derived not from his street toughness but rather his proficiency with a certain armed weapon in the video game *DOOM*.

"Dudes," Shotgun said as we walked into the store. He clasped his fist to mine and gave me a half bro-hug over the counter. He did the same with Moss Murphy. "Did you jump off the rainbow in *Mario Kart* yet? It cuts your track time in half."

"Yep. It was awesome," Moss Murphy said.

He was lying. Neither of us had managed to jump off the rainbow correctly and had only succeeded in launching ourselves into the celestial abyss. Still, Moss Murphy wasn't about to admit his shame and neither would I.

Shotgun gazed around absentmindedly. He looked like he was just coming down from being high.

"Where's Blowpipe?" Moss Murphy said.

Blowpipe was Shotgun's partner in crime, the assistant manager at Sore Thumbs, a Lars Ulrich look-alike with a patchy goatee and near-autistic-savant-level skills when it came to playing *Final Fantasy VI*.

Shotgun plunked his elbows on the counter. "It's a sad story. Blowpipe's in rehab."

"Really?"

"Really, dude."

"What was it?" Moss Murphy said. "Booze? Weed? Bags of glue?"

"It's nothing like that. Blowpipe got addicted to the nudie bar."

Moss Murphy and I looked at each other. "What?"

"Yeah, dudes. They don't tell you this in high school. I mean, they warn you about other addictions: alcohol, drugs, sex, even food. Only, Blowpipe wasn't addicted to any of those. He got addicted to the nudie bar and it got bad. He started going there every night, spending all his money, running up a big tab and getting lap dances on credit. I'm just saying — when the strippers start asking how your mother's thyroid condition is holding up, it's bad news."

Some ten-year-old kid approached the counter and asked for change for a dollar. Shotgun seemed like he was about to give the kid some quarters and then told him, "No can do, little bro," and to go to the K-Mart down the hall. He looked back at me and Moss Murphy. "I thought Blowpipe might get things under control when Club Paradise lost their liquor license on account of serving to minors. The place went downhill real quick. The strippers jumped ship to Springfield and the customers disappeared overnight. All that was left was an empty stage, no booze and some fat old lap dancer named Zelda. But Blowpipe kept going, drinking soda and staying there until all hours of the night. If his mom hadn't dragged him out of there by his ear, in a couple more years he might've put Zelda's grandchildren through college."

"Is this Zelda really that bad?" Moss Murphy said.

Shotgun leaned in close. "I don't care how many 7 Ups they ply me with, I'm not paying ten dollars for that."

Moss Murphy and I nodded like we completely understood.

"Anyways, his parents shipped him off to some rehab facility up north. But you know how those places are. He'll probably come back addicted to painkillers."

A gray-haired man in a suit walked into the store and started checking out the imported Japanese game titles on the far wall. Shotgun gave us a look like he'd spotted a whale who might spend some real money, and the two of us nodded and slinked out the door. We walked over to Mrs. Fields, where Moss Murphy bought two double chocolates with walnuts and three nibblers. I bought a bottle of SunnyD and we walked around the mall, checked out the poster store and then decided to head home to play Nintendo.

Moss Murphy was polishing off his second cookie (it was like dropping lumber into a wood chipper) as we stepped out the front doors. Someone called his name.

"Moss! Moss, over here!"

We turned to see a girl in a green dress standing next to a wiry young man wearing a gray suit, handing out pamphlets outside the door. Moss Murphy waved like he knew the guy and walked over. He shook the man's hand.

"So good to see you outside of church," the young man said.

Moss Murphy introduced me and the young man extended his hand. With supreme reluctance, I shook it and got covered in thirdhand chocolate glop from Moss Murphy's fingers.

"Have you heard the word?" he said.

"I'm sorry?"

"The word," he said. "Have you heard it?"

"Jacob goes to the Passion Lord Church of God," Moss Murphy said.

"Ah," the young man said. "A worthy institution."

"This is Youth Pastor Glenn," Moss Murphy said. "He works at my family's church."

"I'm taking over for Minister Matthew during his absence," Youth Pastor Glenn said. "And this is Samantha."

I recognized the girl in the green dress from school, only she looked different than the mousy, ball-cap-wearing ninth grader I thought I knew. The ball cap was gone. So too was her puffy black coat. Samantha's brown hair was braided like Princess Leia's in *The Empire Strikes Back*, only fancier and long, and her dress clung to her body, accentuating every curve.

Beside me, Moss Murphy's eyes were burning a hole in Samantha's dress. I'd seen that look before, on his birthday last year when his father brought home a pizza box, and inside, instead of cheese and crust and pepperoni, there was a pizza-sized chocolate chip cookie with his name on it. Moss Murphy had turned absolutely giddy at the sight of that giant cookie. But this, the appearance of the girl in the tight green dress with the star-shaped freckles on her nose, put Moss Murphy on another plane of existence.

Samantha ran her hand through her braids and Moss Murphy's eyes glazed over. He looked hypnotized. Mesmerized. Horny and infatuated and serious-yet-scatterbrained at the same time.

"Samantha is helping out with the event we're having on Friday night," Youth Pastor Glenn said. He handed me a pamphlet that read:

Have you heard the WORD OF JESUS?
If you haven't, trust us . . .
It's more fun to hear it with music and cake.
That's right . . . cake! And games and fun!
All teens welcome.
Friday night, July 26th, at 8 p.m.
at the Church of the Lord's Creation
corner of Ascott Street and Jedidiah Avenue

I looked up at Youth Pastor Glenn, who towered six inches above me. His hair was impeccably trimmed, as though each strand knew exactly where it was supposed to be. Below that perfect head of blond hair was a pair of thick black-rimmed glasses, hip, ironic glasses that I couldn't even criticize because they were just so ironic and hip. He had incredibly chiseled cheekbones and wouldn't stop smiling.

"Is Samantha going to be there?" Moss Murphy said to Youth Pastor Glenn.

The girl handed him a pamphlet. "Of course. I'm helping organize."

"I could bring some soda," he said.

"That would be great," Youth Pastor Glenn said.

"Awesome."

"Awesome."

Moss Murphy was uncharacteristically quiet on the walk home. He farted once, but forgot to call out the name of a Mexican delicacy and stared at the clouds when I made jokes about Blowpipe's elderly stripper. Half an hour later, after halfheartedly bogeying three consecutive holes in *PGA Tour 96*, Moss Murphy walked over to the mirror in the far corner of his basement and took a good, long look at himself.

What did he see and was it for the first time? I wondered. Did he notice the unkempt hair, the chubby cheeks, the way his faded *Jurassic Park* T-shirt pressed against his mushrooming man boobs? The small smudge of orange cheese puffs on his right cheek? The remnants of chocolate and little flakes of walnuts in the corners of his mouth? I couldn't be sure. But he must have seen something, because when he turned around, Moss Murphy uttered the words I never thought I'd hear him say.

"I've got to clean myself up."

6
Teen Boy Makeover

The next day Moss Murphy showed up at my front door stinking like Drakkar Noir.

The smell was powerful, like an old Italian fisherman hadn't showered in a week and then doused himself in a gallon of Colgate, sawdust and lavender. I almost gagged. My first instinct was to slam the door and run around back to get some fresh air. Only, Moss Murphy had such a lost-kitten look on his face, I couldn't do it.

I did, however, pinch my nose. "What did you do?"

"Is it bad?"

"Um . . ."

A dense glob of grease held his hair aloft and his dad's white dress shirt was dangling off his shoulders.

"My eyes hurt," Moss Murphy said.

"Wait here," I said, and shut the door.

I ran upstairs and knocked on my sister's door.

"I'm studying!" Caroline yelled.

I tried twisting the doorknob, only it wouldn't budge. Last year, Caroline had gotten smart and installed a door-knob that locked from the inside. Her room was like an island unto itself. No one — not me, my dad or even my mom — could get in unless she wanted us to.

"I need your help," I said.

"Bugger off!"

"It's Moss. He's wearing cologne."

Two seconds passed and then Caroline opened the door. She had an eyeliner pencil in one hand and lipstick in the other. Her room smelled like baby powder, only subtle baby powder, nothing as pungent as what was going on downstairs.

"What do you mean, he's wearing cologne? Is he wearing deodorant too?"

"I don't think so."

"Did he shower today?"

"I can't tell."

"Well, for the love of God, don't let him in the house. Mom would freak out if he sat anywhere except his blanket."

"You don't understand. He needs your help."

Caroline scrunched her nose. "With what?"

The deodorant section at Walmart was intimidating. From a distance, the individual plastic containers looked like Chiclets arranged in a quasi color-coordinated order. Up close, they told a different story — one of rugged machismo, intimidating sports branding and a fear of getting the pit sweats.

It was forty-five minutes after Moss Murphy showed up at my door. Caroline had sent him home to shower off the cologne and "wash that guck" out of his hair before putting the two of us in the back seat of her car and carting us to Walmart, where we quickly found the health and hygiene section.

"What about Irish Springs?" Moss Murphy said.

"It's Irish Spring. Singular," Caroline said. "And don't use it. Not the soap, not the deodorant, not at all. Guys like the smell of Irish Spring. Girls hate it." She turned to me. "I'm right to assume this is about a girl?"

"Yep," I said.

"So, unless you're planning on impressing your gym class, don't go near it." Caroline curled her fingers under her chin. Her face turned all analytical. "I read in *Cosmo* the other day that it's all about pheromones. Pheromones are these invisible things that every person in the world emanates and other people can smell. The better your body is at emanating pheromones, the more people want to have sex with you. The article said that's why supermodels sometimes date average-looking guys. It also said some scents can affect you without you even knowing it. Like, did you know that the smell of cinnamon buns has been proven to increase penile blood flow? Which is essentially a way of saying you're way more likely to get a boner at Cinnabon than you are at McDonald's."

A weird silence filled the aisle.

"What about Old Spice?" Moss Murphy said finally.

"No way," Caroline said. "Our Uncle Ted smells like Old Spice. And trust me — you don't want to smell like Uncle Ted. You only use Old Spice after you turn fifty, and even then you only wear it when you've started tucking your golf shirt into your pleated shorts." She reached into the deodorant wall and pulled out a dark green container. Caroline opened the lid and smelled it. "Use this. It's Degree. And it's not just a deodorant. It's an antiperspirant, so you won't sweat through your shirt." She handed one to Moss Murphy and one to me.

"But I use Dad's Irish Spring," I said.

"I know. I've been meaning to talk to you about that."

"What about shaving cream?" Moss Murphy said.

"For what?"

"For my moustache."

Caroline and I looked closely. "What moustache?" we said.

Moss Murphy pointed to his upper lip. There, just below his nose, was a faint line of dark brown hairs. "Does it make me look sophisticated?" he said.

"It makes you look like you just drank a cup of chocolate milk," Caroline said.

"So I should —?"

"Shave off the peach fuzz. Today," she said.

I laughed out loud and Caroline stared at me.

"You too, Porn 'Stache."

"But Dad says that as soon as you start shaving, it grows back in like a thick patch of weeds."

"You should still shave it off."

"But —"

"Do you want to look like a man or like a guy with an old lady's armpit hair above his lip?"

Moss Murphy and I stared at the floor. Caroline could be quite convincing when she wanted to. We both instinctively reached for the closest shaving cream in the aisle.

"Maybe not that one," Caroline said. "Instead of regular shaving cream, always buy a gel that lathers into a cream." She grabbed two disposable razors and two cans of shaving gel and handed them to us. Then she picked out two tubes of Topol, the smoker's toothpaste, and insisted we brush with it every night; to whiten our teeth she said (even though neither of us had smoked a cigarette in our lives).

"How much money did your mom give you for clothes?" she said.

"Sixty bucks," Moss Murphy said.

"That's not a lot, but it should cover two shirts."

Moss Murphy pointed to the men's section in the far corner. "I bet we can buy five shirts for sixty bucks here," he said.

"Oh, no," Caroline said. "We're not buying clothes at Walmart."

"So, what's she like?" Caroline said.

We were standing outside the change room at Frida's Vintage Clothes and Accessories, a hop, skip and a jump from the mall. Moss Murphy was on the other side, struggling with the three dress shirts and ultra-tight blue jeans Caroline had picked out for him.

"What's who like?" he called from inside the stall.

"This girl you're trying to impress."

We watched Moss Murphy stumble a little underneath the door.

"Her name's Samantha," I said. "He barely knows her. He met her only once and they didn't even talk."

The change room got very quiet. Then Moss Murphy cracked open the door and poked his head out. "That shows how much you know. I've seen her dozens of times," he said, and closed the door.

"Really? Where?"

"At church. Her family's been coming for six months now. She always wears a dress. Sometimes it's a blue dress, other times she wears this pink one with a little bow on the collar, sometimes she wears the green one she was wearing the other day. She's totally hot. And smart too."

Moss Murphy opened the door again. This time he was

wearing the ultra-tight jeans. Yesterday's *Jurassic Park* T-shirt still covered his chest.

"It sounds like you're in love," I said.

"So what if I'm in love?" he said. "I'm fifteen, not twelve. Two hundred years ago, fifteen-year-olds were considered grown men. They could fight in the army and own livestock and take wives and all that other grown-up stuff."

"Have you even talked to her?" I said.

Moss Murphy's eyes grew close together. I couldn't be sure, but he looked like he was thinking about farting on my head.

"If you haven't spoken to her, then you're just *in lust*. You can't be in love unless you at least know what her voice sounds like."

Caroline pushed in between us. "Love, lust — it doesn't matter. It's all the same when you're fifteen," she said. Caroline lifted Moss Murphy's T-shirt and got a better look at those tight jeans. "This will never work. You're muffin topping."

We both looked down. "What?"

"Your bottom half looks like a wrapper and your top half looks like a muffin overflowed in the oven. Don't act so offended. Someone had to tell you. Take those off. I'll find some relaxed-fit jeans. And don't worry," she said. "We'll get you two decent shirts and a pair of jeans."

Moss Murphy clutched his wallet. "I don't have enough money."

"I'll lend you the money," Caroline said. "I can afford it. When I start work after beauty school, I'm going to make a thousand dollars a day."

Caroline hurried off to find another pair of jeans. She was being so nice to us, it made me think maybe my dad was right. Maybe I'd been too hard on her recently. I was trying to come up with some way to thank her, when I noticed that lost-kitten look on Moss Murphy's face was gone. So too was the menacing glare of a few seconds ago. His eyes looked distant, almost like his feelings were hurt. This was weird. I didn't know Moss Murphy and his natural charisma had any feelings.

"Listen," he said. "Just don't make this hard on me. I like Samantha. So what if I want to take her to the movies and have her come over to the house to play *Mario Kart* —"

"Most girls don't like to play *Mario Kart*."

"Well, then we'll braid each other's freaking hair if we have to," he said. "I don't care. I just want her to like me. It would be way easier on me if you weren't such a dick about it."

7
The Wingman's Role

Nancy Sylvester came over that Friday night. When the doorbell rang, my mom opened the front door with such enthusiasm, it was like she was expecting Publishers Clearing House to show up with an oversized check. Nancy Sylvester and my mom huddled around our tiny kitchen table, drinking herbal tea and talking in hushed voices. The whole situation was strange because Nancy Sylvester rarely came over without six other ladies accompanying her, for Tupperware parties, (gratuitous wine consumption under the guise of) book club or some other prearranged social activity.

Also, she and my mom rarely spoke in hushed voices. Nancy Sylvester was a loud lady. Her voice was loud. Her laugh was loud. The creaking sound a chair made when she sat down was loud. Today, however, she and my mom were leaning over their teacups and pausing with sly looks on their faces whenever one of us passed by.

I found my dad out in the garage, listening to Foghat on his cassette player and sanding a piece of wood.

"What's up with Mom and Ms. Sylvester?" I said.

"Beats me," he said.

"It must be something."

He looked up from his work. The board had clearly

been smooth before he got there. "Maybe she's describing the horror of getting caught with a stolen pack of batteries stuffed in her girdle."

I paused, unsure whether or not to laugh. That was, without a doubt, the funniest, most sarcastic, most out-of-character thing my father had ever said. He *looked* different while saying it too. There was a gleam in his eye, something mischievous I hadn't seen before. I wanted to laugh, but I was so stunned that when I finally forced out a chuckle, it came a full second and a half too late and sounded more like a pity laugh than anything. Definitely not what my father was looking for, or what he deserved.

Dad grunted. He started sanding again, slowly and deliberately. "I try to stay out of your mother's business," he said.

"Well, they're up to something," I said.

For a moment, that gleam in his eye returned. "Why don't you go in there and ask them?"

Fine, I thought, and shut the door behind me. I walked up the stairs and into the kitchen, where I poured myself a glass of orange juice.

Nancy Sylvester looked up from her tea. "Oh my, don't you look nice tonight," she said.

My mom looked over at me too.

"Are you going to a wedding? Maybe getting married?" she said, and they both laughed.

I was wearing the new blue dress shirt with the subtle striped pattern that Caroline had bought me. I'd washed my best pair of jeans that morning, taking special care to include three sheets of scented Downy fabric softener in the dryer so my legs smelled good. I also applied four stripes of Degree antiperspirant to each armpit, but held back on applying cologne — so as not to interfere with any pheromones. My hair was gelled just like Caroline taught me: starting with product in the back. I'd washed my face and even popped a pimple on my chin.

I was going on my first ever visit to the Church of the Lord's Creation, the big church across the street, the church these two ladies had probably been talking about moments ago. I'd felt funny about it all week — sort of like frogs were juggling water balloons inside my stomach — but Moss Murphy insisted he needed a wingman if he was going to talk to Samantha. I couldn't turn him down. Being his best friend meant I was his *default* wingman. Whether you're fifteen or thirty or sixty-five, being someone's default wingman is a pretty big deal. Moss Murphy described it as equal parts honor and obligation. I couldn't argue.

"Moss Murphy and I are going to the arcade," I said.

Instead of grilling me for details, my mom looked down at her tea, over at Nancy Sylvester and back up at me again. "Did you know that the Community Advisory Council controls the sign in front of our church?"

"Um, what?" I said.

"The sign in front of our church. Reverend Richard actually has no say in what goes on it. Nancy just informed me of a church bylaw that's been on the books for years now. Apparently, the Community Advisory Council has free rein to put anything we want on the sign."

"Our church has an advisory council? And bylaws?" I said.

The ladies nodded. "Of course. We're both members of the council," Mom said.

"What are you going to put up on the sign?"

My mom stood up and navigated the tight space between the chair and the countertop, then gave me a kiss on the cheek. She wrapped her arms around me. The whole while, she and Nancy Sylvester shared a knowing gaze.

"Have fun at the arcade," Mom said, and kissed me again.

Moss Murphy and his mother were waiting at the edge of their driveway across the street. Moss Murphy's mother — named Elizabeth, but whom everyone called Betsy — was a stick-thin woman with what my father would call unviable birthing hips. She looked waiflike in the fall, frail in the winter, dainty in the spring and anorexic in the summer; the polar opposite of Moss Murphy's dad, who resembled a sweaty Stay Puft Marshmallow Man year round. Back before Moss Murphy and I became friends, I used to joke that he and his dad would let Betsy eat dinner only once they were finished, which of course they never were, so she only got to eat random stray peas and noodle scrapings the Murphy boys had neglected in their haste to get on with the next meal. In reality, Betsy Murphy subsisted on cigarettes and Diet Coke, with an occasional aspirin or Midol thrown into the mix.

Betsy wore oversized muumuu dresses that dangled off her shoulders like bed sheets and, despite her persistent frown each time she spoke to my mother, was actually quite pleasant any time she spoke to me, particularly when she'd bring Rice Krispie squares down to the basement for one of our late-night Nintendo marathons. Above all, Betsy was protective of her only child, Moss, whom she loved unconditionally and, at times, unrequitedly.

Moss Murphy had long grown tired of his mother watching over him like a hawk, flipping her lid at the sight of a single hangnail on one of his fingers, and demanding to know where he was going and "has anyone been mean to you at school?" Moss Murphy endured his mother with clenched teeth, which is why I was surprised he'd asked her to drive us to the big church tonight.

52

He left Betsy smoking a cigarette and met me halfway up my parents' driveway. Moss Murphy was wearing a black dress shirt covered in little white anchors, a single gold chain and dark jeans that actually fit his frame. His hair was spiked and he'd washed his face and shaved off his thin moustache. He looked great. And clean. Very clean.

"Why can't we just walk?" I said.

"I don't want to get all sweaty."

"Fair enough."

"Now, don't forget," he said. "You're my wingman tonight. That means you have to stay by my side at all times. If I get tongue-tied around Samantha, you have to help me."

"Help you how?"

"Change the subject. Make conversation. Tell her what a great guy I am. You know, typical wingman stuff."

I nodded.

"Oh, and if she has a friend, you have to pretend you like her. I don't care if the girl has a goatee and a single black-bean tooth. Make out with her if you have to."

I gave Moss Murphy a funny look. I'd never even kissed a girl, let alone made out with one who looked like a wilde-beest. "Really? Because that's no small thing you're asking," I said.

Moss Murphy shrugged. "The wingman's job is the wingman's job. I don't make the rules."

Caroline came strutting down the driveway in her halter top and tall black boots, her long blonde hair flowing behind her. As she stuck her key in the door of her car, she dropped her makeup compact. Caroline bent over to pick it up, reveal-ing two inches of her bum crack in the process.

A goofy smile spread across Moss Murphy's face.

I jabbed him with my elbow.

"What can I say?" Moss Murphy said. "I have an eye for talent."

Caroline picked up her compact and looked over at the two of us. She sashayed a few steps and stopped in the driveway with her hand on her hip. "Don't you two look handsome," she said.

Moss Murphy blushed. I think I did too.

"Are you seeing that girl tonight?" she said.

"Yep," Moss Murphy said.

Caroline flattened the cowlick at the back of my head. She fixed Moss Murphy's collar and adjusted his gold chain. "How could she resist?" Caroline said. She walked back to her car and had already fired up the engine and pulled onto the street when she unrolled her window and leaned her head out.

"Oh," she called. "I forgot to mention. Moss, whatever you do, don't let this girl watch you eat!" Then she peeled off down the road with Alanis Morissette's "You Oughta Know" blasting out of her speakers.

Moss Murphy's mom — who'd been leaning her tiny elbow against the streetlight this whole while — threw her cigarette butt into a nearby drain. She was getting her keys out of her purse when, from behind, Mr. Murphy opened the front door to their house. Like a bolt of lightning, the ferret scurried outside. Instead of hightailing it for the hills, little Roscoe ran straight to Betsy. He scaled her frail body and nestled in atop her shoulder.

"Lorne! Be careful! What if Roscoe ran into the street!?" Betsy yelled.

Mr. Murphy mumbled a quick apology and shut the door.

Betsy examined Roscoe's eyes. "Moss, did you give Roscoe his drops?"

"He's a ferret, Mom. He doesn't need vitamins."

"It's not vitamins. It's medicine."

Moss Murphy rolled his eyes. "I couldn't find him."

"How hard is it to ferret out a ferret?" I said.

I'd been waiting three years to say that, and was pretty proud of my joke. Only, it fell on deaf ears. Moss Murphy kept rolling his eyes while Betsy glanced back at their house like she was trying to decide whether or not to go back in and give Roscoe his drops.

Before she could decide, my mom came striding down the driveway, purpose in her every step. "Betsy!"

"Hello, Margaret."

Mom's expression turned when she saw the squirming cat-snake. Still, she kept walking until she was face-to-face with Betsy. "I don't suppose you've noticed this business with the signs at church," Mom said in her fake-cheerful, talking-to-company voice.

"Everyone's noticed," Betsy said.

Mom stepped closer. "I hope you don't mind me asking," she said. "But what's going on at the Church of the Lord's Creation? I mean . . . why is everyone over there instead of at the Passion Lord Church of God?"

"Well, there's the air conditioning."

"Yes. There's that. But is air conditioning a good enough reason to switch denominations?"

Betsy stroked little Roscoe's backside. "Let's be honest," she said. "Is there really that much of a difference between Presbyterians and Methodists?" Mom didn't respond, so Betsy added, "Besides, it's not like we've gone Catholic or anything."

"No. Heaven forbid."

"Heaven forbid."

The street got very quiet. Moss Murphy and I were thirty feet away, and still it felt like you could cut the tension with a knife.

"The sermons are better too," Betsy said finally.

"But how exactly?" Mom said.

"Well, without taking anything away from Reverend Richard, Minister Matthew is an excellent public speaker. And ever since Youth Pastor Glenn took over, it's been so enlightening. You don't feel like you're just sitting there listening to someone. It's a truly spiritual experience."

"That's all well and good," Mom said. "But to put down Santa Claus, after all the joy he brings —"

"There's no such thing as Santa Claus," Betsy said, sharper and yet a little quieter so Moss Murphy wouldn't hear. "Youth Pastor Glenn is quite serious about not worshipping false idols. In fact, lately he's been teaching us about the real St. Nicholas. Did you know the real St. Nicholas single-handedly resurrected three children who'd been chopped to pieces by a butcher? If that's not a miracle, I don't know what is."

Mom squinted extra hard. Each time she looked down at Roscoe, her chest convulsed, like her stomach was telling her to get as far away from the cat-snake as possible. "But you used to attend services at the Passion Lord Church of God. You and your family were such loyal Christians —"

"Mom!" Moss Murphy called. "We're going to be late."

"That's okay," my mom said, laughing her fake laugh. "I don't mean to keep you from driving the boys. God bless." Mom took one last look at the ferret and walked back up our long driveway to where Nancy Sylvester was waiting.

Betsy watched my mom leave. She bit her lip and pulled out the keys to her Ford Pinto station wagon. "Let's go, boys," she said. As soon as she turned onto the street, Betsy pulled out her lighter and started fumbling in her purse for a cigarette.

"Aw, Mom. You promised," Moss Murphy said from the passenger's seat.

"I'll open the window," she said.

Moss Murphy grabbed her purse and held it tight. "No way! I can't go to this thing smelling like smoke."

"I'll open the window really wide!"

Moss Murphy squealed like a toddler who'd lost its binky. He gripped Betsy's purse even tighter. This was how we traveled to the Church of the Lord's Creation, with Moss Murphy clutching his mom's purse so tight his arms turned red and Betsy trying to grab it away. All the while, little Roscoe darted around beside me in the back seat.

As we stepped out of the car, Moss Murphy threw his mom's purse onto the passenger's seat. He grabbed two bottles of soda from the floor.

Betsy immediately lit a cigarette. "Do you need a ride home, sweetie pie?"

"No thanks, Mom."

"Are you sure?" she said, looking at me.

Moss Murphy gave me a death stare.

"I think we'll walk, you know — to get some exercise," I said.

Betsy waved goodbye and drove out the way she came, just as Moss Murphy started walking up the path to the Church of the Lord's Creation. At first, my feet didn't want to move. I was standing on the curb, closer than I'd ever been to this monster building, and it felt odd. The church looked even bigger. Its white walls were almost gray, with little holes where pockets of air had formed as the concrete hardened during construction. There was an enormous stained-glass window with the Virgin Mary etched in a turquoise cloak and golden rings over her light brown hair. From across the street, the stained-glass Mary looked just like any other lady from two thousand years ago: barefoot in a meadow, with trees and flowers all around her. Up close, her profile was surprisingly lovely, almost serene.

Above the Virgin Mary was a rainbow, and not just a regular red, orange and yellow rainbow — a multihued kaleidoscopic of colors was cast into the stained glass. I'd never noticed before how much effort went into making something like this.

"Let's go!" Moss Murphy called.

He tossed me one of the soda bottles.

I caught it, but just barely.

"Come on, hurry up!"

I took one last look back at my parents' little Passion Lord Church of God across the street and I nearly threw up. There, carrying a stack of papers and climbing out of his car, was Reverend Richard. There was no doubt about it. I saw him and he saw me. The blood in my veins turned to ice. I was totally busted. What was he doing outside the church at seven forty-five on a Friday night? And why did he have to see me? Reverend Richard must have been a hundred feet away, but I could still make out his downturned lips, the disappointed look in his eyes, the way his shoulders slumped when he realized one of his silent but dedicated soldiers was crossing enemy lines with a bottle of root beer in his hands. Reverend Richard looked down at his papers and back at me. I looked down at my soda and back at him. Then I turned and hurried in through the doors.

The inside of the Church of the Lord's Creation was even more impressive than the outside. The walls were so huge and wide, it felt like if you let a helium balloon go, you would lose sight of it before it ever left the building. The ceiling was essentially one enormous skylight and everywhere you looked there was more stained glass. Everyone from the Bible got equal attention, not just Jesus. There was a panel for Moses and another for Adam and Eve (both with their private parts discreetly covered with fig leaves). There was one depicting David and Goliath (although in the image, the stained-glass Goliath had already been struck by the projectile from David's sling and looked more annoyed than injured, having received only a minor bump on his noggin). There was a mural depicting Noah leading animals two by two into his ark, and a medieval-looking stone statue of John the Apostle. I would have never guessed it was John the Apostle (he might have been Judas, for all I knew) if not for the placard under the statue's feet that spelled out his name in big black letters.

All of this must have cost a lot of money. I wasn't sure how much, but *boatloads* seemed like a safe estimate.

"Wow," I said.

"You haven't even seen the best part," Moss Murphy said. "Don't forget the air-hockey table in the basement."

The basement wasn't at all how I pictured it. I always thought Moss Murphy was exaggerating. I pictured a damp, dingy room with a single flickering lightbulb and dozens of folding chairs stacked against the walls. The downstairs turned out to be even nicer than the upstairs, with dozens of arcade games — air hockey, mini-bowling and *Daytona USA* — along the far wall. They even had my personal favorite, *Puzzle Bobble*, which was essentially *Tetris* if you liked to shoot things.

On the other side of the stairs was a daycare with a play kitchen, a swing set and slides, dozens of beanbag chairs and a toddler dress-up area. No wonder all those families jumped ship. The Passion Lord Church of God couldn't compete with all this if they gave out free bags of Doritos and raffled off a car at the end of each sermon.

While I was so wide-eyed and amazed, Moss Murphy wasn't even looking at the games room. He wasn't looking at me or at the big gold crucifix at the bottom of the stairs. His eyes were focused on one thing only: the girl in the green dress, the one with the star-shaped freckles on her nose. Over by the auditorium entrance, Samantha was smiling at him.

8
Conversion for Heathens

For all his talk about my duties as wingman, Moss Murphy immediately left me behind and walked right up to Samantha. There was an impressive swagger, a skip to his step that spoke of newfound confidence. I watched from the bottom of the stairs as Moss Murphy drew within two feet of the girl in the green dress, my mind flooding with all the opportunities that could arise were my best friend to turn into an all-out ladies' man.

First and foremost, it would mean that from this point on, Moss Murphy would do most of the talking. My chief responsibilities would be to maintain my hygiene and try not to say anything stupid, which would work well if I could pull it off, as I'd long heard women love the strong, silent type. All I had to do was show up, wait for Moss Murphy to chat with some beautiful young lady and hope that her friend — the wingwoman on the other side — wasn't all that unattractive. It seemed like a perfect plan. I couldn't wait.

Then I heard Moss Murphy speak, and instantly I knew things weren't going to be that easy.

"Soda," he said.

Samantha crossed her eyes. "I'm sorry — what?"

He held up the bottle in his hand. "This is Fanta. Jacob has root beer."

Samantha looked down at her feet, around the auditorium, anywhere except Moss Murphy's rapidly perspiring face. "Er . . . that's great," she said. "You two should get inside. The music's about to start."

Moss Murphy's eye was twitching like a frog's leg in a science experiment. I hurried over and the two of us walked in through the auditorium doors.

He waited until we were out of range. "What the hell?" he whispered. "You totally bailed on me back there."

"You took off on your own. Then you started talking about soda," I whispered back.

He shook his head. "You're dead weight. I should have left you at home."

I shook my head back at Moss Murphy. There was no way I was going to let his bad attitude ruin my night. I gazed around the auditorium instead. It was so large, it could have easily fit four hundred people. Tonight, the theater-style seats were empty. Thirty or so teenagers sat in folding chairs in front of the stage. I could see only the backs of their heads, but I still recognized a few of them from school. The Delany sisters were there, two twin girls and a younger sister. The twins wore their hair in giant hair-sprayed beehives while their younger sister had a Tennessee top hat that could have given Calvin Cockfort's curly mullet a run for its money.

Speaking of Calvin Cockfort, he had a glass of soda in each hand. One of his friends must have been looking out for him. Nobody really liked to talk about it, but Calvin Cockfort had developed a severe jock-itch problem to go along with the strange snorting noise he made. The past year or so, it had gotten really bad. He just couldn't stop scratching. At a high school dance a few months back, his buddies kept two drinks in his hands at all times. That way he couldn't scratch himself and scare away all the girls.

Calvin Cockfort polished off the ginger ale in his left hand and before he could set his cup down, Jackie Dog Face hurried over to give him a refill.

Jackie Dog Face was actually Jaqueline Bachmeier, a skinny sixteen-year-old with what could pass for a crew cut. She wasn't that bad-looking. In fact, on the days she wore blue makeup around her eyes, she was actually pretty cute. Nevertheless, about a year ago, a few heartless twelfth graders had nicknamed her Jackie Dog Face and somehow the name stuck. Those twelfth graders had long gone on to join the workforce or to college or just to bum around Europe for a semester or two, while poor Jaqueline Bachmeier was stuck here in Parksville with a mean-spirited and (depending on whom you asked) entirely inaccurate nickname.

It didn't help that she kept wearing her mother's homemade sweatshirts. Just after Valentine's Day last year, Jaqueline's mother held a session at the high school to show teachers and students how to stitch glitter onto the fronts of white sweatshirts, usually in the shape of unicorns or frogs. The price of the sweatshirts was borderline absurd ($22.95 plus tax, plus the cost of glitter, plus a little extra if you spilled the hot glue), and no one attended except the librarian, Ms. Davis. Rumor had it Ms. Davis stumbled upon the session on her way outside to smoke a cigarette and only stuck around because she felt sorry for Jaqueline. Still, Mrs. Bachmeier blamed the poor turnout on the price of the sweatshirts and not on their inherent quality or aesthetic appeal. Either way, Jaqueline Bachmeier was mocked for weeks. No one could believe it when she continued to wear her mother's ugly sweatshirts to school.

Today there was a sparkly panda on her chest.

I was surprised by how many of my classmates went to the Church of the Lord's Creation. There were dozens of them here. And they were all looking at a single person: Youth Pastor Glenn, who was standing on the stage, smiling.

"Moss," he said. "So good of you to come. And you brought your friend."

The entire group looked our way. Moss Murphy, still stricken by selective mutism, waved his bottle of Fanta in response.

Youth Pastor Glenn smiled even wider, revealing innumerable pristine white teeth. "Just set it down with the other refreshments," he said.

We walked over to the far wall where a table of snacks was set up. It turned out we didn't even need to bring the soda. Fifteen assorted bottles of soda pop were already lined up five wide and three deep. Even if every kid in attendance drank three glasses tonight, we wouldn't make a dent in what was already there. We set our soda bottles down anyway. I was about to find my seat when I noticed Moss Murphy staring at something.

It was the largest assortment of cheese puffs I'd ever seen. Someone had taken a punch bowl and filled it with so many Cheetos, they were overflowing, and not just overflowing onto the table, but onto four other bowls containing more cheese-flavored delicacies: crunchy cheese puffs, cheese balls, Cheetos Cheesy Checkers and Moss Murphy's personal weakness, El Sabroso Blazin' Hot Cheese Crunchies. I thought Moss Murphy might start to drool. If he were a dog in Pavlov's laboratory, Pavlov could have finished his dissertation on classical conditioning in a single afternoon.

"Moss," I said. "Moss . . ."

Only, he wasn't listening. Powdered cheese was involved now.

I tried to come to the rescue. I picked up a cinnamon swirl and handed it to him, only Moss Murphy refused to take it.

"Your sister told me not to eat," he whispered.

"Just rub it on your hands," I whispered back.

"What for?"

"The pheromones," I said, thinking about what Caroline had told us about erections in Cinnabon.

"The last thing I need tonight is sticky hands," he said, a little too loudly.

A girl's voice sounded. "Moss?"

We turned to see Samantha pouring herself a glass of 7 Up.

"Would you like some?" she said.

Moss Murphy tore himself away from the giant cheese puff display. He managed to emit a single "Yes, please" and then followed Samantha, drinks in hand, over to the crowd sitting in their folding chairs. I took my seat as well and Youth Pastor Glenn introduced the church band.

The band was comprised of teenagers from the congregation, including their drop-dead gorgeous lead singer, who'd graduated from high school last year and now worked at an insurance office in town. She hadn't quite given up on her dream of rocking out, as evidenced by the single stripe of purple in her hair. The band got up onstage and blazed through an acoustic set of cover songs, each of which followed a pattern. The singer — intermittently tousling her purple-striped hair — would sing the first verse and chorus exactly like the song sounded on the radio. Then she would change the second verse to include the wisdom and ideology of Christ our Lord. It made for a very strange version of TLC's "Waterfalls" and an almost unrecognizable rendition of Elvis Presley's "Hound Dog" — *"I want to be a disciple, praying all the time"* — but the inclusion of AC/DC's "Dirty Deeds Done Dirt Cheap" was a pleasant surprise, and even though the singer tried to make it all about Judas and Jesus and their fundamental disagreement toward the end, they really rocked out.

As soon as they finished, Youth Pastor Glenn got up in his dark blue suit and took the band's applause for himself. "I know some of you don't attend our church regularly," he said. "And it's probably kind of sneaky for me to get up here and preach to a group of teenagers who've been promised rock 'n' roll music and all the snacks they can eat. I don't want you new faces out there to think of this as conversion for heathens. But if you'll just bear with me while I say a few words, we can get to the refreshments."

He paused, but didn't wait long enough for anyone to object. "Today I'd like to speak about tolerance," he said. "I like that word, *tolerance*. It kind of slips off your tongue. And what does it mean? To have the capacity for enduring the actions of others. And do you know who was the most tolerant person of all?" He pointed up to the ceiling. "Our friend JC, up in the sky. Old JC would never say something like 'My tolerance for your behavior is limited.' Rather, he would tolerate. He would endure. Not always in silence, mind you. But with patience.

"I encourage each and every one of you to look at your parents, at your brothers and your sisters and your neighbors." He glanced at me out of the corner of his eye. "Ask yourself — what can I do to understand this person's actions, to listen before I attempt to teach? Make no mistake about it, the words of Jesus Christ are meant to be taught. And I — no, *we* — are meant to teach them. Only, first we must find tolerance in our hearts. Can I hear an Amen?"

"Amen."

"I can't hear you."

"Amen!"

"Excellent," Youth Pastor Glenn said. "Now, let's have something to eat. I believe our own Samantha Dewan has baked a cake for the occasion. After we eat, there's going to be some games. A few parents raised hygiene concerns about bobbing for holy apples. So that one's out. But there will be an air hockey tournament, as well as a game of charades. So thank you for listening and please enjoy the night."

Five minutes later, Moss Murphy and I were chatting by the refreshments table while the Delany sisters arranged teams for charades. Moss Murphy was showing great restraint by eating only a single string of grapes and I could tell it was killing him not to have a fistful of Cheetos in either hand. I was drinking root beer and trying to make sure I didn't slouch, when Samantha's voice surprised us from behind.

"Don't eat the cake."

"But you made it," Moss Murphy said.

Samantha stood over top of her double layer cake. "My stepmom helped me," she said. "Right after we finished icing it, she told me one of her contact lenses had fallen out and she didn't know where it was. We looked everywhere." Samantha pointed at the table. "It might be in the cake."

Moss Murphy nodded confidently. "I'm willing to risk it."

Samantha laughed, and not just a pity chuckle, but a full-blown laugh where she tilted her head and her shoulders shook. Moss Murphy laughed as well. Then something remarkable happened. Samantha touched him on the arm.

It only lasted long enough to count one Mississippi, perhaps two, but it was definitely deliberate. I stared at Samantha's hand on Moss Murphy's forearm with fascination. This girl — this beautiful, slim, delicate-featured young lady with the adorable star-shaped freckles on her nose — was flirting with Moss Murphy. *My* Moss Murphy. The one perpetually covered in processed-cheese crumbs, the one forever licking dried bits of chocolate out of the corner of his mouth, the Moss Murphy whose Mexican food–induced flatulence was, at times, almost canine. Last summer, Moss Murphy had gone an entire week without bathing — and not just a regular week, but the first week of August when the sun was beating down and the sweat was congealing on his lower back — and now this pretty girl was interested in him. I couldn't believe it.

By the look of him, neither could Moss Murphy. He looked down at her hand and blushed. Then he smiled so wide I thought the corners of his mouth were going to touch his ears. I slipped away and slunk out the doors to check out the video games. The first rule of being a wingman, Moss Murphy had told me, was knowing when to get the hell out of Dodge. I couldn't think of a better moment.

I found the *Puzzle Bobble* game outside the auditorium and was happy to see it had been rigged so you didn't need quarters to play. Immediately I started shooting bubbles, trying to connect four of the same color so they'd burst. I was already on level six when two guys I'd never met walked out of the auditorium and started playing air hockey. From the size of them, they looked like twelfth graders.

"I'm telling you — Youth Pastor Glenn's pissed off," one of them said as the air-hockey table warmed up.

"Nah," the other one said. "That guy doesn't get mad.

He's like a robot. No real emotions."

"It's the ones who keep it all inside that you've got to be concerned about," the first guy said. He slammed the puck into the other guy's net.

I glanced over, more to see who scored than to hear their conversation better. One guy gave me a funny look. He lowered his voice a little.

"Things like this don't bother guys like you and me," he said. "But Youth Pastor Glenn? Who spends all his time underlining passages in the Bible? He's hardcore, with all that talk about not worshipping false idols and everything. He doesn't want kids believing in some imaginary man in a red suit."

"Well, he already put that little church in their place. And that white-bearded reverend guy didn't do anything about it," his friend said.

"I'm just saying — Youth Pastor Glenn isn't going to let this go."

I looked over again and this time they could tell I was listening. I would have had some explaining to do if it wasn't for Moss Murphy and Samantha walking up to me at that exact moment. They weren't holding hands or anything, but they looked chummy and were standing a few inches closer than they needed to. They looked sharp, Samantha in her tight-fitting green dress and Moss Murphy with those little anchors all over his shirt, like they were headed over to Sears for a professional couples photo shoot.

"Do you want to play charades?" I said.

Moss Murphy and Samantha giggled.

"Not really," she said, and leaned into my ear. Up close Samantha's skin was warm. Her hair smelled like green apples. She whispered, "Do you want to go to a real party?"

9
Cougars, Canyon Parties and Evil Clowns

Samantha led us through the suburban side streets for ten minutes until we came to a pathway tucked in between two houses. Moss Murphy and I knew exactly where it led. Two hundred feet down and a little to the left was Cougar Canyon, a long, expansive ravine that sat in between the suburbs and the nearby highway. We'd both been to Cougar Canyon dozens of times, especially when we were eleven and would play life-sized G.I. Joe down there.

An urban legend existed that an actual cougar lurked in the ravine, lying in wait for teenagers to sneak into its lair. My dad insisted the cougar story was just a myth perpetuated by our forefathers to create a tourist attraction where there was none. My mother said Dad's conspiracy story was all hogwash and there had once been a cougar in the region but that was before the three-lane highway and nearby smelting plant had driven out most of the local wildlife.

In reality, the cougar was the least of our worries. Even more frightening was the rumor of the evil clown. The story was that some local pervert — dressed up in clown makeup, complete with red nose, impractical shoes and a flower lapel that squirted knockout gas — had been caught molesting children in Cougar Canyon. This seemed much more plausible than a man-eating cougar. However, my father insisted that any evil clown story was derivative of the Stephen King book *It*, in which a clown lures children into the sewers only to terrorize and murder them. Dad said it was straight-up nonsense and besides, anyone brazen enough to dress up in a clown's outfit would have been caught by the police and featured on the front page of the newspaper by now.

"Besides, how would he climb that steep ravine in his oversized shoes?" Dad wondered out loud.

Moss Murphy, Samantha and I all looked down the darkened path. My brain told me there were no man-eating cougars or nefarious clowns down there. But it was like staring into a *Mario Kart* abyss. I wasn't sure about this. The canyon was a great place to explore in the daylight — at night it was full of all sorts of unimaginable horrors.

Moss Murphy was carrying two easy-burn fire logs that Samantha had hidden in the bushes outside the big church. He was definitely going down there. Moss Murphy's libido was directing his decisions tonight. He would follow Samantha off a cliff into a pool of crocodiles if he thought there was even a remote chance of getting to first base with her.

Samantha adjusted her jean jacket. "Come on," she said, and stepped down the path.

Moss Murphy traipsed after her.

"Most horror movies start this way," I said. "Some girl leads a couple of sad-sack teenagers into the woods and they end up getting chopped to pieces by a deranged serial killer. It's a textbook example." I glanced down the path. "How do we know it's not a trap?"

"You don't," Samantha said and walked into the darkness.

Moss Murphy shrugged and followed. I waited a few

seconds, convinced myself that my imagination was running wild and then went with them. We headed down a concrete path. A patch of grass followed and then the deep, long, winding path of stones that led to the canyon. Samantha and Moss Murphy led the way, with me following close behind, for just over five minutes. Our eyes adjusted to the moonlight. Somehow, the overgrowth of trees was twice as frightening coated in moonlight. It felt like we were walking into our own little George A. Romero black-and-white murder fest, with me as the third wheel. And everyone knows the third wheel always gets killed off first, oftentimes to comic effect. It was really starting to worry me until we heard music and voices from deep down in the canyon. It started first as a murmur, then the light from two separate campfires slipped through the trees and the voices grew louder. Samantha led us along a second path and then to a clearing where a full-on party was raging.

There were at least forty young people down here, mostly older teenagers and a few college kids as well. Someone had placed a boom box on a tree stump and girls were dancing around the fire to No Doubt's "Spiderwebs." Around the second campfire, some kids were passing a joint as if it were a collection plate at church. I couldn't believe the scene. Caroline had told me about these kinds of parties. One night, she'd even invited me along, only I'd been too scared to go.

Kids were getting wasted. Over by the tree line, two seniors were making out. The guy had his hand up his girlfriend's shirt. It was Sodom and Gomorrah meets a high school dance, with all the chaperones having cleared out and the smell of cheap weed in the air. It all felt new and strange and exciting. I felt it in the pit of my stomach. I felt different just by being here.

"I brought the fire logs!" Samantha called out to some muted fanfare. She took the logs out of Moss Murphy's hands and set them down on the respective fires. Then she walked over to an open cooler, dug her hands into the ice and pulled out three beers. Samantha handed one to Moss Murphy, another to me and kept the third one for herself. Moss Murphy twisted the cap off his beer and slugged it back like it was a can of Dr Pepper.

"Won't we get in trouble for drinking someone's beer?" I said.

Samantha already had her lips wrapped around her bottle. "My brother bought them," she said. "It's fine. You can each have one."

Moss Murphy and I shared a look. Free beer and a canyon party? Girls dancing to ska punk–infused reggae? There was no question: this was the greatest night of our lives.

I twisted the cap on my beer bottle. When it didn't come off, I examined it in the firelight. It was a regular bottle of imported Heineken. So what was wrong with the cap? I twisted harder, only it wouldn't budge. The spoke marks dug into my palm.

Moss Murphy grabbed the bottle out of my hand. "Watch how a real man does it," he said. He placed his chubby hand on the bottle and twisted so hard I thought he might burst a blood vessel. He kept twisting and when all seemed lost, he twisted some more.

"Here," a voice called.

Over by the fire, a girl was holding up a bottle opener. She was the prettiest girl I'd ever seen. She had red hair, but it wasn't just red or orange, it was the color of leaves in the fall, the color of the early morning sun. Her eyes shined through the moonlight, burned through the amber flames and pierced my soul. Her lips weren't just beautiful, they were perfect, the way they formed a little heart beneath her nose.

I didn't just fall in love at that moment — although I did, and I knew it and more importantly, I *knew* that I knew it — seeing her changed me. Standing there with that bottle of Dutch beer in my hand, I knew my life would forever be divided into two distinct periods of time: before I first saw her and after I first saw her.

I must have been staring because it suddenly occurred to me that all this inner monologuing was taking up a considerable amount of real-life time. The beautiful girl, Moss Murphy and Samantha were all looking at me.

"Do you want to use this?" She waved the bottle opener in the air.

"Yes," I said. "Yes, I do."

I was still standing like a tree that had grown roots. Then I felt Samantha's hand on my lower back, pushing me toward the redheaded girl.

"I'm Mary," she said, taking the beer out of my hand and popping off the cap, just like that.

"Jacob," I said.

Mary took a sip of her wine cooler and glanced down at the vacant tree stump beside her. "Do you want to sit down?"

I took a seat and sipped my beer. It was cold and coarse and slid down my throat like a handful of frozen jumping jacks. As I swallowed, I glanced over at Mary. Her profile was even more fascinating than looking at her straight on. Immediately, I started to worry — about my breath, about whether my hair looked okay, whether I'd applied enough antiperspirant. What if my armpits started to rain? There were so many things to worry about that — left completely alone — I might have gone mad. Then Mary opened her mouth and instantly all my cares drifted away.

"Were you at the youth meeting tonight?" she said. "I was supposed to go, only I had to visit my dad. He's out of town for a while."

I nodded like I understood. A few seconds passed before I realized it was my turn to talk. Was I supposed to ask where she visited her dad? Compliment her shoes? Change the subject entirely?

Luckily, Mary saved me. "Don't you go to that small church?"

"The Passion Lord Church of God? Yep."

"What do they teach there?" she said.

"Um, I'm not really sure."

"What do you mean, you're not sure?"

"Reverend Richard talks a lot about Jesus. He likes to tell us about all the times Jesus was almost stoned to death."

Mary took another sip from her wine cooler. "Some days I'm like that," she said. "Just waiting for the villagers to come and stone me, to get it over with. Do you know what I mean?" I didn't have the foggiest idea what she meant. But I smiled and Mary said, "So do you agree with Reverend Richard?"

Again, I didn't have a clue what she was talking about. I must have furrowed my brow like a bewildered chimpanzee, because she kept talking.

"I mean, do you believe that Jesus Christ of Nazareth was the Holy Spirit embodied in the form of man?" She looked at me with those penetrating eyes.

"I haven't given it much thought," I said.

Mary looked around. The party was still raging. Over by the other campfire, some girl with poor self-esteem had been cajoled into flashing her boobs. I caught some side-boob out of the corner of my eye, but Mary barely noticed. She looked up into the sky and my gaze followed. From down here you could see the stars so clearly, hundreds of thousands of galaxies, supernovas, white dwarfs, black holes and infinite space. Mary's gaze shifted to the flashing girl, the one standing on a fallen tree and letting her breasts out for some fresh evening air. The crowd cheered, and Mary half-smiled and then shook her head.

"Why don't you think about it now?" Mary said.

"About what?"

"About whether Jesus Christ was the son of God."

"Now?"

"All we have is the present moment," Mary said. "The past is just something people remember, and often not all that well." She spread her arms into the air. "You never know what the future will bring. If right now is all you have, why not spend it contemplating the greatest theological question of our times?"

Twenty feet away, another girl was being pressured into flashing. She took the moral high road and instead began yelling at her boyfriend. If my father had been there, he would have said that men are supposed to protect women, not pressure them into brazen displays of public nudity. It was all so distracting, and Mary was still looking at me, her eyes glistening like gemstones in the fire. I started to feel dizzy.

"That's okay," she said, and placed her hand on my shoulder. "I don't want you to think I'm thumping my Bible at you or anything. I know how frustrating that can be. One time I met this Scientologist at the Grand Canyon and he literally spent an hour and a half telling me L. Ron Hubbard's entire life story. By the end, I wanted to pull my hair out. I just wanted to know what you thought. We don't have to talk about this now. Why don't you think about it for a while and then get back to me?"

Mary stood up, walked over to where the girl was yelling at her boyfriend for "not having my back and always acting like a big, dumb ape" and spoke quietly in their ears. I couldn't tell what she said, but it only took Mary a few seconds to elicit a laugh out of the couple. Mary hugged her friend. She playfully punched the boyfriend in the arm and, like water into wine, the impending breakup was defused into some good-natured banter. I was marveling at her, the way she moved, the way she spoke, the depth of her words and her affable approach to an otherwise impossible situation, when Moss Murphy sat down beside me. He looked over at Mary as well.

"That chick has the fattest ass I've ever seen."

"What?" I said.

"Look at her body. The top half of her is normal and then watch as your eyes drift down to her hips. She's pear-shaped. A redheaded pear."

"Moss, *you're* fat. You drink nine cans of soda a day."

"Yeah, but I'm properly proportioned." He patted his round belly and watched it jiggle. "That girl there — she's like a regular girl up top and a fat girl down below. It's weird."

I'd never wanted to punch someone as much as I did at that moment. Looking at Moss Murphy, the moonlight highlighting his round, chipmunk cheeks, six years of friendship were immediately forgotten. Suddenly, he was that same mean kid who used to sit on my head and fart. How dare he criticize Mary? How dare he call her fat? *Moss Murphy was fat.* And he wasn't getting any skinnier. Chances were, he would lose a foot to diabetes someday. And here he was insulting Mary, this angel, this beautiful girl who talked to me like I was a real person, who asked me questions as though I was someone with something to say, someone worth listening to. I couldn't see what Moss Murphy was talking about. Mary still looked perfect to me. Her bum didn't look big at all.

Mary was talking to another friend, a girl I recognized as being Pushkar's daughter, Pia. Pia had sat two seats away from me in social studies that year. I think I'd even borrowed one of her H2 pencils to take a quiz.

Pia and Mary were looking in our direction. Moss Murphy and I glanced at each other and then looked over our shoulders into the woods. There were no two ways about it. Those girls were staring at us.

Moss Murphy nudged me with his elbow. "Now that Pia girl, she's hot."

I tore my eyes away from Mary and took a second look at Pia. She was quite gorgeous. There was something about the symmetry of her face, the positioning of her wide brown eyes over her cute little nose and the way her body hugged her baby-blue No Fear T-shirt that would make any man drool. Pia was thin and she was my age. (Mary, I had to assume, was at least a year older.) But Pia couldn't hold a candle to Mary. Pia was a gorgeous girl, but a girl all the same. Mary was heaven-sent. I could tell from the moment I looked at her. I was a different person than I was when I'd descended the rocky path minutes ago.

I was alive.

I was awake.

I was in love.

The girls walked toward us and Moss Murphy whispered under his breath, "Good Lord, they're coming our way." He started to stand up. "Samantha went to pee in the bushes. I'll go find her."

"You don't abandon your wingman," I said.

Moss Murphy glared at me. As much as I wanted to punch him a few seconds ago, I needed him now. And Moss Murphy knew it. We shifted awkwardly on our log. The girls were ten feet away and then five and then two and then they were standing over top of us.

"You guys know Pia, right?"

We both said, "Hi," and then there was an awkward pause.

"Can we sit down?" Mary said.

Moss Murphy and I bumped into each other trying to make room. We paused and then did it again. It was a full-on *Three Stooges* display and I couldn't believe it was taking place in front of Mary. Finally, we created two spaces. The girls sat down and it went — Mary, me, Pia and then Moss Murphy.

"Moss," Pia said. "Who's that girl you guys came down here with?"

Moss Murphy looked over at Samantha, who'd returned from her pee break and was now dancing around the fire to some old-school Salt-N-Pepa. He told Pia about how Samantha had invited us. "She likes *Mario Kart* just like me," he said. Moss Murphy was describing Samantha's Nintendo skills when I felt Mary nestle in beside me. Her shoulder pressed up against me first, all soft and warm, and then her leg grazed mine. I put my beer bottle to my mouth and downed the final third of my beer in one gulp. The alcohol lit a fire inside my chest and Mary drew even closer.

I remember being so happy, thinking this was the best moment of my life. It was one of those moments where the greatness isn't just in the moment, but in the anticipation of the next moment, of all the moments to come. It was so strange to think I could have been in Moss Murphy's basement trying to discover coding defects in the Hell section of *DOOM*. Instead I was here. Next to Mary. And she was leaning over to whisper in my ear.

Her lips parted. Her bottom lip brushed against my earlobe.

The party slowed to a standstill — Samantha and her dancing friends, the flickering fire logs, the voices all around me.

Then Mary spoke. And everything changed.

"I think Pia likes you."

10
Conjugal Visit Cheetos

Two hours later, Moss Murphy and I were standing in his backyard. He opened the shed where his father kept their firewood and pulled out an emergency stash of Cheetos. He started scarfing them down like a convict going at some poor, overwhelmed girl during his first conjugal visit in a decade. A few minutes ago, Samantha's brother Scott — a college dropout who worked at the lumberyard and lived in his parents' attic — had dropped us off in his rusted, red-striped Camaro. Scott wasn't at all impressed when Samantha insisted he drive us home. He cranked up Slayer's *Reign in Blood* album on the stereo and didn't say a word until we pulled in front of my house, when he mumbled, "See ya," before peeling off down the street.

Samantha waved goodbye from the passenger's seat. As Moss Murphy and I walked into his backyard, he proudly showed me a piece of paper with Samantha's phone number on it.

"Did you get Pia's number?" he said.

"What? Why?"

Moss Murphy scraped the last few bits of cheese out of the bag. He crumpled it up and threw it back in the shed. "Pia likes you. Mary told me right before the two of them bailed."

"They left pretty early, didn't they?" I said.

Moss Murphy licked his fingers. "Mary has a curfew. She probably had to make up some excuse just to get out of the house. It can't be easy being the minister's daughter."

"Mary's dad is Minister Matthew? The minister at your church?"

"Yep . . . at least he was. He hasn't been around for a while."

"Where did he go?"

Moss Murphy shrugged. "Beats me," he said. "Think about it though. If you had six daughters and they were all being homeschooled, you'd probably bail too."

I'd never heard of anyone in Parksville being home-schooled before. When I asked Moss Murphy about it, his nostrils flared. He was starting to get annoyed with all my questions.

"I heard they have a classroom in their garage where their mom teaches them math and science and stuff. Mary's totally sheltered. That's probably what led to her getting such a fat butt." He reached under his shirt to scratch his belly.

"So she hardly ever leaves the house?"

"I think she works at Dairy Queen or something. Anyways, it doesn't matter. Dude, Pia likes you. That's awesome. You can totally score. Maybe even brumsky her chesticles." He sloshed his chubby cheeks back and forth.

I looked up into the moonlight. It had dropped a few degrees outside and I was shivering in the new shirt Caroline had bought me. For all his bluster, and as much as I wanted to punch Moss Murphy in the face for mentioning Mary's backside again, I couldn't argue with him. That Pia girl was beautiful. And if she really liked me, she was the first girl ever to admit it in public. It was amazing how much a decent shirt and a proper stick of antiperspirant had helped my cause. I might be able to kiss Pia, maybe even make out with her. A couple hours ago, I'd seen the first side-boob of my young life and now there was a chance a girl might even let me touch hers. This was cause for celebration. It was a dream come true. Moss Murphy and I should have been high-fiving and dancing a jig in the street.

Still, I couldn't shake that feeling from when Mary's leg touched mine, when her mouth parted and her bottom lip grazed my earlobe.

"It was a big night," I said. "Everything changed."

Moss Murphy nodded. "Everything changed." He looked over his shoulder, grinned and said, "I've been holding this in for hours . . . Guacamole!"

He lifted his leg and let out the longest, wettest, shrillest-sounding fart I'd ever heard. It lasted five full Mississippis (eight if you counted fast, three if you counted slowly) and it didn't end well. Moss Murphy squeaked like he'd cut off the fart midstream. His eyes bugged out and his jaw clenched tight.

"Emergency," he said.

"What?"

"Emergency," he said again, clearer but with ten times the panic.

I looked around. What did he expect me to do? Call 9-1-1?

"Moss, are you going to crap your pants?"

"Shut up!"

"Did you crap them already?"

"Seriously, shut up!" He crossed his legs and leaned forward.

"What can I do?" I said.

"Get the key. The key in the fake rock."

I hurried over to the rock pile by the side door and pulled out his family's spare key, then opened the door to the garage.

Actively perspiring and with a deranged look on his face, Moss Murphy half-hopped, half-sprinted past me and in through the garage. He bashed into the wall and then barged into the house and down the hallway, making enough noise to wake up the neighborhood. The last thing I wanted to do was follow him, so I tucked the key back into the fake rock, shut the door and walked across the street and up the long driveway toward my house.

It was crazy to think that my best friend — the one who may or may not have made it to the toilet on time — would soon go out on a date with an actual girl. My mind raced. I thought about Pia, the way she smiled at me, how I'd be insane not to go out with her, and then about Mary, that tingling sensation on my earlobe.

And I knew exactly what I needed to do.

11
Like Thieves in the Night

"Jacob. Wake up."

It was my dad's voice. And it was early. I glanced over at my alarm clock. It wasn't even 6 a.m. on Saturday morning. My dad was sitting on my bed. He'd turned on the light and all I could see was his round head, those wide eyes.

"Why?" I groaned.

"Your mother needs you."

"It's too early."

"It's never too early for your mother," he said. "Remember, we're a family. And what do families do?"

I pulled the blanket over my head.

"What do families do?" he said.

"They stick together."

"That's right." Dad pulled off my blanket. "We stick together. Now, get up and get dressed. I'm not leaving until you do."

I gave him the most pitiful, sleep-deprived look I could muster. When that didn't work, I scowled at him and climbed out of bed. I slipped on my jeans and slid a hoodie over my T-shirt.

"That's my boy," he said, and slapped me on the back.

Dad was smiling a little too wide for this early on a

Saturday morning. There was something different about him, something I couldn't quite place.

"What?" he said.

I kept staring. My dad's smile slipped away and his face got all serious, like he didn't enjoy being examined at such close range. It took a few seconds, but I finally figured out what was different. Dad had trimmed his eyebrows. Just yesterday they were full and bushy, like collapsed log cabins with random chunks of hair of all different widths and lengths, colors and fullness. They looked thin now. His eyes looked wider and younger underneath. If that had been the only change, I might not have noticed, but he'd also gone to town on his ears and nostrils with a pair of tweezers. For over a decade, my dad had been infamous for the bountiful bouquet of hairs sprouting forth from his nostrils. At times, like right after he'd gotten a haircut, his nose hairs were even longer than the ones at the back of his head. His ears had been pretty bad too, filled with a messy tangle of cobwebs and nests a cockroach could get lost in. They were clear now. His entire face looked cleaner, younger, more earnest.

My mom popped her head in the doorway. "Excellent. You're awake," she said. "Come with me. We need a lookout."

Twenty minutes later, I was standing at the corner of Ascott Street and Jedidiah Avenue, staring at the giant Church of the Lord's Creation, the very same church I'd visited last night. Mom and Nancy Sylvester (who, to suit the clandestine mood, had dressed in black from head to toe) were digging through the back of Nancy Sylvester's trunk and casting guilt-ridden glances over their shoulders every few seconds.

"Is the coast clear?" Mom called.

The park across the street was deserted, the trees

86

slouching a little this early in the morning. Dew coated the grass and a single sparrow fluttered around the drinking fountain. The Church of the Lord's Creation, with its darkened skylights and shadowy stained glass, looked abandoned, as did our little rickety Passion Lord Church of God. The sun hadn't fully come up yet and the orangey-red glow of the electronic billboard coated the ground, casting a sheen on the trees across the way. Nancy Sylvester's face looked pink in the light. The rest of her looked like a mildly obese ninja.

"It's all clear," I said.

My mom paused to look up and read the big sign again.

THERE'S ONLY ONE TRUE MESSIAH
AND IT SURE ISN'T SANTA.
READ THE BIBLE, PEOPLE

She gritted her teeth and got to work. Mom and Nancy Sylvester crept over to the sign in front of our little church and unlocked it with a key. They opened the glass panel and promptly started rearranging letters. It took about two minutes before CHRISTMAS IS ONLY 5 MONTHS AWAY. REMEMBER . . . SANTA'S WATCHING! was transformed into

SANTA CLAUS BRINGS LOVE AND JOY
TO THE HEARTS OF CHILDREN EVERYWHERE

Mom and Nancy Sylvester secured the glass panel and stepped back to view their handiwork. I'd never seen a prouder look on my mother's face. I actually had to give her some credit. Twenty minutes ago, when we'd climbed into Nancy Sylvester's Mazda and zipped down the empty streets with a trunk full of black letters, I'd assumed the worst. I wouldn't have been surprised if my mother had posted a blatant, vile insult or a derogatory dig at the lunacy of building such a large church in such a small town. What she'd posted was actually rather diplomatic. It was genuine and heartfelt. I would have been one hundred percent on her side if it wasn't for the evil twinkle in her eye.

Mom and Nancy Sylvester high-fived. They let out a cheer and then my mom traipsed back and forth on the side of the road, her fists in the air like Rocky, her pupils lit up like fireworks, as if she'd just kicked over a hornet's nest and felt immune to their stings. Nancy Sylvester handed me a camera and I took a commemorative photo. Moments after the camera flashed, the lights came on in the goliath Church of the Lord's Creation. The parking lot lampposts started to hum.

Mom gasped. Nancy Sylvester let out a panicked squeal, and the two of them took off running for the car. I was twice as far away, but I bolted too, worried that in their panic, they might leave me behind. Before we could see who had turned on the lights, I climbed into the back seat and Nancy Sylvester fired up the Mazda.

Like thieves in the night, we peeled off down the street.

12
Love in the Time of Expired Milk Products

There were only two Dairy Queens listed in the phone book and they were so far away, there was no way I could walk in the blistering afternoon heat. I took my BMX bike instead and rode to the DQ down by the highway. When I entered and asked for Mary, a large woman with a prominent mole approached the counter and asked if I was a courier dropping off a parcel. They hadn't heard of Mary at the Dairy Queen attached to the go-kart track either. I was about to head home with my head hung low (and maybe strangle Moss Murphy for feeding me inaccurate info), when I heard someone say, "Hey!"

Over by the doorway, a guy in a windbreaker was eating a Dilly Bar and sending pennies down the Spiral Wishing Well Coin funnel. "She probably works at the mall," he said.

I glanced around, wary of talking to strangers.

"There's no Dairy Queen inside the mall," I said, and opened the door to leave.

"Not inside the mall. At the strip mall behind the Garden Center across the street."

I looked at him funny. This guy was wearing a hat and sunglasses and had his windbreaker hoodie pulled over his head. His skin was littered with stubble and he was holding up the Dilly Bar so I couldn't see his face. Immediately I became concerned. Was he sending me on a wild goose chase? If I showed up at the strip mall behind the Garden Center twenty minutes from now, would he be waiting in his car with a roll of duct tape and a rag covered in chloroform, his eyes shining all crazy like a three-peckered billy goat? I couldn't be sure.

"Thanks," I said.

He took another handful of pennies out of his windbreaker and dropped them one by one into the funnel. "Anything for love, dude," he said. "Anything for love."

I stopped dead in my tracks. This time I recognized his voice. "Blowpipe?" I said.

He pulled his windbreaker in front of his face.

"Blowpipe, I know it's you. I talked to Shotgun the other day."

He didn't say anything.

"Aren't you supposed to be in rehab?"

Blowpipe slouched. He pulled back his hoodie and took off his sunglasses. "I busted out," he said. "Just for an hour or two."

"Why?"

He held up the Dilly Bar. "I needed one of these. It reminds me of Zelda."

Blowpipe's Dilly Bar was largely intact. Up close, it looked suspiciously like a flattened breast with a chocolate swirl doubling as a nipple, so much so that I'd always felt embarrassed each time I ordered one and dared to lick it in mixed company. Blowpipe sneezed and wiped his nose with his sleeve. He looked haggard and scraggly and tired. I felt terrible. What kind of life is it when you're addicted to the nudie bar?

"You should go now, dude," Blowpipe said. "Find your own Zelda. Kiss her. Hold her close. Never let her go."

I opened the door and looked back. "Is there anyone you want me to call? Shotgun maybe? Your mom?"

Blowpipe dropped a nickel into the coin funnel and watched it swirl. "Nah, little buddy. Don't worry. I'll be okay. I just have to get back to rehab in time for curfew."

"Well, good luck," I said.

I stepped out the door, hopped on my BMX and pushed myself a few feet. Before I rounded the corner, I looked back through the window and watched Blowpipe toss the rest of his change into the funnel. He bit down hard on the Dilly Bar, relishing its creamy chocolate shell and soft ice cream center. He was walking up to the counter to order another when I turned the corner and took off for the Garden Center.

It turned out Blowpipe was right. There was a Dairy Queen hiding in that tiny strip mall. It was actually less like a strip mall and more like a cul-de-sac of stores facing one another. There was a nail salon, a Baskin-Robbins, a boarded-up Laundromat, a produce store with a surplus of bananas and, over on one side, a Dairy Queen kiosk. I approached the DQ and was startled to see a woman in her early fifties with three days' stubble on her chin. I glanced down at her chest. Yep, those were women's breasts all right, and her eyes — when seen in the proper light — were actually quite pretty. But her jaw was bristly like my dad's on Sunday morning. Her name tag read Customer Service. I was so stunned, I didn't know what to say.

"What'll it be, honey?"

"Does Mary work here?" I said

"Nope. Just me and Freddy. And he only works nights."

"Oh," I said.

My disappointment must have been written on my face because the large stubbly lady placed her elbows on the counter and gave me a sad look.

"There's another Dairy Queen over by the highway," she said.

"I already tried there," I said, and turned to walk away, defeated.

"Wait." She looked around her counter space and then opened the door to the freezer along the side wall. "Here. Have a Dilly Bar." She handed it to me and I reached into my pocket to pay. "Don't worry about it," she said. "The bar's expired. I mean, technically it's expired, but it's still good to eat. We're supposed to throw them out two weeks before they go bad."

"Thanks," I said.

"No problem, sugar."

I had just unwrapped the Dilly Bar and started to wheel my bicycle away when a voice sounded across the way.

"Jacob! Over here!"

My heart skipped a beat. Mary was standing in front of the Baskin-Robbins, wearing a blue apron and a pink striped hat. She didn't work at Dairy Queen after all; she worked at Baskin-Robbins. Moss Murphy's intel wasn't wrong — it was flawed. I wheeled my bike over, and Mary reached her arms up like she was happy to see me. *Was she really going to hug me?* Then she stretched her arm forward, and I realized she was just shaking my hand. It was no ordinary handshake though. Her hands were cold and smooth even though it was hot and muggy outside, and she clasped my hand between hers and held it tightly.

"A Dilly Bar? From the enemy?" she said.

I glanced back at the Dairy Queen. The smile on the

lady's face had turned into an angry line underneath her nose. "It's expired," I said.

"Really? And you're still going to eat it?"

I'm not sure if it was teenage machismo or a desire to prove I wasn't insane for accepting an expired milk product from a partially bearded woman I didn't know, but I bit right into the Dilly Bar. The chocolate shell crumbled in my mouth and I tasted the ice cream underneath. While it wasn't exactly sour, it wasn't exactly fresh either. I could see how eating an entire tub of it might make me violently ill, but I figured I could stomach a single bar.

"It's still good," I said.

"Well, come in and chat. My manager went home and there're no customers, so I'm all alone."

I followed Mary into Baskin-Robbins, which was less of a kiosk and more like an old-fashioned malt shop. There didn't seem to be room in their display freezer for thirty-one different flavors, but I wasn't about to start counting. I was so stunned that I'd actually found her, my hand was still tingling from where Mary's palm had met mine, and — after two more bites of the Dilly Bar — an unpleasant tang was liquefying in the back of my throat.

Mary walked behind the counter and I sat down on one of the bar stools.

"So, what brings you out past the Garden Center?" she said. "People hardly ever come back here. This mini-mall is dying. They just shut down the Laundromat and there's word the nail salon might close soon, although I'm not convinced it's really on the up-and-up. You know how they say nail salons are the new massage parlors? Happy endings and all? It's not like I see middle-aged guys in trench coats sneaking out of there at all hours of the night, but there aren't any ladies getting their nails done either." She glanced up at a flickering fluorescent light in the ceiling and then back at me. "You don't say much, do you?"

"Um . . ."

"That's okay," she said. "There's something to be said about the strong, silent type."

Aha! I knew it. There was still room in this world for the strong, silent type.

"Anyways," she said, "have you given any more thought to what we talked about?"

I stared at her blankly. The ice cream from the Dilly Bar started to run down my fingers, and Mary handed me some napkins.

"You know, about the greatest theological question of our time. Jesus, God, the Immaculate Conception and all that. I only ask because you go to that little church across the way and my dad says he doesn't know exactly what they teach in your denomination, or what really goes on in there, but I've always wondered. A couple times, I've almost snuck across the street on Sunday morning and slipped into the Passion Lord Church of God to mingle with the congregation, uninvited and all. I never did it though. My dad would kill me. He blew his lid when I insisted on getting a summer job. Imagine what he would do if I jumped ship on the church where he ministers?" She glanced up at that flickering fluorescent light again. "You're a really good listener."

I looked up at the flickering light too. "Is that driving you crazy?" I said.

"It hurts my eyes. Last weekend, it totally gave me a headache, but we don't have a ladder. I meant to bring one from home but I forgot about it until I came into work today."

I glanced around. The stool I was sitting on was the tallest thing in this little shop, and while it was a little wobbly, I felt compelled to help. I braced myself against the counter and stood up on the narrow stool. For a moment, I almost lost my balance, but then I righted myself, all the while holding the dripping Dilly Bar in my hand.

I reached up and the light singed my fingertips. I was about to try again when, from the corner of my eye, I saw the lady from Dairy Queen storming across the concourse. That straight line under her nose was now a full-blown scowl. She looked mad as hell.

"Oh God, it's the bearded lady," Mary said.

"What?" I said from my perch atop the stool.

Mary took a step back. "People say she used to have patches of peach fuzz on her face. Then one day, decades ago, she started shaving it off, and all of a sudden it grew back in all thick and hairy. So she kept shaving more and more. Now she has a full-on beard and when she goes a day without shaving, it looks like five o'clock shadow."

What do you know? My dad was right. As soon as you start shaving, it grows back in like a patch of weeds.

"She and my manager got into a big fight last week," Mary said. "Something about us stealing her business by moving in right across the way. She's been giving me the stink eye ever since."

The bearded lady burst in through the doors. Her face had gone beet red and she didn't look like she'd be calling me honey or sugar again anytime soon.

"Give me back the Dilly Bar," she said.

"What?" I said.

"You heard me. You don't accept a gift from a business and then head straight to their competitor's place to eat it."

"It's expired," I said.

"Hurry up!"

"You can't be serious," Mary said.

The bearded lady pointed an angry finger at her. "You stay out of this, hot pants!" she said.

Mary looked down at her conservative, store-issued slacks and back up at the bearded lady, as if to say, *Hot pants?!*

The stool shook under my feet, and against my better judgment, I reached up again and burned my fingers on the flickering light. I twisted it two more times and — success! The light stopped flickering. I was about to step down off the stool when the bearded lady yanked the dripping, half-eaten Dilly Bar from my hand. The stool wobbled. I regained my balance and thought I might be able to step off with my dignity still intact. Then it wobbled again and before I knew it, I lost my balance. The stool slipped out from under me.

I fell. It was like it happened in slow motion and at the speed of light at the same time. I grabbed for something — anything to break my fall — but only found soft, yielding air. My feet left the stool. It felt like I was floating, but in reality I was barreling toward the ground at 9.81 meters per second (minus wind resistance). I would have been lucky to hit the ground. Instead, my head struck the counter. A sharp pain burst on the side of my eye. Then everything went black.

13
Waffle Cones Everywhere

I woke up slowly. Before I even opened my eyes, I could sense the room: the cool breeze from the air conditioning, the hard tile floor beneath me, the ache on the side of my head. A pair of soft hands cupped my face. They slid along my jaw and grazed my ears, then rested tenderly on my cheeks. *Oh, Mary*, I thought, and my chest flushed with warmth. Even in my woozy state, a surge of blood rushed between my legs. I could have opened my eyes, but I hung on for just a moment, enjoying those soft, cold hands. Suddenly, my head didn't hurt so badly anymore. I could feel Mary holding me, taking care of me, watching over me.

I reached up to cup her face. Something was horribly wrong.

I opened my eyes. "Mom!"

"My baby!" she said, and wrapped her arms around me.

Even in my panic, I could still feel that surge of blood in the tip of my penis. I tried to push her away.

"Don't move," someone said.

I looked over to see a guy in a paramedic's outfit holding a needle. "I'm fine," I said, and tried to stand up. "Don't stab me."

Mom pushed me back down.

I caught a glimpse of Mary. Reverend Richard was standing beside her. He was wearing a gray golf shirt and his beard looked whiter than usual.

"Sit still, son," Reverend Richard said.

I squirmed away and stood up. My legs almost buckled, and I grabbed a stool for support. "What happened?" I said.

"The bearded lady did it," Mary said.

I looked out the window. The kiosk across the street was closed, the bearded lady nowhere to be seen. "How long was I out?"

"Twenty minutes or so," Mary said. "You scared the life out of me, Jacob. I called 9-1-1 right away but then I didn't know what to do and you were just lying there, not moving. I wanted to call your mom, only I realized I didn't even know your last name, so I called the Passion Lord Church of God to ask them, and lo and behold, your mom was already there talking to Reverend Richard."

Reverend Richard nodded. "Margaret, Nancy and I were having a long talk. So we all rushed over."

I looked at the back of the store where Nancy Sylvester was perched on a stool, eating a double-scoop waffle cone with rocky road on the bottom and rainbow sherbet on top. "You ordered ice cream?" I said.

Nancy Sylvester took a long lick of sherbet. "It's been a stressful couple of days."

My mom wrapped her arms around my shoulders and pulled me close. "We hurried right over," she said. "Now, who is this bearded lady and why did she beat you up?"

"A bearded lady did not beat me up," I said.

She lifted her hand to my temple and came back with her fingers covered in blood. "Well, she certainly did some damage."

I reached up and felt the blood too. I tried to be brave in front of Mary, but my face must have been contorting into a full-blown panic because the EMT had to step in and assure me that it wasn't all that bad.

"It'll probably only need a few stitches," he said. He sat me down in the corner and asked all sorts of questions to see whether or not I had a concussion. I told him I knew where I lived and recited my zip code and the day's date. He seemed skeptical and kept probing, but I promised him I didn't feel dizzy or nauseous and that I would definitely go to the emergency room if any of those symptoms appeared.

Then he sewed me up, right in the corner of the Baskin-Robbins. My mom got jealous of Nancy Sylvester's waffle cone and ordered one for herself. She also bought Reverend Richard a caramel parfait, which Mary made swiftly and with care. Reverend Richard feigned disinterest before finally succumbing to temptation, and then he and my mom sat down with Nancy Sylvester to watch the EMT sew four stitches into the side of my head. The needle in his hand had turned out to be freezing for the stitches, not an adrenalin shot as I'd feared. By the time he finally packed up his bag and left, my mom had polished off her waffle cone and now couldn't stop stroking my hair and rubbing my back.

Mary was watching the entire scene with a bemused grin that I knew couldn't be good for me. There was no way she'd ever think of me as boyfriend material if she thought I ran to my mommy each time I got hurt. I tried to push my mom away, which only made her hold on tighter. My only option was to get out of there as fast as I could.

"Maybe I should go home and rest," I said.

Reverend Richard and Mom agreed. Nancy Sylvester lost interest and went outside to check out the mangoes and tangerines at the produce store across the way.

"Here," Mary said as we left. She held up a double-scoop mint chocolate chip waffle cone. "On the house. I promise this one's not expired."

I took the cone and thanked her. Mary tilted her pink-and-blue-striped hat and smiled. Then she leaned in and gave me a soft shoulder-to-shoulder hug and whispered in my ear, "Meet me outside church tomorrow morning. I have something for you."

We left Baskin-Robbins and headed to the parking lot where Reverend Richard put my BMX into the trunk of my mom's car. As I stepped inside, I took a final look and could see a vague outline of Mary rearranging the stools inside her store. I wasn't sure what "I have something for you" meant, but if I contorted the words enough in my head, it almost sounded like she and I had a date.

Maybe the day wasn't such a disaster after all.

That night, however, was definitely a disaster.

My head, while sore to the touch, felt just fine in that I wasn't dizzy or wobbly. Still, my mom insisted I take a nap. A half hour after I went to sleep, she shook me awake. Apparently Candice Collington had called to say she'd read somewhere that if you sleep immediately after suffering a head injury, there's a good chance you might slip into a coma and never wake up.

"What a kind woman," Mom said. "Taking time out of mourning her beloved basset hound to check up on you."

I pulled my blanket over my head and said I didn't feel "the least bit coma-esque."

Still, she demanded I come into the next room and watch *Wheel of Fortune* with her. Mom wrapped her arms around me while I ate fish sticks with her extra-tangy homemade tartar sauce. She made me submit to forcible cuddles all the way through three rounds of Pat Sajak's banter and an entire episode of *Jeopardy!*

When the game shows finished, she said, "Let's watch that program I like, the one with the hip prince."

I raised my eyebrows at her.

"You know," she said. "It has the little fellow who dances to Tom Jones."

"Do you mean *The Fresh Prince of Bel-Air*?"

"That's it. The hip prince. He's funny."

I groaned.

"Aww. How does my baby feel?" she said.

"A little sore."

"Maybe you should go sit on the toilet and see what happens."

"Mom!"

I couldn't believe she said that again. For fifteen years now, anytime I had so much as a sniffle, or dared to cough, or — heaven forbid — sneeze, my mom would tell me to go sit on the toilet and see what happens. As if a sore throat or a head injury could be cured by a particularly liberating session of diarrhea. I'd asked her countless times to stop saying it, and still she insisted. At this point, I'd pretty much come to terms with it. Mom would be telling me to go sit on the toilet until we put her in the old folks' home, maybe even longer, and there wasn't a thing I could do about it.

I wiggled out of her grasp and went to find Caroline to tell her all about my sudden fall and the promise Mary had made. Caroline and I weren't exactly best buddies, but she'd dated dozens of guys and was the closest thing to a relationship expert in my house. I found her out front by her car, adjusting her long black boots and hiking up her green crop top.

"Let me see it," she said, and tried to pull off the bandage covering my stitches.

"No way. You'll poke it or something," I said.

Caroline pulled out her compact. She fished some eyeliner out of her purse and started coloring.

"How can you tell if a girl likes you?" I said.

Caroline didn't even look up. "She'll touch you on the arm."

I thought back to Samantha and Moss Murphy, those two full Mississippis when her hand rested on his forearm. Across the street, the Murphy house was quiet. Mr. Murphy was probably inside eating an entire plate of ribs while his wife, Betsy, smoked a cigarette and tried to cram a suppository inside her belligerent ferret. I hadn't heard from Moss Murphy all day. What if he and Samantha were out together right now? They might be splitting a milkshake with two straws like they used to do back in the '50s. Or maybe they were sitting in a movie theater, holding hands or even making out. Just a week ago, I thought Moss Murphy was destined to die alone, and now my best friend might very well have his tongue inside a girl's mouth. Amazing.

In the distance, a pickup truck peeled around the corner, the twang of country music blasting from its speakers.

"I have to go," Caroline said. She tucked her makeup into her purse and sashayed down the driveway without a single look back. She climbed into the passenger's seat and the truck sped off down the street.

I took one last look at Moss Murphy's house and walked back inside. Mom was sitting on the couch, watching the television and holding a tissue to her eyes.

"What's wrong?" I said.

"It's the hip prince. His birth father doesn't want anything to do with him," she said. Mom patted the cushion beside her. "Come join me. Maybe the little fellow will liven things up again."

"In a minute," I said, and headed out to our back deck where my dad was duct-taping a propeller to a birdhouse.

"What are you doing?" I said.

"Fighting the squirrels," he said.

I knew exactly what he meant. My dad hated squirrels and loved birds. For months now, he'd spent hours staring out our tiny kitchen window with a pair of binoculars, just waiting for his feathered friends to land on the expensive three-tier birdhouse he'd bought at Home Depot. Unfortunately, not a single hummingbird or blue jay had visited, no matter how much birdseed my dad poured into that house. While the occasional crow had been brazen enough to buzz by the portable bird mansion (forcing my dad to chase it off with a broom), for the most part, the squirrels had eaten all his bird food.

"How is the propeller going to stop the squirrels?" I said.

Dad grinned. "They like to climb up this drainpipe, jump on top of the birdhouse and then sneak inside. Now when they jump on top, they'll land on this propeller, go for a quick spin and then fall right off," he said.

I looked closer at my dad's contraption. He'd wrapped duct tape all around the propeller, up and down, side to side, in big wide circles. "How is the propeller supposed to spin?"

Dad scratched his bald head. He tried to spin the heavily duct-taped propeller. When it didn't move, he squinted like he was trying to recall the first forty digits in π.

"How long have you been out here?" I said.

"About an hour."

Now I scratched my head. It shouldn't take an hour to

improperly tape a plastic propeller to a vacant birdhouse. Then my gaze drifted to the house behind us. The Deck Girls were having a cookout. Emboldened by the warm summer weather, Lydia and Leah Fontaine were wearing bikini tops and jean short shorts while cooking Salisbury steak on their hot plate. Leah stood up and stretched, her enormous breasts defying the itsy-bitsy bikini's attempt to preserve her modesty. She looked over at us and waved. Her sister stood up and waved too. I waved back and was about to head inside when I caught a glimpse of my father — he of the recently shorn eyebrows, the unfettered nostrils and ultra-clean ears — and he looked positively giddy, like Moss Murphy at a Mexican buffet. I leaned toward my dad to see if I could get his attention, only he wouldn't have noticed me even if I'd stepped in front of him and started doing the Macarena.

14
Stir Up a Hornet's Nest

My mom wasn't kidding around. There was no way on God's green earth we were going to be late for church that morning, not with the grand opening of the Passion Lord Church of God's new slogan. She and Nancy Sylvester had already exchanged a half-dozen phone calls since breakfast, each filled with mounting pride and a budding righteous superiority. My dad was wearing his best suit — navy blue with an orange tie — and Mom had on a flowery dress and her favorite cardigan. I was wearing my best black polo T-shirt and the three of us were ready to go. Then Caroline stepped out of her bedroom.

"No," Mom said.

"But —"

"No."

"But, Mom!"

Caroline was wearing the shortest skirt imaginable, the kind that would give my Uncle Ted a heart attack. Even a slight breeze — say from a car door shutting too quickly — would expose Caroline's underpants, if she was wearing any. Up top she was showing enough cleavage to get backstage at a Van Halen concert.

"March right back in there and change into something appropriate," Mom said.

"Oh, you'd just love it if I showed up dressed like a nun," Caroline said. "Is that what you want? Me covered from head to toe?"

"That wouldn't be so bad," Dad called from down the hall.

"Shut up!" Caroline and Mom yelled.

Mom lowered her voice and whispered in Caroline's ear. A few seconds later, Caroline slammed her door, and Mom walked down the hall and joined us in the kitchen. She took a sip from her tea.

"Your sister will be along shortly," she said.

Five minutes later, Caroline emerged with the makeup scrubbed off her face. She was wearing a wool turtleneck, a camping vest and a pair of baggy jeans. Her hair was up in a ponytail and she looked incredibly warm.

"But it's summer," I said.

"I'm just preserving my modesty," Caroline said, staring daggers at Mom.

My mother, however, wouldn't be baited into a big battle this morning. She'd already fired a salvo in the holy war with the church across the street. Why clash with her own troops at home? She poured her tea into a travel mug, straightened her cardigan, picked up her purse and walked out the front door.

The drive over wasn't all that bad. Kenny Loggins was on the radio and it was fun to watch Caroline squirm in her stuffy wool turtleneck. She had far too much pride to ask my dad to turn on the air conditioning, so she asked me to ask instead. I couldn't really say no, seeing as she'd just bought me a dress shirt and taught Moss Murphy and me all about personal hygiene. When I mentioned the A/C to my dad, however, he just raised his eyebrows in the rearview mirror and shook his head slowly side to side.

"Sorry," I whispered.

"Go hump a loofah," she hissed back.

"What did *I* do?" I said.

Caroline gave me the same dirty look she'd been giving my mom and blew down inside her turtleneck.

Two minutes later, we pulled into the church parking lot to find it crowded with people. Typically when we arrived at the corner of Ascott Street and Jedidiah Avenue, most of the parishioners would already be inside getting good seats. A few stragglers aside, both parking lots would be ghost towns of empty vehicles. Today, people were standing by their cars. And no one was looking at the tame, diplomatic message Nancy Sylvester and my mom had posted in the wee morning hours. They were staring at the giant electronic billboard in front of the Church of the Lord's Creation.

My dad parked the car, and right away Mom climbed out and charged into the crowd, anxious to get a better look. Dad ran after her, keys in hand. I stepped out with Caroline, who, despite sweating in her warm winter outfit, couldn't wipe the smirk off her face.

The giant electronic sign read:

YOUR IMAGINARY FRIEND IS A LIE.
ONLY JESUS IS REAL.
THIS IS NOT OPEN FOR DEBATE!

Caroline looked back at our tiny little sign espousing the love Santa Claus brings to the hearts and minds of children and then up at the giant red letters in the sky. She started laughing uncontrollably. I tried to cover her mouth, but Caroline licked my palm just like she did when we were kids.

Reverend Richard was standing a few feet away, his mouth dangling open, his eyes as wide as golf balls. He glanced over at Caroline and my dad came running. By now Caroline was bowled over in hysterics and a few little kids had started giggling along. Only, my mom wasn't laughing. My dad wasn't laughing either. He grabbed Caroline by the arm and dragged her inside the church while the rest of us stood staring at the fighting words up on that big sign.

Across the street, a hundred or so worshippers were gathered, and while Mary wasn't there, Moss Murphy definitely was. And he was holding Samantha's hand! I couldn't believe my eyes. How long had I been unconscious yesterday? Was it really enough time for Moss Murphy to go from romantic hopeful to full-on hand-holding boyfriend? He wasn't even wearing his good shirt. Moss Murphy was wearing his purple Hypercolor shirt, the kind that changes color with your body temperature, the very shirt he'd been mocked for wearing during math class that past spring, the one that turned bright pink the more embarrassed Moss Murphy got. I couldn't tell from this far away, but it looked like he'd forgotten to put gel in his hair. He was back to regular old Cheetos-eating Moss Murphy, and still that cute girl with the star-shaped patch of freckles was leaning her head against his shoulder. Had the entire world gone mad?

I couldn't take it anymore: the tension in the air, that look of satisfaction on Moss Murphy's face, the sound of my dad yelling at Caroline from inside the church. I walked over to the car and was planning on sitting in the back seat until church was over, when someone called my name. It was difficult to hear over the noise from the crowds. Then she called again. I turned and saw Mary standing at the edge of the park. She wasn't in her Baskin-Robbins uniform this time.

Mary was wearing a white dress with pink and green flowers at the bottom and a wide black sash around her waist. Her one hand was on her hip while her other hand was leaning against a tree. With her red hair up in a bun, she looked like an angel on earth.

She called my name again.

No one was watching. I slipped away, jogging the last few paces to meet Mary. She put her hands in the air again, only this time I wasn't going to be fooled into thinking she wanted to hug. I reached my hand out to shake hers, just as she went to hug me, and — in a moment of sheer horror — touched her right between the breasts. Not *on* the breasts. My hand didn't touch anything soft or forbidden or wonderful or smooth. The tips of my fingers tapped her rib cage instead.

Mary gazed down at my hand and then up at my mortified expression. "Looking for a cheap thrill there, sailor?"

"I . . . I was going to shake your hand."

Mary put her hand on her hip again. She didn't look the least bit embarrassed. "Don't you know? Once you hug someone, you're supposed to hug hello the next time, not shake hands. It's not like we're strangers anymore," she said.

I thought back to that soft, shoulder-to-shoulder hug she'd given me at the ice cream parlor. It had been so quick and in front of so many witnesses, I'd hardly thought it was precedent-setting. Mary smiled and I wasn't sure what to do. Should I go in for a hug now, after we'd already spoken? That wasn't right. And shaking her hand was off the table, presumably forever. Mary glanced back at the crowd in front of her church, and I realized that our greeting, however bizarrely executed, was complete.

Mary pointed to my bandage. "How's your eye?"

"It only hurts when I think about it."

She pulled on the side of my bandage. Her eyes grew wide at the sight of my four black stitches and the patches of dried-up blood.

"The EMT said it wouldn't leave a big scar," she said. "But wouldn't that be cool? If you had a battle wound to show the ladies for years to come? I mean, you wouldn't have to admit that a bearded lady gave it to you. You could say you got it in a knife fight at the docks or that some jilted husband hit you with a folding chair for sleeping with his wife. Scars are awesome because they're the one thing you're allowed to exaggerate about and it's never really a lie. Because you have proof. The damage is real. The story is yours."

Mary looked across the street. Standing underneath the enormous sign was a young boy. Tears were streaming down his face. He'd clearly figured out that "imaginary friend" was a rather unsubtle euphemism for Santa Claus. The boy's mother went over to console him.

"I had nothing to do with that sign, I promise," she said.

I looked from the crying child to my mother still simmering with rage at the front of the crowd and back to Mary again. For the life of me, I couldn't think of anything clever to say.

"You don't say much, do you?" Mary said.

My heart sank to the bottom of my stomach. This was the second time she'd said that, and I knew it was true. When Mary spoke, the words just flowed, and it wasn't like she was filling up airtime, like my mom and Nancy Sylvester sitting around the kitchen table, talking about apple season and knit sweaters and how to get stains out of teenage boys' sheets. It really felt like Mary was talking *to me*, saying things she thought would interest me. I had to think of something — quickly — before I went from being the strong, silent type to plain old boring.

"I'm perpetually shy," I said.

"Perpetually?"

"It's a curse," I said. Then I remembered something I'd seen on TV. "Besides, I just like listening to you."

Mary tilted her head to the side and made a sound with her lips, the kind people make when they've just seen a newborn puppy. Her hand moved toward my arm in slow motion and all I could think about was how many Mississippis it would stay there. I closed my eyes for just a moment, anticipating her touch. When I opened them, Mary wasn't alone.

Youth Pastor Glenn was beside her, grinning with those white teeth and that immaculately combed hair. I glanced over his shoulder, at the crowd across the street, at the small smattering of trees attached to the park, back at the parking lot where Caroline had broken free of my father's grasp and locked herself in the back seat of the car. Where in the blue heaven had Youth Pastor Glenn come from? Had he been here all along? I'd thought Mary and I were alone.

Discreetly, so Youth Pastor Glenn couldn't see, Mary slipped me a small piece of paper. It went from her fingers to mine and I cupped it in my hand.

"Good morning, Jacob," Youth Pastor Glenn said.

I stared at him, speechless.

"I think Jesus would have enjoyed a wonderful day like this," he said, adjusting his tie.

Mary rolled her eyes. "I've told Glenn a thousand times — conservative Christians would have hated Jesus."

Youth Pastor Glenn gave her a look, but he didn't reply.

"Jesus was a rule-breaking humanist who wasn't *saved*," Mary said. "He undermined the scriptures of his day, and always in favor of empathy. If he were alive now, *Christianity*

Today would write horrible editorials against him. The pope would call him a traitor."

It looked like Youth Pastor Glenn was about to engage Mary in some kind of spirited debate. Instead, he put his arm around her and pulled her close. "That's what I love about this girl. She has her own views on important topics and isn't afraid to speak her mind."

In a brazen display of affection, Mary reached up and touched his hand. Their fingers intertwined and it became clear: they were more than just friends. I thought I was going to barf. Seriously. The maple-and-brown-sugar oatmeal I'd eaten an hour ago lurched up into my throat and it took all my power to keep it from flying out my mouth.

Youth Pastor Glenn used his free hand to point back at the crowds. He didn't seem at all fazed by the sight of the crying child. "It seems there's a bit of an uproar today," he said. "I hope you understand, Jacob. I didn't want to stir up a hornet's nest."

"It's just Santa Claus," I said. It felt good saying it, too. Like someone should have said this to him days ago. I was basking in my minor (though fairly heroic) rebellion when the skin on Youth Pastor Glenn's face grew tight.

"Is it?" he said. "Is it just a fat man in a red suit?"

"Um . . ." I stammered.

"The entire town drives by our little street corner here. I don't want them to think we worship false idols. Do you?"

His piercing eyes burrowed into my soul — emoting, imploring, dissecting me into little pieces right in front of Mary. I suddenly felt underdressed in my black golf shirt. Mary still looked so pretty, like a magazine cover girl, and Youth Pastor Glenn couldn't stop smiling. Whatever his eyes did, his mouth kept smiling.

"No. I don't suppose I do," I said.

Youth Pastor Glenn's eyes returned to normal. "We'd better get back."

They turned and walked across the street. Youth Pastor Glenn moved his arms in big sweeping circles and his congregation started filing into their church. Mary didn't look back at me. Neither did Youth Pastor Glenn. And while Reverend Richard, my mother and the other parishioners on our side still hadn't moved, none of them noticed me. They were too busy staring up at that sign. I was the forgotten man, standing in my Sunday best next to a tree.

I took a few steps toward the church before I remembered the paper in my hand. It was a small piece, folded three times over.

Inside, written in purple ink, was the name Pia.

The "i" had a little heart over it.

Underneath Pia's name was her phone number.

15
Dave's Refrigeration Emporium

Church that morning was an out-and-out gong show. Reverend Richard — looking equal parts haggard and perturbed — delivered his sermon on respect for the elderly as scheduled, despite the angry faces and occasional murmurs coming from the pews. Afterward, he locked himself in his office and insisted on seeing only one parishioner at a time. My mom lined up outside his door with all the other agitated ladies while my dad and I sat on the front steps, sweating in our Sunday clothes. Caroline still hadn't left the back seat of the car but she'd discarded her heavy turtleneck and propped the doors open to create a breeze. I waved to her and she flipped me the bird.

Dad was listing all the foods Mom wouldn't let him eat.

"Corn Pops," he said. "There's too much sugar in Corn Pops, she says. I told your mother — I'll dilute the sugar by mixing the Corn Pops with Rice Krispies. But did she listen? Nooooo. The other day, she gave me a bowl of flaxseed and a shot of wheatgrass for breakfast. Do you know what wheatgrass looks like, son? Like a hippie blew his nose into a shot glass. That's what wheatgrass looks like."

"When are we leaving?!" Caroline bellowed from the back seat of the car.

Dad ignored her. "Pizza Pops. That's another one," he said. "She says there's no room for them in the freezer. So I told her — just take out the Swedish meatballs. They're all freezer burnt anyways."

As my dad moved on to comparing low-sodium turkey bacon to the far superior maple-cured bacon, I watched the congregation pour out of the Church of the Lord's Creation. Lorne and Betsy Murphy walked to their car with Moss Murphy trailing behind. His new girlfriend, Samantha, must have still been inside because she wasn't holding his hand anymore. The other families climbed into their cars as well. As the last few people filtered out, I noticed Mary wasn't among them. She must have been inside too.

My mind filled with horrible images: Mary sitting on Youth Pastor Glenn's lap, his hand nonchalantly — and yet completely brazenly — resting on her thigh. The two of them snuggled up, waiting until no one's watching and then sneaking kisses in the pews.

"So are you in or are you out?" Dad said.

"Pardon me?"

"Will you help me with the delivery tonight?"

I looked my dad right in his hairless nose. "What delivery?"

"Haven't you been listening to a word I said? Honestly, Jacob, sometimes I think your head is permanently up in the clouds. I'm having something delivered tonight. It took a lot of doing to get the company to deliver on a Sunday and I need you to distract your mother for me."

"Um, okay," I said.

"It's very important your mother doesn't see it."

"Um, sure."

"And don't say 'Um' at the beginning of every sentence.

You know your mother thinks it makes our family sound uneducated," he said.

"Er . . . okay."

Dad glanced over at Caroline, who, after taking off her boots and tossing them onto the pavement, had now removed her socks and hung them out the window.

"Also, don't tell your sister," he said. "She's a loose cannon."

Two minutes later, my mom came storming out of the church. She blustered straight past us and over to the car, kicking up little bits of gravel along the way. Mom ignored Caroline completely, climbed inside the passenger's seat and slammed the door so hard I thought the window might shatter. Dad and I exchanged uneasy glances and then slowly made our way to the car. I handed Caroline her boots and we climbed inside. As we pulled out of the parking lot, Mom's eyes did a slow burn on the gigantic church across the street.

"Look at that," she said, and my dad pressed on the brakes.

"At what, honey?" he said gingerly.

"At that rainbow above the Virgin Mary on their stained-glass window. Don't they know that rainbows are gay?"

"That's racist," Caroline said.

"It most certainly is not."

"Well . . . it's discriminatory somehow," Caroline said.

Mom spoke through clenched teeth. "The homosexual community has adopted the rainbow as their symbol of gay pride. It's common knowledge."

I gave my mom and Caroline a confused look. I didn't know there was a flourishing gay community in Parksville, let alone that they'd taken over all the rainbows in town.

"You're crazy," Caroline said. "Tight pants and motorcycle jackets are gay. Rainbows are things kids paint in kindergarten."

"I wish your grandmother was alive to hear you talk like this," Mom said. "My mother wouldn't have put up with any of this: that infernal sign, the arrogant looks from those defectors across the street, that gay-as-the-day-is-long rainbow in front of their church." She turned around and looked Caroline straight in the eye. "I am a tolerant person!" she yelled. "Did you know your Great-Aunt Gladys hated the gays so much, she refused to even speak to men with black moustaches? Do you know how many waiters in Springfield have moustaches? How many restaurants we had to leave before we ever got to eat? Your father and I are nothing if not tolerant and accepting!" Mom looked over at Dad, who was quivering like a frightened gerbil. "Now drive!"

That evening, I sat staring at the telephone in my living room, crumpling and then uncrumpling the piece of paper with Pia's number on it. If I was going to make the call, this was the perfect time. Caroline was locked in her room, listening to the Red Hot Chili Peppers and probably practicing for beauty school by applying her makeup in front of the mirror. My dad was outside waiting for his package to arrive, and Mom was out with Candice Collington and Nancy Sylvester, undoubtedly scheming up some clever response to the blatant heathenism they'd witnessed that morning. Twice now I'd picked up the phone, started to dial Pia's number, then hung up before I could go through with it. Never in my life had I wanted and not wanted to do something so badly at the same time.

If I was being completely rational, I would have written out a list of pluses and minuses that came along with calling Pia. I would have assigned a grade to each relevant factor and summed them all up, shedding significant light on this difficult problem.

The minus side would've contained: (a) I barely knew this girl; in fact, I'd only spoken to her twice, (b) dating Mary's friend would definitely not help make Mary fall in love with me, and (c) even if I did date Pia, and we ended up going steady and moving in together after high school, sharing a life and buying a house and growing old together, it would be just like the "Perfect Mate" episode of *Star Trek: The Next Generation* where Captain Picard meets a beautiful alien played by Famke Janssen, and even though Famke Janssen knows she has to marry someone else, she bonds to Captain Picard and commits to love him for the rest of eternity. Ultimately, I would always be thinking about Mary, even if Pia and I were old and sitting on the couch together watching reruns of that very same *Star Trek* episode.

There were plenty more minuses to list. However, one plus point trumped all the negative points: there was a girl out there — a real, actual human girl, and a pretty one, no less — who might let me kiss her and (who knows?) maybe even get to second or (gasp!) third base.

I would be a fool to resist.

I dialed Pia's number and heard it ring.

The deep-down cowardly part of me briefly considered hanging up, but I was so worried she might use *69, I made up my mind to see this through. I would talk to the pretty girl. And that was that.

"Hello."

"Hello. Is this Pia?"

"No."

"Is Pia there?"

Pause. "Who's calling?"

"It's Jacob. Pia gave her number to Mary, who gave it to me."

There was a second pause in which I cursed myself for doling out so much unnecessary information. Clearly, I would not fare well in an interrogation setting. The pause seemed to go on forever until finally the woman said, "One moment," and set down the phone.

I stood up in my living room and played with the phone cord until a second voice came on the line.

"Hello."

"Hi. Is this Pia?"

"No. This is Priya. I'm Pia's sister."

Something seemed strange. "How old are you, Priya?"

"Six."

"Is your sister there?"

"My Aunt Alpana wants to know what your intentions are."

"I'm sorry?" I said.

"Your intentions. What are your intentions with my big sister?"

Someone yelled in the background. "Give me the phone, you little brat!"

The little girl giggled. "Bye-bye," she said.

There was a thump and then some yelling in a language I didn't recognize. It got very quiet, then Pia picked up the phone.

"Jacob, is that you?" Pia said.

"Yes."

"It's so good to hear from you," she said. "Listen, I can't talk right now. My aunt and my sister are literally jumping at the phone. But do you want to stop by and see me tomorrow?"

"Stop by your house?"

I pictured a scene in which I was blocked from entering the front door by a difficult six-year-old and a vigilant, over-protective aunt.

"No. Stop by the AMPM. I work there for my father in the summer," she said.

"Sure," I said. Before I could say anything else, my dad burst into the living room with a frantic look on his face.

"It's go time!" he shouted, and then ran out the way he came. He wasn't gone for a half-second before he appeared again, his eyes wide like saucers, waving his arms in the air. "The delivery guy just showed up, and your mother and that damned Nancy Sylvester are going to be home any minute!"

I barely had time to say goodbye and hang up before Dad dragged me outside where a delivery truck was idling. A man in brown shorts with a long goatee was pushing a cart up our driveway. The box on the cart was much smaller than I expected.

"You got *that* delivered?" I said. "Why didn't you just throw it in the trunk of your car?"

Dad gave me a death stare. "The purchase came with free delivery. You don't turn down free delivery."

"You do if it's going to get you busted," I said.

He shook his head. "Your generation will never under-stand the value of a dollar."

Dad grabbed my arm and rushed me down the driveway. We met the man in the brown shorts halfway and my dad made a big showing about how fast the delivery truck had to be off the street. The delivery guy proceeded to take his time, setting the cart down and searching his paperwork for the right invoice for my dad to sign. The delivery guy was stroking his goatee and adjusting his clipboard when Dad pulled out his wallet and gave him ten dollars. Suddenly, miraculously, the right invoice appeared. Dad signed it and the guy trotted down the driveway and pulled away in his truck.

Before we could breathe a sigh of relief, from around the corner, the front end of Nancy Sylvester's Mazda appeared. Dad immediately tried to pick up the box, only he lifted with his back and not his knees. He reeled in pain. The panicked look in his eyes increased tenfold. I crouched down and picked up the box.

"Thanks, son," he said, holding his lower back.

"Where does it go?"

"The garage."

I started walking toward the open garage.

"No! It goes there later!" Dad yelled/whispered. "Put it beside the house for now, between the bikes and the firewood."

I shuffled around the side of the house just as Nancy Sylvester's Mazda pulled up.

"Hello, dear!" my dad said.

I heard my mom step out of the car.

"Why are you outside? And why are you holding your back?" she said.

"I . . . I . . . hurt myself fixing the birdhouse and I couldn't find any Advil. I thought you might have some in your purse."

Nancy Sylvester's Mazda pulled away.

"Goodbye!" Mom called.

I peeked around the corner just in time to see my mother gather her eyebrows. She turned her head to the side, as if trying to figure out what my dad was really doing hanging out in the driveway. Mom fished around inside her purse and handed him a travel-sized bottle of pills.

"Let's get you inside. You can lie down on the floor and rest your back while we watch *Wheel of Fortune*," she said.

Mom took his arm and together they walked inside.

At the last moment, Dad looked back and gave me the *okay* sign. I took one final look at the box, waited a few seconds and then followed them inside.

The label on the box read: Dave's Refrigeration Emporium.

16
Sweet, Sweet Pain

Pia never specified what time I should stop by the AMPM, and the last thing I wanted was to arrive at the store and see her father standing behind the counter with a suspicious look on his face. For the most part, Pushkar was a pleasant, even jovial, guy. Last year, when my dad asked him to play Saddam Hussein in the church's annual Operation Desert Storm reenactment, Pushkar not only didn't complain about the (rather imprecise) racial stereotyping, he showed up at the park on the corner of Ascott Street and Jedidiah Avenue dressed just like the Iraqi dictator. His costume included military shoulder patches and a black beret, and he had a big smile on his face, delighted to be included.

During the reenactment, however, Pushkar grew frustrated with a series of glaring historical inaccuracies and started shouting that the whole production should stop immediately so the details could be worked out. My dad's drinking buddies were too sloshed on moonshine to listen, and I had the misfortune of standing a few yards away from Pushkar as he kicked over a McDonald's orange-drink container and screamed at the eleven-year-old palace guardsmen. Pushkar eventually calmed down, drank some homemade hooch and got in the spirit of things, but for those tense few minutes, his eyes turned yellow, the hair on his ears stood up and his voice sounded like a demon from the netherworld.

I definitely didn't want him to see me calling on his daughter. At least, not if I could avoid it. In the past, I'd seen Pushkar working nights at the AMPM and I assumed he'd be doing the same today. Two p.m. was the time I chose. It was in the middle of the day, so it gave me the best chance of finding Pia alone at her father's store. It was also long enough after lunch that I wouldn't interrupt her eating a spinach salad or anything, and it was far enough away from dinner that she wouldn't assume we'd be going to eat at the Sizzler across the street, which, incidentally, I couldn't really afford.

I put some gel in my hair and applied five layers of antiperspirant to my left armpit and eight to my (more troublesome) right. As I retrieved my bike from the side of the house, I noticed a patch of flattened weeds in the spot where my father had removed the Dave's Refrigeration box. Earlier that morning, I'd heard him tinkering around inside the garage before he left for work, only I'd been too busy watching *The Price Is Right* with my mom to go see what he was doing.

I wheeled my BMX out front and saw Moss Murphy shooting hoops in his driveway. Samantha was with him.

"Hey, Jacob!" she called, and then sunk a jump shot.

Samantha was wearing jean shorts cut so short, the tips of her pockets were hanging out. Up top, a tank top with a picture of an Andy Warhol soup can clung to her chest. I was 99.999999 percent sure she wasn't wearing a bra.

Samantha sank another jumper. "I'm killing him today," she said.

Moss Murphy had a Slurpee in his hand and a twitch

about his eye. He lumbered over even slower than usual, dragging his leg like he was quarreling with hemorrhoids. "She's good," he said. "The girl never told me she was a ringer."

Samantha tossed the ball to Moss Murphy. He barely moved to catch it and the ball bounced off his shoulder and rolled over to the curb.

"Moss, can I use your bathroom?" she said.

"Of course," he said. "Just make sure you don't let the ferret out."

Samantha looked at him sideways. "Is that a poop joke?"

I laughed but Moss Murphy turned bright red.

"No. There's really a ferret inside the house. His name's Roscoe. He's sick all the time," he said.

Samantha gave him an even funnier look and then walked up his driveway and stepped inside. I set my bike down, picked up the basketball and tossed it to Moss Murphy.

"Don't!" he yelled, and batted it away.

"What the hell?" I said.

"You don't know what's going on," Moss Murphy said. He waved me closer and I walked over so he could whisper in my ear. It felt strange, the two of us standing so close in the middle of the street, without a single soul within earshot, but Moss Murphy's eyes looked misty and he seemed like he needed to get something off his chest.

"She touched it," he said.

"Touched what?"

"You know . . . *it*."

I looked him up and down. "I'm afraid you're going to have to spell this out for me," I said.

"My dink. She touched my dink, okay? Last night we were sitting on the couch and my mom went upstairs to give

Roscoe his bath. I figured this was my chance. I checked my breath and everything and then I went in to kiss her."

"That's awesome."

"No, it isn't," he said. "It's the opposite of awesome. She told me she's saving her mouth for the man she's going to marry."

"And by saving her mouth, you mean . . . ?"

He glanced back at the house. "She doesn't even want to kiss a guy until they're engaged. And even then, the poor bastard might have to wait until a minister pronounces them man and wife."

"Bummer," I said. "But wait — she still touched your dink?"

"She said she knows teenage boys have urges and that she wanted to help me out. So she started unbuttoning my pants."

"Well, that's the awesome part then."

He whispered even quieter in my ear. "Dude, she gave me the most painful handjob of my life. I'm not kidding. It was excruciating."

"How do you know that's not the way it's supposed to be?" I said. "I mean — you say it was the most painful hand-job of your life, but let's be honest. It was the *first* handjob of your life."

Moss Murphy took an angry sip of his Slurpee. "I've given myself enough handjobs to know that's not how it's supposed to feel. It was ten minutes of terrible, horrible pain. At one point, she stopped for a second and whispered, 'You like that, don't you?' and then started up again. It was five more minutes of twisting and squeezing."

I couldn't help myself. I laughed out loud.

"It's not funny," he said. "A few minutes ago, she said she

126

couldn't wait to 'help me out' again tonight. There's something wrong here. I think she has something against me."

Just then, the Murphys' front door opened and Samantha emerged with Mrs. Murphy behind her.

"Moss! I invited Samantha to dinner!" Betsy called.

"That's great, Mom."

"We're having cheese-and-bean quesadillas!"

"That's great, Mom."

Samantha said something to Betsy and then came gliding down the driveway. Her soft, tanned skin glistened in the afternoon sun. Her long legs were silky smooth and she had the sweetest smile. Still, I could only look at one thing: her right hand. The Crusher. The Squeezer. The Immobilizer.

Samantha picked up the basketball and tossed it to Moss Murphy. He made a halfhearted attempt at dribbling, but I could tell he was still having trouble getting around.

"So, are the three of us going to play twenty-one?" Samantha said.

"Sorry," I said, climbing on my bike. "I've got to go."

Moss Murphy gave me a pleading look that said *Don't Leave!* but I was already halfway down the street. Pia was waiting for me.

17
At the Car Wash, at the Car Wash . . . Yeah

Years ago, the AMPM was just a dingy little corner store three blocks from the mall. It was called Brave Bill's Pop Shop and there used to be soft-serve ice cream instead of slushy machines and only a single 7 Up sign out front. Brave Bill eventually retired as sole proprietor. Rumor had it he moved to Vegas to risk his entire life's savings on one hand of blackjack. Rumor also had it that he hit on thirteen, busted out and ended up living in a van down by the river. Brave Bill's Pop Shop became the Blue Bird, which was essentially the exact same store with a different name and a picture of a blue jay painted on the 7 Up sign. The Blue Bird did install two video game consoles: *Mortal Kombat II* and *Dragon's Lair*.

When I was seven years old, I loved *Dragon's Lair* more than life itself. *Dragon's Lair* was the first successful laserdisc arcade game. It was essentially an interactive movie in which a knight named Dirk the Daring attempts to rescue a scantily clad princess from the evil dragon Singe. The princess was locked up in a wizard's castle and by clicking buttons, a player could direct Dirk the Daring's heroic attempts to save her. I should mention that I never managed to save the princess. I did get far enough in the game to see her a few times, which

I thought would be great, but actually turned out to be a little annoying. It turned out Princess Daphne took up a lot of screen time, and I wasn't quite old enough to appreciate how surprisingly slutty she looked (think Anne Heche's face on Pamela Anderson's body).

The game was almost impossible to beat, what with spiders leaping onto Dirk's head, venomous bats that chewed him to pieces, an electrocuting throne and all manner of murderous trapdoors and steep cliffs that led to Dirk's doom, and to me inserting another quarter to try my luck again.

The crazy part was that it was actually fun when Dirk the Daring died, because he would turn into a skeleton and look amazing for a few seconds right before the game refreshed. *Dragon's Lair* was all I could think about as a young boy. I had a poster of Dirk the Daring on my wall and my mom even gave me my allowance in quarters so I could bike over to the Blue Bird, buy a ginger ale and keep trying to rescue the princess.

The AMPM that replaced the Blue Bird wasn't just a convenience store anymore. Instead of video games, it had a state-of-the-art automated car wash out back. While the old-school car wash across town still used spinning brushes to wipe vehicles clean, the AMPM's car wash used water pressure alone. And even though a touchless car wash wasn't quite as much fun as sitting in the back seat of your parents' car and watching a zillion blue brushes flap against the windshield, it was safer, did less damage to a vehicle's paint job and provided a high-tech experience, all for three dollars and forty-nine cents.

I pulled up to the AMPM to see a single blue car sitting outside. The rest of the parking lot was empty. Quickly, and from a distance, I did a drive-by to see if Pia was working and whether she was alone. With the afternoon sun in my eyes, I walked up to the window and cupped my hands over my face. There she was, the pretty girl who'd sat two seats away from me in social studies last year. Pia was standing behind the counter, fiddling with the cash register.

She looked up and gasped, like she was surprised to see me.

I waved and the startled expression drifted from her face. With one last look for Pushkar, I opened the door and stepped inside.

"Oh my God, I thought you were the Parksville Peeper," Pia said.

"The Parksville Peeper?"

"You know, the guy who's been sneaking around, peeping in ladies' windows."

"There's a guy peeping in ladies' windows?"

"Apparently," she said.

I walked up to the register and smiled. Pia smiled back. Only, she didn't say anything. Now that our conversation about the Peeper was over, it seemed we didn't have anything to say to each other. I glanced from side to side, up at the security camera, down at the row of chocolate bars, searching for something — anything — to talk about. Nothing came to me.

In Baskin-Robbins the other day, I didn't have to say a word. Mary just started talking. She asked me questions. She was interested and interesting at the same time. Pia just stared at me like I was a movie screen and she was waiting for the show to start. I cursed myself for ever calling her, for showing up without specific talking points in mind, for not practicing my banter ahead of time, for being so dull that I couldn't launch into a two-minute monologue if my life depended on it.

A nervous orange surge swelled in my stomach. Right before it leapt into my throat, Pia spoke.

"What happened to your eye?" she said.

I touched the bandage on the side of my head. "A bearded lady took my ice cream."

"Really?"

"Really." I really should have made something up.

Pia leaned her elbows on the counter. She glanced down and I saw a small television set next to the cash register. There was a VCR hooked up and a still frame of an airplane on the TV. "I was just watching *Top Gun*," she said.

In my head, a comment started to form, something about Tom Cruise and Meg Ryan and that guy who played Goose. At a certain point, the comment got quite close to being clever. When it left my mouth, however, it emerged as a single semi-stuttered word.

"G-G-Goose," I said.

"That's right. Goose and Maverick," Pia said.

A second passed and then the front door jingled. A middle-aged man entered and walked over to the Gatorade section of the long refrigerator. I stepped back to check out the energy bars while the man paid for his Gatorade, a pack of spearmint gum and a two-pack of lighters. Before he handed over his money, he mumbled something under his breath.

"Excuse me?" Pia said.

The man whispered.

"We don't have the new issue of *Penthouse*," Pia said. She thumbed the edges of the magazines in black plastic bags behind the counter. "We have the Australian *Playboy*. We also have the new *Naughty Neighbors*."

The man adjusted his baseball cap to better conceal his eyes. "I'll take that one," he said.

"*Naughty Neighbors?*" Pia said.

"Well, it's only neighborly," he said in a desperate attempt at humor.

Pia didn't laugh though. She was all business. She scanned the magazine, placed his purchases into a plastic bag and took his money.

While she was counting his change, the most surprising sight appeared outside the window. It was far away and the sun was in my eyes, but I was positive I saw Blowpipe walking down the far sidewalk. He must have escaped rehab again. This time he was carrying a backpack and what looked like a walking stick. I watched him approach a large middle-aged woman from behind. Blowpipe tapped her on the shoulder and the woman jumped. He said something to her. I couldn't read his lips, but it must not have been anything good because a half second later, the woman swung her purse. It hit him right between the eyes and Blowpipe took off running like a frightened animal.

What on earth was going on? Was he still searching for Zelda? I wished Moss Murphy could have been there to confirm the Blowpipe sighting, because he'd never believe me if I told him.

"Jacob?"

Pia's customer had left with his dirty magazine and we were alone.

"Sorry about that," she said.

"That guy was . . . creepy."

"I guess. He comes in here every other week. I kind of feel bad for him." She glanced around the empty store. "Do you want to watch *Top Gun* with me?"

"Sure."

Pia sat back on her stool and I leaned against the counter.

She fast-forwarded her VHS tape until she found the scene she was looking for. "This makes the movie worthwhile," she said, and pressed play.

The TV cut from the classroom scene where Tom Cruise tells Slider he stinks (cue Slider comically sniffing his armpit) to the studly pilots playing volleyball on the beach. Pia watched with spellbound eyes and I could tell why. The *Top Gun* volleyball scene is the finest, purest soft-core porn for women of all ages. There are shirtless hunks with waxed chests. A strapping, in-his-prime Tom Cruise breaks a sweat while a young, bleach-blond Val Kilmer struts his stuff. Even the big oaf who played Slider is completely ripped. (As a footnote, women everywhere should thank the movie's director for insisting that Goose keep his shirt on.)

Pia dangled her finger under her lip as she watched the trick photography help the five-foot-seven Tom Cruise implausibly spike a volleyball over a regulation-size net. She watched the camaraderie, the slow-motion shots of the oiled-up bodies. Her chest heaved when the scene ended and Tom Cruise hopped on his motorcycle and rode off into the sunset.

Pia pressed pause on the remote control. She walked out from behind the counter and grabbed my hand. "Come with me," she said, and led me outside. She put up a Back in 5 Minutes sign on the door and locked it with a key.

"Where are we going?" I said.

"I promised my aunt that I would wash her car."

For a moment, I couldn't place the look in her eyes. Then it came to me. I'd seen it the other night when my dad checked out the Deck Girls. Pia pressed a few buttons on the car wash, then threw me the keys to her aunt's car.

"I'm not old enough to drive," I said.

"It doesn't matter," Pia said. "We're on private property. Besides, you only have to drive ten feet or so."

Pia climbed into the passenger's seat and I slid behind the wheel. I inserted the key and fired up the engine just like my dad taught me in our driveway, then I eased the car forward a few feet. The gas pedal was more sensitive than I'd expected and we hopped a little bit. Pia put her hand on mine and helped guide the wheel.

"A little closer," she said. "Now stop."

Pia shifted the car into park and pulled the keys out of the ignition. Below us, railings grabbed hold of the wheels, and up above, sprinklers positioned themselves. Within seconds, the car was surrounded by water. In sweeping swells, it sprayed from all around until we couldn't see out the windows anymore.

"I set it on super-long clean. We have ten minutes," Pia said.

Then she pounced.

In retrospect, I should have known something was up, but I was totally stunned when she climbed on top of me and stuck her tongue in my mouth. This was my first kiss and I didn't know what to do. Should I move my lips up and down? Suck a little? Nibble playfully? Just sit back and let her mouth do all the work? It was very confusing. And wet. And warm. Also, my happy parts were on fire.

Pia grabbed my hand and put it under her shirt. For the first time, I cupped an actual breast. I only touched it over her bra, but it was so incredibly soft and yet firm all at once. I kissed Pia back too, and I think she liked it; at least, she didn't complain. Thirty sweaty, saliva-filled seconds passed and then she slipped back onto the passenger's seat and started undoing my belt.

"I don't have one," I said, then immediately realized it sounded like I was talking about a penis and not a condom.

"That's okay, we don't need protection," she said, and pulled my pants down to my thighs, exposing my bits and pieces in front of a real live girl for the first time.

She cupped it in her hand and leaned over like she was going to use her mouth. In that moment, I wasn't thinking about Mary. I wasn't thinking about the world outside this tiny water-covered car. All I was thinking was — *Holy Crap! I'm actually about to get a blowjob. Like, this is really going to happen!!!!!*

Pia giggled, a sweet and yet completely nefarious giggle, then she leaned even closer. She looked up and our eyes met.

"You have to do one thing for me," she said.

"Anything," I said.

"If we're going to be boyfriend and girlfriend, you have to convert to Hinduism."

"I'm sorry . . . what?"

She shifted in my lap. "Don't worry, there's no real conversion ceremony. In fact, most Hindus don't even think outsiders can convert. Still, it would help if you read a Deepak Chopra book. And started doing yoga."

"Sure, I guess," I said.

"And if anyone asks, especially my father, you have to tell them that deep inside you're a Hindu, not a Christian. Okay?"

I looked over at the wide, blurry splotches of water on the window and then at that lust-filled look in Pia's eyes. Things were getting out of hand. My parents would freak out if I suddenly came home and announced I'd converted to some strange foreign religion. And were Pia and I even boyfriend/girlfriend yet? My experience with women was pretty limited, but even I knew that one blowjob in the front seat of a car — mid-car wash or not — did not bond two people together for all time. Did Pia even really want to be my girlfriend? We'd barely said twenty words to each other. Committing to this now was crazy. It was foolish. It was a morally reprehensible thing to do.

But then again, she did have my penis in her hand.

"Okay," I said. "Sure. That sounds great."

Pia giggled again and then leaned over. I felt her mouth wrap around me and then — OH MY GOD! A moment ago, I'd felt exposed. Now I was on my own personal highway to the danger zone. Half a second passed and then, just as I was easing back in my seat, getting comfortable and wondering about the orgasm-notification protocol, a terrible clank sounded outside. The sprinklers suddenly shut off and Aunt Alpana's car lurched to a stop in the middle of the car wash.

I looked back, to the right, even forward. Then I looked out the driver's-side window and there, glaring at me with yellow eyes, was Pia's father, Pushkar.

18
The Arranged Marriage
of a Christian and a Hindu

A few months back, right before summer holidays started, some girl got pregnant. She didn't even go to my high school. She went to the high school across town — the small high school, the one without a cafeteria — and while I never actually met her, for two weeks the pregnant girl was all my mom would talk about. Her name was Paula and she went to the giant Church of the Lord's Creation. Apparently she'd had sex with some guy on her father's living room sofa and had gotten pregnant because he "forgot" to put on a condom; although how someone can overlook something as basic as wrapping a piece of plastic around his penis, I'll never know. My mom never said a word to Caroline about poor pregnant Paula. She would always speak to my dad at the dinner table while secretly hoping Caroline got the message.

"The poor girl got herself in trouble," Mom said as she pushed her Country Harvest carrot, peas and corn medley onto her spoon. "The parents are making them get married. It's the only right thing to do." She waited for Dad to chime in, only he'd suddenly gone mute. "I hear poor pregnant Paula bought her wedding dress before she even tried on her prom dress."

Caroline couldn't take it any longer. "Okay, Mom! We get it!" she shouted. "No sex before marriage."

Mom took a sip of her Diet Coke. "I wasn't talking to you," she said, and proceeded to describe the store where poor pregnant Paula was seen trying on her wedding gown.

Caroline let out an exhausted groan. "Do you want me to wear a chastity belt? Would that make you happy?"

"That's not such a bad idea," Dad said, trying his best not to gag on my mom's overcooked casserole.

Mom poked Dad in the elbow with her fork. Caroline laughed, and Dad poked her in the elbow. I choked a little on a toughened piece of casserole cheese, only everyone thought I was laughing and I got stuck with forks in both elbows.

My mom continued, undaunted. "A moment of passion, a lifetime of burden . . ."

Caroline and I received the message loud and clear, although it probably wasn't the exact message my mother was going for: if you're going to have sex, for the love of God, don't let your parents find out.

"Sit still," Alpana said.

Pia's aunt was applying Polysporin to the new cut on the left side of my face.

I was a mess. The right side of my face still had a bandage covering my stitches and now the left side had two separate cuts and a huge black eye. It was a real shiner. That Pushkar could punch like Mike Tyson when he wanted to.

Three shots, that's how many he'd given me when he pulled open the car door; two to my face and a third to my stomach for good measure. His eyes lit up like tiny yellow suns. His teeth gnashed the air, and then, as quickly as it started, it was over. He yanked me out of the car, made me stand under the dripping car-wash contraption and said, "I need to talk to your parents."

That's where we stood, or rather sat, now.

I was sitting on the couch in Pushkar's living room. Pia and Pushkar were sitting across from me, while Pia's little sister was doing a puzzle on the floor. For five minutes now, Aunt Alpana had been fussing over the cuts above my eye.

"Ouch," I said.

"Be a good boy," Alpana said.

"Be a man," Pushkar said.

After he'd closed down the AMPM and drove Pia and me home in his SUV, Pushkar sat us down on opposite couches and told us to "Keep quiet" and then went upstairs and changed into a suit and a tie. He combed his hair and took a few deep breaths before calling my dad and telling him in vague terms what he'd seen.

Aunt Alpana finally applied a Band-Aid to my cuts and sat down beside Pushkar to wait for my parents to arrive. The room was air-conditioned and the couch was soft and slippery; my rear end kept sliding down into the crack between the cushions and I kept having to pull it back out, which only led to Pushkar giving me more dirty looks. We sat in silence for thirteen and a half agonizing minutes before the doorbell rang.

The little girl Priya and Aunt Alpana ran to answer the door. Pia tried to move too, but her father grabbed her arm. We heard voices in the front hall, then my family appeared. Not just my dad, or even both my parents. My sister was there too. Caroline had the silliest grin on her face.

Pushkar shook my dad's hand. "Donald."

"Pushkar."

He shook my mom's hand as well. "Hello, Margaret. It's good to see you again. I wish it could have been under different circumstances."

My parents stepped into the room. My dad was wearing his blue suit and my mother had her best cardigan over her checkered-pattern dress, all this despite the scorching temperature outside. They sat down beside me and each gave me a different look: my mom one of exasperation mixed with disappointment and my father a simple head nod that told me everything would be okay. Neither of them seemed taken aback by my new bandage and black eye.

Caroline sat down beside my mom. Her eyes drifted to the coffee table between the two couches. In the center was a bowl of fruit and on top of the apples and oranges was a single ripe banana. I could only hope, for all our sakes, that she didn't pick it up and start eating it.

Pushkar cleared his throat. He told the six-year-old to leave the room and asked Aunt Alpana to bring his guests some lemonade.

"Lemon or pink grapefruit?" she said.

"It doesn't matter," Pushkar said.

"I like pink grapefruit," Caroline said.

My dad looked like he wished he had a fork to poke Caroline in the elbow.

"Pink grapefruit it is," Aunt Alpana said, and walked down the hall.

Pushkar rubbed his hands together. "Now, let's get down to brass tacks. As I told you on the phone, I found your son engaged in carnal relations with my daughter."

"Father!" Pia said.

"Be quiet," Pushkar said. "I found them in the front seat of Alpana's car. They were in . . . an unholy state."

140

"Well," my dad said, "we have to remember — they're just kids."

"If your boy was Jewish, he would be considered a man already."

"We're not Jewish," Mom said. "We're Christian."

I bit my lip, not sure whether I was Christian or Hindu now.

"Nevertheless," Pushkar said. "My family's honor is at stake."

My dad looked at me. He stuck his thumb right onto my black eye.

"Ouch!" I said.

"There's a lot more where that came from," Pushkar said.

"It looks like you've already gotten a fair measure of revenge," Dad said. "Perhaps cooler heads can prevail. I'm not sitting here furiously angry that you struck my son. And I think the boy learned his lesson. Maybe we can . . . oh, I don't know, call it even?"

That yellow hue returned to Pushkar's eyes. The hair on his ears curled. "The children shall be married. It is the only way to preserve Pia's honor."

Caroline laughed so hard she snorted. My mom elbowed her and Caroline had to cover her mouth to keep the laughter at bay.

"Married?" I said.

"No way!" Pia said. "Besides, Father, if I may speak truthfully, things between Jacob and me are strained. We're not as close as we used to be."

"What?!" I said.

Mom shushed me.

"We've barely said six words to each other in our entire lives," I said.

She pinched me hard.

"Now listen," my dad said. "Jacob is only fifteen. And Pia is . . . ?"

"Sixteen."

"Exactly. They're far too young to get married. And besides, it's a fact of life these days. Teenagers are going to have sex."

Pushkar pointed an angry finger at my dad. "Now you listen to me, sir!"

"We never had sex," Pia mumbled.

Everyone looked at her.

"What was that?"

Pia threw up her hands in exasperation. "We never had sex, okay?" she said.

My mom stood up to leave. "Well then," she said. "I don't see what we're doing here."

Pushkar stood up too. "This isn't over. They were engaged in immoral congress."

"Your daughter said they didn't have sex," my dad said.

The room grew silent, and Caroline looked from Pushkar to my parents and over at Pia. "Well then, what the hell happened?"

A deathlike silence followed in which I could hear the blood circulating in my veins.

"I gave him a blowjob, okay!" Pia yelled. "Is everybody happy? Now you know!"

From the hallway, a little voice giggled.

"Hee-hee. Blowjob," Priya said.

"Go to your room!" Pushkar bellowed, and the six-year-old took off running.

Just then Aunt Alpana entered with a tray full of lemonade and started handing out glasses. My mom and Pushkar had to sit down to get out of her way.

"I'm sorry, dear," she said to Caroline. "We only had lemon flavored."

"Is it Minute Maid?" Caroline said.

"I believe it's organic."

Caroline took a sip and stuck out her tongue. "Blah. Gross."

Dad glared at her. At this point a fork wouldn't have been enough. He would have stuck her with King Neptune's trident if he'd had the chance.

Pushkar took a sip from his lemonade and so did my mom. Aunt Alpana set a glass down beside me, only there was no way I was touching it until this debacle was over.

"You have every right to be upset," Dad said. "But I don't think marrying off a couple teenagers is an appropriate solution."

"It seems your son just wants to get the milk for free," Pushkar said. "He is not willing to buy the whole cow."

Caroline whispered under her breath. "Technically, Pia was the one doing the milking."

"What was that?!" Pushkar said.

The silly grin slipped off Caroline's face. A moment passed in silence before Pia whispered in her father's ear. He listened for a second and then brushed her away.

"I will settle for restitution," Pushkar said.

My family exchanged confused glances.

"What do you mean, restitution?" Dad said.

"Your boy has done a disservice to my daughter. He has brought shame to my family. I want restitution."

"Are you talking about a pound of flesh?" my mother said.

"The boy will work in the store," Pushkar said. "For free."

"Um, what?" I said.

"Fifteen shifts of seven hours each. That will be his penance."

Mom cupped her hand over my dad's ear. "It will be good for his résumé. Jacob's only ever had a paper route, after all."

My dad nodded. He reached across the coffee table and shook Pushkar's hand. "Agreed," he said. Then the two men stood up and, strangely, started making small talk.

"So what's this I hear about Santa Claus being crucified outside your little church?" Pushkar said. They walked down the hall and went outside where Pushkar started showing Dad his new barbecue.

Mom finally put her hand up to my eye to check the damage. "How do you feel, sweetheart?"

"I'm a little woozy," I said.

"Maybe you should go sit on the toilet and see what happens."

"Mom!" I said.

Pia and Aunt Alpana giggled.

Caroline tapped her fingers on her glass. She suddenly looked bored now that the show was over. "Can we go?" she said.

"Don't be rude," Mom said. She took a sip from her organic lemonade and told Alpana how much she liked the drapes. Aunt Alpana, in turn, complimented my mother's dress. With the adults lost in idle conversation and Caroline playing with the ice in her drink, I looked over at Pia. We'd been avoiding eye contact since Pushkar caught us inside Aunt Alpana's car. Pia stared at me now, those pretty eyes unwavering. She put her fingers to her mouth and blew me a little kiss.

"Maverick . . ." she said.

Five minutes later, we were standing at the front door.

My mom and Alpana were exchanging phone numbers. Pushkar and my dad were chatting about this year's Gulf War reenactment.

"I hope this doesn't change your mind about playing Saddam Hussein," my dad said.

Pushkar shook my father's hand. "So long as we imbibe spirits, our spirit will be fine."

"I'm sorry?"

"Yes," Pushkar said. "I would be delighted to participate."

He took my hand. His fingers — like sturdy Bavarian sausages — gripped down hard. "I will see you tomorrow morning at the AMPM," he said.

19
Presbyterians vs. Methodists

Just after sunrise the next morning, there we were again: Mom, Nancy Sylvester and I, standing beside our little church sign with the glass panel swung open and Mom and Nancy Sylvester fussing over the placement of the black letters. I'd barely had time to wipe the sleep out of my eyes before my mother dragged me out of bed.

"We need a lookout," she said.

"Again?" I said.

"Again."

Before I left the house, I passed Caroline stumbling on her way to the bathroom. She smelled like baby powder and Smirnoff Ice.

"Are you seriously going with them?" she said.

"I have to."

"When you see Nancy Sylvester, ask her how many cats she has," Caroline said. "I bet she's lost count."

I slipped past her, and Caroline went into the bathroom to pee and possibly throw up. Twenty minutes later, I was standing lookout in the chilly morning air. The ground was covered in dew and the tip of the sun sat on the horizon like a flat red balloon. I glanced around and, for the first time, wondered why my mom kept bringing me here. Technically, she didn't need a lookout. Aside from a few crows picking through litter at the park, the place was deserted. The big church, for all its imposing size and intricate stained glass, looked abandoned. It was just me and two scheming middle-aged ladies, awake an hour before we needed to be.

I started to think. Perhaps I wasn't just here as a lookout. Maybe my mother had brought me along because this — the righteous indignation and small-town ethos of fighting The Man — was the family business. If Don and Margaret were in the mob, I would already be laundering money and helping them throw bodies into the lake. I wasn't on these early morning trips to guard Nancy Sylvester's ten-year-old Mazda. I was here because one day, years from now, when Mom was old and senile or dead and gone, I was expected to continue her crusade.

I left my post and walked up to them.

"Why am I here?" I said.

Mom shifted an X next to an M. "Because we're a family. And family sticks together," she said.

"No, seriously. Why?"

Mom looked me straight in my black eye. She paused, then said, "Because of the Parksville Peeper."

I glanced around. "Um, are you serious?"

"Don't say 'Um' when you begin a sentence. People will think our family's illiterate."

"Fine, whatever. Now, what about the Peeper?"

Nancy Sylvester looked at me as if I were five years old. "Haven't you heard?" she said. "There's some creep going around town peeping into windows. Everyone's worried. Their modesty is at stake."

"But don't peeping Toms usually peep at young girls? Like, wouldn't this guy peep in Caroline's window or stalk the Deck Girls or something?"

Both ladies immediately stopped fussing over the letters and stared at me. I couldn't be sure, but I think I'd offended them as women.

"You're never too old for someone to sneak a peek at your undercarriage," Nancy Sylvester said.

I stared at her curiously. Twelve. I suspected she had at least twelve cats.

Mom and Nancy Sylvester turned around and continued placing letters. A quarrel erupted over how many words should be in each line, and I walked over to lean against Nancy Sylvester's car. I was fiddling with my new bandage when a pickup truck came flying down Ascott Street at fifty miles an hour, headed straight for us.

Dear God, I thought, *it's the Peeper.*

"Mom! Ms. Sylvester!" I yelled.

My mother closed the glass panel and secured the lock. When she turned around, instead of looking worried or afraid, her face lit up like a Christmas tree. Nancy Sylvester was wearing a grin too, one that stretched from ear to ear. The two ladies high-fived and ran over as the vehicle pulled into the parking lot. We all watched Candice Collington step out of the truck. The women hugged, then began hauling gear out of the back.

"Jacob, a little help here, please," Mom said.

I carried a case of bottled water and set it down beside the sign. The ladies set down some tent poles and a large tarp next to a few chairs and an ice-filled cooler with Tupperware sticking out.

"What's going on?" I said.

"We're setting up camp."

"You're kidding."

"Look me in the eye and tell me I'm kidding," Mom said.

Her jaw was clasped shut. Her posture was rigid. Candice Collington looked serious as well, but then again, she'd really only expressed two emotions since the Good Lord took Old Rex away: super solemn and hysterically upset. All things being equal, I suppose it was better to have her looking at me so seriously. Only Nancy Sylvester couldn't stop smiling. She wasn't even dressed up like a ninja this time, her bright yellow blouse a sign that this was no longer a covert mission.

"Okay, so you're not kidding," I said to get them to stop staring at me.

They insisted I help them set up the tent, which turned out to be a tall sunshade held up by four poles. We each grabbed a pole and positioned it next to the sign. Just when I thought we were done, Candice Collington pulled a second tarp-looking contraption out of her truck. She set it down at the edge of the road and walked over to me, bicycle pump in hand.

"If only there was a strong young man around here to help," she said.

I looked from Mrs. Collington to the large red-and-white ball of plastic. It suddenly occurred to me what was going on: she wanted me to inflate a giant Santa balloon. I didn't even have to look at my mom to know what she was going to say. *A gentleman helps a lady, every chance he gets. No exceptions.* I took the bicycle pump, attached the cord to the ball of plastic and started pumping.

It took forever. At least, it felt like it took forever, what with me pumping like a madman while the ladies stood behind me, chatting about all sorts of random topics: the price of car insurance, when exactly pomegranates were in season, how to purchase a giant inflatable Santa Claus at a bargain-basement price in late July.

About halfway through pumping, as the inflatable balloon began taking shape, the women fell silent. They walked out onto the street and stared at the red-and-white figure behind me. I looked up too.

No one said anything for the longest time. Then Nancy Sylvester blurted out, "Is that really Santa Claus?"

Candice Collington crossed her arms. "It sure ain't Rudolph."

"Then where's his beard?"

The women exchanged confused glances.

"I don't know," Candice Collington said. "Maybe Summertime Santas don't have beards."

"I've never heard of a Summertime Santa before," Nancy Sylvester said.

My arms were pretty sore. I looked down at the pump and then over at my mother.

"Keep pumping," she said.

"But —"

"Keep pumping."

I took the pump in both hands and pushed up and down again a few hundred times. When I finally finished, I was dripping in sweat. My hands were sore and I could barely feel my arms. In front of me, at the edge of Jedidiah Avenue, stood a giant inflatable Mrs. Claus. There was no denying it. From her beardless face, down to her white apron lined with little green Christmas trees, to her red dress and back up to her gray hair in a poofy bun atop her head, the four of us were staring at Santa's better half.

Candice Collington's eyes quivered. I felt pretty bad for her. First her beloved basset hound Rex lost a life-and-death battle with a raccoon. And now this.

My mom clapped her hands together. She laughed her fake laugh. "This is better."

"How is this better?" Nancy Sylvester said.

"Think about it," Mom said. "Mrs. Claus is the brains behind the operation. Do you think Santa gets anything done by himself? A man couldn't deliver presents all around the world without a woman's help. What if he got lost after the first house? He'd just drive around in circles, refusing to pull over and ask for directions. You ladies know how husbands are."

Candice Collington nodded.

Nancy Sylvester nodded too, even though she didn't have a husband. "Mrs. Claus is the brains."

"She's the manager and he's the employee," Mom said.

"That's right. She's the general and he's the private." Nancy Sylvester laughed so hard she cried. "She's the master and he's the servant!"

Mom touched her on the shoulder. "I wouldn't go that far, Nancy."

The women chatted for a while. It took a couple minutes, but eventually Candice Collington came to terms with her discount/impulse purchase. They pulled a few more supplies from the back of her truck and then posed in front of the inflatable Mrs. Claus, with me as the reluctant photographer again.

"Smile," I said, and snapped the picture.

All three flashed wide, triumphant smiles. And why wouldn't they smile? On the sign beside them, spelled out in black letters, was a new slogan:

PRESBYTERIANS GET PRESENTS ON XMAS.
METHODISTS GET LUMPS OF COAL.

20
The Friend Zone

"Does your eye hurt?"

"Yes."

"Good."

That was the longest exchange Pushkar and I had during my first shift at the AMPM. During those first few hours, only a handful of customers came into the shop, some to buy cigarettes, others to pick up a bottled water or a donut. Most of them came in to get their morning coffee. They all chatted with Pushkar like long-lost friends, exchanging pleasantries and discussing the weather — "It's going to be a scorcher today." "Ah, you should try India, my friend. This would be winter in India."

Pushkar didn't let me work the cash register. He didn't even let me stand at the front of the store. The moment I arrived (six minutes early, just to be careful), he led me to the storeroom and told me to move a dozen large crates of Mountain Dew from one corner to the other.

"Can I use the dolly?" I said.

His eyes flashed yellow. "No."

When I finished lugging the crates, Pushkar came back, surveyed my work and said, "It was better before. Move them back." So I spent another thirty minutes carrying the heavy crates and placing them back in their original position. When I went out to find Pushkar, I knew from the look on his face exactly what he was going to say. He poked his head into the storeroom, lent a passing glance and said, "On second thought, move them back."

And so it went for the next three hours. When I showed up at the AMPM that morning, I'd hoped this might work out for the best, that Pushkar would hand me a blue AMPM smock, nod approvingly as I slipped it over my shoulders, then teach me how to use the cash register. The two of us would grow to appreciate each other, my past transgression — no matter how egregious — fading into history as the hours and days passed. Eventually, I might even become an irreplaceable member of his staff. Pushkar would put his arm around my shoulder. "Sales of magazines are up twenty percent," he'd say. "The fruit punch Gatorade has been flying off the shelves and it's all because of you."

Only, it wasn't to be. I was his slave and he knew it. Who could I complain to? My father would only tell me to suck it up. After all, hadn't he brokered me a sweetheart of a deal? I couldn't go to the police. They might want to hear more about what had gone on in Aunt Alpana's car. There were probably some government agencies that might be interested — the workers' compensation board, the department of labor perhaps. Only, there was no way they'd ever be on my side. City Hall was right around the corner and three of Pushkar's regulars that morning were wearing fancy suits and ID badges.

I had to face the truth. No one was coming to save me. This was my penance, not so much for letting Pia seduce me — no fifteen-year-old could ever be blamed for that — but for being careless enough to get caught. While my mom fought her holy war across town, I toiled away in the back room of my own atonement.

After I'd moved the cases of Mountain Dew nine separate times, Pushkar handed me a mop and a scrub brush. "The toilet's waiting for you," he said.

When my shift ended at 4 p.m., I bolted out of the store as fast as my legs would carry me. I was drenched in sweat and my hands were covered in grime. Pushkar had made me clean out the old soap scum behind the car wash and then sent me back to the storeroom for more manual labor. I'd hoped Pia might arrive at some point and her father might show a shred of mercy, only she never appeared. It was just me and Pushkar. Me and the mop bucket. Me and those backbreaking crates in the storeroom.

Afterward, instead of heading home to shower or maybe even borrow one of Caroline's heart-shaped bath bombs and take a long, relaxing soak in the tub, I unlocked my bike from the pole at the side of the store and rode it straight to Baskin-Robbins.

I didn't show up looking like a completely filthy animal. About two blocks from the Garden Center, I stopped at the public fountain with the dolphin squirting water from its blowhole and washed my hands and my face. Two new moms were sitting nearby breastfeeding and they gave me funny looks, but that didn't stop me from running some water through my hair.

Dairy Queen was closed and the bearded lady was nowhere in sight, but Baskin-Robbins was open. I pulled up outside and stepped into the store. My heart skipped a beat when I saw Mary wiping down a counter. Only, she wasn't alone. A gray-haired woman was standing behind the display freezer while a family of four — a big burly dad, a mom with a flower in her hair, and a boy and a girl — were eating ice cream at a nearby table. I waved hello to Mary.

She brought her finger up to her lips. "Shhh."

The older woman looked at me. Her name tag read Delores. "Welcome to Baskin-Robbins," she said, then stared at me expectantly.

I glanced over at Mary, who was absolutely no help. Her eyes were glued to the counter, a tiny smile tugging at the corners of her mouth.

"What'll it be?" Delores said.

I scanned the flavors. I really hadn't planned on ordering anything, especially not ice cream. Pushkar hadn't offered me a lunch break and I was too afraid to ask for one, so the last thing I'd eaten was a blueberry bagel out of Candice Collington's cooler that morning. In the eight hours since, my stomach had been gradually gurgling, and the thought of pouring ice cream into that empty space made what was left of that bagel climb up into my throat.

What I really could have gone for was an order of Dairy Queen French fries, those thin, almost-crispy-but-just-right-in-the-center ones that came in a red basket. I glanced out the window at the abandoned DQ kiosk and then down at the ice cream in Baskin-Robbins' display freezer. My choices were pretty slim.

"I'll take a single scoop of tiger tail in a waffle cone," I said.

Delores served me my ice cream and helped me at the register. I walked over to the corner of the store and sat down. A few seconds passed and then the little girl at the next table dropped her cone on the floor. Before you could count to five, she launched into a hissy fit the likes of which I hadn't seen since the bearded lady demanded her Dilly Bar back.

Mary put her arm on the little girl's back. "We'll get you a fresh cone, sweetie," she said, which prompted the girl's mom to say, "God bless you," which prompted Delores to scoff under her breath. The little boy ignored all this and started showing Mary how he could count to twenty (of course, he got completely confused between thirteen and seventeen). The only person who didn't say a thing was the little girl's father, and I was pretty sure that was because he was trying to peer down Mary's blouse.

Mary brought over a new pink-bubblegum ice cream cone and the little girl hugged her. Before slipping back behind the counter, Mary rearranged the napkin holders on the table beside me. "Delores doesn't like it when my friends stop by," she whispered.

"Okay."

"I'm off in twenty minutes. Do you want to go to the mall?"

"Okay."

Mary and the little girl's mom started chatting about how long this Baskin-Robbins had been open. I took a few licks of my ice cream, then wandered outside where I tossed my waffle cone into a nearby trash can. My stomach was still gurgling, only this time louder, like it was yelling at my brain not to eat any more frozen dairy products.

I wandered over to the produce store, where I bought a bag of salt-and-vinegar chips and a can of Sprite. Thirty seconds later I was sitting on the curb outside, wolfing down the chips like I hadn't eaten in a year. The moment I took my final bite, a wave of regret came over me. What was I thinking? It was bad enough that I showed up at Mary's workplace a sweaty, disheveled mess. Now I'd added vinegar breath to the equation. At the canyon party the other day, Moss Murphy and I had been at our cleanest, finest-smelling best. Our bodies were showered. Our hair was gelled like the male models in Caroline's *Cosmo* magazine. Our armpits were covered in layer upon layer of antiperspirant.

How could I be so naive this time? So unprepared?

I took a large swig from the Sprite and whooshed it around inside my mouth. That didn't quite do the job, so I took another swig, tilted my head back and gargled. No one was nearby, so I spat out the soda and did it again. The lady in the produce store crossed her eyes. I stepped a few feet away and repeated my carbonated vinegar cleanse. My mouth now tingled with sugar and all I could taste was the Sprite, but was that enough to give me fresh breath?

I'd just spat out another mouthful when a voice sounded behind me.

"Jacob?"

It was Mary. She was standing there in her adorable pink-and-blue-striped hat, her blue Baskin-Robbins shirt and regulation khakis. Mary was biting her lip and looking at me like I was a crazy person. I had to do something. I couldn't just set down the can of Sprite and pretend this never happened. And I couldn't let her go on thinking I was a filthy, dirty spitter, a gobber, a horker with absolutely no regard for the ground other people walk on. I had to think up a lie and think it up quick.

"I swallowed a bug," I said.

"Oh, no."

"I think it's caught in my throat," I said, continuing the lie to its logical conclusion.

"That's terrible," Mary said. "My sister once got a dragon-fly caught in her esophagus. We had to go to the hospital and everything."

"Is she okay?" I said.

"She's fine. That was years ago. The doctor removed it with a tube and she got to eat yogurt for a week."

"Thank goodness," I said.

Mary came closer. She put her hands on my jaw and tilted my head so she could see the back of my throat. The entire time I was terribly afraid she would get a lethal whiff of vinegar.

"I think I see it," she said.

"Really?!"

Mary let go. "Maybe you should just swallow it."

"You're kidding."

"I hear bugs are a delicacy in Thailand."

I laughed a little, only the longer Mary looked at me, the more I realized she was serious. I would have swallowed right away — how hard is it, after all, to swallow an imaginary bug? — only now I was worried about what she'd seen in the back of my throat. It couldn't have been a blueberry from the bagel that morning. Maybe it really was a bug. Maybe this was the universe's way of punishing me for lying: afflicting me with my own fake affliction.

Mary was still giving me a concerned look. There wouldn't be time to find a mirror and have a good look. I lifted the can of Sprite, poured it down my throat and — bravely and courageously — swallowed the imaginary bug.

"I think it's gone," I said.

Mary took off her striped hat, revealing her pretty red hair. "Do you want to help me buy some jeans?"

"Of course," I said.

"Excellent," she said. "And on the way to the mall, you can tell me what happened to the other side of your face."

"Does my bum look fat in these jeans?"

"I'm sorry, what?" I said.

"Don't avoid the question. Does my bum look fat in these jeans?"

Mary and I were standing inside the Gap store at the mall. She'd just emerged from the change room looking radiant as always, her Baskin-Robbins khakis discarded and replaced by a pair of tight black jeans. On the way over, I'd told her the story about how I hurt my eye — "Out of the blue, the car wash just malfunctioned, it was the weirdest thing" — and now she was looking at me expectantly, twisting her lower lip between her teeth and leaning on one leg.

Never before had a girl asked me a question like this. I looked at Mary's bum and realized I was trapped. If I said, "Maybe a little," then I was being an inconsiderate jerk. If I said, "Not at all," then I was a big fat liar. The truth was: if I stared directly at her bum, maybe it looked slightly larger than average in those jeans. But this was a trivial point, and the size of Mary's bum in no way detracted from her beauty. Rather, it *added* to her beauty — the way Mary's lower back arched, the angle of her hips, her denim-covered backside in all its curvaceous glory. Mary was gorgeous all the way from her head down to her feet. She had the softest hair I'd ever seen. Her eyes didn't just sparkle, they made you want to get behind them, to see the world the way she saw it. Her mouth alternated between a tiny back-of-a-Hallmark-card heart and a kissable string of red licorice. It baffled me how Mary could focus on the size of her bum when she was always the

159

prettiest girl in the room.

I could tell by the look on her face that I didn't just need to come up with a proper response, I needed to come up with one quickly. In no way was "I hear guys like a little junk in the trunk" going to cut it.

"Your bum looks terrific," I said.

Mary smiled. She tilted her head. "Really?"

"I wouldn't lie."

"Thanks," she said. "For someone who doesn't talk a lot, you always know exactly what to say."

She hiked the jeans up a little, checked them out in the mirror and ran her hand along her backside. "It's all in the pockets, you know. The smaller the pockets, the bigger your bum looks. Don't get me wrong, I know I'm fighting genetics here. But look at these tiny little pockets. You couldn't fit a credit card in these things. What was the designer thinking?"

The salesperson who'd been helping us came over with two more pairs of jeans for Mary to try on. She thanked him and stepped back into the change room while I sat down on the bench and watched in awe. The black jeans fell to the floor. Through the opening at the bottom of the change room door, the ultra-small pockets dangled around Mary's bare ankles. She lifted one foot and shook her ankle to get the other leg free. Just four feet away, Mary was standing with her legs bare, half-naked really.

I couldn't help but imagine what she looked like in there, what color her panties were. Were they white and covered in little red hearts? Or were they soft and lacy, the kind the girls wore on the late-night chatline ads? Maybe she was wearing a G-string. My heart gasped. My fingertips felt numb.

I watched Mary's bare ankles shimmy into a pair of blue jeans and all I could think about was a single thread slipping between her cheeks and disappearing into a Narnia of hot, unbridled flesh. I had half a mind to pry open the door and kiss Mary right then and there, Youth Pastor Glenn be damned. I glanced back into the store. The salesperson was chatting with another customer. No one was watching. I could really do it. Just last week, I'd watched Al Pacino in *Carlito's Way* break down his lover's door and kiss her ravenously. She totally melted in his arms. It wasn't out of the realm of possibility. Mary could melt in my arms the very same way.

I rolled my tongue around the inside of my mouth, cleared out the residual salt and vinegar taste and was just standing up when Mary hit me with a bombshell from the other side of the door.

"You know," she said, "I think you're fast becoming my very best friend."

Instantly, my plans for Mary melting in my arms, for our great, unbridled moment of passion, came crashing to the ground. Her words resonated like an atomic bomb. I had just been officially, irrevocably lobbed into the Friend Zone, a bottomless pit of sorrow and longing from which there was no return. I leaned back in my seat and Mary opened the door.

"I'm serious," she said. "It's hard in life to find someone who truly gets you. Every time I say something, I feel like you understand. You never argue for the sake of arguing. You'd never believe how many people like to argue." She modeled the jeans in the mirror. "Do these look like bell bottoms? Don't answer. I know they do. I could tell before I even tried them on. Jacob, you look kind of tired. Are you sure you didn't get a concussion?"

"I'm fine."

"But how do you know? In less than a week, you've been attacked by a bearded woman and a malfunctioning car wash. You might have a brain injury and not even know it. Plus, you just started a new job. That can be kind of stressful." She stepped back inside the change room. "I'm curious, how much do they pay you at the AMPM anyway?"

"Um . . ." I said.

"Is it more than minimum wage? I hope so. That phrase absolutely drives me nuts — *minimum wage* — as if your employer is saying that your effort and loyalty are worth the very least he's legally obligated to pay. And worst of all, it's not like you can slack off at McDonald's or Baskin-Robbins or anything. They expect you to work hard, whereas in the back of your mind, you're always thinking, *Hey, buddy, you're paying me the absolute minimum wage, I'm going to put in the absolute minimum effort.*"

Mary stepped out of the change room in a pair of dark blue jeans. She checked her backside in the mirror and grinned when she saw how wide the pockets were. "I think we have a winner," she said.

"They're awesome," I said.

I thought she'd forgotten all about the AMPM. Then she said, "So how much does the AMPM pay?"

A swirl of panic spread in my chest. There was no way I could tell her I was working for free. Even if she believed that I was simply padding my résumé with volunteer work, Mary seemed like the type to storm into the AMPM and demand to know why Pushkar was taking advantage of me. No matter what I said, the truth would come out: the incomplete fellatio in Aunt Alpana's car, Pushkar's fist striking me in the head, the *Top Gun* volleyball scene, Pia's impish giggle, my hasty conversion to Hinduism. There was no way Mary would ever dump Youth Pastor Glenn and agree to love me for all eternity if I told her the truth.

Mary looked down at the price tag on her jeans. "I have to work two shifts at the ice cream shop to pay for these," she said. "Oh, I totally forgot to ask — did you ever call Pia?"

"Um . . ."

"Well, did you?"

"Um . . ."

"It's okay if you didn't. I understand. But if you did, I want to hear all the juicy details."

Four Mississippis passed in utter, tongue-tied silence.

"I was wondering," I said. "Can you tell me the difference between a Presbyterian and a Methodist?"

21
Quite the Public Menace

You can tell a lot about a person by the way their car smells. For instance, my dad's car smelled like motor oil and the lingering aroma of instant coffee. My mom's smelled like vanilla. Nancy Sylvester's ten-year-old Mazda smelled like kittens and spilled milk. And Caroline's car smelled like fruit punch and hairspray.

Mary's car smelled like fresh-baked cinnamon buns and the softest, faintest perfume.

"You'll have to excuse the clutter," she said as I climbed into the passenger's seat. "I share this car with three of my sisters. Also, my little sisters sometimes climb in the back seat and have a tea party."

Mary was right. Her car was cluttered. But it wasn't filthy. The 1982 Trans-Am that sat in Moss Murphy's driveway contained a cornucopia of filth: random candy bar wrappers, empty Taco Bell containers, weeks-old banana peels and, in the corners of each seat, a quasi–trail mix of sunflower seeds, stray M&Ms, dirt and cracker crumbs. Mary's car, in contrast, was covered in beauty products. There were two combs on the front seat and three eyeliner pencils, various scrunchies, a pink compact, a blue compact and several tea-cups strewn about the back seat.

"It's not that bad," I said, pulling a bobby pin out from under my leg.

With my BMX sticking out of the trunk, Mary drove us over to the corner of Ascott Street and Jedidiah Avenue. Along the way, she quizzed me about the sign my mother had put up.

"I can't remember the exact quote," I said. "I just know it was meant to stir up trouble."

"And your mom and her friends are just sitting there, waiting for trouble to occur?"

"I guess."

Mary gunned it around a corner. She slowed down for a second and then gunned it again. During the ten-minute drive, Mary stayed completely calm behind the wheel. Down low, however, she had a lead foot. Mary didn't just speed. She accelerated from zero to sixty in the blink of an eye. She passed cars without checking her blind spot, she changed lanes in the middle of intersections and, worst of all, she didn't slow down for corners. A dozen times, I found myself holding on for dear life. It turned out Mary was quite the public menace on the road. You would never have known it from the absentminded way she fiddled with the radio, the way she chatted as though she was sitting at a kitchen table, having a cup of tea.

"Did you know there's a talking donkey in the Bible?" she said.

"Really?"

"Yep. For real. People don't like to talk about it, but there's this one part in the book of Numbers, which I think is the fourth or fifth book of the Hebrew Bible or something, where this donkey keeps getting hit by this guy Balaam. And the donkey just starts talking, like you and me, telling Balaam to stop beating him up. Isn't that insane?"

Mary yanked the steering wheel and we flew around a corner, narrowly grazing the curb and almost hitting a mailbox.

"There are all kinds of other crazy things in the Bible. Like in Exodus, there's this part where fathers are told to sell their daughters into slavery. And in Leviticus it tells you to never get a haircut and that men aren't allowed to shave their beards. There's also this other part, I think it's in Exodus too, but don't quote me on that, where it says that if you work on a Sunday, you're supposed to be put to death."

"Really? On a Sunday?"

"Well," she said, "technically it says you're supposed to die if you work on the Sabbath. But the thing is, Jews and Christians have never been able to agree on what day the Sabbath is supposed to be."

The light in front of us turned red and Mary slammed on her brakes. She slipped three hair elastics off the car's emergency brake and tossed them in the back seat.

"What do you think?" she said.

"About the talking donkey?"

"Well, yes. About the historical inaccuracies. You know — stuff people might have believed two thousand years ago, but that, nowadays, you'd need a bottle of snake oil to sell it to them."

The light turned green and Mary floored it, nearly clipping a cyclist.

"I suppose if Jesus wrote it, it had to be true," I said.

Mary slammed on the brakes, right in the middle of the road. "Jesus didn't write the Bible," she said.

The cyclist caught up to us and flipped Mary off, though she didn't seem to notice. The car behind us honked. Only, Mary didn't move. She just kept staring at me with those wide green eyes.

"You should probably drive the car," I said.

The other car revved its engine, pulled up alongside us and its driver yelled, "What the hell?" before speeding off down the road.

Mary waited two full Mississippis before putting her foot on the gas and flying down the road again. "I'm not sure what Reverend Richard's been teaching you," she said. "The Old Testament was written hundreds of years before Jesus was born. Most of the New Testament was written within the hundred years or so after Jesus died. Basically, it was written by a bunch of Jesus's followers, plus James and Jude, who were Jesus's half-brothers. Don't even get me started on how the son of God can have half-brothers."

She turned down Ascott Street.

"If Jesus didn't write it," I said, "then why believe anything it says?"

"Hold on," Mary said. "Dismissing the entire Bible is even more insane than believing in the talking donkey part. The thing about the Bible is that it's full of Jesus's teachings. There's some amazing stuff in there. It's just like anything else in the world. You have to sift through the dirt to find the gold."

She pulled up next to a group of twenty or so people standing underneath Candice Collington's tent. Only, there could have been a thousand people outside and Mary wouldn't have noticed. She was staring straight at me. Mary set her hand down on the emergency brake and her thumb grazed the edge of my hand. It wasn't just a passing glance. Her hand rested there, touching mine, and I wondered: was she secretly counting Mississippis in her head? Did girls' brains even work that way? Did Mary's?

The rest of the world faded away and I was alone with

the smell of Mary's soft skin, her breath against my face. She looked so sincere, and when she spoke, it felt like I was the only other person in the world.

"The Bible always makes me think about Heaven," she said. "And the thing about Heaven is that it's peaceful. It's free. Everyone up there is naked and clothed at the same time, and they see each person as someone who matters. There's no mocking. Two angels don't gang up on another angel and pick on him. They don't make fun of anything. The fun is all around. It's never-ending. Sometimes though, late at night, I wonder . . . if every joke is funny, if every Salisbury steak tastes like filet mignon, how do the angels know it's good? How do they know they're in the Promised Land? Isn't there a small part of them, the smallest part perhaps, that wants to escape? Don't they need to suffer — even *want* to suffer — for a moment or two, so that when the bliss comes, they'll know it?"

I wanted to kiss her right there on the side of the street. I didn't care who was watching. Mary's lips parted and then came together softly, like watermelon-colored pillows. Her eyes focused and they didn't.

I edged closer and Mary didn't move. Better yet, she didn't recoil in horror. I shifted my hand ever so slightly along the emergency brake so there could be no confusion. Our hands were really touching. I closed my eyes and parted my lips. The Friend Zone be damned: this was going to be the one moment, out of all the possible moments, that I would seize.

Knock. Knock. Knock.

"What's going on?"

A pair of chiseled cheekbones appeared outside Mary's window. It was Youth Pastor Glenn. The destroyer of moments. His mouth contained an infinite number of teeth

— incisors and molars, translucent enamel — all ready to chomp down on me. Up close, leering through the window, he looked like a bizarre, colorless monster.

"Are you two taking in the scene?" he said.

Mary took her hand off the emergency brake and stepped out of the car, our brief moment forgotten. I stepped out too.

There were two dozen people gathered on the lawn outside my parents' little church, most of them milling about the sign that read PRESBYTERIANS GET PRESENTS ON XMAS. METHODISTS GET LUMPS OF COAL. They were drinking out of paper cups and chatting. A few of them were eating hot dogs and listening to Elvis Presley's version of "I Believe in the Man in the Sky" on a boom box. Toward the church steps, Candice Collington was operating a hibachi barbecue. The giant Mrs. Claus I'd worked so hard to pump up was half-deflated, and Mrs. Collington's husband was peeling off strips of duct tape and strategically placing them across leaks in Mrs. Claus's apron.

I searched the crowd for Reverend Richard, curious as to what role he played in all this, but he was nowhere to be found. My mom was there, standing beside the church sign, right in the thick of things. To my surprise, a woman in a pink pantsuit was holding a microphone up to her chin. A few steps away, a cameraman pointed a large video camera at her. Mom was beaming. Her hands were animated and beside her, Nancy Sylvester was bursting with pride.

"Is she . . . ?"

"Giving interviews to the press?" Youth Pastor Glenn said. "Yes, I believe she is."

Mary, Youth Pastor Glenn and I walked closer. When my mom saw me, she smiled and waved. Then her mouth formed a thin, angry line when she saw Mary and Youth

Pastor Glenn. She gave me a look like *What are you doing?!* I shrugged and pointed at the camera crew as if to say *What are you doing?!* Then the reporter asked my mom a question and she turned back to talk to the lady, all smiles again.

My stomach was still grumbling after barely eating all day, and I was about to see if Mary wanted to sneak into the crowd and get some hot dogs when Youth Pastor Glenn spoke.

"It never fails to amaze me, the unbridled optimism of the unaware."

Mary shook her head. "You're speaking in riddles again, Glenn."

He checked his watch. "Just wait."

Thirty seconds passed in which the three of us stood at the side of the road, watching my mom give her interview, watching ladies carry folding chairs out of their cars and set them up underneath the sun tent, watching Candice Collington and her husband quarrel over whose job it was to scrape the hibachi grill. Youth Pastor Glenn checked his watch again while Mary and I exchanged uneasy glances.

Then it happened. Suddenly, the giant billboard across the street changed. Just seconds ago, it had been filled with red letters — YOUR IMAGINARY FRIEND IS A LIE. ONLY JESUS IS REAL. THIS IS NOT OPEN FOR DEBATE! The color transformed from red to a brilliant swimming-pool blue. The sign grew so bright, it took over the sky.

My mom gasped. Her friends gasped too. The cameraman swung his camera around and started filming as the reporter rushed to the street and began reporting.

All the while, Youth Pastor Glenn stood beside me, his arm around Mary, those innumerable teeth flashing wide and white in his mouth.

The sign read:

WHEN WILL YOU PEOPLE LEARN?
CONVERTING TO PRESBYTERIANISM
DOES NOT MAKE A FAT MAN IN A
RED SUIT CLIMB DOWN YOUR CHIMNEY

22
Jesus vs. Gandhi

At home, someone was cooking pork chops. A big whiff of fried meat wafted through the air when I walked in the front door. It was like smelling a shower fart: pungent, surprising and nearly impossible to escape.

A clang rang out from the garage and then my dad hollered. "Margaret? Is that you?" There was another clang and then the sound of something spilling. "Are you there?"

"It's me! Mom's not home yet!" I yelled back.

I followed the smell to the kitchen where Caroline was frying up two enormous pork chops and three strips of bacon. She was wearing her purple sports bra and a pair of spandex shorts and standing as far away from the pan as possible.

"You should put on a shirt," I said. "One time, I cooked bacon without a shirt on and it kept spitting at me."

Caroline scrunched her nose. "Maybe the pig in the pan was upset because a lower life form was frying him up."

I flipped her off, only she didn't look up from the pan. "Are you wearing running shorts or a girdle?" I said, a little cruelly.

"I'm curious — when you hump a loofah, do you give

it a name like Shirley or Rebecca? Or do you prefer the romance to be anonymous?"

"What's got you in such a bad mood?"

Caroline pointed to the clock on the wall. It was quarter past six. "Mom wasn't home to cook dinner and all I could find in the freezer was pork chops. I suppose you're going to want some."

"No thanks. I had three hot dogs at the protest."

"Oh God, they're serving hot dogs there?" she said.

"I hear there might be a mini-donut stand tomorrow. You can say what you want about Mom's friends, at least they know how to eat."

"Anyways, don't call it a protest. They're not protesting anything. It's not like Mom's turned into Gandhi overnight."

The pan spat at her, and Caroline jumped out of the way.

"What would Gandhi say about your pork chops?" I said.

She put her spatula down. "Pfft, Gandhi. Yeah right, like he went on a hunger strike. The same with Jesus Christ — you know, Mom's invisible best friend. I don't believe his BS either. Two thousand years ago, people were like animals. They used to poop in the street. And I'm supposed to believe that everyone listened to the one guy who was all sweetness and light? That's bull crap. You know what would happen if you put Jesus and Gandhi in the same room? They'd get into a fistfight, a real one with biting and kicking and Gandhi pulling Jesus's hair, because they'd both want to be in charge. That's what Mom and Youth Pastor Glenn are like right now. Both of them want to be in charge of what everyone thinks."

"Is Youth Pastor Glenn running things at the big church now?" I said.

"It sure as hell isn't Minister Matthew."

Minister Matthew. That was Mary's dad.

"How do you know?"

"This guy I'm seeing, Dennis, told me all about it the other night. He goes to Youth Pastor Glenn's church. Dennis is super smart. He and I might even become boyfriend and girlfriend."

Caroline was still giving me a nasty look. I thought about leaving, then I said, "Just because some guy puts his hand up your shirt, it doesn't make him your boyfriend."

Caroline grabbed an apple and whipped it at my head. When that missed, she picked up an egg timer. Before she could throw it, the bacon spit a burning gob of fat onto her back. Caroline cursed. She started frantically wiping it off.

"Karma," I said.

Caroline hurled the egg timer. I don't know what came over her — if the spirit of Cy Young briefly inhabited her body or what — but the egg timer came at me fast, spinning through the air like a dreidel on crack. It hit me square between the eyes.

A half-second later, I hit the ground.

"Oh, crap!" Caroline yelled. She came running. "Does it hurt?"

She grabbed me by the shoulders and helped me into a chair. Caroline held a handful of Kleenex against my face to stop the stream of blood seeping from my nostril.

"Ouch," I said.

"Jacob, I didn't mean to."

"Why does everyone keep hitting me?" I said.

Caroline's voice softened. "Well, you kind of deserved it when Pushkar hit you." She touched the other side of my face. "And what happened here? Did you really tell some woman she has a beard and then throw a chocolate-dipped cone at

174

her?" Caroline twisted a chunk of Kleenex and slid it up my nose. She ran her hand through my hair, all maternal-like.

"I never told her she had a beard," I said. "And it wasn't a chocolate-dipped cone. It was an expired Dilly Bar."

Caroline laughed softly, consolingly. "The Dilly Bar's a rip-off. For thirty cents more, you can get a chocolate-dipped cone, which has even more ice cream, plus the cone."

"But they glue the wrapper on to the cone," I said. "You end up eating the glue."

She leaned my head against her shoulder. I glanced up into her eyes and was surprised to see how concerned she was, how sorry she was to have beaned me in the nose. Just a few moments ago, I'd hurt her with my words as much as I possibly could, teasing her about yet another guy feeling her up. That wasn't right. Caroline was sensitive about her past, about her future in Parksville. And all I'd ever done was make mean jokes about her.

Caroline looked into my eyes and suddenly we realized how close we were. Everything — her arm around me, my head on her shoulder, the gentle way she was stroking my hair — felt awkward and weird. Caroline stood up quickly. She adjusted her shorts and checked on her pork chops. The fried-meat smell had gotten worse and more familiar at the same time. Caroline used a pair of tongs to lift the pork out of the pan and set it on a plate.

"No vegetables tonight," she said with a smile.

"Vegetables suck," I said, pulling the Kleenex out of my nose and checking for blood.

Caroline handed me an extra-crispy piece of bacon, then looked closer at my nose. "You'll be fine," she said. "There's no mark."

I was about to stand up and find a mirror when my dad

appeared behind me. He looked like he'd shaved since he came home from work, and those nostrils and ears were still curiously trimmed. He was wearing a new shirt, the same kind of dress shirt Caroline had bought for me. Despite his bald head, Dad looked hip. He looked ten years younger. He looked like he was up to something.

"Jacob, can you help me in the garage?"

I wiped away the last bits of blood from under my nose. "Um, sure."

"And tarnation, Caroline," he said, "open a window. There's a giant cloud of smoke in here."

Caroline flipped on the fan over the stove and carried her plate of fried pork into the living room to watch television while she ate. With no good reason not to help, I followed my dad into the garage. As soon as we got inside, he shut the door and a big smile spread across his face.

"I don't actually need your help. I just wanted to show you something," he said. Dad walked over to the corner where he kept his power tools. He shifted three pieces of plywood out of the way, and there it was: his very own refrigerator. Dad absolutely beamed when it came into view. He opened it up and started pulling out groceries. "Check it out. Strawberry jam, spicy salsa, imported mustard. And in this little freezer: ice cream sandwiches and Pizza Pops." He pointed to the piece of bacon I was eating. "What is that, some kind of tofu-infused, gluten-free turkey bacon?" he said. "You don't need to suffer anymore. Look at this." He held up a package wrapped in brown paper. "Maple-cured bacon. The expensive kind, with extra salt."

The piece in my hand tasted like regular bacon, not something from a vegan food store, but I wasn't about to say anything. My dad was so excited, he sounded like an infomercial salesman hopped up on caffeine.

"And what are you going to eat that bacon with? Your mother only keeps seven-grain bread in the kitchen." He pulled a loaf of bread out of his fridge. "This is six-grain bread. Don't you see? The superfluous grain has been eliminated."

Superfluous grain?

"I don't think you're supposed to keep bread in the refrigerator, Dad."

"Sure you are."

"Actually, I think it makes the bread go stale faster."

"Poppycock," he said.

Poppycock?

What word was going to fly out of his mouth next? *Balderdash? Hornswoggle? Fiddlesticks?*

"All I need is a hot plate, maybe even a toaster oven, and I'm all set," he said.

"Set for what, Dad?"

He opened his mouth but didn't say a word. He just stood there, making a strange sound, like a soft A turning into a U. Maybe he was momentarily tongue-tied. Maybe a crisis of conscience had suddenly overcome him. More likely, I think that for the first time, my dad faced the truth about what he'd been doing. Over the past week, he'd been slowly moving into our garage, and not because it was such a fantastic destination, which it wasn't, but because he was moving away from us. He was moving away from Mom.

He closed his mouth and that six-grain bread fell limp in his hand. I wish I could say that I gave him a big hug, that I told him everything was going to be all right, that I suggested he go talk to his wife and that, for the love of God, he finally build her that state-of-the-art kitchen she'd always dreamt about. But I didn't. The truth was, all I wanted to do was get out of that garage as fast as I could. I wanted to get away *from him*. I barely recognized my father anymore.

I took a single step toward the door, when Caroline appeared in the frame.

"You won't believe it," she said. "Mom's on the news."

We all hurried into the living room and stared in stunned silence at the TV. Mom really was on the news. That reporter and her cameraman had been the real deal after all. Mom was pointing at her sign and rambling on about how Santa and Jesus were equal in the hearts and minds of children everywhere, while a separate image appeared in the corner, one of the giant sign in front of the Church of the Lord's Creation, the sign that read WHEN WILL YOU PEOPLE LEARN? The reporter asked Mom a series of questions, and Mom tried her best to remain calm under the glare of the camera's light.

The most amazing sight on our television wasn't even my mother. It wasn't her beloved church sign. It wasn't Youth Pastor Glenn's slogan in the upper left frame. It was the letters in the bottom corner: CNN. This wasn't just the local news picking up the story. The entire country was watching.

From the look on my mom's face, from the twinkle in her eye and the fighting words coming out of her mouth, I could tell — this war was only getting started.

23
Pious Pancakes

When I awoke the next morning, the smell of pork chops had been replaced by the warm, inviting aroma of pancakes. I entered the kitchen to find my mother flipping her home-made flapjacks. She must have gotten home after I went to bed and woken up before anyone else. Despite getting less than six hours sleep, Mom was rushing around, singing Joan Osborne's "One of Us" and pouring glasses of juice.

"Good morning, sweetie pie," she said. Mom kissed the bandage on the side of my head.

"Ouch," I said.

"How's my big, strong workingman today?"

"I'm not even being paid," I said. "It's like slave labor."

"You never know where opportunities will lead," she said, and set down a plate of pancakes for me. Mom had arranged them in the shape of a teddy bear. She'd even fried up two crispy little pancake eyes and placed a chocolate chip in the center for its nose, the way she did when I was little.

"Thanks," I said.

"We do things for each other in this family," she said. Then she walked to the top of the stairs. "Donald! Caroline! Breakfast!"

My dad came lumbering down the stairs in his bathrobe,

all unshaven and smelling like stale socks. Caroline came down too, wearing an Oasis T-shirt that barely covered her underpants. Dad grunted and sat down to read his newspaper. Caroline grunted too. She pulled a piece of cantaloupe out of the fridge and dug into it with a spoon.

"I'm glad we're all so cheery," Mom said.

Dad and Caroline both perked up a bit when Mom placed a stack of pancakes in front of them. Caroline wasn't even fazed when she saw that Mom had organized hers into the shape of a cross. "Pious pancakes taste the best," Mom said, and kissed her on the cheek. Caroline rolled her eyes and turned her plate around so her pancakes looked like a sword. Dad set his newspaper down and reached for the syrup, when my mom grabbed his wrist. She handed him a second bottle, one with Aunt Jemima on it.

Caroline and I stopped eating. Dad looked at the syrup bottle with wide, astonished eyes. Along the label, in yellow letters, were the words Butter Rich.

My dad didn't know quite what to say. For years now, Aunt Jemima syrup had been first on my mom's unwritten list of banned foods. While she and my dad often argued about what types of jam to keep in the cupboard, Dad knew better than to bring up the Aunt Jemima. He'd long made peace with the idea of pouring Mom's generic store-brand maple syrup on his pancakes. And yet here was his wife, handing him a plastic container of Butter Rich syrup like it was no big deal. And there was my dad, he of the whittled-down eyebrows, the stylish new clothes and the secret stash of perishable goods tucked away in the garage. They stared at each other and then my dad said, "Thank you, Margaret." His voice sounded different. It sounded softer, gentler.

Mom said, "You're welcome, Donald," and sat down with

her own plate of pancakes. She used the generic store-brand syrup (which, incidentally, tasted like corn syrup mixed with baking soda) and let my dad pour his Aunt Jemima himself.

"Doesn't anyone want to ask about my big day yesterday?" Mom said.

"I'm sorry, dear," Dad said. "How did things go at the church last night?"

"Terribly. That damned Church of the Lord's Creation put up the most offensive slogan on their sign. It said that converting to Presbyterianism doesn't make a fat man in a red suit come down your chimney."

We all stared at our plates. The three of us already knew the details — the new slogans, Mom's appearance on CNN — but it was best not to ask too many questions.

"I mean, really! Do they think we're that stupid?" she said.

We kept staring at our plates.

"The thing I don't get is that most Methodists aren't all that different than the rest of us. They're *supposed* to teach their kids about Santa Claus. And what about the children? Has anyone stopped to think about *them*? That infernal fluorescent sign could be doing all sorts of permanent damage to their impressionable little minds. I mean, how is a mother supposed to explain all of this to her five-year-old child? Mark my words, Youth Pastor Glenn is trying to start a cult. Pretty soon all his disciples will be wearing the same shoes and chanting in tongues."

Mom leaned back in her seat. Her voice shifted. She sounded reflective, almost wistful. "Other than that, last night was amazing. It really was. A news crew showed up and everything. And you won't believe it, but it wasn't just a crew from the *Village Gazette* or anything. A CNN news crew showed up to interview me." She paused to let the information sink in. "Our little church's struggle against oppression is national news."

"That's weird," Caroline said. "Are we supposed to believe that a CNN news crew was just sitting around Parksville, waiting for two churches to get into a fight?"

"Oh, they weren't in town to interview us, at least not at first. They came to do a story on the Parksville Peeper. Apparently one of the houses the Peeper peeped into belongs to the second cousin of a member of the House of Representatives. The Parksville Peeper got a good, long look at this young girl undressing. She called her dad, who called his cousin, who has a brother-in-law who's a producer at CNN. And presto! They came to town. Only, they couldn't find the Peeper, so they came to talk to me." She lowered her voice. "Between you and me, Nancy Sylvester is getting a little too excited for her own good. But she has a videotape of us on CNN. I'm heading over to her house before I go back to church today."

"You're going back?" Caroline said.

"Of course I am."

"Why?"

Mom crossed her arms. "Because injustice anywhere is a threat to justice everywhere."

"What?" I said.

"Are you quoting Martin Luther King?" Caroline said.

"Martin Luther King, *Junior*, actually," Mom said.

I glanced over at my dad. On any other day, he would have jumped right into the fray. Today, however, he just sat there with a sheepish look on his face. Maybe he was tired. Or maybe all the hoopla at the church made him think better of opening his mouth. If you asked me, he felt guilty for already having a bottle of Aunt Jemima Butter Rich syrup hidden behind the weed whacker in the garage. Either way, he kept his mouth shut.

"You can't misquote Martin Luther King whenever you feel like it," Caroline said.

"Martin Luther King, *Junior*," Mom said. "And I'm quite sure I didn't misquote the man."

"You're misusing his words."

Mom stabbed her fork into a big slice of pancake. She spoke with a mouth full of corn syrup. "Either way," she said, "I know persecution when I see it. And I won't stand for it."

The rest of breakfast went by quickly. Dad finished his pancakes and then lumbered upstairs to shower. Caroline gave up on her pious pancakes after two or three bites and proceeded to chip away at the cantaloupe until she'd scraped out every last bit of orange. Mom spent five minutes quizzing me about my duties at the AMPM. She actually looked proud — or was it relieved? — that I was working my first ever job. I didn't have the heart to tell her Pushkar was forcing me to do meaningless manual labor, so I lied and told her I'd been learning how to use the cash register.

"I'm also learning how to spot shoplifters before they steal anything."

"That's my boy," Mom said.

Caroline muttered under her breath and went back to bed.

"What time do you start work this morning?" Mom said.

"Nine o'clock."

She flipped two more pancakes onto my plate, then sat down beside me. Mom put her hand on my wrist. "I know," she said.

"Know what?"

"I know, Jacob."

Our eyes met and it was like I was looking at her for the first time. Here was this woman, the one who'd given birth to me, who'd burped me and fed me and changed my diaper, who'd raised me. Somehow, slowly, without a single exact moment to say when it happened, my mom had blended into the wallpaper in our house. Her face, her voice, the way she smelled and moved and carried herself, were all just background scenery to me. And the strangest part was, it wasn't her fault. She was still Margaret, the devout churchgoer, the mama bear whose sole objective in life was to protect her two little cubs; the same woman who thought Pat Sajak's banter was "beyond clever," who passionately insisted a moustached Alex Trebek was smarter than a clean-shaven one. I was the one who'd changed.

What did she know? Mom knew about Pia and the car wash, the incomplete fellatio, why Pushkar beat me up. But did she know that Pia made me convert to Hinduism? How I'd been slaving away in Pushkar's storeroom? Did she know I loved Mary more than anything? How I would walk a hundred miles in my bare feet over razor blades and rusty nails just to get her to love me back? Did she know about Moss Murphy? The incredibly painful handjobs?

These past few weeks, I'd been living a secret life. And up until this moment, no one in my family knew what I'd been doing. They didn't know *who* I was anymore. All along I'd thought that since the moment I met Mary, everything inside me had changed. And maybe that was true. But I hadn't started *being* a different person until I started acting differently, until I went to the ice cream shop to talk to Mary in the light of day, until I climbed into the front seat of Aunt Alpana's car and kissed a girl for the first time.

Now my mom knew what I'd been up to.

"I'm sorry," I said.

"It's okay, Jacob. We all make mistakes." She rubbed my back. "All men betray. All lose heart," she said.

Wait, was she quoting *Braveheart* now?

Mom started clearing the table. "I can see the allure," she said. "The air conditioning, the stained-glass rainbow, the arcade games in the basement."

"I'm sorry . . . what?"

"Jacob, I know you went into the Church of the Lord's Creation. Candice Collington's neighbor saw you there watching a concert. Don't worry. I'm not mad. In fact, this might work out for the best." She looked down at the bottle of Aunt Jemima in her hand. Mom breathed in deep and when she breathed out, it was like it wasn't enough. The weight of the world was still on her shoulders. She set the bottle down on her tiny counter space. "What time do you finish work?"

"Four p.m.," I said.

"Excellent," she said. "Because I have a job for you."

24
Taste My Samosas

If my first shift at the AMPM was the most exhausting, back-breaking work of my young life, my second shift was all about psychological abuse. I walked in ten minutes early (take *that*, Pushkar!), expecting to lug some more crates around the storeroom. It turned out Pushkar didn't have any manual labor planned. His purpose had shifted.

In his hands was a hot-dog costume, the kind that crazy people wear on Halloween, where the bun goes along your back, all the way from your shoulders to your hamstrings. The actual hot-dog wiener wraps over your head and covers your torso, finishing somewhere around your crotch.

"Put this on," he said.

"You can't be serious," I said.

Pushkar's pupils pulsed.

"Do I look serious?"

"Um . . ."

"I ask you, the young man who dishonored my family in my sister's car in the car wash that I own, do I look serious?"

I took the hot-dog costume. Along the front was a long, wobbly serving of mustard. Pushkar watched as I slipped it over my clothes, right there in the middle of the AMPM. The suit was tight and its polyester material felt strange, like I was surrounded by static.

Pushkar allowed himself a quick grin. "Now hold this," he said, and handed me a sign that read:

COME IN FOR HOT DOGS!
Only 99 Cents!

I glanced at the rotisserie next to the slushie machines. Pushkar already had six wieners roasting. This wasn't just about humiliating me. The man was serious about selling hot dogs.

"Now go outside and stand on the street corner," he said.

"But —"

"Time is wasting."

"I heard it's going to be hot today."

"You're correct," Pushkar said. "The temperature should be in the mid-'80s today."

"What if I die of heat stroke?" I said.

Pushkar paused to think. "If you die, I will pray for your eternal soul."

I wanted to say that his prayers would be of small comfort to me. That this was cruelty beyond measure and that I wouldn't stand for it. I wanted to club him over the head and make a break for it. Only, I didn't. I couldn't. I put the sign over my shoulder and walked out the door, past the bike rack and all the way to the street. I stood at the edge of the sidewalk and held up the sign for passing traffic to see, humiliated, debased, thinking things could never get any worse.

Then Pushkar poked his head out the door. "Sway your hips!" he said. "Draw some attention to yourself!"

A small part of me thought perhaps he was kidding, that at any moment, he might double over with laughter, run up and pat me on the back, telling me the hazing was over and "Welcome to the AMPM family." But his eyes were like steel. He wasn't joking.

I held the sign up over my head. Slowly at first, building momentum until I got faster and faster, I began swaying my buns.

Three hours later, I felt like I'd lost half my body weight in sweat. I managed to find a bit of shade in the shadow cast by the AMPM sign, but the relief proved fleeting and whenever I glanced back at the store, Pushkar was at the window, glaring at me. For the first time in my life, I endured the catcalls of strangers. It was surprising, even a little shocking. The few times I'd passed by a teenager on a street corner holding a retail sign, the last thing on my mind was unrolling my window and hurling insults at him. Yet it happened time and time again. The first was some guy in a dirty pickup truck. He pulled up next to me, yelled, "Pansy!" and took off. *Okay*, I thought, *maybe he has Tourette's.* Then two guys in a sedan drove by and yelled, "Halloween's over, jackass!" *Fair enough*, I thought. It was only when a lady walked by pushing a stroller and mumbled, "Get a life," that my feelings started to get hurt.

Eventually Pushkar emerged from the AMPM with water. Not water in a bottle, or water in a cup, mind you, but a bucket of water. Pushkar set the bucket down on the sidewalk. "Drink," he said.

I picked it up and smelled it. "Is it toilet water?" I said.

Pushkar rubbed his chin philosophically. "You will never know, my friend." He turned and walked back inside.

The water looked clear. It certainly didn't smell like toilet water. I took a sip and then another. It felt so good sliding down my throat, I didn't care what kind of bacteria might be lurking within. I removed the hot-dog cowl and dumped some over my head. It was the best feeling in the world. Back at the AMPM window, Pushkar was still watching. I took a few more sips and then set the bucket down on a patch of grass, pulled the costume back over my head and lifted the sign again.

An hour later, a patch of clouds mercifully pulled in front of the sun. The temperature dipped and a light summer rain started. I couldn't believe my luck. I stayed there for five hours, with only one short bathroom break in the middle, before Pushkar called me inside. He told me to take off the costume and, surprisingly, gave me a free lemon-lime Gatorade out of the refrigerator.

Five minutes later, Pia walked in the door. It was the first time I'd seen her since the sit-down on her father's couch. A few customers were getting their coffee and Pushkar was busy at the cash register.

Pia walked right up to me. "I hope my father isn't working you too hard."

"Um . . ."

Pushkar shuffled over quickly, suddenly all smiles. He put his arm around my shoulder. "The boy is a revelation," he said.

"Is that so?" Pia said.

"We're getting along like green eggs and ham. Right, Jacob?"

I wiped the sweat off my forehead. "Right," I said.

Pia snuck me two extra bottles of Gatorade and I drank out of the hose behind the store before I rode my bike home. I thought for sure that as soon as I walked into the house, I'd have to pee like a racehorse. But no. Barely a trickle came out. My body had absorbed the Gatorade like a parched cactus. I took a quick shower, shaved — my paper-thin porn 'stache was now a thing of the past — and changed before hopping back on my bike and riding over to the church.

I arrived to find that the inflatable Mrs. Claus had given up. She was fully deflated now, with patches of duct tape sticking off her apron as she lay collapsed at the side of the road. Mom and Nancy Sylvester were in the middle of a spirited debate over whether Mrs. Claus's deflation was an act of God or deliberate sabotage. Candice Collington kept interrupting them, insisting they head over to Walmart and order a replacement. Their friends were milling about, somewhat interested but trying not to get involved, while at the park across the street, the reporter in the pink pantsuit was smoking cigarettes with her cameraman and checking her watch every thirty seconds.

A hand touched my shoulder. "Would you like a samosa?"

It was Aunt Alpana, the woman whose front seat I'd defiled.

"No, thank you," I said.

She held up a plate of deep-fried delicacies. "Are you sure? They're scrumptious."

I sniffed the samosas. They certainly didn't smell scrumptious. "What's in them?"

"Let me see," Aunt Alpana said. "There's potatoes, onions, some grated ginger, lentils, cilantro . . ."

Grated ginger? Lentils? Cilantro? None of these were mainstays of my regular diet of chicken fingers and pancakes. They sounded more like the ingredients Moss Murphy used to fart on my head.

"I think I'll wait for a hamburger," I said.

She lifted the plate so the samosa smell sailed toward my nose. "The hibachi broke. There are no hamburgers today."

Aunt Alpana was dressed extra fancy. A thick layer of makeup was caked on her cheeks and she was wearing big hoop earrings and an extravagant necklace.

"What are you doing here?" I said.

"Jacob! How rude!" my mom shouted. She'd slipped away from Nancy Sylvester and had somehow snuck up right behind me. Mom took a samosa and bit into it. She seemed to enjoy the explosion of grated ginger and lentils in her mouth. "I invited Alpana," she said between bites. "Now, be polite. Have a pierogi."

"It's a samosa," Aunt Alpana said.

Mom looked down to inspect exactly what she was eating. Her gaze shifted to me. Mom's eyes said: *Eat the samosa and eat it now, mister!* I took a piece and put it to my lips. As I opened my mouth, I still hoped there might be some way to get out of this, that I could fake a coughing fit or simply tuck the samosa in my pocket for later, but looking at Mom's somber stare and Aunt Alpana's enthusiastic eyes, I really had no choice. I took a bite.

"What do you think?" Alpana said.

I hadn't swallowed yet. A few lentils and a stray pea were swirling around the back of my mouth. "It's good."

"Just good?" Mom said.

"You can really taste the cilantro," I said.

Aunt Alpana smiled. She leaned toward my mom. "Now, where is this Ted you told me about?"

"Uncle Ted?" I said.

"Yes," Mom said. "I thought Alpana and your Uncle Ted might hit it off."

Aunt Alpana launched into a long explanation about

191

how she was a widow, but not really a widow, as her husband had left her to move to Mexico and become a professional wrestler. Apparently Pushkar insisted on telling everyone her husband had died in an ice-fishing accident, even though they lived nowhere near a frozen lake. Alpana hadn't seen him in four years, and while India's parliament stated that divorce was expressly forbidden, Alpana pointed out that she and her estranged husband no longer lived in their birth country and an annulment could be assumed based on equal parts "continuous desertion" and "valid mental illness." Aunt Alpana said someone must be mentally ill to join an unregulated Mexican wrestling league and roll around in a pair of tights with a bunch of fat sweaty men named Pantalones Loco ("Crazy Pants") and Enojado Perro Misterioso ("The Mysterious Mad Dog").

"I could also seek an annulment based on venereal disease or leprosy," she said.

"Does your husband suffer from either of those?" Mom said, as though the two afflictions were mutually exclusive.

"Maybe one, maybe the other. Who knows? It's been a long while since I saw him," Aunt Alpana said.

I surveyed the crowd. "Uncle Ted isn't here."

"May I ask what he does for a living?" Aunt Alpana said.

"He sells used cars."

"Pre-owned cars," Mom said.

Aunt Alpana nodded. I took another bite of the samosa, which I'd decided wasn't all that bad, while Mom gestured for the news crew to come over. The reporter in the pink pantsuit stamped out her cigarette and hurried over with such gusto, I thought she might trip in her high heels.

Mom pulled me aside. "Don't you have to be somewhere?" she said.

"I'm already here."

"You're supposed to be over *there*." Mom pointed to the big church with its colossal sign. She looked dead serious again.

Aunt Alpana, for her part, looked disappointed that my creepy Uncle Ted wasn't around to taste her samosas. I glanced at my watch. The youth meeting was set to start in ten minutes. But before I could head over, Reverend Richard pulled up in his car. He looked exhausted. His hair was a mess and his wrinkled jacket made him look like he'd crawled out from under a rock. Reverend Richard made a beeline for my mother. I waited by her side, eager to see what happened when Reverend Richard and the fast-moving reporter converged.

Mom put her hand on my back and pushed me toward the Church of the Lord's Creation. When I resisted, she gave me the same look as when I got sent to my room as a little kid: *You'd better move!*

I shoved the last of the samosa into my mouth and marched across the road. I was going to the youth meeting at the big church tonight. To spy on Youth Pastor Glenn.

25
Story of a Young Man, Undercover

"What happened to your hair?" I said.

Moss Murphy ran his hand through his newly shorn locks. "Samantha gave me a haircut. I tried telling her that Vince at Great Clips always cuts my hair, but she really wanted to do it," he said. He took a sip from his can of Dr Pepper. "How does it look?"

I didn't know what to say. He'd gotten butchered. Samantha must have had something against him after all, because it looked like she'd used garden shears in the back and toenail clippers in the front. The left side was noticeably shorter than the right and there was a single long strand dangling down his forehead.

"It looks pretty good," I said.

We were standing beside the snack table in the auditorium downstairs. Moss Murphy had arrived with Samantha, but now she was up on the stage, talking to Youth Pastor Glenn, twirling her hair and tilting on one leg. All the usual suspects were there. Calvin Cockfort was holding a soda in each hand (to keep the scratching at bay) and chatting with one of the Delany sisters. Jaqueline Bachmeier was wearing a sweatshirt featuring a glittery monkey. Another fifteen or so teenagers were milling about. Only Mary was nowhere to be seen. When my mother first insisted I become a double agent, I agreed in large part because of Mary. Even if she was dating Youth Pastor Glenn, at least I could spend time with her. Now Mary wasn't even there.

"The handjobs stopped," Moss Murphy said.

"Pardon me?"

"Samantha still hasn't kissed me. And now she won't even give me the handjobs. Don't get me wrong. Part of me is glad it's over. And while I'm kind of afraid — and I mean *physically afraid* — of it happening again, another part is sad she doesn't want to do it anymore." His eyes misted up a little. "Last night we just sat on the couch and watched *Top Gun*. She wouldn't even come near me."

"Really? *Top Gun*?" I said. "What about the volleyball scene?"

"What *about* the volleyball scene?"

"Didn't it get her all riled up?"

Moss Murphy looked at me like I was insane.

"Have you tried baking cinnamon buns?" I said.

"What?"

"You know, like Caroline said. To get her in the mood."

Moss Murphy narrowed his eyes. "I think you seriously misunderstand how this whole pheromone thing works," he said.

Up on the stage, Samantha's hand was on Youth Pastor Glenn's arm. I wasn't sure how long it was there, but infinity-plus-one Mississippis seemed like a good guess.

"I'm sorry, buddy," I said.

Moss Murphy stuffed a handful of Cheetos in his face. He spoke with his mouth full. "What's the point? What's the point of anything?" he said. He chewed a bit and kept talking, but I didn't hear a word he said. Mary was at the door. And she was radiant. She was wearing a low-cut shirt — sans modesty panel — and her new jeans with those big pockets. A girl who looked like her younger sister was with her. Mary didn't see me right away. She waved to Youth Pastor Glenn, then Samantha went over and gave Mary a hug.

"You know what happened, right?" Moss Murphy said. "Youth Pastor Glenn fingerbanged Mary."

"Bullshit," I said.

"It's true. He did it in a tent during the spring youth camping trip. That's the word on the street, anyways."

"How do you know?" I said.

"Everyone knows."

I looked from Mary over to Youth Pastor Glenn. There was no way I could ever imagine her letting him do that.

"It's time, people!" Youth Pastor Glenn said.

Moss Murphy and I took our seats in the front row. Mary and her sister sat behind us and a little to the left. At first, I thought Samantha was going to sit with the girls. Then she climbed over the seats and sat down right in Moss Murphy's lap. He turned red — with embarrassment or arousal, I wasn't quite sure.

Samantha looked up at Youth Pastor Glenn.

Youth Pastor Glenn looked back at Samantha.

"Leave some room for Jesus there, Moss," he said.

Everyone laughed and Samantha hopped off Moss Murphy's lap. The crowd settled and Youth Pastor Glenn said, "Thank you all for coming to this Wednesday-night event. We've changed up the schedule a bit since I took over for Minister Matthew and I appreciate your patience as we iron out the kinks under new leadership."

The way he said "new leadership" sounded definitive, as though Minister Matthew was never coming back. I tried to catch Mary's eye, but her gaze — and everyone else's — was fixed on Youth Pastor Glenn.

For the next ten minutes, Youth Pastor Glenn delivered a sermon entitled "Dinosaurs: God's Big Mistake or Part of the Almighty's Plan?" He started by claiming there was no way to prove that dinosaurs were millions of years old, as science had led mankind to believe. He went on to suggest the first dinosaurs appeared at the same time as Adam and Eve. "People assume dinosaurs are ancient because they're not mentioned in the Bible," Youth Pastor Glenn said. "But what these so-called 'scientists' fail to acknowledge is that the term *dinosaur* wasn't even invented until 1841, hundreds of years after the Bible was written. So how could the word *dinosaur* be in the Bible?

"In reality, God created dinosaurs along with all the other animals on the sixth day," Youth Pastor Glenn said. He let out a chuckle. "That's a pretty big job, even for the Lord. No wonder he needed so much rest on the seventh."

The audience chuckled too.

I was shocked by how politely these teenagers sat through the whole sermon. Instead of asking how Noah managed to cram two Tyrannosaurus rex onto the ark alongside the giraffes and hippos and all the other random beasts, the crowd nodded along. Several times, I wanted to raise my hand to say something, only I kept flashing back to the piercing look Youth Pastor Glenn had given me after I suggested, "It's just Santa Claus." The last thing I wanted was to lose a staring contest in front of everyone.

And besides, I was still undercover. I had to keep a low profile.

As Youth Pastor Glenn switched from dinosaurs to floods and Genesis and how a flat earth wasn't all that inconceivable

197

an idea, I started to see his allure as a public speaker. His voice ebbed and flowed in a way Reverend Richard's never did. At times he looked like a sincere young man. At other times, in those moments when he gazed up to the heavens, his expression shifted, his skin tightened on his face and he looked almost wild, like a whiskey-addled tent preacher. The whole while, the crowd sat captivated.

Maybe it wasn't just the extravagant new building and meat-locker levels of air conditioning that kept parishioners coming to this side of the street. Maybe they came to see Youth Pastor Glenn talk. The other day, Reverend Richard looked like his voice was putting his face to sleep. It was like I could hear the sound of Pac-Man dying each time he sighed. This Youth Pastor Glenn was different. If Reverend Richard was the past, he was the future.

I snuck a quick glance at Mary. I caught her gaze and she said *Hello* with her eyes. In my mind, her eyes didn't just say hello. They said, *Hello, Jacob darling. I've missed you. Thanks for going jean shopping with me. You're a scintillating conversationalist. Do you want to know what color my bra is?*

Then again, maybe her eyes were just saying hello.

After the sermon, Youth Pastor Glenn had us all sit around in a circle and share something for which we were thankful. This is where I completely tuned out. I didn't care that Calvin Cockfort's uncle was paying for his deviated-septum surgery. Or that Jaqueline Bachmeier was grateful that that awful Gennifer Flowers was out of Bill Clinton's life forever and that our president finally had the chance to work scandal free. My ears perked up when Mary's sister spoke. She was thankful for her family and for her big sister Mary and for Youth Pastor Glenn filling in so admirably for her father these past few weeks.

As one of the Delany sisters spoke, I noticed Mary and Youth Pastor Glenn exchanging looks across the circle. They were mouthing words back and forth. Every few seconds Mary would shake her head and Youth Pastor Glenn would cup his hands over his mouth and almost whisper. I elbowed Moss Murphy to see if he knew what Youth Pastor Glenn was saying, only he was too busy staring longingly at Samantha to notice. Samantha, for her part, was too busy staring longingly at Youth Pastor Glenn to look back at Moss Murphy.

The sharing circle was almost complete and Calvin Cockfort was speaking again. It was difficult to pay attention, what with all the looks being cast around the circle and the fact that Calvin Cockfort kept reaching down and scratching his crotch every few seconds, but I think he was describing his aspirations to get involved in "retail electronics." Before he could finish, Mary stood up and walked out the auditorium doors. Calvin hesitated, then kept talking.

A few seconds later, Youth Pastor Glenn stood up too. "Excuse me. Something requires my attention. Please continue," he said. Then he walked out of the room. The auditorium doors closed behind him.

We all looked at one another.

"Should I keep going?" Calvin Cockfort said.

Jaqueline Bachmeier didn't reply. She merely handed him a can of soda to keep the scratching at bay.

Two seconds later, the yelling started. Outside the auditorium doors, Youth Pastor Glenn and Mary were having a heated argument. Their voices were muffled and I couldn't make out exactly what they were saying. Youth Pastor Glenn seemed angry and Mary seemed upset. He kept asking her questions and then cutting her off before she could answer.

After thirty seconds, Samantha tiptoed over and put her ear to the door.

"What are they saying?" Moss Murphy said.

"Shhh!" Samantha waved her hand at him, seriously annoyed.

The fight went on for another minute or so. Then it became quiet. Almost too quiet. For a second I thought maybe Youth Pastor Glenn had hit her. Maybe Mary hit him back. Maybe at that very minute Youth Pastor Glenn was carrying Mary's unconscious body to the trunk of his car for discreet disposal. I pictured myself heroically leaping into action, tackling Youth Pastor Glenn and punching him square in the nose, Mary awaking in my arms, staring deep into my soul and saying, "Jacob, I knew you would save me."

That is not what happened.

Mary opened the door with tears in her eyes. Her sister ran over and Mary whispered in her ear, then they left holding hands. A few seconds later, Youth Pastor Glenn entered through the very same door.

"Where were we, people?" he said.

Youth Pastor Glenn ushered Samantha back into the circle and, strangely, the sharing started up again as if nothing had ever happened. Two more Delany sisters shared what they were thankful for. Calvin Cockfort finished his thoughts. Moss Murphy even took a turn, thanking Samantha for all the joy she gave him. He went on to express his gratitude to the veterinarian who prescribed antibiotics to his mother's ferret. "That happy little guy might live a few more years," he said.

The whole while, we all kept one eye on the door in case Mary came back.

She never did.

26
The Green Flash

Early the next morning, a figure appeared at the edge of my bed. It was dark and at first I could only make out a hazy silhouette. The red numbers on my alarm clock told me it was 4:47 a.m. I'd been asleep for six hours, but in my semi-conscious state, it felt like just minutes had passed since my head hit the pillow.

The figure poked me hard in the leg and I shot up in bed.

"Mary?"

"No."

Was it Pia? Had a girl really snuck into my bedroom in the middle of the night? Was I about to be ravished? Was I *ready* to be ravished? My mouth tasted like glop and I was a little sweaty, sleeping in my boxer shorts.

I turned on the lamp and saw that the enchanting figure wasn't Mary. It wasn't Pia either. It was my sister, Caroline. Suddenly, she wasn't so enchanting. Caroline sat down beside me. She rubbed her eyes.

"Wake up, loser," she said.

"Go away," I said, and lay back in bed.

"Seriously, wake up."

"There better be a nuclear war going on outside for you to get me up this early."

"There's no war," Caroline said. "But there is a girl throwing rocks at your window."

I crossed my eyes at Caroline, not sure whether to believe her. Only, the Caroline I knew couldn't keep a straight face. If she were joking, she would have already smirked in spite of herself. I stood up and parted the blinds. Mary was outside my window, standing on our front lawn, waving up at me.

"She was throwing pebbles at my window, thinking it was your room," Caroline said. "I thought it might be the Parksville Peeper, so I ignored it at first. Eventually I got up and she asked me if Jacob lives here."

I looked from Caroline to Mary and back to Caroline again. "What should I do?"

"I don't care," Caroline said. "I'm going back to sleep." She walked to the door. Before she left, she ran her hand through her messy hair and said, "Don't forget to use a condom, stud."

I flipped her the bird. She flipped me off back and then stepped into the hallway. Outside, Mary was still waving. I put on a pair of jeans, a T-shirt and a hoodie, and hurried over to the bathroom, where I ran a sliver of toothpaste across my teeth and whooshed it around my mouth. Then I tiptoed downstairs, avoiding the creaky steps near the bottom. When I opened the front door, Mary was there.

"Hey."

"Hey."

"Is everything okay?" I said.

Mary paused. Her eyes turned brittle and for a moment it seemed like she might sit down on my front step and unload her heart to me, confess exactly what had happened between her and Youth Pastor Glenn. Then she said, "Everything's good."

A longer pause followed in which I wondered whether

my parents were going to wake up and find us standing there. I wondered whether I should invite Mary in, whether something terrible had happened, like someone dying or a horrible accident. It couldn't be all bad, I decided, because at least she was turning to me in her moment of need. And wasn't that all I wanted? Wasn't that what everyone wanted? Someone to need us in their time of need?

Mary took a small step forward. "Do you want to see the green flash?" she said.

"Is that like a superhero?"

"Not even close," she said.

"What's the green flash?"

"Come with me and I'll show you."

Ten minutes later, we were flying down the highway in Mary's car. At this hour the roads were pretty much deserted. With the cars off the streets, Mary's driving wasn't quite the public menace it usually was. She did scare the life out of me a few times as we worked our way out of the suburbs, but once we got on the highway, it was clear sailing.

Mary explained the green flash as she drove. Apparently it was a meteorological phenomenon she'd seen on the Weather Channel. During sunset and sunrise, the sun's light travels through more of the earth's atmosphere to reach your eye, and a prism effect is created. If you're on a long, uninterrupted horizon, perhaps sitting on a prairie or at the edge of the ocean, you might be lucky enough to see something called astronomical refraction, where the sun suddenly changes color from reddish-orange to greenish-blue. A green flash shoots up into the sky and then disappears, as if it never happened.

Mary told me that for hundreds of years, sailors had reported seeing green flashes at sunrise. Their minds weak with scurvy, their stomachs unsettled after weeks onboard a ship, the sailors thought the green flash might be mermaids being born or souls coming back from the dead. Mary said these were just old wives' tales and that the anchorman on the Weather Channel had broken down the scientific reasons why it occurs. She also warned me that green flashes are rare and almost impossible to see, so we might not have any luck this morning. I gave her a curious look that said, *Why are we driving in the dark to see something that probably isn't there?*

Mary switched lanes without signaling. "The rarest things in life are the things we covet most," she said. "Shouldn't all our efforts go toward seeing what we've never seen before?"

"Well, all right then," I said.

We were heading to an abandoned airfield thirty minutes outside of town. Mary described its runway as "super long" and the horizon as clear. The sun was supposed to rise at 6:07 a.m., which would give us at least fifteen minutes leeway between when we arrived and when the green flash might occur.

Mary sounded a little like a tour guide as she gave me all the details, then we lapsed into a comfortable silence. I felt content sitting there, listening to Mary breathe. The radio was off and the only other sound was the air coming through the vents. It was just the two of us again, going to see an astrological phenomenon that may or may not appear. I couldn't have been happier.

"I'm sorry I woke up your sister," Mary said finally.

"That's okay," I said. "She wakes me up all the time. She snores when she's drunk."

Mary laughed. Only, I wasn't kidding. On the nights Caroline stumbled in smashed out of her mind, she sounded like a busted wood chipper.

"I'm glad I didn't throw rocks at your parents' window," she said. "I might have interrupted them having sex."

I looked over at her and she looked over at me. Against my will, I pictured my parents kissing, my dad giddily traipsing to their bedroom door, his hard ding-a-ling swinging in the air, him locking the door, then looking back at my mom and saying, *Well, Margaret, where were we?*

"You're blushing," Mary said.

"I'm not."

"Yes, you are. I've seen your parents, you know. They're both still pretty young. I bet they're passionate. A little debauched. Virile."

"You're going to make me barf," I said.

Mary laughed. She reached over and touched my shoulder. It stayed there for one and a half Mississippis. "What is it?" she said.

"Nothing."

"You looked like you were about to say something."

"I wasn't," I said. "I mean . . . I was. It's just, this one time I heard my dad call my mom a sexy nickname. It really freaked me out."

"What was it?"

I looked over at her but I didn't say a word.

Mary took a turnoff going east. Instead of slowing down, she sped up as we flew over the off-ramp.

"That's fine," she said, "if you don't want to share."

"It's embarrassing."

"Well, lots of things in life are embarrassing," she said. "Farts are embarrassing, but everybody farts. Even Oprah Winfrey blasts off a little wind now and then."

Mary burst out laughing. I couldn't help myself. I laughed too. Then, almost too quickly, we stopped.

"You can't bring up something like that and then not tell me," Mary said. "It's cruel. It's against the social code we all live by. You know, the one that keeps us from becoming mass murderers or running around the mall with our underpants on our heads."

"I didn't know there was such a thing," I said.

"Well, there is."

"Still, I can't say."

"Okay," Mary said. "I'm not going to force you. Just remember, if you follow this pattern of mentioning things and then keeping them to yourself, you're just a hop, skip and a jump away from strolling through the mall in your underpants. Or murdering someone. Is that how you want to be known, Jacob? As the Underpants Murderer?"

The car got quiet. Mary zipped past a pickup truck and left it in her dust. Ahead of us, the road was clear for as far as the eye could see. It felt like the outside world didn't exist, like we weren't driving down the highway at all, like we weren't even in a car. The headlights and the steering wheel, the vents blowing cool air, all vanished, and it was just Mary and me sitting side by side, an island unto ourselves.

"Sugarboobs," I said. "My dad called my mom Sugarboobs."

Mary's mouth hung open. The air in the vehicle changed. It felt supercharged, electric. I didn't know what she was going to do, if she was going to stick out her tongue and yell "Gross!" or pull over and leave me on the side of the road. Then Mary laughed; a pure, joyous, effortless laugh. And I laughed too. I laughed as hard as I'd ever laughed before.

The rock at the edge of the airport was enormous. It wasn't just a boulder. It looked like a chunk of earth had burst out of the pavement into the early morning air. It also looked like a bit of a hazard. Why launch planes next to something they could crash into? Mary handed me a blanket and I gave her a boost. Together we scaled the rock face. It was still dark when Mary lay out the blanket and sat down. She'd chosen a secluded spot. There was no one around and it was completely dark. The nearest streetlight was half a mile away.

I settled in next to her. "How long until it happens?"

She checked her watch. "Ten minutes or so." Mary looked back at the car, at the abandoned building behind us and then at the unbroken horizon. "I walked in on my grandparents having sex when I was fourteen."

"That's impossible," I said.

"Trust me, it's possible. They're in their early sixties. That's still pretty young. They came to visit for Thanksgiving one year and my dad sent me looking for them. So I went to the guest room and I guess I forgot to knock. I opened the door and there they were, in the middle of the day, doing it."

"That sounds . . . harrowing."

"Good word, Jacob. And yes, it was harrowing. It freaked me out big time."

"What did you do?"

"I screamed. I said sorry. Then I shut the door. What else was I supposed to do?"

Mary's eyes shone bright even in the dark. I had yet to see this miraculous green flash, but for the life of me, I couldn't imagine it being more beautiful than her eyes. Even when she was talking about horrifying grandparent sex.

"The worst part," she said, "was that they were doing it, you know . . . from behind."

"Like doggy style?"

"Well, they're not dogs, Jacob. But that's what they were

207

doing. They were both facing me. My grandma had this hypnotized, almost satisfied look on her face, like . . . like . . .”

"Like she'd just polished off a box of Ferrero Rochers?”

"Yes! Exactly. And my grandpa looked all serious, as if he was trying to do math in his head or something. Right before I screamed, my grandma looked me in the eye and said, 'Oh, hello dear.'” Mary held in a chuckle, then shook her head. “I mean, I get it, we're all sexual beings, and good for them, I suppose, if they're still enjoying themselves in their sixties and everything. I just wish they'd locked the door. I mean, who visits for Thanksgiving, then has sex in your house in the middle of the day without locking the door?”

Mary's question must have been rhetorical, because she kept talking. "I suppose it's part of God's plan. He puts us down here on earth, with these private parts that match up so perfectly to the other sex. How could he not want us to do it? Like, even saints like Mother Teresa have urges. It's not as if Jesus Christ took the form of man and then didn't feel the need to clear the pipes every once in a while.”

"Clear the pipes?” I said.

"You know, to get himself off. We're all given these physical cravings, and Lord help us, they start when we're teenagers, sometimes even preteens, so we don't know what to do with them. And then our parents tell us to keep it in our pants. And meanwhile my grandmother is writing erotica. Don't laugh. I'm not kidding. When I caught them doing it, my sister told me she'd found a short story my grandma was working on. It was straight-up erotica. It wasn't even subtle. There was no plot, just an English lord walking into a farmhouse and catching an innocent young maiden changing her corset. Then suddenly it's all bow-chicka-wow-wow.”

She stared into the sky. "Sometimes I think my father

208

became a minister as a reaction to all the free-spirited hijinks going on in his house growing up. It's funny. We always rebel, don't we? I mean, if your parents are total Ward and June Cleaver cookie-cutter stereotypes, then of course you're going to go wild. But when the parents are the wild ones, the kids often go the opposite way. It's human nature." She nudged me in the shoulder. "What are *you* rebelling against, Jacob?"

I didn't even pause. "You're the minister's daughter," I said. "What are *you* rebelling against, Mary?"

Mary laughed. She ran her hand through her hair. "Touché. Well played."

The horizon started to brighten.

"I don't know what it is about you, Jacob," Mary said, "but every time I'm with you, I start monologuing like a supervillain. You know, in a movie when the bad guy has the superhero on the ropes, and death and destruction are moments away, yet somehow the good guy convinces the supervillain to start telling him all about his plans for world domination and how his parents never loved him and how if it had only been him in the superhero's position, the public would love and adore him, and hate the superhero? That's what you do. You get me monologuing."

I couldn't believe it. Mary had just made a comic book reference. I needed to hold on to this girl and never let go.

In front of us, the sky morphed into shades of gray. The horizon was so clear, it felt like it wasn't even real, like we were watching it on some large-screen, high-definition television. Except it was real. It was spectacular.

"Don't forget," Mary said, "if you stare at the sun too long, you might go blind. So look out of the corner of your eye. Then, just when it changes color, stare right at it. Oh, and don't blink. The weatherman said if you blink, you might miss it."

The sun appeared like a tiny red orb peeking over the horizon. I forced my eyes open. And then it happened. Quickly, in an explosion of color, it turned green. Not just green, but blue-green and lime and olive and the color of shamrocks right in the middle. The green flash stayed for a fraction of a second and passed by so quickly, I thought my eyes were playing tricks on me.

Mary squealed with delight. "Did you see it?"

"I did. I really did."

I kept looking at the sunrise, watching from the corner of my eye as the red orb revealed itself more and more. Maybe this is how one acquires depth, I thought. By experiencing moments. I could have been lying in bed, asleep with my head against my pillow. Instead, I was up and I was watching. I was thinking.

This was all Mary's doing. She didn't wait for moments to appear. She seized them. She woke up early. She threw pebbles at the window of a house she'd never visited before. She drove us here. Mary picked me, out of all the souls on earth, to watch the green flash with her.

I decided I should make things happen. I was finally going to kiss Mary. We were going to share a moment. Because what does anyone have to share, if not moments?

I leaned over and, instead of kissing her, placed my hand squarely on her thigh. I don't know what came over me. It was like my hand operated independently of my body, like it had its own agenda. And once it was on her thigh, there was no going back. I could feel her warm skin through her jeans, the contours of her flesh, her body next to mine. *I* knew my hand was there. Of course I did. It was *my* hand. Mary knew it was there too. It was on *her* thigh. Only, we both refused to acknowledge it. We kept watching the sunrise, like it was about to do something unexpected, like at any moment, the sun might dip back down and reemerge all beautiful and green again. Yet we knew it wasn't going to change. The sun rises slowly. It can't be rushed. All the hoping in the world won't hurry it up.

Nine long Mississippis passed before Mary spoke. She didn't look over, but her voice was clear as day.

"Jacob, do you remember the book of Luke, passage 14:10?"

My hand still hadn't moved from her upper thigh. "No," I said.

She stared straight ahead. "Really? You don't remember what the host said to the friend in Luke 14:10?"

"I'm sorry. I don't."

"That's a shame," Mary said.

Time passed so slowly, it couldn't be counted in seconds or Mississippis. All I wanted was to take my hand off Mary's thigh. But removing it would mean admitting it was there in the first place. So I left it where it was. The sun rose. Mary watched the sky turn blue. I sat beside her, racking my brain for what on earth the host said to the friend in Luke 14:10 and why Mary had mentioned it. I couldn't remember even a thin outline of the plot of the book of Luke, let alone that particular passage.

The sky was fully bright.

"We should go," Mary said.

I took my hand off her thigh. Two seconds later, it was like I hadn't touched her at all.

We slid off the giant rock, stepped into Mary's car and she drove me home. I arrived before anyone in the house had even woken up. I left my shoes at the door and hurried into the living room, where I pulled my mother's well-worn Bible out from under the coffee table. Upstairs my parents were stirring. The sound of Caroline snoring leaked through her door.

I flipped to the book of Luke and found the passage. With my head filled with the image of my hand resting just inches away from Mary's personal holy land, I read what the host said to the friend in Luke 14:10.

It read: *Friend, move up higher, then shalt thou have glory.*

27
No Christmas This Year?

Work was torture that morning. I never got back to sleep after Mary dropped me off, and Pushkar had no sympathy for my tired looks and sleep-deprived sighs. The moment I arrived, he put me into the hot-dog costume and I got back to waving my sign. An hour into my shift, Pia and her Aunt Alpana drove up to the store. They stepped out of their car and rushed over.

"What is this?" Aunt Alpana said.

Pia put her hand on her hip. "You know, my father wore that costume for Halloween."

I didn't want to say anything to get Pushkar upset, so I kept swaying my hips and waving my sign until eventually they went inside. I couldn't see what they were saying, but moments after the women got their coffee and drove away, Pushkar called me over. He had me strip out of the hot-dog costume and follow him into the storeroom. Pushkar pointed to the crates of Mountain Dew and told me to "Get lifting!"

The manual labor didn't end until my shift finished at 4 p.m.

As I was walking out the door, Pushkar approached. I'd removed the sweat-stained bandages from either side of my face during my shift and Pushkar paused to look at the damage he'd inflicted. He handed me a sheet with a list of dates scribbled on it. Pushkar's penmanship was so bad, his ones were indistinguishable from his twos. The *g* in August looked like the symbol for infinity.

"Is this my schedule?"

Pushkar nodded.

I squinted hard. "Is this a two or a one?"

Pushkar peered at the sheet. He raised his eyebrows like even he wasn't sure. "It's a one," he said finally. "I don't need you here every day. You have most of this week off. But trust me, you will work your fifteen shifts."

I tucked the sheet into my pocket and had turned to leave, when Pushkar said, "Jacob, have you ever heard the expression 'walking on eggshells'?"

"I think so."

He rubbed his fist slowly, purposefully. "Just remember, my friend, your shells have already cracked."

I hopped on my bike and pedaled out of there as fast as I could. When I got home, before I could sneak upstairs and take a nap, my mother asked me to help her chop vegetables in the kitchen.

"We hardly ever do anything together," she said.

She made room for me on her tiny counter space and I picked up a piece of celery and a knife. It was actually kind of nice, standing there chopping vegetables with her. I'd become so used to her obsessing over the church signs, always having some bizarre motivation behind what she was doing, that I'd forgotten what it was like to spend time with my mom. I was just thinking that we should do this more often when she said, "So, how's my little 007?"

"Um, what?"

"You know, how's my double agent doing? Have you

discovered anything interesting about the Church of the Lord's Creation?"

"Not really," I said.

"There must be something."

"I don't know what to tell you. It's not like they drink goat's blood and sing 'Kumbaya My Lord' while Youth Pastor Glenn throws virgins into a volcano."

Mom pursed her lips. "Don't be ridiculous. If there was an active volcano in Parksville, I'd have heard about it by now." She chopped her vegetables faster. "You don't have to help if you don't want to."

"I *do* want to help. It's just hard to go undercover when everyone knows who you are."

"That's fine. Abandon your mother in her time of need," she said.

I thought for a second. "Youth Pastor Glenn says that Noah put dinosaurs on the ark."

Mom smirked. "Really? That's impossible."

"I know."

"Imagine the trouble a bunch of dinosaurs would cause on a boat," Mom said. "How on earth are the sheep and the goats and all the chickens supposed to survive the flood when you've got a T. rex biting off their little heads?" She laughed so hard, she snorted.

"What are we making?" I said in a desperate attempt to change the subject.

"Oriental food," Mom said.

"That's racist!" Caroline yelled from the other room.

"It's a stir-fry. Stir-fries are from the Orient!" Mom yelled back.

Caroline appeared at the kitchen door with her face covered in grayish-black glop. She was playing with her lips in front of a hand mirror. "You're supposed to say Asian. That's more politically correct."

"What's that stuff on your face?" I said.

"It's hot sesame cream. It's supposed to heat up to your body temperature."

"Are those sesame seeds in it?"

"Yep, black ones." She read the label on the container. "They've got all sorts of stuff in here: methylparaben, parfum, butylparaben —"

"Butylparaben? What's that?"

"I don't know," she said. "That's probably one of the things they teach you in beauty school. There's a lot to know. They don't pay makeup artists a thousand dollars a day for nothing."

I nodded. For the first time, Caroline's beauty-school aspirations made sense.

Mom was furiously dicing a carrot beside me. "*Oriental* is a properly fine word," she said. "I'm not going to say *Asian* just because the multicultural police are everywhere these days." Mom set her knife down and looked right at Caroline. "Last month you told me I couldn't use the word *Indian*. But Alpana's an Indian and she's my friend. She doesn't mind if I use that word."

Caroline threw her hands in the air. She looked like she wanted to kick something. "Of course Alpana doesn't mind. She's from India! You're not supposed to use the word Indian, you're supposed to say Native American!"

"That doesn't make any sense."

"It makes sense because they're not from India. When that slave trader Christopher Columbus arrived in America, he was so confused he thought he was in India and started calling everyone with dark skin Indians."

Mom lifted her hands as if to say, *Simmer down*. She brushed her carrots into a pan and started skinning an onion. "Whatever our politics, let's be respectful of Christopher Columbus in our house. He is an American hero. End of story."

"Christopher Columbus wasn't American. He was Italian."

"Well, he's American in my book, and that's what counts."

Caroline stormed away, leaving Mom and me working elbow-to-elbow in the kitchen. Mom rolled her eyes at Caroline and I rolled mine back. I'd finished with the celery and was trying to figure out how to chop a leek when Caroline came storming back.

"You always do this, Mom," she said. "You put people on a pedestal when they don't deserve it."

"That's not true, dear," Mom said.

"It is true. That's what you've been doing all week with Santa Claus. You do it all the time with Jesus." Caroline pointed at me. "Tell her, Jacob. Tell her what Mary said about Jesus."

I flashed Caroline an angry look. She and I had eaten cereal together that morning and, in my sleep-deprived state, I'd spilled my guts over Mary. Caroline knew all about the green flash, what Mary said about Jesus and the Bible, how I'd put my hand on her thigh, what the host said to the friend in Luke 14:10.

"Mary?" Mom said. "Which Mary? The one from Baskin-Robbins? The minister's daughter?"

Caroline crossed her arms. "That's right."

"Have you been spending time with Minister Matthew's daughter?" Mom said.

"You told me to investigate," I said sheepishly.

"Oh. So first you climb all over poor innocent Pia in the

217

car wash and now the minister's daughter?"

"Quite the little Casanova, isn't he?" Caroline said.

I wanted to bean her between the eyes with an egg timer. Instead, I put my head down and kept chopping the piece of kale or iceberg lettuce or whatever it was.

"What exactly did this Mary say about Jesus?" Mom said.

I kept chopping.

"Jacob?"

"I don't know," I said. Mom kept staring at me and I felt an interrogation coming on. I decided it was better to give her a little information rather than let her get worked up and demand to hear it all. "Mary told me that Jesus was a rule-breaking humanist who undermined the scriptures of his day. She said it's been so long since Jesus died that we probably don't know a thing about who he really was."

"Is that so?"

"It makes sense," Caroline said, picking a sesame seed off her nose.

"What else did this Mary say?" Mom said.

This time I looked her straight in the eye. "Mary said the Bible wasn't even written by Jesus and that most of it was written by men hundreds of years after Jesus died. She said that nowadays everyone's trying to take advantage of Jesus's legacy. Like all those religious call-in shows. Mary said the only reason someone would have a religious call-in show is so they wouldn't have to go out in the real world and get a job. Like Cousin Stephen."

Mom stared daggers at me. I'd brought up Cousin Stephen in a deliberate attempt to distract her. My dad's cousin didn't work. He lived on disability payments because of what my mother called "the mildest case of carpal tunnel syndrome in history." I hoped Mom might change the subject to how it wouldn't kill Cousin Stephen to pick up a few shifts a week at the gas station, but she was fixated on one thing.

"There's nothing but blasphemy at the Church of the Lord's Creation. Blasphemy, heresy and sacrilege."

Caroline sat down at the kitchen table, grinning like the cat who'd eaten the canary. "Tell her what else Mary said. About what Jesus does when he's alone."

"Caroline!"

I growled at her, but Caroline was so amused, she didn't care.

My dad appeared at the doorway. He'd been out on the back deck, fixing his birdfeeder again. Dad was wearing a brand-new button-up shirt and drinking a Zima. He smelled different. The Irish Spring was gone, replaced by the unmistakable aroma of Drakkar Noir. "What's going on?" he said. Dad looked around the room. He sensed the tension and turned to leave.

"Not so fast," Mom said, stopping him in his tracks. She pointed a radish at me. "What did Mary say Jesus does when he's alone?"

I didn't speak. I didn't even move. It suddenly felt very hot inside. I pictured myself making a break for it, elbowing my dad out of the way and running out the front door. I could've probably made it too. The element of surprise was on my side. Eventually though, I would have to come home. And Mom and Dad would be waiting for me. If there's one thing I knew about my mother, it was that she only got more upset as time went by. So I stayed in the kitchen, refusing to talk. I would keep my mouth shut until the Rapture if need be.

"Mary said Jesus was a masturbator," Caroline said.

Mom slapped me hard on my chest. "Jacob!"

"Caroline said it!"

Dad chuckled.

"It's not funny, Donald," Mom said. "Those heathens have been filling your son's head with all sorts of perversions. And this minister's daughter sounds like the Whore of Babylon."

"She's not a whore," I said, picturing Mary and Youth Pastor Glenn lying side by side in a tent, his hand reaching down low, his fingers crawling toward Mary's personal private paradise.

"Well, she's a liar. That's for sure," Mom said.

Caroline was playing with her lips in front of her mirror again. "I'm thinking about getting collagen injections," she said to no one in particular.

"You'll do no such thing," Mom said.

"It's the latest craze," Caroline said. "Soon everyone's going to have them."

"Then they'll all look like streetwalkers together."

"Mary's not wrong," I mumbled.

"What's that?" Mom said.

"Mary's not wrong," I said, clearly this time. "If Jesus was a real person, then he must have peed and pooped and . . . you know, done other stuff just like a regular human being."

"Are we still talking about this?" Caroline said.

Mom grabbed the leeks out of my hand and threw them into the frying pan. She didn't care if they were diced or not. "It's high time you had a chat with Reverend Richard," she said.

"Aw, Mom."

Mom looked over at Dad, who was leaning against the doorframe and polishing off the last of his Zima. Mom was preparing this special meal for him and there he was, gulping down his sparkling New Age drink from his secret refrigerator, as if his wife hadn't been serving him Butter Rich pancakes all week.

"Do what your mother says," Dad said.

"There's no way I'm talking to Reverend Richard," I said.

Mom put her hands on my shoulders. "It's for the best."

"I'm not going."

Her eyes shifted from wide and concerned to narrow and unforgiving. Her jaw grew rigid. "If you don't go, there's no Christmas this year."

Caroline stopped playing with her lips. My dad stood up straight.

"You can't be serious," I said.

"Try me," she said. Mom stared at me with those unflinching eyes. In the background, a commercial was playing on the living room television. Out the window, the Deck Girls were making macaroni and cheese. I couldn't believe my mom would make such a threat, especially after all the trouble she'd been going through at church this week. For a moment, I considered calling her bluff.

Then memories of my mother's baking flooded my mind: pecan pies and candy-cane cookies, third servings of turkey and buttery mashed potatoes with sweet peas. I pictured Christmas gifts from years gone by: Lego sets, Castle Grayskulls, multiple Mario games, even that Snoopy snow cone–maker Caroline refused to share. Christmas morning was magical. It was the happiest day of the year, a thousand times better than any picnic in July. And how many more Christmases did I have left to still be a kid?

No argument was worth missing Christmas morning.

"Fine," I said. "I'll talk to Reverend Richard."

28
The Ejaculation Schedule of the Messiah

Reverend Richard's office was small and stuffy. His desk was clean but the rest of the room was cluttered with random stacks of paper and half-filled cardboard boxes. A rickety cabinet sat to my left, overflowing with a hodgepodge of books. The Old Testament and New Testament were side by side, of course. Next to them were three volumes of the *Encyclopedia Britannica*, a threadbare copy of *The Very Hungry Caterpillar* and various *Reader's Digest* anthologies. Reverend Richard had thumbtacked dozens of photographs to the wall. Some, like one of him and my mother sharing a toast at a church picnic, were quite recent, while a smattering of Polaroids was at least twenty years old. The young, beardless Reverend Richard in those photos looked so full of life, so unsuspecting, completely oblivious to what lay ahead.

I tried to get comfortable in my seat, only it was stiff and lumpy and it creaked every time I moved. It had been ten minutes since Reverend Richard's secretary sat me down in his office. In that time, I'd thought of several ways to defuse whatever my mother had told him. I could always play dumb. That's what my father did last month when he was pulled over for speeding through a playground zone. (It didn't work, not even when he batted his eyes at the grim-faced lady cop.) I could also cry. Very rarely is someone eager to scold a crying teenager. If things got really bad, I could always pretend to be the victim of a grand scheme, one involving Reverend Richard's nemesis, the Church of the Lord's Creation, adults with malice in their hearts and perhaps even the news crews outside.

As good as these options were, in the end I decided to face the subject head-on. Any attempt to sidetrack or confuse Reverend Richard would only result in more awkward meetings, and I wasn't keen on being involved in this one.

The longer I sat there, the more my mind started to drift. I pictured the fragile look in Mary's eyes when she arrived at my doorstep the other day. After watching the green flash together, it wasn't inconceivable that Mary and I might become boyfriend and girlfriend. In a perfect world, we might even double date with Moss Murphy and Samantha. I imagined the four of us in our best clothes, making small talk as we waited to be seated for a big night out at our local Outback Steakhouse.

I glanced over my shoulder, out the open door and into the hallway. Where was Reverend Richard? There was only so much nervous anticipation I could take. My mind really started to drift. A Superman sticker attached to a dusty box on the floor reminded me of the old comic books my dad kept in the hall closet, the ones I used to read as a little kid. In some of them, Superman and Lois Lane would have a baby (usually a boy), and it would be fifty percent career-minded crack investigative reporter and fifty percent Kryptonian, powered-by-the-yellow-sun do-gooder with truth, justice and the American way billowing through its indestructible little veins.

Of course, due to continuity concerns and a lack of promising storylines, these hybrid Superbabies would never last. They'd be explained off as dream sequences or alternate-world hypotheses. But I would always remember. Even at seven years old, I wasn't the kind of kid who could just forget about an adorable little Superbaby in his red cape, inadvertently using his super-strength to lift the couch and bump it into Lois's vacuum cleaner. I was attached to those Superbabies. I liked them. I wanted to see more of them and thought it was the world's biggest rip-off they didn't stick around longer.

I was considering writing DC Comics a sternly worded letter, when footsteps sounded in the hallway. A few seconds later, Reverend Richard entered. I sat upright in my chair. The Superbabies vanished from my mind and the reason I was here flooded to the front of my brain.

Reverend Richard took his seat and apologized for keeping me waiting. He folded his hands on his desk. His gaze drifted skyward before settling right between my eyes.

"I've just had an interesting talk with your mother," he said. Reverend Richard ran his hand through his beard, as though searching for the right words. "You see, Jacob, masturbation is like potato chips. You've never seen a person eat just one potato chip, have you?"

I shifted in my chair. "I don't think I have."

"That's right. Once you pry open a bag of chips, dip your hand in and eat the first one, there's no going back. Most people, regardless of their station in life, will eat the entire bag." Reverend Richard's hands shifted up and down, a steeple forming and collapsing. He spoke in a slow, measured tone. "This pointless self-abuse will not relieve your carnal desires. It's a temporary solution to a spiritual problem — a counterintuitive solution, one that only intensifies the appetite for salacious activity, which in turn leads to more self-abuse. Furthermore, such behavior often begets the viewing of pornography."

He fished a well-worn copy of the New Testament out of his desk drawer. Reverend Richard flipped to a dog-eared page and asked me to read a passage from Job 31.

I looked down and, with no other option, read out loud. "'If I have lurked at my neighbor's door, then may my wife grind another man's grain —'"

"No!" Reverend Richard grabbed the Bible. "Not that part." He searched for the right passage.

Now I was really confused. "How does a wife grind another man's grain?"

"It doesn't matter," he said. "Read this passage. From the top."

"'I made a covenant with my eyes not to look lustfully at a young woman.'"

"Do you see?" Reverend Richard said. "In our purpose of serving the Lord, we must not look lustfully. We must not think lustfully. To be righteous is to be free of such burdens." Reverend Richard flipped to another dog-eared page. "Here. From Corinthians 6:18 — 'Flee from sexual immorality. All other sins a man commits are outside his body, but he who sins sexually sins against his own body.'" He closed the book and set it on the desk. Reverend Richard paused to let his words sink in.

I, however, had no idea what he was talking about. The office felt even stuffier with the two of us in here and I could smell the half-eaten Subway sandwich sticking out of his garbage can. What he was saying was a bit over my head and at no time did he address the real reason why my mother had sent me here.

Reverend Richard cleared his throat. It had been seven or eight seconds since either of us spoke, a short while if you're waiting in line at the grocery store, a long while if a middle-aged man in a white collar is staring you down.

"Listen, Jacob. I'm not about to tell you what to do with your body. That's between you and God. But maybe it would be a good idea to keep those things private. Private from your friends. Private from your family."

"You're talking about keeping a secret."

His eyebrows formed a question mark. It took him a moment. "Are you referring to the sermon I delivered three weeks ago?" he said. "The one that quoted Ecclesiastes 12:14 — 'For God will bring every deed into judgment, with every secret thing, whether good or evil.'" Reverend Richard ran his fingers through his beard again. "There the Bible is referring to *big* secrets. Secrets that can harm our neighbors and shake the foundations on which families stand. I assure you, in that particular case, God wasn't talking about self-abuse."

I didn't know what to say. I couldn't remember the sermon he was talking about. My mind drifted again, this time to how pretty Mary had looked when she came into the auditorium the other day, her low-cut shirt, those tight-fitting jeans with the appropriately sized back pockets, the warmth of her thigh.

"Jacob?" Reverend Richard said.

"Yes?"

"Do you have anything to say?"

I stammered a little. "I'm not sure what my mom told you," I said. "But I'm not here because I have a problem with self-abuse. I'm here because I want to know whether Jesus was like everyone else."

"How do you mean — like everyone else?"

226

"Maybe I don't need to know." I went to stand up.

Reverend Richard glued me to the seat with his eyes. He leaned forward in his chair. It occurred to me there would be no miracle interruption, no one coming to save me. Reverend Richard wasn't going to let me out of that room unless I told him why I was really there. I closed my eyes and when I opened them, I just blurted it out.

"Was Jesus a masturbator?" I said.

Reverend Richard's eyes opened wide like flying saucers. He ground his teeth together and his expression shifted to that of a grizzly bear agitated by a bumblebee. Slowly, he stood up from his desk and looked out his window. It wasn't a panoramic view by any means. His office was on the second floor, overlooking the church parking lot and, in the distance, not his beloved park, but the monolithic Church of the Lord's Creation and their enormous pulsing sign. A rivalry he couldn't escape.

When Reverend Richard turned around, his face was a dreadful pink color. His hands were shaking. He slammed his palm on the table, shockingly, violently. "How much of this am I expected to take?!" he yelled. Reverend Richard clenched his fists. He'd completely lost it. "I come in here, not just on Sunday like everyone thinks, but every single day of the week. And I listen and I advise and I try to help people. But all I hear is sin, sin, sin. It's like I'm dealing with wild animals!" He stopped and looked at his clenched fists, as though he'd just realized what he'd said.

Reverend Richard sat down on the edge of his desk. He tried to compose himself. "You wouldn't believe what I have to deal with. Just this week I had some lady come in here complaining about a rash on her you-know-what. And she asked me if it was the Lord's vengeance. And I'm

227

like — *How on earth could the Lord place his vengeance onto your private parts?* Oh, and this is the best part. Then she admits she's been sleeping with the milkman. The gall-darn, freaking-fracking milkman! I didn't even know there were milkmen in this day and age. Is that even still an occupation? How long and hard did she have to look to find a milkman in the year 1996? And then her husband comes in the next day complaining about some —" here he made air quotes, "'mysterious and unexplained symptoms.' And do you know what? I'm not allowed to tell him. I'm not even supposed to tell you. The conversation was privileged. I'm like a lawyer with forty insane clients, half of whom couldn't find their hands if they put them in front of their faces."

I exhaled, thinking he was winding down. Only, Reverend Richard was just getting started.

"I've got shoplifters and adulterers. In the past year, I've dealt with not one, not two, but *three* Community Advisory Councils, because most of these women can't get along. I swear, if I wasn't here to intervene, this place would be like a women's prison on the day all their cycles synced up and they ran out of Prozac." He pointed out the window. "They're posting unrepentant blasphemy on the sign across the street. My career is in a shambles. And my home life — do you think that's any better? My eighty-year-old mother has completely lost her marbles. Most of the time, she thinks I'm her dead brother Frank. Just last week she climbed on top of a piano at the old folks' home and started singing like Marilyn Monroe. An orderly had to bribe her with a Snickers bar to get her down. I mean, you can call it Alzheimer's, but she's just straight-up bat-crap crazy and has been for a good six years.

"And then you come in here, Jacob, asking me whether our Lord and Savior Jesus Christ used to masturbate. Well, color me happy. Isn't this the best day of my life? A teenage boy wants to know the ejaculation schedule of the Messiah."

Reverend Richard put his shaking hand on my shoulder. Perspiration coated his face. He leaned in close and looked me dead in the eye.

"I like you, Jacob. I love all the sheep in my flock." He paused and I watched his pupils expand until there wasn't any color left. "But so help me God, if something doesn't change and change soon, one of these days — not today, and maybe not tomorrow, but soon — I'm going to lead the lot of you straight off a cliff."

29
The Final Countdown

I stumbled out of church, bewildered and confused. I hadn't been there ten years ago when Brave Bill sold his corner store and lost his entire life's savings on one hand of blackjack, but at that moment, I kind of knew how Old Brave Bill felt. My legs were rubbery. The hot summer air pressed against my skin.

And there was a circus to behold.

Three news vans were parked outside. I counted six cameramen, and the female reporter had multiplied into several pantsuited reporters now — one in pink, another in blue and another in green, each with big blonde hair and black roots, holding microphones and interviewing anyone willing to stand in front of a camera. My mom's friends had multiplied as well, from fifteen to almost fifty.

Across the street, a second group had gathered, this one in the parking lot of the giant church. They were sitting in lawn chairs and having their own cookout with a half-dozen hibachis. A couple of them were carrying homemade signs, mostly stuff about not worshipping false idols and advice for Presbyterians to read their Bible. One even had a picture of Santa Claus crossed out with a big red X and the real St. Nicholas pulling three little children from a boiling cauldron underneath.

My mom was right in the middle of things. Her precious church sign was covered in a bed sheet from our hall cupboard and, judging by the general hubbub and electricity in the air, it looked like a big reveal was only moments away.

I staggered over to Dad and my Uncle Ted.

"Jacob, my boy!" Uncle Ted grabbed my hand. "Don't shake hands like a wet fish," he said.

I increased my grip, but it was no use. Uncle Ted was already squeezing too hard.

"What happened to your face?" he said.

I'd almost forgotten about my stitches and black eye. "A bearded lady attacked me."

Uncle Ted burped into his fist. "I thought a jilted husband beat you up for washing his wife's car," he said.

My dad patted me on the back. His face beamed with pride. "The boy was getting busy with a young lady in a car wash."

"Dad!"

"You don't say? Congratulations, Jacob." Uncle Ted shook my hand again. He scanned the crowd. "Tell me, is your sister around?"

I rolled my eyes. For three Christmases now, Caroline had been extra-wary of hugging Uncle Ted and scared to death of being trapped under the mistletoe with him. "He's so obvious," she would say as Ted lurked by the doorway.

"I don't know where she is," I said.

Uncle Ted frowned. He was holding a plastic cup filled with red wine and his white dress shirt was open to reveal a set of gold chains like a plate of spaghetti on his chest. His face looked like Joe Pesci's — if Joe Pesci's likeness had been carved onto a potato, the potato had been dipped in orange paint and then stamped on Uncle Ted's head. Uncle Ted wore shoulder-padded suit jackets from 1989 that probably fit seven years ago but now made him resemble a beer keg on stilts. He had a pencil-thin moustache and ear hair for days.

"Did you hear what's going on?" Dad said to Uncle Ted. "The big church is planning their own Operation Desert Storm reenactment for the same day as ours."

Uncle Ted took a sip of red wine. "Are we going to switch days?"

Dad looked at the assembled mass in the other parking lot. How many of his former drinking buddies were now his mortal enemies, I didn't know. "They're kidding themselves if they think we're going to change days," he said. "They probably don't realize we have an authentic-looking Saddam Hussein."

I looked over my shoulder, worried that Pushkar might be within earshot.

Uncle Ted looked around too. "Margaret mentioned I might be able to meet Saddam Hussein's sister."

"Ah, yes," Dad said. He waved over Mom, who in turn waved over Aunt Alpana. Alpana rushed over with a plate of samosas.

"Ted, this is Alpana. Alpana, this is Ted," Mom said. Mom had a twinkle in her eye. Surprisingly, so did Aunt Alpana.

"It's a pleasure to meet you," Uncle Ted said, and kissed Alpana's hand.

Aunt Alpana blushed. She even curtsied a little. "Would you like a samosa?"

Uncle Ted grinned. His moustache grinned too. "I've been looking forward to tasting your samosas all week," he said.

I couldn't stand to watch these grown-ups flirt anymore.

I turned around, planning on sneaking off the premises and walking home, when Mary appeared right in front of me.

"Hey," she said.

"Hey," I said, a little stunned.

"I know, it's crazy. I snuck across enemy lines. I just wanted to see what life was like on this side of the invisible fence." Mary looked over at Candice Collington and her husband setting up a new hibachi, at the reporters in their pantsuits interviewing parishioners wearing red Santa Claus hats. She saw Nancy Sylvester diligently guarding the sheet-covered sign. "Is that the lady who robbed the radio station?" she said.

"She stole a pack of Triple-A batteries from RadioShack."

"Oh."

"I hear she still feels really guilty about it."

"As well she should," Mary said. From the smile in the corner of her mouth, it felt like, had Mary been the store detective on duty that day, Nancy Sylvester would have been let off with a warning.

I thanked her for taking me to see the green flash and was about to pull her aside and tell her what Reverend Richard had said, when my mom broke away from the group and headed straight toward us.

"Jacob," she said, "you haven't introduced me to your friend."

I gave her a funny look. They'd clearly met at Baskin-Robbins the other day. "Mom, this is Mary. Mary, this is Mom."

"It's Margaret," my mom said, shaking Mary's hand.

Mary smiled. "I saw you on the news. You looked great. Very well-spoken," she said. "Also, I love your church."

"You do?"

"Of course. There's something so picturesque about your little chapel here. I've always meant to sneak over and hear a sermon."

"Isn't your father Minister Matthew?"

"He is," Mary said.

Mom rocked back and forth on her heels, not sure what to make of this minister's daughter. "I was so sorry to hear about your father, I hope he feels better soon."

"Thank you," Mary said.

I looked from Mom to Mary. No one had told me Mary's father was ill.

"You know," Mary said, "I'd love to take a peek under that blanket, to see what your new slogan is before the big reveal. Unless, of course, you're worried I'm a spy."

Mom let out a big fake laugh. "A spy? What a ridiculous notion." She looked over at the sign. "I suppose it wouldn't hurt to let you have a peek a few minutes early."

Just like that, Mom and Mary walked over to the sign. I watched from a distance as Mom tried to coax Nancy Sylvester into letting Mary have a quick look. My dad and Uncle Ted were still talking. Aunt Alpana had left to hand out more samosas and two others had taken her place. It was Pushkar — yellow-eyed, unsmiling Pushkar — and beside him was Shotgun from Sore Thumbs.

"What's going on?" I said.

The four of them looked at me like I was gate-crashing their private party.

"We're talking about the reenactment next week," Dad said. "Keith here was just telling us the big church is planning on using laser-tag equipment."

"Keith?" I said.

Dad pointed at Shotgun.

"That's right, dude. They're upping the ante this year," Shotgun said.

"That's why Keith came to meet us today."

Shotgun grinned. His eyes were glassy. I think he was a little stoned. "I've got a line on paintball equipment," he said.

"Paintball?" I said.

All four of them nodded their heads like they'd just discovered uranium or something.

"Couldn't somebody get hurt?"

"Well, yes. Yes, they could," Shotgun said. He turned to my dad. "It's not cheap. A few hundred rounds of paintballs will really cost you."

Uncle Ted hitched up his belt. "Do you know how many pre-owned vehicles I sold last month?" he said.

Shotgun looked even more stoned as he tried to estimate Uncle Ted's gross domestic sales.

Pushkar put his hand on Shotgun's shoulder. "Let's talk money."

All four of them gave me that look again. I slipped away from their little secret society, wandered over to the barbecue area and got myself a double-fudge Yoo-hoo. As I cracked it open, I saw Reverend Richard watching from one of the upstairs windows. Over by the sign, Mom had finally convinced Nancy Sylvester to let Mary have a peek.

In the park across the way, a single heavy figure was lurking. I could hardly believe my eyes. It was the bearded lady from Dairy Queen, the one who'd swiped my expired Dilly Bar. She was wearing beige jogging pants and a big brown hoodie that made her look like a pregnant Wookiee. The bearded lady and I made eye contact and then, quick as a cat, she snuck off into the trees. I was still searching for her when Mary came over.

235

"What are you looking at?" she said. "Did you see the Parksville Peeper? I hear he's been everywhere this week."

"Nope, no Peeper," I said.

Mary scanned the tree line. "Your mom invited me over for dinner."

"Really?" I said.

"Yeah. I couldn't believe it either."

My mother was getting ready for her big reveal. She flashed me a sly look, like she was keeping her friends close and her enemies closer. "It's time!" she yelled. The parishioners stopped their conversations and gathered around. The reporters in their pink, blue and green pantsuits all stood in line, and their cameramen hoisted their cameras on their shoulders. My mom stood beside her beloved sign, bed sheet in hand.

Then Nancy Sylvester shrieked — a wild, startling shriek. She pointed across the road.

Youth Pastor Glenn was standing in front of his giant sign. His congregation were on their feet, steel in their eyes. Above Youth Pastor Glenn, the slogan had disappeared. In its place was the number 5,000. Then the number 4,999. A few seconds passed before the number 4,998 appeared on the screen.

I looked from Mary to my dad to my mom. Each was more stunned than the last. The reporters rushed to the other side of the street and began frantically reporting. You could have heard a pin drop on our side of the road.

The countdown was on.

30
To Catch a Peeper

I never dreamt in color. Even when my *Mario Kart* addiction was in full swing and my unconscious brain was frequented by spinning turtle shells and rainbow racetracks, or during those torrid days of eighth grade when Ms. Tarvis would point at the blackboard and expose her toned midriff, when I woke up in the morning, all I could remember were shades of gray — vivid, intense shades of gray, but shades of gray all the same. I would be the *Mario Kart* champion of the world. Ms. Tarvis would squeal in ecstasy as I inserted *Tetris* block after *Tetris* block into her bellybutton. But I couldn't remember a single red or blue.

Hours after the countdown began, I awoke with a start. It was past midnight. My bedspread was coated in moonlight, and I could still see the colors from my dream.

I leaned back in bed. Twice, maybe three times in my life, I'd awoken in a hazy state, slipped back into sleep and found I could control my dreams. It was the most amazing feeling in the world. One time I could fly. I pushed off the ground and suddenly I was floating. Everything was hovering around me: cars, people, staplers, ice cream cones; only I could zip between them. I could spin circles in the air, like Superman without the cape.

The other dreams were erotic in nature and, truth be told, I'm not proud of everything I did in my semiconscious state. Suffice it to say that both Ms. Tarvis's midriff and the side-boob of the hostess at our local Outback Steakhouse were left satisfied, slightly sticky and perhaps reeling a bit from the experience.

These dreams proved fleeting. I remember waking up slowly, then a flash of panic as I lost control, clinging to the sensation for as long as possible. Then it was over. Each time I tried to fall asleep again, hoping to repeat the unrepeatable, grasping at one more perfect moment, like an addict unable to recapture that perfect high.

On this night, I couldn't control the dream, but when I woke up, I recalled colors for the first time. Mary was wearing a summer dress adorned with poppies: ruby-red poppies and dark mahogany poppies, poppies speckled like strawberries and poppies that lay in lush swells like crimson-red lips.

We were walking in the park near my school, watching two dogs chase a Frisbee. The park transformed into winter, and snow fell — languidly, spectacularly — in wondrous wide flakes all around. The dogs were no longer dogs but wolves, and they were sprinting into the frost-tinged woods. A thousand shades of silver emerged from the snow. The sun glistened.

Mary and I ran into a clearing and suddenly it was summer again. We were at the corner of Ascott Street and Jedidiah Avenue. Reverend Richard was there, dancing cheek to cheek with Caroline. They were wearing burgundy suits made of the softest velour and Caroline had butterflies painted over her eyes. Mary and I laughed joyously at the sight of them. The greens of the trees, the shifting shades of sapphire in the sky, the nuanced auburn in Mary's hair, it was all so mesmerizing.

Then the enemy arose across the street — Youth Pastor Glenn and his posse: Calvin Cockfort and his mangy mullet, the Delany sisters and a couple jocks backing them up. They were gray and black and white and transparent, their faces painted in stars. Youth Pastor Glenn was dragging a cross and the rest were marching in his wake.

As they drew closer, Mary buried her head in my chest. I felt her breath against my neck, saw her copper-toned hair up close. The evil horde drew near, moaning like zombies. From the back, the bearded lady appeared, hurling expired Dilly Bars in the air. One of them struck me in the temple, splitting my stitches open. Still I stood my ground.

I would stand with Mary until the end of time.

I would never, ever let her go.

Then I woke up.

I lay back in bed, my mind awash with colors, amazed at how even now they seemed so bright and wide and wild and real. I hid under my covers in a desperate attempt to get back to sleep. Only, it wouldn't come. I was trying too hard. It's impossible to recapture a moment when you're preoccupied with controlling it.

I rolled out of bed and walked to the bathroom to pee. Caroline was snoring like an ox. I closed her door and tip-toed downstairs to have a bowl of cereal. My mother usually allowed only three different cereals in our house at a time. "These cupboards are too small to hold dozens of boxes," she would say. Typically, it was Shreddies, Rice Krispies and — depending on my mother's current digestive temperament — either Corn Flakes or Raisin Bran. Imagine my surprise when I opened the cupboard door and discovered a brand-new box of Count Chocula.

I held it like Indiana Jones gripping the Holy Grail. It had been a decade since a sugary cereal had made an appearance in my mom's kitchen. When I was five, we won a box of Franken Berry in a raffle at my elementary school Halloween party. On the way home, Caroline and I passed the box back and forth in the back seat of Dad's car, running our fingers along the monster's pink electrodes and checking out the ad for Boo Berry on the back. "If you want to taste something delicious," Dad said, "try the Count Chocula. It's amazing."

It had been ten long years. I looked up the stairs. This was clearly a treat Mom had bought for Dad. Did I dare break the seal?

Damn right I did. I tore open the package and helped myself to a big bowl of chocolatey goodness. I had just poured the milk and sat down at the kitchen table, when I looked out the window. Something was moving on the neighbors' deck. I took a closer look. With the moonlight shining and a street lamp nearby, it was bright enough outside to see the Deck Girls' tent rustling back and forth. Then a figure emerged.

He was facing away from me at first, but when he turned my way, I saw his face. I saw his bald head glistening in the moonlight. My heart leapt into my throat.

It was my dad. Donald. The man who raised me.

I almost choked on my Count Chocula.

My dad was the Parksville Peeper.

31
The First Supper

The next day, all the talk was about the countdown on the giant sign. An evil genius must have programmed it, because the countdown was irregular, meaning you never knew when the next number was going to appear. Sometimes it would tick down in a matter of seconds — 4,145 ... 4,144 ... 4,143 — and other times it would take five minutes before the next number arrived. The crowds outside the two churches were spellbound. It wasn't like they could set their watches, go home and veg out in front of the TV until the clock reached zero and it was time to come back. My mom and her friends had to keep a constant vigil.

I was a little surprised when Mom pulled herself away long enough to make dinner. Nancy Sylvester had just called from the church secretary's office to give an update from the front lines. Apparently the countdown was now in the mid-3,000s.

"They completely stole our thunder," Mom said.

Nancy Sylvester's muffled voice sounded on the other line.

Mom cut her off. "The slogan we were going to use won't cut it. We need to think of something really clever, something to totally put them in their place. Then, the moment after their clock hits zero, we pull off the sheet and wham-o! They're all stunned and depressed."

Mom kept the phone to her ear while she checked on the roast beef. Mary was coming over for dinner. In fact, she was supposed to arrive any minute. I'd showered, shaved and put on a clean shirt. I even let Caroline apply a little foundation around my black eye. Now all I had to do was wait.

"It's all about shock and awe," Mom said into the phone.

I slipped away and paced the hallway. Two minutes later, the doorbell rang.

"I'll get it!" I yelled.

Caroline poked her head around the corner. "Go get her, lover boy," she said. She flipped me off before I had a chance to say anything back and then disappeared upstairs.

When I opened the door, Mary was standing there in a retro '50s sock-hop dress. She was so drop-dead gorgeous, I shuddered. I was still amazed that she was here to see *me*.

Mary handed me a loaf of bread. "It's stoneground wheat," she said. "I wanted to bring a marble rye, but the bakery was all out."

I was impressed. Mary wasn't just beautiful, she was classy. She knew not to show up empty-handed. Then I looked to her left. Moss Murphy was with her. And he looked terrible. His new form-fitting clothes were gone. In their place were dirty sweatpants and his old Hypercolor shirt. Moss Murphy's haircut made him look a convict, the kind the other prisoners picked on in the lunchroom, and sometimes the showers. He smelled like an old dishcloth and the tips of his fingers were covered in orange glop.

Mary touched Moss Murphy on the shoulder. "I found him in the street."

Moss Murphy scratched his armpit where a bright pink

splotch had formed on his Hypercolor shirt. "Can I come over for dinner? I'm starving," he said.

Did he really think I needed a wingman? I didn't need a wingman. Wingmen are for when you're out on patrol or flying over enemy territory, not for when you have the target in your sights. I had half a mind to send him home. Only, I could never do that in front of Mary. She would think I was mean and cruel, a dastardly villain and a bad friend. Plus, Moss Murphy had such a sad puppy-dog look on his face, I couldn't turn him away.

"Mom!" I called. "Can Moss come over for dinner?"

My mom poked her head around the corner. She looked like she would have said no, if not for Mary. "Is it okay with your parents?"

"They sent me over here. My mom has no time to cook because Roscoe's really sick."

"Roscoe? The cat-snake?" Mom said.

"It's a ferret," I said.

Mary turned to Moss Murphy. "Your mom has a sick ferret?"

He gave her a look that said, *Doesn't everybody?*

"What's wrong with him this time?" I said.

Moss Murphy ran his foot along the ground. "He ate a tube of Vaseline and now it's drooling out his back end. It's pretty gross. He has to wear a diaper and everything."

"Poor Roscoe," I said.

"Poor Roscoe? What about me?" Moss Murphy said. "I'm the one who has to put on his diaper. Have you ever tried to pin down a ferret and force him into a diaper? It's not easy."

Mary and I looked at each other. For a split second, I thought she was going to burst out laughing.

"Of course you can come to dinner, Moss. You're always

welcome in our home," Mom lied through her teeth. Like a flash, she took off in search of the Moss Blanket.

Mary and Moss Murphy stepped inside and I led them into the living room where my mom was furiously searching through a pile of blankets. Before she could drop a flame-retardant sheet over the easy chair and set out a bowl of candies, Moss Murphy plopped himself down on the chesterfield. He leaned back and put his orange-stained hand on one of my mom's fancy throw pillows. Mom's eyes bugged out at the sight of his unwashed jogging pants. Her nose turned up at his smell. It took all her power to suppress her disgust.

"Does anyone want an iced tea?" she said.

"Sure," Moss Murphy said.

"Yes, please," Mary said.

I handed Mom the gourmet loaf of bread.

"Is this from you?" she said to Mary.

"Yes, ma'am."

"Well, thank you," Mom said. She gave the bread a good sniff before stepping into the kitchen.

Mary sat down on the couch. "How are things going, Moss?"

"How does it look like they're going?"

"Truthfully?"

"Truthfully."

Mary paused. For a second, I thought she was conjuring up a compassionate reply, equal parts encouraging and authentic, to soothe his wounded soul. Instead, she said, "You look like shit."

If there was a single moment that I knew I was one hundred percent, completely, head-over-heels in love with this girl, this was it.

Moss Murphy stared at Mary in disbelief. His eyes misted

over. "I know," he whimpered. "Samantha won't return my calls. I think she's going to break up with me."

"Oh, Moss," Mary said, and gave him a big hug.

Mom came bustling in with two iced teas in her hands. She took in the scene, with Moss Murphy tearing up and Mary holding his cheese-covered hands. I happened to cough a little at that moment and she looked over at me.

"Are you okay?" she said.

"I'm fine. Just a tickle in my throat."

"Maybe you should go sit on the toilet and see what happens."

"Mom!"

"Suit yourself," she said. She handed an iced tea to Mary and another to Moss Murphy. "Come on kids, dinner's ready."

Mom had overcooked the potatoes and undercooked the roast beef. This suited Dad just fine as he liked his protein still mooing on his plate, but Mary and I both chose end pieces. Caroline turned up her nose the moment she walked into the kitchen and made herself a garden salad while my mom cut herself a nice big piece of meat and then never touched it the entire meal. Moss Murphy, for his part, devoured everything on his plate. The six of us didn't really fit in our little kitchen. My dad had to push the table away from the wall and Moss Murphy was practically sitting in the hallway.

We made small talk for a while. I should have been paying close attention to my mom's passive-aggressive attempts to destroy Mary. Instead, I kept staring at my dad. His eyebrows and nostrils were immaculately trimmed. I shuddered, thinking about what other parts of his body might now be hairless and smooth. Dad was wearing a brand-new golf shirt and he smelled even more like Drakkar Noir, as if after days of applying it, the cologne had seeped into his pores. I still couldn't believe he was the Parksville Peeper. Then again, if the man was willing to set up a top-secret studio apartment in his garage and think his wife was never going to catch on, he was capable of anything.

"So, Mary, I hear you're homeschooled," Mom said. "What's that like?"

"It's good," Mary said. "My mom has her teaching certificate and we go to class every day, just like everyone else. I'm a year ahead in my studies."

Mom crossed her arms. "Really?"

Mary nodded. "We take standardized tests and everything. Plus, we do a lot of music. I play the piano and my sister Jane is learning the bassoon."

"The bassoon?"

"You know." Mary mimicked blowing on a woodwind instrument.

I have to say, it was a little erotic.

"What do you want to be when you grow up?" Mom said. Before Mary could respond, Mom pointed at Caroline. "Caroline here is going to be a makeup artist."

Caroline beamed with pride. "It pays a thousand dollars a day."

"Really? That much?" Mary said.

"There's a lot more that goes into it than people think."

"I'm going into finance," Moss Murphy said. "Or maybe personal training."

We all looked at him funny.

Mom touched Mary on the arm for 0.002 Mississippis. "No one will think less of you if you haven't figured out your future yet," she said.

Mary wanted to respond, only she'd just taken a bite

of roast beef. Her molars toiled for a few seconds before she could swallow. "I'm not really sure yet," she said. "I just know I don't want to go into sales or marketing. My big sister is in marketing and she comes home with all these horror stories about office politics and bowing down to The Man. It scares me a little. I suppose I've got a little Lloyd Dobler in me."

"Lloyd Dobler?" Mom said.

"You know." Mary held an imaginary boom box over her head. She hummed the pre-chorus of Peter Gabriel's "In Your Eyes," then took a bite of overcooked potatoes.

"I'm not familiar with this Lloyd Dobler," Dad said. "Is he from Parksville?"

I gave him a dirty look. A filthy, evil, mean, dirty look. Who was he to talk to Mary when he'd been peeping all around town?

Unfortunately, Dad didn't notice.

"He's a character in *Say Anything*. It's a movie. Duh," Caroline said.

Mary set down her fork. "I've been thinking about this a lot lately, and it seems to me that all products are marketed toward youth," she said. "It's like, forty years ago, a bunch of New York advertising guys got together and decided youth was the most important thing. And I suppose that makes sense. If you get a person hooked on Pepsi at age six, they'll probably drink it until they're eighty. It's just that . . . young people are kind of stupid. We *are*. It's a scientific fact. I read in *TIME* magazine that teenagers' brains change so quickly, at certain points in our development, some of us can be declared medically insane."

"And that makes you not want to work for The Man?" Mom said.

Mary took a sip of iced tea. "I just don't want to actively participate in a consumeristic society that worships youth and neglects anyone over the age of forty-five. I mean, doesn't experience count for anything these days?"

Mom stared at Mary, gape-mouthed.

Dad took a sip of his Zima.

Moss Murphy stood up to get a second helping of under-cooked meat from the kitchen counter.

"I'm not an anarchist or anything," Mary said. "I just don't want to put on a pantsuit and carry a file folder around an office thinking I'm super important, drinking my overpriced Starbucks latte and bringing home the Benjamins at the cost of my physical well-being and, ultimately, my immortal soul."

Mom stuck her fork in a potato and held it in midair. "So you're planning on serving ice cream your whole life?" she said.

This was a cruel dig and I wouldn't have been surprised if Mary fired one right back. Mary, however, couldn't be baited.

"Maybe. If it comes to that," she said. "Lately I've been thinking about going into acupuncture."

"Is that where they stick needles into your skin?" Mom said.

Mary nodded. "It's an ancient Chinese medicine."

No one said anything. We all kept eating for close to a minute.

"I had a Chinese friend once," Dad said.

"That's racist," Caroline said through a mouth full of salad.

"How can it be racist if he was my friend?"

"It's racist to call someone Chinese."

Dad rolled his eyes in Caroline's direction and looked at Mary. "Medically insane, you said?"

Caroline picked up her fork like she was going to jab my dad with it, causing Dad to pick up his fork right back. I wanted to yell *Stab the Peeper!* as loudly as I could, but thought better of it. My mom had to touch both of them on the arm to get them to calm down.

"Come to think of it," Dad said, "he might have been Korean. Or maybe Japanese."

"It's even more racist when you don't know," Caroline said.

Dad ignored her. "Anyways, my buddy's name was Fuj. We went to a Lynyrd Skynyrd concert one time back in high school."

"Are you still friends?" Mary said.

"Oh, no," Dad said. "But I heard Fuj is running a car dealership in Springfield. It's quite successful."

Moss Murphy came back to the table with his plate stacked so high, I thought an avalanche of roast beef and potatoes might come tumbling down at any moment. He lifted his plate to get past my dad. Before he reached his seat, he gave me a funny look.

"Are you wearing makeup?" he said.

I covered my black eye where Caroline had applied the foundation.

"You *are* wearing makeup," he said. Moss Murphy snickered. He went to plant his backside in his seat when disaster struck. He was so busy laughing, he misjudged the distance between the table and his chair. Moss Murphy missed the seat entirely. He fell straight back and his mountain of food came crashing down. *Boom! Splat!* Moss Murphy knocked into Caroline and then crashed to the floor, covered in roast beef and potatoes.

Caroline shrieked because Moss Murphy had spilled gravy all over her jean shorts.

Mom shrieked because Moss Murphy braced himself to stand up and now there was a big orangey-brown handprint on her wall.

Dad took another sip of his Zima.

And Mary looked at me. "Dinner's more fun in your house than it is in mine," she said.

After dinner, Mom and Mary became surprisingly chummy. Mom took Mary on a tour of the house, describing her dream renovations along the way. "Over here, I'd like a marble fireplace. And this wall should come down entirely. Once the kitchen's renovated, the living room will become a sitting room."

Dad couldn't bear to listen to any more renovation talk and took off to be alone in his man cave while Moss Murphy, Caroline and I did the dishes.

"This stinks," Caroline said. "Your girlfriend should be in here scrubbing this pan, not me."

"She's not my girlfriend," I said.

Moss Murphy opened the fridge. After spilling his food and the chaos that ensued, he'd helped himself to a second plate and then, while the rest of us were listening to Mom tell Mary her side of the whole sign debacle, Moss Murphy got up for thirds.

He held up a Tupperware container he'd found in the vegetable crisper. "Can I eat this?" he said.

I thought it might have been corn. Or maybe chickpeas.

"I guess. If you want," I said.

Moss Murphy sat down at the table and dug into the cold yellow pellets with a spoon.

Caroline, still scrubbing that pan, could only watch for so long. "Remember, Moss, it's only food. It's not love."

"Bite me," he said, and kept chowing down.

As Caroline dug around the cupboard for a heavy-duty scrub brush, Moss Murphy snuck a quick peek at her bum in her tight gravy-stained shorts. His eyes didn't linger long. He seemed to have lost the will to ogle.

I patted him on the shoulder and cleared the rest of the table. "So, what do you guys think?"

"About Mary?" Caroline said. "She's awesome."

"She's great. I mean, fat ass aside," Moss Murphy said.

"Moss!" Caroline said.

"Jacob's only asking because he wants to rub it in," Moss Murphy said. He waved his hands in the air. "Look at Jacob, living on cloud nine, where the unicorns feed him Smarties and the squirrels steam-clean his socks."

"Don't listen to him," Caroline said. "You're a lucky guy and I think Mary's perfectly proportioned."

That was perhaps the nicest thing Caroline had ever said. I switched places with her and took over scrubbing the roasting pan while she rinsed off the plates and put them in the dishwasher. From upstairs, I could hear Mom telling Mary about the renovations she had planned for the master bedroom. Her voice competed with the sound of Dad playing his Foghat cassettes in the garage and Moss Murphy chewing his mystery pellets. I stopped scrubbing for a second and realized how happy and excited I was. It seemed like Mary might actually like me. Her argument with Youth Pastor Glenn the other day was probably the best thing that had ever happened to me. Even though I'd been in the next room, it was a turning point in my life.

Mary had to like me; otherwise, she wouldn't be here.

I poured some liquid soap into the pan and bore down with the scrub brush. Pinned to the wall in front of me was a family photo from my Cousin Candice's wedding. I was ten years old when Cousin Candice married a guy named Paul. The wedding was pretty fun. There was a chocolate fondue fountain, the groom and his best man sang a Fine Young Cannibals medley and my dad let me have a few sips of wine.

I still remembered the speeches from that night. Everyone who got up to the microphone kept saying how lucky Candice was to have met Paul. They went on and on about what a great guy he was. It got to the point where Paul was embarrassed by all the attention. However, not a single person mentioned how great Cousin Candice was. No one said how fortunate Paul was to have met her. The message was clear: Candice was the lucky one. Paul was the great catch. I didn't ask my cousin how she felt that night (I was only ten years old, after all), but I imagine she left the wedding feeling like the Rhoda to Paul's Mary. The Jan to his Marsha Marsha Marsha. The Megadeth to Paul's Metallica.

The longer I stood there scrubbing that pan, the more Caroline and Moss Murphy's words sunk in. If Mary really did like me . . . why? I looked at my reflection in the window. My black eye had turned off-green in the past twenty-four hours and the foundation Caroline had applied only made it look worse. I had stitches over my eyebrow and two nasty-looking cuts on the other side of my head. Plus, I was at least a year and a half younger than Mary. Youth Pastor Glenn was older than her. If she was really considering becoming my girlfriend, she'd be dropping three years in boyfriend age.

Mary was pretty. She was kind and sweet and funny. Why would she come to my house, out of all the houses in Parksville, for dinner tonight?

"Jacob?"

Mom and Mary were standing in the hallway.

"Your friend here has some excellent ideas," Mom

said. "Maybe she can do interior design along with her acupuncture."

I scoped out Mom's face. Her gaze was straightforward. Not once did she scrunch her nose or shift her jaw. She actually meant it. Mom had come around to liking Mary.

"I have to go home," Mary said.

I stood there with soap bubbles on my arms.

"Be a gentleman, Jacob," Mom said. "Walk the young lady to the door."

Caroline and Moss Murphy jeered me.

"Yeah, step up to the plate, buddy."

"Prove that chivalry isn't dead."

I wiped off the bubbles and tried to maintain my dignity while walking Mary down the hall. Mary looked a little embarrassed alongside me.

At the front door, she thanked my mother for a wonderful meal and then Mom left. Mary slipped on her shoes and stood in front of me. She didn't back away at all. This was my chance to kiss her. Butterflies spun circles in my stomach and my legs felt heavy. I started wondering exactly how moist my lips were supposed to be, whether it was bad manners to lick them ahead of time, how much pressure I was supposed to apply. Mary stepped toward me. I moved forward a bit and then, out of the corner of my eye, I saw three sets of eyes watching us from down the hall. There was no way I could do this in front of Mom, Caroline and Moss Murphy. Judging by Mary's expression, neither could she.

She gave me a warm, soft, inviting hug; not a friend-hug, a real one.

I whispered in her ear. "Why?"

Mary glanced at the three snoops down the hall.

"Why me?" I said.

Mary stepped back a little and took my hands in hers. Mississippis abounded. "Because," she whispered, "you're the only boy I've met who would never hurt me."

"How do you know?"

She looked at me with those wide green eyes. "I just know."

32
To Confront a Peeper

Hours after Mary left, I still felt a glow where she'd hugged me. My mom had left as well, escorting Moss Murphy out the door before returning to keep vigil on the church lawn. Caroline and I watched *Wheel of Fortune* and *Jeopardy!* without her. Aside from my father crashing around inside the garage, it was a quiet night in our house. Then the telephone rang.

"If it's Dennis, tell him I'm out," Caroline said.

"Why?"

"I'm playing hard to get."

We had no call display and when I picked up the phone, I didn't know who it was. Most likely, it was one of our long-lost relatives who'd been calling nonstop ever since Mom appeared on CNN. It might have even been Moss Murphy, inviting me to play *Mario Kart*. Deep down, I hoped it was Mary.

"Hello?"

"It's me. My father's not home. Come over now."

I glanced at Caroline. She was completely captivated by the season finale of *Melrose Place* she'd taped months ago and had watched at least six times. By this point, Caroline practically knew the dialogue off by heart.

"Who is this?" I said.

"Jacob! You know who this is. It's Pia."

"Oh. Hi."

"So, are you coming over or not?" Pia said.

"Well . . ."

"Your big fat uncle took Alpana to the movies and my father's at Priya's dance rehearsal. We'd have the whole place to ourselves." I didn't say anything, so she upped the ante. "I'm sitting here in my bra and panties. There's this bottle of baby oil and I just don't know what to do with it."

I pictured Pia's face right before she climbed on me in the front seat of her aunt's car. Her sweet yet completely nefarious giggle still rang in my ears.

"I don't think it's a good idea," I said.

"But you converted for me," she said.

"Well, to be honest, I haven't even bought the Deepak Chopra book."

"Have you at least tried yoga?"

"Not yet."

"Why not?" she said.

"I'm not really bendy. I don't think my body would stretch that way."

Pia took a sharp breath. "I'm beginning to think you're not taking this relationship seriously," she said.

"But, at your father's house, you said things were strained between us. That we weren't as close as we used to be."

Caroline gave me a curious look and I moved as far away as possible without the phone cord snapping.

"You know what?" Pia said. "I'm glad my father put you in that hot-dog costume. You got exactly what you deserved. I don't know what I was thinking. You don't look anything like Tom Cruise."

A pause followed in which I could hear her breathing on the other line.

"At least I'm taller than Tom Cruise," I said.

Pia fumed. It felt like flames were coming through the receiver. "Is that a joke? Are you making jokes?"

"Sorry."

"Tom Cruise is a living legend, Jacob. A superstar. What have you ever done in your life?"

The door to the garage opened and my dad waved me over. When I shook my head, he waved me over again, this time with his stern-father expression.

"I have to go," I said.

"Don't bother showing up at the AMPM again," Pia said.

"I have to. Your father would be mad."

"What about me?" she said. "Don't you care about making me mad?"

My dad was hovering now. He had an excited look on his clean-shaven face that even his stern-father expression couldn't conceal.

"Hurry up," he said.

Pia slammed down the phone before I could say another word. The dial tone sounded.

"Now! Come on!" Dad said.

He dragged me into the garage. At first it didn't look like anything had changed. Dad's Foghat cassette was playing in the corner and his mini-fridge was still concealed by several planks of wood. There was a white cardboard box resting on Dad's workbench and he'd moved his lawnmower, but other than that, there was nothing to see.

"Check it out," Dad said. He pushed the lawnmower aside and pulled out the workbench drawer. A click sounded and a second drawer opened. Dad yanked on it pretty hard and out unfolded a cot, complete with a blanket, pillow and bed sheet.

I glanced over my shoulder to see if I'd been caught on *Candid Camera.*

"Isn't it awesome?" he said.

I took a closer look. How did he even install this contraption? For a man whose handiwork had, thus far, consisted of improperly duct-taping a propeller to a birdhouse, he'd sure transformed into MacGyver awfully quick.

"You're kidding, right?" I said.

Dad gave the pillow a good fluff. "Kidding about what?"

"About sleeping out here."

He waved his hand in the air. "Pfft! I'm not going to *sleep* out here. This is just a place to take naps."

I looked over at his concealed mini-fridge, then down at Dad's pop-out cot. It occurred to me that if he won the lottery tomorrow, Dad would get his own apartment. He would leave his wife and kids in a heartbeat.

"You haven't seen the best part," he said. He lifted the white cardboard box to reveal a disco rainbow globe light. I'd seen one of these before at a high school dance, only my father's was different. It had little pictures of fish on each bulb. "Now watch this," he said, and turned the globe on. Instantly, the garage was coated in spinning psychedelic fish.

In the corner, Dad's Foghat cassette finished. He walked over, inserted an AC/DC cassette and pressed play. The opening chords of "Rock 'N' Roll Damnation" bounced off the walls.

"I saw you," I said.

Dad didn't hear me. He was too busy rocking out to AC/DC and watching the goldfish spin.

"I saw you coming out of the Deck Girls' tent," I said.

This time, his entire face turned white. He turned off the disco globe and when the colored lights disappeared, it was like a giant mosquito had landed on his back and sucked out all his blood. Dad glanced from side to side with this unnerved look in his eyes and then shut the door that led back into the house. He unfolded a lawn chair and sat down.

I couldn't believe it. This wasn't how I envisioned this playing out at all. My dad was supposed to deny. He was supposed to be snide and condescending and turn the conversation back to why I was watching him at the neighbors' house. That's what people do, isn't it? When accused of even the smallest wrongdoing, they lash out, they criticize and get defensive. Their faces twitch with anger. They don't suddenly transform into ghosts.

Dad turned off the cassette player and pointed to the fridge in the corner. "Go fetch me a Budweiser."

He looked so serious, I couldn't say no. I shifted the boards out of the way and pulled out a beer.

"Get yourself one too," he said.

I handed Dad the cold beer. He cracked it open and took a short sip, then a long swig.

"Sit," he said, pointing to another lawn chair.

I slid the chair over and sat down across from my dad. My beer can fizzed when I opened it. I lifted it to my mouth and tipped it back, felt that odd sting of bubbles and alcohol — like mouthwash, only ten times stronger. It slid down my throat the way ginger ale does when you're sick, curing and scratching at the same time. This was the first time Dad and I had ever really shared a beer.

He took another sip and leaned forward in his chair. "I don't know how to describe it, son. I just never expected to become *this guy*. I never thought I'd be forty-three. Don't get

259

me wrong, I always knew I'd get older. Only, I never expected it would be like *this*.

"I know it's hard for you to believe," he said, "but I used to be a very different guy. I was cool. I had long hair. I used to get loaded and smoke cigarettes outside Brave Bill's Pop Shop. These two guys named Fuj and Soup were my best friends in the whole world and we would pick up girls and party all the time. Soup even had this avocado-colored vw van. The thing puffed black smoke and sometimes it barely ran, but it was so awesome. Soup dubbed it the Big Bright Green Pleasure Machine, after a Simon and Garfunkel song. Do you know Simon and Garfunkel, Jacob?"

He stroked his chin wistfully, but he didn't wait for me to answer.

"We charged the stage at the Lynyrd Skynyrd concert in '74. Soup, Fuj and I charged the rail, do you know what I mean?" He shook his head. "I haven't talked to those guys in years. I made up that thing about Fuj running a car dealership. I have no idea what happened to him. And all I know about Soup is that he got fat and moved to Minnesota."

He paused like he was trying to remember his old friends' real names.

"I'm not sure when it all changed. But things are different now. I'm just an average Joe working an average job. I have a boss who does horrible things and then tells me how happy I should be about it. And did I tell you I'm not allowed to eat raspberries anymore? That's right. The doctor says the seeds pocket in my bowels. If I eat a bowl of raspberries, I'm going to be stuck on the toilet, bunged up for days. That's the real reason I want strawberry jam. But will your mother listen to me? Nooooo."

He hesitated, like maybe he was finished, then he kept going.

"Do you know the worst part about middle age? Things have started to sag. I won't get too graphic, but suffice it to say I can't wear boxer shorts anymore. I have to wear briefs for the support."

Dad leaned back in his lawn chair and took a long, slow sip of his beer. In that moment, it occurred to me that in my whole life, I hadn't spent thirty seconds thinking of things from his perspective. Children take from their parents. It's their existence in a lot of ways. Children take their parents' time, they take their parents' money. Without even realizing it, they take a part of their parents' essence away. It was like Dad was a part-time player on the stage of life, with my sister and me and my mom in the starring roles, and my dad — who worked five days a week, who drove me to my soccer games and paid for everything and who was on call twenty-four hours a day to defend our family with his life — was just there as occasional comic relief.

Dad rubbed his neck. Guilt dripped off him like sweat off a marathon runner. For the first time, he looked human, like a real person, not just my dad but a flawed individual who'd given up Lynyrd Skynyrd concerts and hanging out with his buddies for his family. I felt a strange compassion for him. Still, it didn't excuse what he'd done.

Peeping was peeping.

He turned his beer can around in his hand and picked at the tab on top. "She listens to me," he said. "I don't know how else to describe it. Your mother and I got together when we were very young, before either of us figured out who we really were. I never meant to turn to the arms of another woman."

Now I was completely confused. "Who listens to you?"

"Leah Fontaine."

"Oh my God," I said. "Are you having an affair?"

Dad held up his hand. "Not an affair. I never slept with her."

Oh man, did I have to listen to another fingerbanging story?

"I just kissed her. One time."

"You kissed a twenty-year-old girl?"

Dad bowed his head. No matter how hard he tried to look remorseful, I could see he was a little proud of himself. His panicked look was all but a memory. He took another sip of beer, no doubt recalling what the Deck Girl's lips tasted like, her warm breath, the smell of her alone in her tent. I felt lightheaded just looking at him. Dad wasn't sleeping with Leah. He was having an emotional affair, one that led to kissing, that made him do crazy things like try to secretly move into the garage. I pictured Leah Fontaine in my mind. Her enormous breasts aside, she wasn't even the cute one. Plus, she had a lisp. And who could forget that bad check she wrote at Target? I wondered what Dad would have done if the Deck Girls' father had caught him sneaking out of his daughters' tent.

"So you're not the Parksville Peeper?"

Dad laughed with a little too much gusto. "What gave you that idea?"

"I thought you were peeping at the Deck Girls."

He shook his head and took another sip of beer. It got quiet in the garage, so quiet I could hear the refrigerator humming in the corner. My dad scratched a patch of stubble on his neck. That little hint of pride drifted from his eyes.

"You have to decide," I said. "It's just . . . it's not fair to Mom. If you want to get your own place and live some kind

262

of wild bachelor life, fine. Whatever. I'll come visit you and everything." I gestured around the garage. "But you can't live here. You can't have a girlfriend and a wife."

Dad suddenly looked like he was about to cry. "I don't know what to do. Maybe I should talk to Reverend Richard."

"No!" I said. "Don't talk to Reverend Richard."

Dad wiped his eyes. He lifted his beer can toward me. At first, I thought he might be finished and want another. Then I realized what he was doing. I lifted my can and we cheersed in midair.

"Jacob," he said.

"Yes?"

"Until I figure things out, don't tell your mother."

33

Locker Room Pepsi-Beers

The next morning, Mom insisted I help deliver breakfast to her friends. Together we climbed into her car and drove to a local pastry shop called the Flaky Croissant to pick up two dozen bagels. Mom spent fifteen minutes inside exchanging pleasantries with the lady behind the counter (who, despite the store's name, sounded more Italian than French). As we stepped outside, Mom made a sour face at the rival bakery down the street. "We would have spent our money at the Dreamy Danish, if only their owner was more sympathetic to our cause," she said.

We headed over to the grocery store to pick up juice and bottled water, then drove down Ascott Street where we parked beside the Passion Lord Church of God. The whole while, I kept staring at her face, watching her mouth move, waiting for a well of emotions to burst forth, for the lines around her eyes to reveal what she knew, how she felt about what my dad had done. You don't just go from tyrannically oppressing your husband's daily diet to buying him boxes of Count Chocula cereal without doing some serious soul-searching.

Only, if Mom was torn up inside, if she was merely suspicious or if her heart was breaking piece by piece as the seconds ticked by, she never let on. She kept handing out bagels and little packets of cream cheese like nothing was wrong. We didn't have the kind of relationship where I could ask her, *So, Margaret, how's your marriage? Are you feeling fulfilled? Is your husband happy? Like, really happy? Does he have a wandering eye? Do you sometimes think things might've been better if Caroline and I had never been born?*

I couldn't ask and Mom would never tell. And while she put on a brave face around her friends, it was clear when Mom and Dad were in the same room. Something was wrong. Their marriage wasn't so much held together by glue — more like Post-it Notes and Scotch tape. At the very least, Mom suspected something was up. Perhaps this battle with Youth Pastor Glenn, the line she'd drawn in the sand over the biblical importance of a man in a red suit, was the battle she *could* fight. The battle at home — the one she *couldn't* fight — was the one no one would win.

"Jacob, be a dear and take this to Reverend Richard," she said.

Mom handed me a blueberry bagel and two packets of cream cheese. I hesitated but thought better of arguing. Mom hadn't asked how my talk with Reverend Richard had gone the other day, and it was best not to reopen that can of worms. If Reverend Richard asked me how things were going, I'd say, "Great. Never better." If he persisted, I'd say, "So, how's your mother doing these days?" If he really persisted, I'd say, "I think I'm getting a rash on my private parts. Can you have a quick peek and tell me if it looks like the wrath of God?"

When I couldn't find him in his office, I left the bagel on Reverend Richard's desk and walked downstairs to pee. There were two washrooms in the Passion Lord Church of God's basement, one for men and another for women. Unfortunately, the women's washroom had been out of order for the better part of a year. My father blamed Nancy Sylvester's high-starch diet. Others blamed the old pipes running underneath the building. Either way, the entire congregation had to share a single toilet. I arrived at the basement to find a lineup of six people (two women, four men) waiting outside the lavatory.

Candice Collington's husband was among those assembled. He did not look amused. "Your uncle's been in there for half an hour."

A voice sounded from the other side of the door.

"Jacob? Is that you?" Uncle Ted said. "Come here, boy."

I edged over and stood beside the door. "What's up, Uncle Ted?"

"Don't tell anyone, but those damn flaming samosas got me. For days now, it's felt like fire ants have been crawling around inside my butt," he said.

I glanced over my shoulder. Uncle Ted was speaking as clear as day. Everyone in line now knew about his blazing bowels.

"I used to keep Pepto-Bismol tablets in my wallet," he said. "But I finished them off last week when I got the runs at Arby's."

"Okay, Uncle Ted."

"Jacob? Are you still there?"

"Yes, Uncle Ted."

"This might take a while. I'm dropping some serious heat in here. Is there any way you can disperse the crowd?"

The lineup stared at me. Candice Collington's husband seemed particularly put out.

"Sorry, everybody," I said.

Only, no one left. They'd all heard Uncle Ted clearly. Even Reverend Richard probably heard him upstairs. I shuddered, thinking about what awaited these six unfortunate souls once Uncle Ted finally cleared out of there. Without another word, I jogged up the stairs and hurried across the street to the Church of the Lord's Creation.

Their washroom was a palace. The tile floors were sparkling white and there were five stalls and three urinals to choose from. By the door, two La-Z-Boy recliners were set up next to a long mahogany table, giving the room a trendy, hangout vibe.

Just as I was finishing up, Calvin Cockfort walked in. He reached down and scratched his crotch. There was nothing discreet about it. He gave his groin a good, long, satisfying scratch and really moved things around.

I hurried over to the sink and washed my hands.

Calvin Cockfort snorted and unzipped his pants. "Did I tell you I'm getting involved in retail electronics?" he said as I dried my hands. "It's not just about radios and Walkmans anymore. There's a whole growing industry. I'm getting in on the ground floor."

"You don't say?"

I slipped out the door before Calvin could begin his next sentence and stepped into the hallway, intent on searching downstairs for Mary. Before I could take five steps, Youth Pastor Glenn appeared in front of me. He was wearing a gray suit and a black tie. Every hair on his head was flawlessly in sync.

"It's Wednesday. Are you coming to the youth meeting tonight?" he said.

I hesitated. "I'm not sure yet."

"You know, Jacob, we've never really spoken."

I started twitching nervously. Whenever Youth Pastor Glenn was around, I suddenly felt like a stuttering sidekick, like Garth from *Wayne's World* or Beavis without my BFF Butt-head to back me up. Youth Pastor Glenn stood in front of me in a perfect alpha-male pose, one foot slightly ahead of the other, shoulders back, head held high.

"Come with me. I'd like to show you something," he said. When I didn't move, Youth Pastor Glenn beckoned with his hand. He smiled, softly this time. "Don't worry. I won't bite."

I followed him up a spiral staircase to the second floor. The skylights were brighter up there and Youth Pastor Glenn's gray suit looked silvery-white. We walked down a hallway and entered what appeared to be a control room. Inside, the walls were covered with monitors and there were two soundboards, one equipped with a microphone and another with so many dials, a sound engineer could mix a dozen versions of "Bohemian Rhapsody" on it at the same time.

Youth Pastor Glenn slumped back in a tall black chair. He took off his glasses and undid his tie. "Oh, my aching back," he said. "Do you know what's good for an aching back, Jacob?"

"Advil?"

"Pepsi-beer." Youth Pastor Glenn reached into a mini-fridge next to the mixing board and pulled out a cold glass, a can of Pepsi and a can of Busch beer. He popped the tabs and poured a half-beer, half-Pepsi concoction, then took a big sip. "Ahhhh," he said. "I know. It should probably taste disgusting. I had my doubts before I tried it too. But Klaus kept talking about Pepsi-beers on the *Midnight Metal Madness Hour* and I just had to try it. I'm kind of hooked now."

Youth Pastor Glenn pushed a chair over to me and I sat

down across from him. I watched him take another sip. It was strange seeing him like this, so casual, leaning back with his loosened tie, breaking the law with his blatant underage drinking.

"Is the *Midnight Metal Madness Hour* a religious program?" I said.

He laughed so hard, a little Pepsi-beer shot into his nasal passage. Youth Pastor Glenn wiped his nose with his sleeve. "It's a radio show on Sunday nights. They play all the new metal bands. Seven years ago, they played Nirvana before anyone had heard of them. I think they played 'Floyd the Barber' off *Bleach*, which, trust me, sounds nothing like 'Teen Spirit.'"

"You like heavy metal?" I said, legitimately surprised.

Youth Pastor Glenn looked down at his suit. He flipped his tie over his shoulder. "I know. It's hard to believe, isn't it? You want to hear something funny? Back in high school, I used to listen to Judas Priest on my Walkman all day long. I even wore their *Ram It Down* concert T-shirt wherever I went. Then last year, my buddy told me that their singer Rob Halford is totally gay. Like, the biker from the Village People kind of gay. And all I could think was — oh man, I wore that *Ram It Down* shirt every day for years."

We both laughed. Youth Pastor Glenn was nothing like I'd thought he was. I'd always assumed he was a sanctimonious goody-goody bent on world domination. It turned out he was the coolest guy on earth.

"Do you want a Pepsi-beer?" he said.

"Sure."

He pulled another glass out of the fridge and poured one for me. We cheersed just like my dad and I had done the night before, and I took a sip. The Pepsi-and-beer concoction tasted strange, almost like root beer but with a more off-putting bite. I didn't want Youth Pastor Glenn to think I didn't like it, so I took another sip. The monitors on the wall were showing a live feed from the basement. Mary and Samantha were down there, folding cards at a long table.

"Ah yes," Youth Pastor Glenn said. "The video cameras. We've got three outside and another eight inside. Minister Matthew said he was putting them in for security reasons, but really, it's more of a Big Brother thing." He pressed a red button on the small soundboard and leaned into the microphone. "Ladies, this is your Lord and Savior speaking," he said. "Make sure you fold those flyers evenly. You wouldn't want the pensioners and shut-ins to think we're getting careless around here."

The girls looked up at the video camera. Mary looked back down quickly, but Samantha smiled and waved.

"She's hot, don't you think?" Youth Pastor Glenn said, only he didn't say which girl he was talking about. He put his foot up on the mixing board, leaned back and stretched. "I'm curious," he said. "What do people in your church think happened to Minister Matthew?"

I shrugged. I had no idea what had happened to Mary's father.

"Can you keep a secret?" he said. "The guy's in rehab. It's a bad scene. They had to ship him to someplace in Springfield. I'm not sure if he's ever coming back."

"That's terrible," I said. I hesitated and then I said, "Was he addicted to the nudie bar?"

Youth Pastor Glenn laughed so hard he spat his mouthful back into his glass. "Who goes to rehab for the nudie bar?" he said. "Minister Matthew is an alcoholic. It got pretty bad. He was slurring and almost falling over during mass, downing a bottle of Jim Beam in the morning and pounding back vodka all afternoon." Youth Pastor Glenn looked up at the monitor, at Mary and Samantha downstairs. "Minister Matthew wasn't a violent drunk, but I don't think he was the easiest guy in the world to live with. That's probably why Mary believes in fairy tales."

"How do you mean?"

He cracked his neck. "You know, looking for a dream guy to stand up and sacrifice everything for her. That's why she's so into Jesus. Jesus took one for the team, so to speak. And that's what Mary's looking for some guy to do."

"To get crucified for her?"

"No." He chuckled. "Put it this way: some girls are looking for a knight in shining armor to whisk them off into the sunset. Other girls, like Mary, are looking for a guy to stand up to oppression, to fight the power, to make some kind of ultimate sacrifice for them. And I kept telling her, 'The real world doesn't work that way.'" Youth Pastor Glenn looked up at the monitor again. "That's why Samantha is a better pick for me. Don't look so surprised. She might be young, but she knows how to be a woman."

I gazed at Samantha's image in the monitor. I wanted to say, *Moss Murphy's mangled genitals might disagree with you*, but decided against it. There was something else I wanted to know.

"What happened between you and Mary?" I said.

"Do you mean the other day, that big fight?"

I shook my head.

Youth Pastor Glenn smiled wide. He downed the last of his Pepsi-beer and poured himself another. "You're talking about the camping trip. That rumor that's been going around." He swirled his glass so the Pepsi and beer mixed together. "It's kind of an unfair question, don't you think? You're asking me to share, but you haven't shared anything with me."

"I don't have anything to share," I said.

"There must be something."

I thought of Pia and the car wash. The incomplete fellatio. Pushkar would kill me if he found out I was bragging around town. "Nope. Nothing."

Youth Pastor Glenn tousled his hair. It felt like we weren't in a control room or a church, more like a locker room, a couple of old buddies swapping stories about our sexual escapades.

"Tell me, Jacob, what would you do if you were alone with Mary?"

I took a swig from my glass. The room suddenly felt small.

"I won't tell you, if you won't tell me," Youth Pastor Glenn said. "If you were alone in a tent with Mary, would you fingerbang her?"

"Yes," I said.

Youth Pastor Glenn lifted his glass and we cheersed in midair.

"What if that big ass of hers got in the way?" he said.

Youth Pastor Glenn leaned back against the soundboard. Something clicked in the background, but he didn't seem affected by it.

I took a long drink from my Pepsi-beer. Suddenly I felt lightheaded, emboldened, like a real man.

"If Mary and I were alone in a tent," I said, "I'd fingerbang her all night long. With a great ass like that, I'd be like a surgeon in there. I'm skilled that way."

Youth Pastor Glenn laughed under his breath. Slowly,

272

what started as a genuine guy-to-guy chuckle turned strange as he strained not to make a sound. He tilted his head back and slapped his knee. I suddenly got the impression he wasn't laughing *with me* anymore. He was laughing *at me*. Youth Pastor Glenn looked down at the soundboard he was leaning against. His elbow was pressing the big red button, the same button he'd pressed moments ago to speak to the girls.

We both looked up into the monitor. Instantly, my heart sank to the bottom of my stomach. Mary and Samantha were staring in shocked silence at the video camera. They'd heard every word I just said.

Youth Pastor Glenn lifted his arm and I heard a second click.

"Oh, no. How did *that* happen?" he said. Then he couldn't contain himself any longer. Youth Pastor Glenn started laughing hysterically. He barely managed to stand up and straighten his tie. He flipped his hair back into place. His laughter and that best-buddy vibe vanished and now he stood perfectly still, perfectly poised, perfectly aware of how he'd duped me into running my big mouth. His voice regained that self-satisfied, sanctimonious air. "Thank you, Jacob. It's been a pleasure doing business with you," he said, and went to leave.

Up on the monitor, Mary was hurrying toward the stairs. As quickly as I could, I brushed past Youth Pastor Glenn, ran through the hallway and down the spiral staircase. At the bottom step, I caught a glimpse of red hair rushing by.

"Mary!" I called.

She was thirty feet away, standing by the front doors, tears streaming down her face.

I stepped toward her and Mary put up her hand.

"Don't!" she said, her voice cracking. Then softer, "Just don't."

I wanted to say I was sorry, that Youth Pastor Glenn had tricked me, that I thought we were just trading locker-room banter. Mary's eyes stopped me before the words even reached my mouth. There was nothing I could say and nothing she wanted to hear. She looked down at her feet and then up at me one last time. Mary turned and ran out the doors.

34
Sickly Humping Ferrets

It was just after midnight. Moss Murphy and I were in his parents' basement, playing *Mario Kart* just like we used to do every night. Moss Murphy was Bowser and I was Mario. I was dropping banana peels on the track and he was pegging me off with projectile turtle shells. Nothing had changed. Only, everything had changed. Samantha had fled into the arms of Youth Pastor Glenn. Mary wouldn't return my calls and most likely hated me beyond all reason. Moss Murphy and I were a sad-looking pair and even video games couldn't make us happy anymore. Still, we tried to pretend like nothing was wrong. Moss Murphy even engaged in a little trash talk.

"Do you know how gay you are?" he said. "You're so deep in the closet, you can see Narnia."

I bounced Princess Peach off a mushroom. "It's a wardrobe, not a closet, dumb-ass," I said.

Moss Murphy snorted. "Only a gay man knows the difference between a wardrobe and a closet."

The Moo Moo Farm level finished and we entered the Koopa Troopa Beach. Right away I slipped off a ramp and spun out on a crab. I was so out of practice, even my favorite red controller wasn't helping.

Moss Murphy saw I was down and pegged me with a turtle shell anyway. "You're still gay," he said. "Not that there's anything wrong with that."

"You're so far in the closet, you're finding Christmas presents," I said.

Moss Murphy won the level. I finished third, one behind a computer-operated Luigi. It was a difficult defeat. Losing to another player is one thing, but losing to mid-1990s AI was downright embarrassing. I did my best to refocus as we entered the Kalimari Desert. Still, thoughts of Mary, thoughts of my dad and Leah Fontaine, kept cropping up.

"Are your parents happy?" I said.

"What do you mean?"

"Like, are they happy with each other?"

Moss Murphy glanced upstairs. We hadn't seen his parents all night. The only movement was Roscoe the ferret slinking around behind the couch, looking to swipe a Cheeto from Moss Murphy's bowl.

"I guess so," he said. He paused the game to scratch his stomach. Moss Murphy dug at his bellybutton until he pulled out a multicolored Cosby sweater of lint. He wiped it against his shirt and dug for more.

Moss Murphy was wearing one of his dad's XXXL T-shirts. Lorne Murphy bought his shirts at the comic book store in Springfield and they were always strange — things like Chewbacca playing tennis or a frog humping a radish. Today, Moss Murphy was wearing one with a clown's face on Buddha's body.

"But how do you know?" I said.

"My dad lets my mom cheat at *Jeopardy!*," he said. "She tapes it and watches it before he comes home from work. Then, when they watch it together after dinner, she suddenly

276

knows all this stuff she would never know in real life, like who the king of Prussia was in 1806. My dad knows she cheats but he doesn't say anything."

"What's your point?"

"I'm just saying — you have to really love someone to let them cheat at *Jeopardy!* for fifteen years straight and not say anything."

We kept playing for another two minutes before Moss Murphy set his controller down halfway through the level. Bowser just sat there as all the other racers zipped by.

"Samantha dumped me," he said.

"I heard."

"She was only using me to make Youth Pastor Glenn jealous. That's why she never kissed me."

"I heard that too."

Moss Murphy shoved a handful of Cheetos into his face and spoke with his mouth full. "How am I supposed to compete with other guys?" he said. "There are dudes out there with muscles and water beds. College kids. Men with cars." He ran his fingers through his POW haircut. "That Youth Pastor Glenn has everything a girl could want. He looks like Kirk Cameron, only with straight hair and glasses."

I tried to make him feel better. "Youth Pastor Glenn looks like Kirk Cameron's reflection in a spoon."

"Whatever," he said. "He's dreamy and sublime and we both know it." Moss Murphy picked up his controller and pressed restart. Seconds later, Bowser was flying down the Luigi Raceway.

I knew what Moss Murphy was saying. No matter what you have to offer, there's always some guy out there who's better looking than you, smarter than you, richer than you. Youth Pastor Glenn probably had a glistening set of six-pack abs. He dressed in suits and had that immaculate haircut. It was almost impossible to find a flaw. Still, I tried.

"That Glenn guy isn't perfect. If you look really closely, one of his nostrils is slightly larger than the other one. A fraction of an inch more and he'd be freak-show material."

"Whatever. You're just jealous because he fingerbanged Mary." Moss Murphy held up three fingers. "Two in the pink and one in the stink."

I gave him the evil eye, only he was still racing and didn't seem to notice. The basement lights were dim and the bright colors from the game cast a wicked sheen over Moss Murphy's face. His eyes looked beady. His thin lips were drawn inward, like he'd been sucking on a lemon.

"I bet she groaned when he did it," he said.

"Stop it, Moss."

"*Oh, Glenn, pick a hole, any hole.*"

"Seriously," I said. "Cut it out."

He cast me a cheeky look. "I should tell Mary that you still keep action figures under your bed. That just a couple months ago, you brought out Hulk Hogan and the Honky Tonk Man to wrestle a tag team match against Skeletor and Beast Man."

I gritted my teeth. Inside my chest, a fire had ignited.

Moss Murphy laughed. "You better not leave your toys on your mattress. Mary might squash them with that fat ass of hers," he said.

Slap!

I hit him. My open palm smacked Moss Murphy square across the face.

He looked stunned, in complete shock that I actually did it. Years ago, back when Moss Murphy used to bully me, I never fought back. I'd always been too timid, too weak, too afraid.

I wasn't afraid anymore.

"What the hell?" he said.

I slapped him again, harder this time. "Don't ever say that about Mary again," I said. "Or I'll kick your ass."

Moss Murphy's face morphed from disbelief to outrage. His brow furrowed. His eyes turned red. He jumped on me, slapping me and pushing me to the ground. "How dare you?!"

"Get off me, you fat bastard!"

I rolled him off, but only briefly. Moss Murphy was so strong. He put me in a headlock and squeezed as hard as he could. I did everything I could to break free. I pinched his arm and hit him in the kidneys. Finally, I bit him in the stomach and Moss Murphy let go. We stood four feet apart, staring each other down. Suddenly, we weren't friends anymore. We were enemies. Maybe deep down, we'd always been enemies. Only now we were finally admitting it.

I swung wildly and punched him square in the ear. Moss Murphy staggered.

"Jesus Christ! You really hit me!" he said.

Furiously, frantically, I tackled Moss Murphy and clawed at his face. I swung another fist and missed. Moss Murphy turned me over and still I kept fighting, positive I was going to win. Angry always beats strong, doesn't it?

Actually, no. Moss Murphy shoved his sweaty arms into my face. His fat legs restrained my feet. I smelled his stinky armpits and his gross Cheetos breath. He grabbed my wrists and pinned me to the ground. "Say uncle, bitch," Moss Murphy said.

"Never!" I screamed back.

I squirmed until one wrist came free and then I socked Moss Murphy flush in the jaw. I hit him as hard as I could, as hard as I wanted to hit Youth Pastor Glenn, as hard as I wanted to hit myself.

Moss Murphy reeled momentarily. His face went from red to purple.

"That's it! You're dead," he growled.

He slapped me upside the head over and over again. Moss Murphy ground his elbow into my stitches. As blood trickled down my cheek, a strange, furry feeling shimmied up my leg, like a little pair of hands or feet. Moss Murphy's sickly ferret was humping my leg.

"Get it off! Get it off!" I yelled.

Moss Murphy looked down. He cackled. "You like it, don't you?"

He shifted his weight and flopped his big fat butt on top of my head. I knew what was coming, only he was so heavy, there was no way I could stop him. Moss Murphy farted — a long, shrill, wet fart right in my face.

"Huevos rancheros!"

He farted again.

"Chimichangas!"

He let another one rip.

"Tostadas!"

The ferret kept humping my leg.

Moss Murphy farted so much and for so long, it was like he'd been saving up his gas for years, just waiting to unload it on me. The smell was terrible, like being trapped inside a condemned seafood restaurant, and all I wanted to do was get away. Down at my ankle, Roscoe was humping away like it was the freaking Fourth of July.

Finally, I kicked off the ferret. He flew in the air and smashed against the TV set where the *Mario Kart* music was still playing. Roscoe's diaper slipped all the way to the end of his tail.

"Roscoe!" Moss Murphy leapt to his feet and picked up the ferret. His face twitched as he tried to pull the diaper back onto Roscoe's limp body. "You kicked my ferret!"

"You farted on my face!"

We stared each other down again. Part of me couldn't believe things had gone this far. Another part thought this should have happened a long time ago. How dare he say those things about Mary? The other day on my mom's couch, it was Mary who'd consoled him, Mary who hugged his stinky body and took his cheese-covered fingers in her hands.

I pictured the look on Mary's face when she ran out of the big church, the disappointment etched in her eyes.

Oh God, what had I done?

Moss Murphy looked up from his injured ferret. "I don't think we should be friends anymore," he said.

"Fine by me," I said. "I don't even know why we were friends in the first place."

Three seconds later, I was out the door.

35
$1,000 a Day

I snuck in through the sliding glass door on our back deck, careful not to wake my parents. Caroline was out — her car was gone when I walked up our driveway — but my mom was a light sleeper and the last thing I needed was her waking up and catching me looking like Mike Tyson after a Buster Douglas uppercut. Moss Murphy had ripped my T-shirt and torn open my stitches. I checked them in the bathroom mirror and saw a little stream of blood running down my cheek. I cleaned myself up a bit, applied a dab of Polysporin and was rifling through the empty milk container where my dad kept the Band-Aids when I heard Caroline come in through the front door. This was early for her. Usually when she went out on a date, she wouldn't come home until at least 2 a.m.

I had just placed a new bandage over my eye when I heard Caroline crying. I found her in the kitchen, standing in her boots next to the open fridge door.

"Caroline?"

"There's no yogurt," she said, sobbing. "All I want is a yogurt." Caroline shut the fridge and sat down at the kitchen table. She rubbed some Kleenex against her eyes.

"One second," I said, and ran into the garage. I removed

the boards in front of my dad's mini-refrigerator, grabbed two yogurt cups from inside and hurried back.

"Here." I handed her a grape yogurt and a spoon.

Caroline didn't even ask where the mystery yogurt had come from. She opened it and took a bite, with tears flowing down her cheeks.

"Did some guy hurt you?" I said.

"No," she said. Caroline peeled off her fake eyelashes and tossed them on the table. Her face scrunched up into a little red ball and she burst into tears, real tears, a river of them. I pulled my chair beside her and wrapped my arm around her. Caroline tucked her head against my chest. She wiped her nose with her hand.

"I went out for drinks with Patricia, the lady from the beauty school," she said between sobs.

"Did you not get in or something?"

"It's nothing like that. Patricia and I went out to talk about the industry, you know, to do some networking. She was telling me all these horror stories about perverts she's run into and clients who stiffed her on bills. Finally I asked her why she teaches at the beauty school when she could make a thousand dollars a day doing photo shoots. And she looked at me like I was insane or something. Then she started laughing."

"So, it doesn't pay a thousand dollars a day?"

Caroline's face scrunched up again. "Not even close." She cried so loudly, I thought Mom would come running downstairs. "Most girls, when they graduate beauty school, they end up working at the freaking cosmetics counter at Walmart or something. They make minimum wage, plus some crappy commissions for doing makeovers on old ladies."

Caroline shoved a scoop of yogurt into her mouth.

Neither of us said anything for a while. Out the window, two flashlights were moving around. For a second, I thought it was my dad again. Then I realized it was the Deck Girls going for their midnight pee.

"I'm so stupid," Caroline said.

"You're not stupid."

She gave me a look that said, *Don't lie to me. I'm completely stupid.*

"Why did you think it paid a thousand dollars a day?" I said.

Caroline polished off her yogurt and pried open the second container. She looked relieved that it was strawberry and not grape. "Patricia said the only way girls make that much money is if they do porn shoots."

"What do you mean 'do' porn shoots?"

"They overpay the makeup artists on porn shoots because no one wants to do them. Patricia said that a lot of times, the makeup artist gets paid more than the girls on camera. She said even the fluffer gets paid more than the actresses."

"What's a fluffer?"

Caroline sucked on her spoon. "You don't want to know."

I leaned back in my seat. "I didn't even know they did porn shoots in Parksville."

"They don't," she said. "You have to go to Springfield. That's where the money is." Caroline picked up the yogurt container to see how many calories she'd just ingested. She ran a Kleenex under her nose. While she'd pretty much stopped crying, it felt like at any moment she might start up again.

"What are you going to do?" I said.

"I don't know," she said. "I'd rather die than do makeup on porn shoots. Maybe I'll get pregnant and have a baby.

Don't laugh. Half my friends are doing that. Maybe I can trick Dennis into marrying me." She paused and stared at the spoon in her hand. "Who am I kidding? Dennis is a dork."

Caroline looked out the window, past the Deck Girls climbing into their tent. The moon was nearly full. It was so bright in the sky, we could see the patches of gray, the darkened craters, the enormity of everything outside this little room.

"I'm not college-smart," Caroline said. "The problem is, I'm smart enough to know I'm not that smart. I don't want to live in Mom and Dad's house forever. Only, there's no way I can support myself on minimum wage." She lay her head on the table, defeated, exhausted.

I don't know what came over me, but I took her hand in mine and lay my head down beside her. Caroline and I sat there for a long while, holding hands and waiting, maybe for her to come up with another plan, maybe for Mom and Dad to wake up, maybe for the sun to rise.

36
Village People

The next morning, Mom was making a terrible racket downstairs. I pulled myself out of bed and found her digging in the hallway closet. A pile of old comic books lay scattered on the floor. Mom's head was inside a cardboard box and her backside was in the air.

"It's too early," I said.

She handed me a six-pack of Christmas ornaments and stuck her head back in the big brown box. "Too early for what?"

"For all this noise."

She rummaged around some more. Mom tossed out a stuffed Rudolph the Reindeer and two stockings before yelling, "Aha!" She yanked on a string of Christmas tree lights, only they caught on something. Mom pulled as hard as she could and when that didn't work, she stuck her head back in. She finally untangled the lights, then started stuffing Christmas decorations back in the box.

"What are you doing?" I said.

"They're for the sign," she said. "Last night, Nancy and I came up with the perfect slogan. What we need now is a little pizzazz. We're going to attach Christmas lights and use sparklers. Sparklers, Jacob!" She wiped some dust off an old ornament and chucked it back in the box. "I also need an extension cord. Maybe two." Mom paused. Then her eyes lit up. If she were a cartoon character, a lightbulb would have gone off over her head. "Maybe we've got some fireworks left over from the Fourth of July," she said, and started digging again. Mom quickly grew frustrated. "Who organized this closet anyway?" she said, knowing perfectly well that my dad had rifled through that very same closet yesterday while looking for the replica nineteenth-century army musket he'd brought to last year's Desert Storm reenactment.

I gave up and walked into the kitchen to have breakfast. My dad had polished off the Count Chocula in less than twenty-four hours, so I poured myself a bowl of Shreddies. I was about to add milk when I heard voices coming from the garage. I snuck over to take a look, half-expecting to find Dad and Leah Fontaine sucking face on his pullout cot. Instead, my dad was in full battle attire. He was dressed up in his army fatigues, complete with helmet, camouflage face paint and his prized army musket.

He wasn't alone. Pushkar was with him and he was dressed up too, as Saddam Hussein. Pushkar had shaved his beard and left a thick moustache in its place. He was wearing a brown jumpsuit with red-and-gold epaulets on his shoulders. On his head was a black beret featuring a prominent gold pin. Pushkar was talking with my Uncle Ted, who was wearing a Hawaiian shirt and holding a pair of army fatigues in his hand, like he wasn't sure whether or not to put them on.

"What's going on?" I said.

"Jacob, my boy," Dad said, far too enthusiastically for this early in the morning, "we're trying on our outfits for Saturday's big reenactment."

Uncle Ted and Pushkar nodded.

"It's only two days away?" I said.

"Damn right!" came a fifth voice.

Moss Murphy's dad walked in through the open garage door. He was wearing his hard hat and a greasy old T-shirt that read I'm Not Gay, But $20 Is $20. Part of his belly was sticking out underneath, and he was so sweaty he looked like he'd been lounging in a sauna all morning.

"Good morning, Lorne," Dad said.

Moss Murphy's dad looked at Pushkar and Uncle Ted. He scratched his backside. "I'm joining you bastards," he said.

"But . . . you go to the Church of the Lord's Creation."

"Truth be told, we only go there for the air conditioning," he said. "I wouldn't even go to church if it wasn't for Betsy." He glanced across the street to make sure his wife couldn't hear. "She's been praying day and night for that damned ferret of hers to get better."

A wave of guilt sailed through my chest. "Is Roscoe okay?" I said.

"The thing has a sprained neck. Plus he got into the Vaseline again last night."

Roscoe ate another tube of Vaseline? Maybe the Murphys would be better off if they locked up their petroleum jelly–based lotions and ointments.

"And you want to join our reenactment?" Dad said.

"Damn right. There are two things I look forward to all year: McRib season and playing Santa Claus at my company Christmas party. Now, McDonald's can threaten to take away the McRib all they want. But it'll be a cold day in hell before I let some skinny little nerd like Youth Pastor Glenn take Santa Claus away from me."

Dad looked at Uncle Ted, who looked at Pushkar, who looked back at my dad.

"You're in," they said.

Lorne Murphy shook my dad's hand and all four of them started chatting about their plans for the reenactment.

"It will have to be spectacular, considering Youth Pastor Glenn's reenactment will be at the same time," Dad said.

I was stepping back into the house, when I saw a strange figure walking up our driveway. It took me a second before I recognized Shotgun. He looked different than he did standing behind the counter at Sore Thumbs. He was wearing a Jamaican rastacap with dreadlocks sticking out the back. Over his shoulder was a big, heavy duffel bag.

"Keith!" Dad called. "Did you bring the equipment?"

"Fo' rizzle," Shotgun said. He lugged the duffel bag into the garage and dropped it on a lawn chair. Before he could say another word, Dad began rooting through the bag, pulling out paintball gun after paintball gun.

"Are these automatics?"

"Some of them," Shotgun said. His eyes were glazed over, like he'd just smoked a big bowl of Acapulco gold.

As Dad passed out the paintball guns, I walked over. "What's with the hat?"

"Oh, this?" Shotgun said. "It's National Bob Marley Day."

My dad and I exchanged skeptical looks.

"Are you sure about that?"

"Pretty sure," Shotgun said. "It's Bob Marley Day in Newfoundland."

"What's Newfoundland?"

"It's what they call Canada, since they found it."

We all raised our eyebrows at him.

Shotgun pulled me aside. "I swear it's true. Blowpipe told me."

"When did you see Blowpipe?"

"I bailed him out of jail last night," he said. "Blowpipe got arrested for peeping."

I glanced over at my dad. He was like a kid in a candy store, trying out paintball cartridges and horsing around with Moss Murphy's dad.

"Is Blowpipe the Parksville Peeper?" I whispered.

Shotgun ran his hands through his fake dreadlocks. "I always knew it was true. I just didn't want to admit it."

"Wow. You think you know a guy and then it turns out he's been a pervert all along."

"It's not like that," Shotgun said. "Blowpipe wasn't peeping in all those windows so he could see boobies and pootie and whatnot. He was looking for Zelda."

"Zelda, the elderly stripper?"

"One and the same," Shotgun said. "Only, she's not elderly. She's just late-middle-aged. It's like when people say she's obese. She's not obese. She's just fat." Shotgun shook his head. He looked torn-up inside. "Blowpipe got obsessed with Zelda. And the more I think about it, Zelda was obsessed with him right back. Only, Club Paradise closed down and he didn't know where to find her. He kept sneaking out of rehab and peeping in all those houses, trying to catch a glimpse of her. Then, last night, he got caught. Some lady hit him with a bat."

"No."

"Totally, dude. Do you know that lady, the one whose dog got eaten by a raccoon?"

"Candice Collington?"

"That's her," Shotgun said. "Blowpipe peeped in her

window, looking for Zelda, and the lady smashed him with a baseball bat. When I bailed him out of jail, Blowpipe had his arm in a sling."

"Where's he now?"

Shotgun shrugged. "Wherever the tumbleweeds took him."

My dad brushed past us and removed the planks of wood from the corner so he could show off his hidden refrigerator. He pulled the cot out of his workbench and turned on his disco rainbow globe light. Fish started swimming on the walls.

"Whoa," Shotgun said, all dazed and confused.

Dad walked over to his cassette player. When the AC/DC tape wouldn't play, he turned on the radio and the soulful sound of Rick Astley's "Never Gonna Give You Up" filled the room.

"Jacob!" Uncle Ted said. "Have you really been wearing this?"

Pushkar was holding up the hot-dog costume he'd forced me to wear. The men were having a good chuckle about it.

"Put it on," Pushkar said, laughing. When I didn't move, he said, "Put it on," again, this time with those hard yellow eyes.

I shook my head.

Uncle Ted and Lorne Murphy looked disappointed they wouldn't get to have a laugh at my expense.

Pushkar softened a little. "If you try it on now, I'll give you a day off next week."

My first instinct was to say no. I didn't need a bunch of middle-aged weekend warriors making fun of me. Then I thought about Pia, how angry she'd been on the phone the other night. If Pushkar was capable of psychological torture and slave labor, what was his daughter capable of?

The less time I spent around her, the better. I took the hot-dog costume and stepped into it.

"Whew! Shake it, honey!" Moss Murphy's dad yelled to the amusement of all around.

Uncle Ted swayed his hips like there was an invisible hula-hoop around his waist.

This wasn't going to end well if I stayed inside the garage. I took the hot-dog costume around to the side of the house instead. The weird polyester material still felt strange each time it touched my skin. I pulled it over my T-shirt, fully prepared to be humiliated. As I stepped in front of the house, my mother walked into the garage.

"Donald, I need an extension cord," she said.

The last word — *cord* — barely escaped her mouth.

Mom was stunned.

She was flabbergasted.

She was dumbstruck.

She took in the scene, fully and completely: Dad's man cave, exposed for the first time. She saw the refrigerator, the pullout bed, the rainbow-colored disco fish swirling around the room. Mom heard the sweet tones of Rick Astley playing on the radio. She saw her husband wearing army fatigues and standing speechless in the center of the room. Beside him, Pushkar was dressed up like Saddam Hussein. Shotgun was milling about in his Jamaican rastacap with dreadlocks sticking out the back, while Uncle Ted and Moss Murphy's hard-hatted dad were holding their paintball guns, wearing Hawaiian and twenty-dollar-blowjob shirts.

Mom dropped her Christmas lights.

"Honey . . ." Dad said.

"I . . . I . . ."

"There's a reasonable explanation."

"You . . . you've turned the garage into a gay bathhouse!"

"No! I swear."

Mom made the sign of the cross. When that didn't work, she made it again.

"You're the Village People!"

Just then, I came into view. Mom looked at me in the hot-dog costume and she lost her mind.

"Jacob!" she cried. "Not you too!"

"Mom . . ." I said.

"Donald! What have you done to our son?!"

Mom shrieked at the top of her lungs and took off running with my dad in hot pursuit. She scampered into the house, grabbed her car keys from the front hall and came running out so quickly that the string of Christmas lights twisted around her ankle. She collided with my dad and a mad scramble ensued, with Dad trying to pull Mom close and Mom screaming hysterically, struggling to break free. They toppled over and just when it seemed like Dad had a firm grip around her waist, Mom slugged him in the nose. She crawled along the cement. It looked like she was going to get away, only Dad grabbed the Christmas lights around her ankle.

"Help!" Mom yelled.

"Tarnation, Margaret!" Dad yelled back.

Mom looked up at me with pleading eyes. Somehow she saw past the hot-dog costume and saw her son standing there, her only boy. "Help your mother," she said.

I looked at my dad, madly pulling on the string of lights, then my mom, clawing the pavement in a desperate attempt to escape. Long gone were the days when I could stand idly by. I wasn't that guy anymore. I had to make a decision.

I kicked my dad's arm with my bare foot. When he didn't let go, I kicked him again. Dad's eyes screamed at me — TRAITOR! — but he couldn't hold on any longer. The string of lights came loose. Mom scrambled to her feet and ran to her car in a frenzy, panting like a dog.

In a flash, she hopped into the driver's seat and pulled out of the driveway.

Dad chased after her.

"Margaret!

"Honey!!

"SUGARBOOBS!!!"

The tires screeched and just like that, Mom was gone.

Dad pulled out his keys. He ran to his car and opened his door, panic dripping from his camouflage-painted face.

"Jacob, come with me," he said.

The motley crew in the garage stared at me. Uncle Ted, Pushkar, Moss Murphy's dad and Shotgun were all stunned, shocked, even a little dismayed. I didn't know what to do.

"Your family needs you," Dad said.

37
Drop the F-Bomb

For fifteen years, I had never heard my dad say the F word. Not when someone cut him off in traffic, not when he stubbed his toe or spilled his Coffee-mate all over the kitchen floor. Not even when he caught that scruffy dude in a leather jacket sneaking out of Caroline's bedroom window at two in the morning. Never. Not once. Until six months ago.

It was a Thursday afternoon and Dad was waiting for a FedEx package that was already three days late. It was hugely important for his work and he was getting worried, so much so that he'd been showing signs of stress. He forgot to shave. He called me by his brother's name and he got a severe case of the fumble fingers, dropping anything he picked up. The man was on edge.

I was upstairs reading a comic book (*X-Men Adventures* Vol. 3, No. 4, the one with a spandex-clad Jean Grey bursting out of the ocean on the cover), when a knock came at the door. My dad ran to get it, thinking the FedEx guy had finally arrived. It turned out to be Girl Scouts selling cookies. Dad slammed the door in their faces. He stormed down the hallway. Then it happened. He stood right in the center of the house and yelled "FUCK!" as loud as he could.

I sat straight up in bed. My first thought was, *This is the greatest day of my life.*

I threw my comic across the room and ran downstairs. Dad was still fuming. He had picked up a figure of Abraham and was twisting it in his hands.

"You said the F word!"

"I'll say plenty more than that!" he bellowed.

"Wait, wait, wait," I said. "When I was seven, you grounded me for saying the F word. I didn't even know what it meant and you still stuck me in my room with no television for five whole days." I put my hand on my hip. "You're grounded, mister."

Dad hurled the Abraham figurine at me. He missed (he'd always had terrible aim) and it smashed against the wall and broke into little pieces. Before I could say anything else, Dad marched toward me. His cheeks were bright red. His eyes were boiling like kettles. I took off running, slammed my door and hid behind my desk chair.

An hour later, I found my mom picking up pieces of Abraham in the hallway.

"Dad said the F word."

Mom passed me a handful of shattered porcelain and kept digging in the carpet. "Your father was very upset," she said.

"I know, but he said *the F word.*"

She tapped me on the cheek and made a face like it was no big deal. "He always says it, dear. Just not around you kids."

I probably should have been proud of my father. He'd gone fifteen years without cursing in front of his kids. I should have patted him on the back and praised his self-control. Instead, I told Caroline about it. She was a little surprised at first. Then a smile formed on her face, a wicked, Grinch-like smile. She told me to wait until dinner.

Mom was on her second glass of wine and busy insisting Caroline fill out her beauty school applications. Dad hadn't said a word since he'd hurled Abraham at me.

"Dad," Caroline said. "Could you please pass the fucking butter?"

Mom fell silent. Dad looked up from his roast chicken.

"What did you say?"

"Could you please pass the fucking butter?"

Mom jabbed Caroline with her fork. "We don't talk like that in this household."

"Apparently we do," Caroline said. "Right, Jacob?"

I stared at my plate, scared to death of what my dad might say.

Instead of yelling, Dad kept chewing his chicken. Twenty long seconds passed with the four of us eating in silence, before Caroline set down her knife and fork.

"What does it take to get a fucking soda around here?" she said.

Dad hit the roof. He shook the table with both hands, yelled "Tarnation!" at the top of his lungs and sent Caroline scurrying upstairs.

No matter how mad he was, and no matter how much Caroline deserved it, Dad didn't drop the F-bomb again that night. For six months, he refrained from using it, no matter how stressed he was. Until that day in the car, chasing after Mom.

"Fucking hell! What the fucking hell? Fuck this! This whole week has been a total clusterfuck!"

Dad slammed his fist on the steering wheel and unleashed another barrage of profanity. It was like once one F word slipped out, the floodgates opened. Dad slammed his fist again. He took a sharp turn and my head bonked against the window.

"Put on your fucking seat belt!" he yelled.

I don't know if you've ever sat in a car — with you in a hot-dog costume and your irate father in army fatigues — chasing your hysterical mother down a series of winding side streets as she floors it through playground zones and runs over residential lawns, leaving skid marks for days, but if you ever do, I don't advise using that moment to take stock of your life. It's better to keep quiet, turn on the radio and ignore your father's panic-stricken ramblings. *Do not* start wondering what steps in your life have led you to this. There are times to be emotionally aware, times to be mindful of who you are and what you're doing. This was not one of those times.

Mom turned down Somerset Crescent. At first her route was erratic, like she was trying to lose us and couldn't figure out which way to go. Now she was traveling a familiar path. Dad took his foot off the gas when he realized Mom was headed in the direction of Ascott Street and Jedidiah Avenue. We watched her speed away.

"We'll let Mom get there first," Dad said. "Give her a minute to calm down." He unrolled his window and took a few deep breaths. "Things have been difficult for your mother lately. It's not easy going through The Change."

I looked at him funny. He was talking as if the whole thing was Mom's fault. And this was the first I'd heard of Mom going through menopause, if that's what he meant by "The Change." I suppose some telltale signs had been popping up recently. Mom had been a little on edge. More than once, I'd noticed her hovering in front of the open refrigerator door to soak in the cold air. Come to think of it, just last month the stack of shiny silver-wrapped tampons in my parents' bathroom — the ones featuring empowering, inspirational sayings like *Live Fearlessly!*, *Be Unstoppable!* and *You Go, Girl!* — had been replaced by a trio of scented candles (Calm, Extra-calm and Quiet Tapioca).

Still, whether Mom was staring down the barrel of The Big M or not, she wasn't to blame for what had just happened back there at the garage.

Dad cleared his throat. "I'm proud of you, son."

I looked down at my hot-dog costume, at the mark on Dad's arm from where I'd kicked him just minutes ago. Although I'd suspected it for a while, now I was sure. The man was going insane. "Why?"

"Because you stuck up for your mother. You made a choice, and while I might disagree with the choice you made, you did what you needed to do to protect your family. You saw your mother in distress and you helped her."

I undid my seat belt, pulled off the costume and threw it in the back seat.

Dad's fingers were twitching, the adrenaline still pumping through his veins. He tried tapping along to the music to distract himself. The radio was playing Jackson Browne's "You're a Friend of Mine." "Boy, that Clarence Clemons sure can play the saxophone," he said. When I didn't respond, he started explaining that Clarence Clemons played in The Boss's band (whoever The Boss was).

The car got quiet.

"I ended things with Leah," he said.

I wasn't sure what to say. The church was in view and

we could see Mom's car, only we couldn't see her among the crowd.

"You're the only one who knows what happened," he said.

"I won't tell."

"I know. You're a good son."

We pulled into the church parking lot and Dad got out and began searching. Before long, he spotted Mom over by her beloved sign, standing with Aunt Alpana and Nancy Sylvester. Alpana was rubbing Mom's back while Nancy Sylvester stroked her hair. Mom looked like she was crying. Before she could get a word out, Candice Collington ran up to the group and yelled.

"I hit the Parksville Peeper with a baseball bat!"

Mom looked at her strange. She wiped her eyes.

"Wham-o! Right in the arm!" Candice Collington said. "He cried like a little girl."

"Margaret!" Dad hollered.

The women looked at my dad. They didn't know what he'd done, only that he'd done something terrible. He started speed walking toward them and, like Flo-Jo sprinting toward a nail salon, Mom took off running toward the park. Dad trotted after her as fast as he could.

I was fully planning on joining the chase when I realized I had no shoes. I was standing in my bare feet, wearing the T-shirt I'd slept in the night before and a pair of blue jeans. With nothing else to do, I leaned back against my dad's car and took in the scene. The crowd was pretty big for this early in the morning. Aunt Alpana was handing out breakfast burritos while Candice Collington stood beside her with a Santa Claus cap on her head and a big smile on her face. Striking a peeping Tom with a baseball bat appeared to have done wonders for alleviating her lingering grief. Across the street,

300

the number on the giant sign in the sky read 2,341. It hadn't moved since I arrived.

Below the sign, Mary was reading to a group of children gathered on the lawn. I started walking toward her without even the foggiest idea what I would say. I knew only that I needed to apologize. Deep down, I don't think I'd ever been so scared. What do you say when you know you were wrong? I'd been rude. Inconsiderate. Thoughtless. A damn fool. For me to have any chance to repair what I'd done, Mary would have to find it in her heart to forgive me.

Mary was holding a Curious George treasury and reading about George wreaking havoc at the beach. Four little girls and two boys sat captivated by the monkey's tale. Mary still hadn't seen me when a familiar figure walked by. It was Shotgun. He'd ditched the rastacap and fake dreadlocks and was carrying another duffel bag over his shoulder.

"Shotgun," I said.

He kept walking.

"Shotgun . . . Keith!"

I yelled so loudly, Mary looked up from her book. She paused a moment and then kept reading. Shotgun finally stopped and waved. He adjusted his heavy duffel bag.

Up above, the electronic sign ticked down to 2,340. Whispers darted through the crowds while Shotgun looked up at the sign with wonder. He smelled like he'd just blazed up a big fat doobie in the car. I was pretty sure he was baked out of his mind.

"What are you doing here?" I said.

Shotgun looked down at my bare feet. "The better question is, what are *you* doing here?" he said.

"I just got here with my dad. Remember? You were at my house when I got in the car wearing the hot-dog costume."

"That was yesterday, dude."

"No. That was twenty minutes ago."

Shotgun squinted. "I really think it was yesterday."

I shook my head. Trying to reason with a stoned person is like trying to herd cats through a hula-hoop. "What's in the bag?" I said.

Shotgun's eyes drifted up and to the left. "It's . . . um, the laser-tag equipment I promised that Glenn guy."

I put my hand on the duffel bag and felt the barrel of a paintball gun. Shotgun shifted his feet and hundreds of paintballs rattled around the canisters inside. I couldn't believe it. Shotgun was a double agent, selling to both sides of the street.

"I'm just trying to stack papers, dude," he said.

"Pardon?"

"You know. Make money."

Someone called his name.

"Keith! Over here!"

It was Youth Pastor Glenn, waving his hands in front of the Church of the Lord's Creation. Shotgun shrugged like there was nothing he could do. He hoisted the bag higher on his shoulder and kept walking. As he and Youth Pastor Glenn entered the church doors, several small children ran past me. Mary had finished reading.

"Hi," I said.

"Oh. Hi."

"It's Thursday morning," I said, looking at the crowd. "Shouldn't these people be at work?"

Mary picked up a stack of children's books and refused to look me in the eye. At that moment, all I wanted was to apologize for what I'd said, not just for getting caught, but for even speaking that way about her when she wasn't around. I wanted to tell Mary she was the most beautiful girl I'd ever seen, that she was funny and smart and kind in a way I'd never known. Instead, this came out of my mouth:

"I heard about your dad."

Mary shuffled the books in her hands. "Why would you bring that up?"

"To see . . . to see if you wanted to talk about it," I said.

"Oh, so you want me to open up and bare my soul to you?"

"I don't know. Maybe."

Mary's lips trembled. "You seriously expect me to tell you what it's like to watch my drunk dad stumble around the house every night? What it's like to hear him yell at my sisters? To find him passed out on the floor in the middle of the day? For hundreds of people to watch him slur his words and fall over during Sunday mass?" Her voice cracked. "Why would I share anything with you? Wouldn't you just turn around and tell your best buddy Glenn?" She rubbed her forehead hard. Her eyes looked puffy, like she hadn't slept.

"I never meant to hurt you," I said. "I never meant to embarrass you. It wasn't Youth Pastor Glenn's fault. It was mine."

Mary's gaze was glued to her feet. It felt like I was the last person she wanted to talk to in the entire world. Still, I had to try.

"I have this aching pit of regret in my stomach and all I can do is tell you I'm sorry. From the bottom of my heart, I am so sorry."

I'd barely finished my sentence when a gasp erupted from the crowd. Heads turned. News cameras pivoted. People clamored for a better view. The countdown on the giant sign was zipping by. It started at 2,339 and descended to 2,109 in

303

the blink of an eye. It kept counting down until it reached 1,951 and then stood pat. The uproar subsided but all eyes remained glued to the sign.

Youth Pastor Glenn was standing over by the church doors. His subtle smirk told me everyone was wasting their time watching the clock tick down. It wouldn't reach zero until the morning both churches reenacted Operation Desert Storm at the park across the street.

Mary bit her bottom lip. It felt like ages since either of us had spoken. "Those are just words," she said.

"But I mean them. Every one of them."

"And I appreciate it. I really do. But sometimes words just aren't enough." She turned to walk away.

"Wait." I grabbed her arm.

Mary looked at my fingers around her wrist. Her eyes were so calm, so disheartened, I felt ridiculous for touching her, for approaching her in the first place, for thinking she would ever want to be with someone like me. I let go.

"Maybe we were just meant to be friends," I said.

Mary looked me in the eye. "Maybe we weren't meant to be anything."

She turned and walked into the Church of the Lord's Creation.

38
Definitely a Goose

The next morning, my alarm clock rang like normal. I rolled out of bed and showered, put on my clothes and combed my hair just like any other morning. I walked downstairs and ate breakfast. Someone watching from a distance would have thought it was a typical day. Only, every action, every movement, from washing my hair to pouring Shreddies into my bowl, to lifting the spoon to take a bite, was coated in an aching, somber gray. My head felt foggy. My arms felt heavy. Worst of all, I thought this feeling would never end.

Last year, a goth girl attended my high school. Her name was Kristen, but she insisted everyone call her Rain. Rain dressed in all black. She had black hair and black finger-nails and wore black makeup around her eyes. She carried a black purse and wrote with a black pen. I wouldn't have been surprised if she'd had a selection of black tampons in her pocketbook. Underneath her name in the yearbook, she'd written, "I wear black on the outside because I feel black on the inside." Everyone thought it was funny. In fact, some jackass in her grade had heard what she'd planned to write and made sure his yearbook slogan read, "I wear plaid on the outside because I feel plaid on the inside." It was sort of true. That guy always wore plaid lumberjack shirts to school.

Everyone had a good laugh at Rain's expense. Only, I didn't think it was funny. I believed her. Poor Kristen/Rain probably did feel black on the inside.

As much as I sympathized, I never identified with her. If anything, I'd always felt *almost* on the inside. Like I was almost smart, almost funny, almost good-looking, almost deserving of having friends, almost worthy of falling in love. That morning, going through my regular routine, I finally knew what Rain was talking about. I felt black on the inside. A big lump of coal was sitting square on my heart and I had no idea how to burn it off. It's one thing to make a mistake. It's another thing to betray the one you love.

The feeling wasn't mutual. Mom and Dad were in the kitchen, giddy as schoolchildren that morning. I didn't know what Dad said at the park yesterday, but thirty minutes after he chased her across the street, they emerged holding hands and they hadn't let go yet. Mom was eating yogurt and grapefruit. Dad was biting down on a Pizza Pop, the two of them snuggled up like lovebirds. Last night I tried to convince myself they were moving furniture in their bedroom until 2 a.m., even though deep down I knew what was really going on.

Good for them, I suppose. I only wished I didn't sleep in the next room.

I arrived at the AMPM right on time — 9 a.m. exactly — expecting to find Pushkar standing behind the register with all sorts of unpleasant tasks prepared for me. It had been several days since my last shift and I could picture the soap scum that had built up behind the car wash. I was mentally preparing myself for a day of grueling manual labor when, to my surprise, I saw Pia standing behind the counter. Right away, she smiled and waved me over. I didn't trust her, not for a second. Her hands were under the counter and she could have had anything in them: a boomerang, a flask filled with acid, an Uzi.

I froze in place.

"Don't just stand there. Come here," she said.

I still didn't move. If Pia was anything like her father, her mood could change at the drop of a hat.

Pia leaned against the magazine rack.

"You're not scared of me, are you?" she said.

"Maybe."

She waved her hand in the air.

"Oh, get over yourself, Jacob. I've forgotten all about the other night. There's a new man in my life now. In fact, there he is now."

I turned around to see Samantha walk in through the AMPM doors. Behind her was her brother Scott, the college dropout who worked at the lumberyard and lived in his parents' attic. Scott was carrying a Starbucks coffee cup and a slice of banana bread in his hands.

"Hey babe," he said.

Pia batted her eyes at him.

Samantha and her brother walked up to the counter. Pia took the coffee, said thank you and kissed Scott right on the mouth.

"Where can I take a leak?" Scott said.

Pia pointed to the back of the store. "Thanks, babe," he said, and then sauntered into the employee restroom. While Scott was gone, Samantha asked if she could take her brother's Camaro through the car wash. Pia pressed a button under the counter and Samantha disappeared, leaving Pia and me alone again.

"So, you and Scott, eh?"

307

Pia grinned. "Let's be honest. Scott looks much more like Tom Cruise than you ever will."

I watched Scott come out of the employee restroom. He was tall and skinny with white pimples on his cheeks and red ones on his nose. The guy had no chin. He did, however, have a thick head of black hair. All told, he was definitely a Goose, not a Maverick. Only, I wasn't about to argue. Scott was still drying his hands on his jeans when he walked up and stood between me and Pia. The two of them looked at me like I was a third wheel.

"I'll give you a few minutes," I said, and stepped outside.

The sun was shining. The Operation Desert Storm reenactment was just a day away and the weather promised to be excellent. Even if Pushkar showed up to work today, I wouldn't have to wear the hot-dog costume. I'd left it in the back seat of my father's car on purpose, so Pushkar couldn't make me stand outside in the summer heat, covered in polyester.

A truck pulled up to the AMPM and a milkman got out and started hauling cases onto a cart. The milkman had a discoloration on his neck. It was probably a birthmark, but I couldn't help but think back to my conversation with Reverend Richard. That birthmark might have been a hickey from one of my fellow parishioners. I opened the door for him and the milkman wheeled his cart inside where Pia was talking to that headbanger Scott.

That gray feeling was still pumping through my veins and I was thinking of heading home for the day when I saw Samantha sitting against the wall, twirling her brother's keys in her hand.

"Hey," I said.

Samantha barely looked at me.

There was no one else around, so I sat down beside her. The ground was still damp with morning dew and Samantha was a bit of a mess. Her hair was tangled and her skin was so pale, those star-shaped freckles looked like a constellation.

"Are you okay?" I said.

She stared into the bright morning sky.

"No."

"What's wrong?"

Samantha didn't answer for the longest time. She just kept twirling those keys, looping them around and around, until finally she said, "Have you ever just wanted to be loved?"

I wasn't prepared for that response. It seemed far too candid for this early in the morning.

"Are you talking about Youth Pastor Glenn?"

The keys stopped twirling.

"He doesn't care about me at all," she said. "He says he still has feelings for Mary. And there's not a single thing I can do about it. I was up all night, thinking about him."

"Is that why you're sitting outside an AMPM at 9:15 a.m.?"

"Scott wanted me to come with him." Samantha poked me in the arm. "Why are *you* sitting outside an AMPM at 9:15 in the morning? Wait. Don't tell me. Is Pushkar still mad at you?"

"You know about that?" I said.

"Everyone knows about that."

"Even Mary?"

Samantha nodded her head slowly, as if to say I'd be a fool to think otherwise.

"She didn't care, you know," Samantha said. "Mary didn't care what happened between you and Pia. Just like you shouldn't care about what Glenn did to her on that camping trip."

I looked at her curiously. Moss Murphy's ex-girlfriend seemed to know a lot more about my love life than I thought she did.

The doors opened and the milkman exited with an empty cart, leaving Pia and Scott inside. Scott's rusted, red-striped Camaro was sitting a few feet away. I wondered how long it would be until those two were going through the car wash together.

Samantha stood up to leave.

"You were loved," I said.

"What?"

"You were loved. Moss loved you more than anything in the whole world."

Samantha looked down at her feet.

"He probably hates me. I was so mean to him. I never wanted to kiss him because I was trying to stay pure for Glenn."

"And yet you gave Moss all those painful handjobs."

Samantha gasped.

I cupped my hand over my mouth. I don't know what it was — the gray feeling in my veins, the strangeness of talking to this girl I barely knew, the fact that we were standing mere feet from where Pushkar punched my lights out — but the words slipped out and once they did, I couldn't take them back.

The remaining blood fled from Samantha's face. She looked like she might faint.

"What do you mean, painful?" she said.

There was no sense in holding back now.

"You know, with the squeezing and the twisting and the sudden switches in rotation."

Samantha crossed her arms. She kicked at a pebble on the asphalt.

"Moss never complained."

"He was probably in too much pain to formulate actual words."

I thought she might laugh or at least crack a smile, but Samantha barely even blinked.

"And he really liked me?" she said.

Samantha suddenly looked so young. In reality, we were both young. Up until this moment, it hadn't felt like it. For weeks, I'd felt like an adult, mature enough to make my own decisions. Only now did I really feel like a kid caught up in things too complex for my young mind to comprehend. I felt like hugging Samantha, pulling her close and standing together, with her head against my chest, shielding her from the wind, like on a movie poster. But it would have been weird and strange and I couldn't bring myself to do it.

"Moss *loved* you," I said. "The guy gave up snack foods for you. Moss loved you more than anything in the whole world. And he would still do anything to get you back."

39
Home Renovations

The rest of my shift went by quickly. Pushkar never showed up that day and Pia, now that she'd run into the arms of that headbanger Scott, was a delight to work with. She showed me how to operate the cash register and even let me ring up a few purchases on my own. When things got slow, we watched '80s movies on her mini-television set. "One day I'm going to be the Molly Ringwald of Bollywood," she said. I had no idea Pia even wanted to be an actress. It's amazing the things you learn about a person when you take car wash–fellatio out of the equation.

Still, no matter how nice it was to hang out with Pia, that gray feeling remained in the pit of my stomach. Random thoughts flooded my brain, like that I should move to Canada or fake being eighteen and join the Marines — anything to get away from the guilt and regret I felt over Mary. I still felt the same as I rode my bike home.

As I pulled up to my parents' house, the wreckage of my dad's man cave was piled on the curb. At the end of the drive-way, my dad had dumped his mini-fridge and his pullout cot. Even the disco fish light failed to escape a last-minute reprieve. Dad had piled some other junk with it: a few old planks of wood, some cardboard boxes and a broken lawn chair that looked like Uncle Ted had put his rear end right through it.

I was dropping off my bike at the side of the house when I heard voices around back.

It was my dad and Pushkar. And they were holding sledgehammers.

The mere sight of Pushkar with a sledgehammer made me want to run for the hills. Dad and Pushkar seemed to realize this. They exchanged a sly smile and then Pushkar stepped toward me, hammer raised.

I didn't just flinch. I recoiled in horror.

"Hahahaha!"

"Don't worry, son," Dad said.

"The boy is — how does one say? — yellow with the fear of a coward," Pushkar said.

I was halfway gone when they coaxed me back with promises I wouldn't be hurt. Pushkar even set down his hammer. He put his hand on my shoulder.

"What do you know about this boy Scott?" he said.

"Not much."

"Come now. You must know something."

I pictured Pia's new Maverick in my head. "He dropped out of college and he lives in his parents' attic."

The hair on Pushkar's ears curled. "What else?"

"He's a headbanger. He listens to Megadeth and Slayer. Some Screaming Trees too."

Pushkar's hand clenched into a fist. The man didn't need a sledgehammer to inflict some serious damage. "I'm not familiar with these Screaming Trees," he said.

"They're a rock band. They wear flannel and have long hair."

"Are they any good?" my dad said.

"They suck."

Pushkar shook his head. "If only Pia would date a decent young man like you."

At first I thought he was joking. Only, Pushkar's eyes were pensive. He rubbed his Saddam Hussein moustache like he was pondering the world's greatest questions.

"I thought you hated me," I said.

Pushkar let out a boisterous laugh. "I admit, you did not start off well with me," he said. "But you handled yourself well this past week. You are a good young man. Much better than this headbanger Scott."

Dad smiled at me. The smile went on a little too long, and I started to get seriously embarrassed.

"What's with the sledgehammers?" I said.

Dad pointed at the outside wall of the house. "We're going to build your mother's dream kitchen." He lifted his sledgehammer like he was about to take a big swing.

"Do you have a permit?" I said.

"Of course. I got one years ago."

"Is it still valid?"

Dad's face formed a question mark.

"Is this a load-bearing wall?" I said, suddenly concerned about what was on the other side, things like the kitchen cupboards and the sink.

Dad and Pushkar exchanged baffled looks, as though this had never occurred to them before.

"It'll be okay," Dad said, and hoisted his hammer again.

He was really going to swing it this time, when a different voice stopped him.

"Donald!"

It was Lorne Murphy, Moss Murphy's obese dad. He was wearing his hard hat again and a shirt with a picture of a gopher holding a lightsaber. Surprisingly, Moss Murphy was trailing close behind. I hadn't seen him since our big fight.

"Hold the phone," Lorne Murphy said. "You didn't think you were going to extend this kitchen without me, did you?" He shook my dad's hand and spoke in his ear. "I feel pretty bad about yesterday, with Margaret and whatnot. Let me help. Get things done right."

My dad gazed up at the wall he was just about to destroy, the incompetent handyman inside him waging a war with practicality. Deep down, he knew an unassisted renovation would be a complete disaster. But he'd done things his way for so long, it was hard for him to accept help. He pulled Mr. Murphy aside for a private chat. Pushkar walked over to examine the wall more closely, leaving Moss Murphy and me alone.

Moss Murphy pulled my favorite red Nintendo controller out of a plastic bag and handed it to me. "You left this at my house the other day."

"Thanks."

We both looked at our feet.

"Are you going to the reenactment tomorrow morning?" he said.

"Probably. You?"

"I have to go. I'm helping my dad with the sandbags."

"Sandbags?" I said.

"Yep. Hundreds of them."

Neither of us said anything for the longest time.

"How's Roscoe?" I said.

"His neck's all better and we finally took off his diaper. It's just, now he's got pinkeye. The vet thinks he might have lupus too."

"I'm sorry."

"My dad's planning on buying a parrot if Roscoe dies. I suppose there are a lot of bad words I can teach a parrot to say."

Moss Murphy ran his sandals along the grass. He had a Band-Aid over his ear where I'd hit him. A few feet away, our fathers were talking about purchasing materials at cost. Pushkar was tapping the wall, searching for beams he might not want to strike, while in the other yard, the Deck Girls were arguing over who got to eat the last Eggo waffle they'd heated up on their hot plate. I still didn't know what Moss Murphy was doing here. It wasn't just tense between us — it was awkward. I didn't think anything could change things back to the way they were.

Then Moss Murphy farted. A small, squeaky one, like something a puppy would let loose after a bowl of ALPO.

"Chimichangas," he said.

Moss Murphy farted again, louder this time. This one seemed premeditated.

I couldn't help myself. I laughed.

"Enchiladas," he said.

I laughed again, so hard I couldn't stop myself. I punched him in the arm. Moss Murphy punched back.

"How's your ear?" I said.

"It hurts," he said, and we both laughed.

Dad and Mr. Murphy returned from their powwow.

"Lorne is going to supervise the renovations," Dad announced. He handed me the sledgehammer. "Why don't you take the first swing, son?"

The sledgehammer was heavier than I expected. Everyone was looking at me: the Murphy boys, my dad, Pushkar. Even the Deck Girls were watching.

Leah Fontaine called from their deck. "What's cracking, Donald?"

We all looked up. She and her sister were wearing string-bikini tops and jean short shorts. Leah was dangling her enormous breasts over the banister. I expected my dad's face to turn white, for him to look worried about what Leah might say, what her sister knew. Instead, he looked annoyed.

"One second," Dad said. He walked over to the box containing the paintball guns. Dad hoisted one in the air and fired three paintballs. *Bam! Bam! Bam!* The Deck Girls screamed and ran for cover. A pellet struck the banister, leaving a big red blotch, while two more careened off the Deck Girls' tents. Dad fired two more shots as Lydia and Leah Fontaine hightailed it through their parents' sliding glass door and into the protection of their father's living room. Lorne and Moss Murphy cheered. Pushkar looked pleased.

Dad set the paintball gun down and strolled over, cool as a cucumber. "You ready to take that first swing, son?"

I ran my fingers along the heavy wooden handle. The outside of my house was staring at me, all faded brown paint and flimsy siding. Behind it was pink insulation, maybe a thin coating of cement, then a layer of drywall and, on the other side, my mother's cupboards — the tiny kitchen she'd desperately wanted to renovate for over a decade now. My dad was doing the right thing. This was his penance. And my mother deserved it. She'd fed the man Butter Rich syrup while he locked lips with another woman. This house, this wall, had stood for so long untouched, intact but insufficient. Change had to come from somewhere. And sometimes, the only way to change what you've always known is to take a big hammer and swing it with abandon.

I lifted the sledgehammer over my head. My shoulder strained under its weight. For a moment, I thought I might falter. Then I steadied myself. I gripped the handle as hard as I could.

I swung wildly.

40
Jesus Sighting in My Bedroom

That night, Jesus came to me.

Okay, he didn't literally come to me. I wasn't awoken by a vision of a bearded guy in robes, speaking of peace and light and harmony. A mystical image did not appear in my Corn Flakes, or in the fog on the bathroom mirror or anywhere else.

I was lying in bed, the blanket covering my ears to drown out the sound of my parents moving furniture in the next room, when I had an epiphany. Suddenly, my entire worldview changed, and I *knew* it had changed. It was like that moment at the end of "Livin' on a Prayer" when Bon Jovi switches keys and you realize there was another level he could have been singing on all along.

Why hadn't I seen it before? All those people crowded around the church weren't fighting because they thought Jesus could actually see them from up in Heaven. It wasn't like they were trying to win a ticket to the afterlife dance. (Although, technically, some of them probably were). More likely, they were all so worked up about the signs, about whether children should be allowed to believe in Santa Claus or be taught the true history of St. Nicholas, about whether Methodists were right or Presbyterians had it all figured out, because they were trying to live their lives the way Jesus lived his or, at the very least, in a way that followed his teachings.

All along, I'd thought the big theological pissing match was about proving the other side wrong. Youth Pastor Glenn wasn't trying to do that. My mother (currently moving an ottoman back and forth at the speed of light in the next room) wasn't interested in that. They were trying to prove themselves *right*, trying to live biblically, divinely, righteously. Sometimes, I suppose, the only way people can feel righteous is to show that someone else is wrong.

I thought back to that first night I met Mary, the big question she asked me about whether Jesus Christ of Nazareth was the Holy Spirit embodied in the form of man. In her heart, Mary didn't care whether I thought Jesus was really the son of God. She cared whether or not I'd actually given it some thought. So I thought about it. I sat up in bed, stared out my window and contemplated awhile. I took myself completely out of the equation and asked the big questions.

It frightened me in a way no other kind of thinking had frightened me before. I suddenly wondered whether this existence I'd been living was truly real, whether it was all an elaborate game of some kind, with us humans running around the earth like mice in a maze while the gods drank brandy and smoked cigars in the sky, or whether our universe was just a molecule at the end of a giant's nose, and heaven help us all if he sneezes. I wondered what happens when we die, if we ascend to another plane of existence or if there's pure, unadulterated nothingness at the end of the line. I'd jumped enough *Mario Kart* rainbow raceways to know what plummeting into the black abyss is like.

The sum of all my pondering and spiritual reflection was: I had no clue, none whatsoever. All these questions only begat more questions, not answers. The one thing I knew was that Jesus gave people hope. It didn't matter if you were Caroline with her dream of escaping our parents' house and making a thousand dollars a day, or Youth Pastor Glenn with his aspirations of saddling up as close to the Holy Spirit as he possibly could. Jesus gave each of them something to aspire to, an idol who could never fall from grace.

Mary wanted to debate what Jesus was like when he was alive because she wanted to know more about the icon everyone idolized. She needed to humanize him to believe in him. Jesus had sacrificed himself for our sins. And it's not like anyone else had even come close. Her minister father — that pillar of the community — was in rehab. Youth Pastor Glenn was a self-centered jerk only interested in another carnal romp in a tent. And I'd hurt her on the inside, where it counts. She'd given me the ball and I not only fumbled it, I kicked the damn thing into the crowd.

"No more, Jesus," I said.

I would never betray again.

I would become the man Mary needed me to be.

I would redeem myself.

41
Operation Desert Storm

The next morning, I walked downstairs to find Dad already in his army fatigues and my mother wearing a camouflage hat. They looked like two peas in a pod, hurrying around the kitchen, packing food into a cooler and synchronizing their watches. I would have thought my mother would be stressed to the max, what with the three-foot hole in her kitchen wall and the fact that Youth Pastor Glenn's sign would be ticking down to zero this morning. But she had a big smile on her face. "It's going to be a day of reckoning," she said to no one in particular.

I was still half-asleep when a knock came at the front door.

Dad blustered down the hall. He opened the door to find Lorne and Moss Murphy on our front step. Lorne Murphy was dressed in army pants and a gray Union Army coat that barely fit over his shoulders, while Moss Murphy was wearing the black dress shirt Caroline had bought him. His hair was gelled to the nth degree and I could smell a hint of Drakkar Noir on him. Both Murphy boys appeared ready for battle.

"The sandbags are loaded and I have Saddam's throne ready to go," Mr. Murphy said. He pointed to a rental truck at the end of our driveway. Mr. Murphy hoisted a replica musket over his shoulder. "It's time to lock and load."

Dad grinned like George Peppard, loving it when a plan comes together. He put his hand on my shoulder. "You're going to help us set up, right?"

His face was so full of life, I couldn't say no.

"Sure. But can I shower first?"

Dad and Lorne Murphy exchanged glances, like I'd be costing them some serious time.

"Caroline?!" Dad yelled.

A few seconds passed and then she popped her head around the corner.

"What's with all the noise this morning?" she said.

"I need you to drive your brother to church."

Caroline looked at my dad in his military tactical vest, at Mr. Murphy with his belly sticking out under his T-shirt, and at Moss Murphy and me standing there, helpless at the whims of our fathers.

"Okay," she said.

Dad's mouth was already open, ready to argue. "Er . . . what?"

"I said okay. Fine. I'll drive him to church."

Dad didn't know what to do. He wasn't used to Caroline being so reasonable. Lorne Murphy mumbled that they'd better hurry up.

"Margaret! Let's go!" Dad yelled.

Mom hurried out of the kitchen, carrying the cooler and two purses over her shoulder. There was a general kerfuffle as my parents put on their shoes. Seconds later, they were out the door.

I turned to Caroline, who looked like she'd already been up for an hour.

"I need ten minutes to shower and change," I said.

"Fine."

"Then you'll drive me to the church?"

Caroline shook her head. "There's somewhere else we have to go first."

I didn't realize we were going to Springfield until we were already on the highway.

"Dad's going to be furious if we miss the reenactment," I said.

Caroline didn't bat an eye. "Don't get your panties in a knot," she said. "It's Saturday morning. There's no traffic. We'll be there and back in an hour and fifteen minutes. There's something I really want to show you."

A few miles later, the highway became gridlocked. It took us forty-five minutes to drive three hundred feet. I expected to find a five-car collision at the end, with ambulances flashing their lights and firefighters pulling out the Jaws of Life to free children from a turned-over pickup truck. Instead, a poultry van had lost its cargo. A single truck driver was hauling cages off the road and chasing down chickens as passing motorists hollered at him to get out of the way.

"Poor guy," Caroline said. "Maybe we should stop and help."

It was already 8:15 a.m. We should have been at the reenactment an hour ago.

"Just keep moving," I said.

Next thing I knew, we were pulling into Springfield. It wasn't the biggest city in the world, but compared to Parksville, it was a burgeoning metropolis. The farther we drove into town, the more convinced I became that Caroline was driving me to some guy's house. I pictured her introducing me to a middle-aged divorced banker with a potbelly and a diverse stock portfolio, or some artist with a French name and an English accent — someone other than the tavern folk and carnies she usually dated.

We pulled up in front of a white building with the words Holistic Wellness Education Center emblazoned in large letters.

"What's this?" I said.

"It's where I'm going to school in the fall."

We stepped out of the car.

"Is this the beauty school?"

"It's a beauty school for the soul," Caroline said. "Some of the things Mary said really got me thinking. Beauty school is a place where they teach you how to pretty people up on the outside. The Wellness Center teaches you to pretty people up on the inside."

"So you're going to learn acupuncture?"

"Acupuncture. Chiropractic adjustments. Alternative health remedies. They teach all of that here. I don't have to pick a major my first semester."

I scratched my head. "When you graduate, how much does it pay?"

"Not a thousand dollars a day, that's for sure. But the more I think about it, being a makeup artist or a stylist would have been a job. This is a career."

It was now 8:39 a.m. We'd missed the setup. If we didn't hurry, we'd miss the reenactment too.

"Couldn't you have just shown me all this on a pamphlet?" I said.

"I suppose. I just wanted someone to see the center, to know what's been on my mind lately."

Caroline was holding herself close. Her neck was hunched and she was leaning to the side. Every muscle in her body looked tense, like a series of elastics, each connected and stretched to the point of breaking.

In all our years living under the same roof, Caroline and I had never really been what you'd call *friends*. We'd been frenemies. We'd been co-conspirators (often joining forces to gang up against my dad). We'd even occasionally been partners in crime. But we were entirely different people. Had we not been related by blood, and the two of us happened to pass each other on the street one day, we both would have walked right on by.

But she was still my big sister. Caroline hadn't brought me here just to see the outside of this building. She brought me here because she needed someone's approval. Lord knows she wasn't going to get it from Mom or Dad. Our parents were both too caught up in their own lives to think about her. Even if Caroline never graduated from the Wellness Center — and odds were, she'd grow frustrated with their hippy-dippy BS in less than two weeks — she needed her brother to tell her that it would all work out in the end.

I wasn't going to let her down.

"I think it's awesome," I said.

"Really?"

"Yeah. It's a way to help people. You've always been good at helping people, Caroline."

She gave me a half-hug that turned into a headlock.

"The building's closed. But do you want to see the grounds?" she said. "They have bonsai trees in the back and there's a ceremonial rock garden in the shape of a giant face."

I glanced down at my watch again. "Sure," I said. "Let's have a look."

We arrived at the corner of Ascott Street and Jedidiah Avenue at 9:37 that morning. Part of me still hoped we'd be early. It turned out we were right on time.

Two groups had gathered on either side of the park across the street. My dad's small ragtag collection of weekend warriors was hunkered down behind a barricade of sandbags. On the other side, Youth Pastor Glenn's troops outnumbered them four to one. Caroline stopped her car on the street and the two of us stepped out. Saddam Hussein's throne was set up on a platform in the center of the field like last year, only it was completely abandoned. Pushkar and the seven kids they'd dressed up as Iraqi soldiers were squatting behind Lorne Murphy's sandbag wall, right next to my dad.

Above, the giant scoreboard was ticking down. It was at 99. Then 98 . . . 97. There was only a minute or so to go and the news crews knew it. Five pantsuited reporters with bleach-blonde hair were speaking into microphones, cameras pointed at them. My mom and Nancy Sylvester were standing by their sign, holding the bed sheet in one hand and lit sparklers in the other, waiting for the right moment to unleash their response.

I glanced around, expecting the Parksville police to be hovering nearby, ready to seize control of the situation at a moment's notice. Only there wasn't a single police officer, park ranger or traffic warden in sight. In retrospect, I should have known. On the way out of Springfield, Caroline and I had seen that poultry van that lost its cargo on the other side of the highway. A dozen police officers were chasing chickens along the edge of the road, waving their arms and bumping into one another like Keystone Cops. They would never make it here in time.

No one was coming to intervene. The inmates were now

fully in charge of the asylum.

The sign kept ticking.

"Screw this," Caroline said. She hopped in her car. When I wouldn't follow, she did a quick U-turn and floored it down Ascott Street.

I scanned the crowd but couldn't find Mary anywhere.

The giant sign was at 87.

I ran past Mom and Nancy Sylvester and through the patch of trees. There, next to a small pine tree, was the biggest shock of all. Moss Murphy and Samantha were going at it like it was nobody's business: lips smacking, tongues flying, totally making out. It was mindboggling, amazing and a little gross at the same time.

"Oh, hi, Jacob," Samantha said.

Moss Murphy had his hand up her shirt. "Don't go in the park," he said. "It's going to get nasty."

Samantha giggled. Moss Murphy's hand swam around under her shirt and she giggled some more. I couldn't have been happier for them.

"It's good to see you two kids together," I said, and ran over to my dad.

"Jacob!" His eyes bugged out. Instead of looking mad at me for being late, he seemed relieved to have another soldier in his army. Dad handed me a paintball gun.

"This is crazy," I said.

"No, it isn't," a girl's voice said. I looked down to see Pia dressed up as a soldier in the Iraqi Republican Guard, leaning against the sandbag fortress next to her dad. That headbanger Scott was with her, a petrified expression on his face. Beside him, Candice Collington and her husband were dressed up like Barbara Bush and George Bush Senior. Mr. Collington was sweating profusely. In his presidential getup, he was a prime target and he knew it. Even Reverend Richard was there, clutching a paintball bazooka and mouthing a silent prayer.

I took the gun from my dad.

Across the park, a set of eyes met mine. It was Youth Pastor Glenn. The collection of teenagers behind him looked like a well-armed militia.

"You don't want to do that, Jacob!" he hollered.

"No one's wearing the proper safety gear!" I shouted back, thinking of helmets or, at the very least, goggles.

"We're not going to need it." Youth Pastor Glenn spread his arms to show how greatly they outnumbered us.

The giant sign ticked down to 10. Then 9. Not even Jesus himself could have stopped what was about to happen.

As the sign ticked down to 8, then 7, Mom and Nancy Sylvester gripped the bed sheet tighter. They swirled their sparklers in the air, ready to reveal their slogan the moment the clock hit zero.

6 ... 5 ... 4 ... 3 ... 2 ... 1.

The slogan appeared. Before we even had a chance to read it, Mom and Nancy Sylvester tore off their sheet, exposing their counterargument for the world to see. My eyes opened in wonder. The giant billboard in the sky didn't say anything clever or cruel. It simply read:

BE KIND TO YOUR NEIGHBORS
AND LOVE ONE ANOTHER

All eyes immediately turned to our side's sign. My mom gasped. Nancy Sylvester shrieked. She burned herself with a sparkler trying to cover it up. Only, the cameras had already captured their message.

DON'T LISTEN TO A WORD THEY SAY.
NEITHER SANTA NOR JESUS WOULD EVER
AGREE WITH THAT B.S.

As the reporters furiously reported, Mom slapped her hand to her forehead. Youth Pastor Glenn had played her. Whether he'd snuck a peek at her slogan, or whether he just knew the best way to get her goat, he'd won the battle of the signs with insincere kindness. Mom rushed over to the sandbag barricade. She grabbed the paintball gun out of my dad's hand and stormed the field. It took all Lorne Murphy's strength to pull her back. Mom kicked a little before relenting.

"Well then, what are we going to do now?" she said.

I looked from Dad to Youth Pastor Glenn. The truth was, I don't think either of them really knew. A historically accurate reenactment of Operation Desert Storm would definitely not be taking place today. But a full-scale war? Was that really possible? We were in uncharted territory. Both sides were armed and ready. The news cameras were pointed in our direction. Only, no one had fired the first shot and it felt like no one wanted to be the one to fire the first shot. A minute passed in complete silence before a single figure walked out onto the field.

She emerged from the trees like a wide-loaded vision. At first, I could barely believe it was her. But it was. The bearded lady from Dairy Queen walked right into the park. She stood beside Saddam Hussein's throne and held her hand above her eyes, scanning the crowds.

"Zelda!" a voice screamed.

From out of nowhere, Blowpipe ran onto the field. He must have escaped rehab or jumped bail or somehow gotten away. The bearded lady opened her arms. I stood there in complete shock. The bearded lady — Baskin-Robbins' arch nemesis, the one who'd stolen my expired Dilly Bar — was really Zelda, the late-middle-aged stripper, of Club Paradise fame, Blowpipe's obsession.

"Travis! Oh, my sweet Travis!" she exclaimed. Zelda wrapped her arms around Blowpipe and they embraced in the center of the park. Blowpipe winced a little as she bore down on his sling, but he looked so happy, ecstatic even.

For a moment, I thought this tender reunion might bring us all together, and that we, as a community, might find common ground in the shared love of these oh-so-different human beings.

Then Candice Collington opened fire.

"That's the Parksville Peeper! Get him!" she yelled.

Before anyone could grab her, Candice Collington charged the field. Her curly gray Barbara Bush wig flew off and still she ran, firing paintball after paintball into the air. Candice Collington's aim proved terrible and she missed Zelda and Blowpipe completely. A stray paintball flew into Youth Pastor Glenn's throng, covering Calvin Cockfort's mullet in bright green glop.

Calvin Cockfort stepped forward. Instead of two sodas to keep him from scratching his balls, he had a paintball gun in each hand. He must have gotten involved in retail electronics after all, because he was wearing a RadioShack shirt. He lobbed five retaliation shots in the air and unleashed a raucous scream.

Nancy Sylvester shrieked, Calvin Cockfort's T-shirt no doubt reigniting the memory of her battery-swiping trauma. Three paintballs ricocheted off the sandbags, another struck me on the arm. The fifth hit that headbanger Scott right between the eyes. He started crying like a baby.

Zelda and Blowpipe, seeing that the world was against them (and no doubt wanting to consummate their love), took off running. Only Candice Collington chased after them, her flowery First Lady's dress wafting in the wind. She almost ran into Nancy Sylvester, hurrying back to church to repent for her long-remembered sin.

My dad saw the purple paint on my arm and fired a shot back at Calvin Cockfort. Several of Youth Pastor Glenn's troops returned fire. The shots were scattered, with all of us wary of starting an all-out conflict. Slowly, more shots were being fired. Another paintball struck that headbanger Scott on the side of the head. He cried so hard, Pushkar slapped him.

Things were getting out of hand when I saw Mary climbing the platform in the center of the park. Mary scaled Saddam's throne, stood high above and looked at both sides. She waved her hands in the air. The paintballs stopped and the news crews drew closer. The park grew quiet as we all listened to what she had to say.

"People, please! What are you doing? Someone is going to get hurt."

She pointed to our first casualty, Pia's headbanger boyfriend Scott. The guy couldn't stop sobbing and Pushkar looked like he was thinking of slapping him again.

"Do you all want to end up like that?" Mary said. "What do you think my father would say if he was here? What do you think Jesus would say? This is madness! We were put on this earth to love one another, to care for one another, to find common ground even when it's hard to see. Can any of you tell me what we're even fighting about? Is it about a jolly man in a red suit? Is it about proving ourselves right for the benefit of these cameras? Why are we fighting?"

No one moved. Silence filled the park. Slowly, Youth Pastor Glenn stepped away from his armed forces and approached the throne.

"This is your chance, Glenn," Mary said. "You can unite this town and end all this petty bickering. You can be the hero."

Youth Pastor Glenn ran his hand through his perfectly coiffed hair. He lowered his paintball gun and shifted his foot along the grass. He really seemed to be considering this, so much so that my father stood up. So did Pushkar. Dad lowered his gun. He and Lorne Murphy stepped out onto the field. Dad motioned for me to come with him.

"What do you think, Glenn?" Mary said.

Youth Pastor Glenn was within ten feet of the throne now. He balled his hand against his chest, looking embarrassed, even contrite. Then he opened his mouth.

"I think you read too many fairy tales, Mary," he said. Youth Pastor Glenn's eyes drew sharp and narrow. He lifted his gun and fired a single shot that struck Mary hard in the chest. Mary reeled. Her eyes — which moments ago had been filled with peace and love and the hope for harmony — opened wide in shock and disbelief. And Youth Pastor Glenn wasn't done. His troops rallied to his side. Calvin Cockfort appeared, and so did the Delany sisters. Jackie Dog Face and her glittery unicorn sweatshirt were there front and center, and a half dozen assorted jocks pulled up the rear. Youth Pastor Glenn gave them all a look. They readied their paintball guns.

"NOOOOOOOO!" I yelled at the top of my lungs. I leapt up onto the stage and climbed the throne to stand in front of Mary. "Don't hurt her. If you have to hurt someone, hurt me," I said, and lifted my arms in the air.

In retrospect, I don't know what I was thinking; perhaps that they'd all recognize me from my sporadic appearances at their youth group, that the sight of my already-bruised and bandaged face would elicit such sympathy that they'd lower their weapons, that — despite their mob mentality — there was no way a dozen teenagers would unload their paintball guns into one of their own.

No matter what was running through my head, I'd guessed wrong.

They fired their paintballs. Dozens — hundreds of them — hit me: in my chest, in my face, even right between the legs. It was like the onslaught Tony Montana suffered at the end of *Scarface*, only it was happening to me. Each paintball hurt more than the last and the more they fired, the more they kept firing. Shouts sounded behind me. Pushkar's guttural battle cry rang throughout the park. The distant sound of police sirens whirled. Paintballs fired the opposite way. Still they pelted me. Only, I didn't feel them anymore. I didn't feel anything anymore.

I fell back and collapsed on the platform. Every inch of my body was covered in paint — blue paint, orange paint, green paint, purple — even my face was covered. Thank God they didn't hit my eyes.

Mary leaned over me and wiped the paint away. A projectile hit her in the shoulder and she barely seemed to notice. "Jacob! Are you okay?"

I heard a thousand different sounds: paintballs exiting canisters, Pia's wild screams, parents weeping over their fallen wounded. But I saw only one thing: Mary's face, her beautiful green eyes, her auburn hair, those lips shaped like a perfect little heart. After everything that had happened, I'd still never kissed her. I'd never listened to what the host said to the friend in Luke 14:10.

"Jacob, speak to me!" Mary said.

"I'm sorry," I said, my voice barely a whisper.

Mary glanced at the chaos raging all around. "You're sorry? You took a paintball barrage for me. I never thought anyone would do anything like that for me."

Another paintball hit me in the leg, but I was already numb. I needed an ambulance pretty bad. "I'm sorry about what I said inside the church. Can you ever forgive me?"

Mary drew closer. "Oh, Jacob, don't you know? Forgiveness doesn't happen all at once. Forgiveness happens in stages. Don't worry. We'll get there."

It took all my power to lift my head. My bottom lip brushed against her earlobe. I breathed in deep and whispered the words I'd always wanted to say. "I love you."

I tucked her hair behind her ear. Our eyes formed mirror images as the paintballs sailed through the air like distant shooting stars. I felt her breath against my skin, smelled the scent of strawberries in her hair. She closed her eyes and when she opened them, it was like the green flash shining again and again. Translucent tunnels. Unimaginable beauty.

"I think . . . I think I love you too," she said.

Then she kissed me.

Thank Yous

Thank you to Wendy for being my first reader, for believing in my work and for showing me what it's like to still live the dream. Thank you to Hanna (age 8) for being kind and imaginative and for occasionally listening to your daddy. Thank you to Claire (age 6) for your creativity and joy. This book's for you, kiddo.

Thank you to Jen Hale for your patience, insight and support. Jen isn't just an editor; she's part BFF and part therapist. I couldn't have written this novel without her. Thank you also to everyone at ECW Press, who continue to bravely publish new Canadian fiction.

Thank you to my cousins Joanne Knox & Jim Witty, who read every word I write with enthusiasm and (surprisingly) without complaint. Thank you to my aunts Joan Witty & Anne Craig. I grew up feeling like I had three mothers and with my mom having passed away, I am incredibly lucky to still have you two. Thank you to John Dewan, my Uncle Johnny, for his honesty and his support, and for $20 in an envelope every Christmas morning throughout the entire 1980s.

Thank you to Clare Maloney & Angela Kruger, who, despite displaying a lack of foresight by dating me in high school, have become two of my oldest and most reliable friends. Thank you to Sarah Le Huray for your encouragement and for keeping me sane while watching the kids at the playground. Thank you to Brian Simmers and his awesome trophy wife, Nicole Harvie, for always having my back.

Thank you to Cara Hills for your helpful comments and for high-fiving me the night *The Last Hiccup* won the CAA Award. Thank you to Christie Durnin and Shannon Waterton Dyck for spiritually proofreading this book. Thank you to Larry Meades and Don Meades for your continued support. And thank you to Joalina Tolentino and Wayne Edward Gilchrist for being Awesome with a capital A . . .

Lastly, thank you to the Canada Council for the Arts for your support.

In spring 2014, my mother-in-law Margaret Helsdon passed away. Margaret was the best supporter a writer could ever hope for. She regularly mailed my books to her friends all around the world. Margaret — the children miss you, I miss you and thank you from the bottom of my heart.